THE BURNS WAR

THE FIRE SALAMANDER CHRONICLES BOOK TWO

N. M. THORN

N.M. THORN

THE FIRE SALAMANDER CHRONICLES • BOOK TWO

The Burns War

By N.M. Thorn

Copyright © 2019 by N.M. Thorn. All rights reserved.
nmthornauthor@gmail.com
This is a work of fiction. Any resemblance to actual persons living or dead, businesses, events, or locales is purely coincidental. Reproduction in whole or part of this publication without express written consent is strictly prohibited.
Cover art design by www.originalbookcoverdesigns.com

PROLOGUE

* * *

*September 7, 1812. Nightfall.
Borodino, Russia.*

THE HEAVY STENCH of death was lingering over the field like an ominous cloud. Every square inch of the land was covered in mangled bodies of horses and people, French and Russians alike, mixed into one horrid mass. The ground was soaked with spilled blood. The mound of corpses was growing thicker toward a large hill, Grand Redoubt, that was towering like a dark omen in the center of the field.

Most of the soldiers were dead, but some were still alive, grunting and moaning feebly, their faces twisted in unbearable pain. Covered in blood, torn legs and arms were spread all over the field. Severed heads were staring into space with their empty, dead eyes. The broken blades, gun-stocks and armor, among other debris were scattered all over. A grim flock of black birds was circling the field of the battle, their ear-piercing screeches cutting through the silence of the night.

A lonely man stood at the edge of the battlefield, observing the horrifying view, his face void of emotions. The cold evening breeze rushed through the field, lifting the dust in the air and carrying over the nauseating stench of death. The man lifted his right hand, tucking it beneath the lapel of his military jacket and frowned.

"Peace lies in Moscow," he whispered, shaking his head. He lost thousands of his men today, including two of his generals. But his enemies suffered much greater losses. He won. Moscow was within his reach now, just seventy-five miles away. As the Russian forces were retreating, he could almost see his La Grande Armée marching through the streets of the ancient city and despite the gruesome surroundings, his heart leaped with joy.

"Isn't your celebration a bit premature, Emperor?"

A cold deep voice sounded behind Napoleon, making him snap around. A tall man dressed in red stood between him and his tent, erected at the edge of the battlefield. The man stared down at him without blinking, his deep-seated eyes glowing with a menacing red light. His massive arms were crossed over his chest and his flaming-red hair was flowing around his face, emitting crimson sparks as the wind was playing with it. A hardly noticeable layer of shimmering red light was surrounding his body.

"The Red Man," whispered Napoleon. He blanched and crossed himself, taking a few unsteady steps back.

The thin lips of the Red Man stretched into a glacial smirk and his glowing eyes narrowed.

"I warned you against invading Russia, Emperor, didn't I?" he growled, taking a step forward.

Napoleon measured the Red Man with his eyes, his fear slowly subsiding as he took a step forward, putting his hands on his hips. The first time the Red Man appeared to him was years ago, at the battle of the Pyramids in Egypt. Then he showed up at the battle of Wagram. And every time the man demanded that he stop the war in Europe, warning and threatening him. And now he was here again, mocking him, trying to intimidate him with his terrifying disposition and his menacing words... But this time, the mysterious man looked a little different. More real, corporeal. He could even feel the heat emitted by the Red Man's body.

Napoleon chuckled. "Look at the sky," he said, pointing up. "Do you see it?"

"What am I supposed to see?" asked the Red Man, shrugging his enormous shoulders.

"My lucky star!" exclaimed Napoleon. "It guides me and supports me. And as long as I can see it, I can't be defeated. Yes, I won today. The Russians are crushed. General Kutuzov is pulling back the leftovers of his once mighty army. Only seventy-five miles are separating me from Moscow and everything that lies within its ancient walls."

"Your victory is pyrrhic, Emperor," rambled the Red Man. "Stop your stargazing and look around." The man waved his hand at the battlefield. "Over seventy thousand corpses are lying on the ground, paving the path to your victory. How many more have to die so you can march through the streets of Moscow?"

"As many as needed!" shouted Napoleon, slamming his fist into the palm of his hand. "The Russians are defeated. By me and my La Grande Armée! A few more days at the most and Tsar Alexander will surrender and sign a peace treaty, complying with all my conditions. He wouldn't want me to march farther into his lands, spreading destruction and causing devastating casualties. I will stand in history as one of the greatest military minds, regarded with the kind of respect and admiration as only Alexander the Great and Caesar had been."

"The Russians are far from being defeated and they will never surrender," objected the Red Man dryly, shaking his head. "If you still didn't notice, the Russians would rather die than surrender to you. Yes, you will breach the Moscow's walls and open the doors of the Kremlin, but you will never win this war. Hundreds of thousands will perish on both sides. And why?" He shifted closer, now towering over Napoleon. "Why is it so important for you to take Moscow? And I do not believe that it's only your vanity and ego that are driving you into this horrendous campaign."

The heat that surrounded the Red Man's body wrapped around Napoleon, making him sweat in his thick jacket. He raised his hand and wiped the perspiration off his forehead but didn't step back, holding the steady gaze of the Red Man.

"You're right," Napoleon replied after a short pause, "it's not only my vanity and ego, as you put it so eloquently. Although I must admit that the prospect of seeing this hostile, barbaric nation at my feet sounds pleasing. However, it's not the only reason that drives me toward conquering Moscow. There are many secrets hidden behind the thick red walls of the Kremlin. Many secrets, many riches and many mysterious devices…" Napoleon stopped talking and took a deep breath, his eyes staring East, in the direction of Moscow. "But out of everything that is hidden in the Kremlin, there is only one device that I want. Once I have it in my hands, I will be unstoppable. And this is worth everything! All the losses, sacrifices, pain and death. Everything! With this miraculous device in my hands, I will make Paris the capital of the world."

For a few minutes, both Napoleon and the Red Man remained silent. The Red Man glowered down at Napoleon, his thin lips curled in distaste. Then he shook his head and a deep sound, almost a growl, rumbled in his chest.

"You're a dangerous maniac, Emperor," he hissed through his clenched teeth. "I know the magical device you're referring to and I assure you—this device is well protected and guarded from the likes of you. Neither you nor any other unworthy human will ever put their greedy hands upon it."

Napoleon waved his hand dismissively and smirked, displaying full disregard to the words of the Red Man. "If you truly believed that this device was safe, you wouldn't be here right now, working so hard to make me turn my army around and leave. So, your words mean nothing to me," he said calmly. "I always get what I want. I can guarantee you that no later than the middle of September, I will sit on the throne in the Kremlin with that powerful device in my possession." He raised his arms up, like he was already holding the world in his hands.

The Red Man laughed, his laughter dripping with mockery. "And *I* can guarantee you that your Russian campaign will be your undoing. You have my warning, Emperor. Now farewell."

The Red Man stepped back, his glowing body melting into a wall of fire and a second later he was gone. The darkness descended upon the bloodied battlefield and patches of dark stormy clouds partially obscured the sky. Napoleon looked up at a small opening in the clouds and smiled sadly. In this little window he saw the stars that were surrounding the thin line of the new moon.

"As long as my lucky star is gazing upon me, your words do not scare me, Red Man."

He turned around and walked away toward his tent.

* * *

September 16, 1812.
Moscow, Russia.

IT WAS EARLY MORNING. The sky was still dark, but the ominous red flares of small fires that were rising here and there illuminated the dark city with a sinister red glow. The Master of

Power, Mrak Delar, was standing in front of a window, his obsidian eyes reflecting the red gleam of fires. Silently, he stared at the ancient city, regret shadowing his handsome face.

A young woman stood behind him, silently waiting for him to turn around. She was dressed in men's clothes and her long golden hair was hidden beneath a hat. In this outfit, she looked like a teenage boy.

After a few minutes, Mrak Delar turned around and sighed.

"What a beautiful ancient city," he said quietly, shaking his head. "It's a shame to see it devoured by fire. I don't like to get involved into the affairs of other realms, but both my mentor and the Destiny Keeper were right. It has to be done. The magical artifacts and devices that are hidden beneath the Kremlin cannot fall into the wrong hands. Most of them I concealed, and they should be well protected from the fire by my enchantments. But there are a few that I can't take a chance with. They cannot remain within the city walls while Napoleon Bonaparte and his army are here."

He stopped talking and his eyes moved down to the woman's chest, lingering on a large pendant that was attached to a silver chain. The pendant was quite unusual. It looked like a double-headed medieval axe. The blades of the axe were decorated by delicate golden inlays and the handle had a few barely visible words in *drevnerusskij*—old Russian language—engraved on it. The woman followed his gaze and her arm went up to her chest, her fingers wrapping around the pendant.

"Countess," said Mrak Delar, "you need to leave the city immediately. Unfortunately, I don't know this land well enough, so I can't teleport you. You are a witch. Can you open a portal?" She shook her head no with a guilty look on her face. He sighed and continued, "Outside the city gates, you will find a loyal man with two horses waiting for you. He will accompany you on your journey. Ride to the Ural Mountains toward the city of Yekaterinburg. About twenty-five kilometers, northwest of the city, you will find a place called *Chertovo Gorodishche*—Devil's Settlement. The Wardens will meet you there."

The woman gasped and crossed herself, fear reflecting in her large blue eyes. Mrak Delar pursed his lips gazing heavenwards.

"It's just a name, Countess, there is no Devil there," he said shaking his head. "You are brave enough to walk through the burning city, infested with Napoleon's soldiers. You are not afraid to ride thousands of kilometers through this wild land. But you are showing signs of fear when I tell you the name of a place? And I thought you already went through the Guardian's training and was initiated as a Guardian Witch."

"Yes, Master, I was. And you're right. I'm sorry," said Countess Demidova, her cheeks burning with a hot red blush. "But I can't leave you here alone. It's too dangerous. Come with me."

He smirked, his obsidian eyes getting warmer as he gazed at her. "I'm the Master of Power. Neither the elements nor humans with their mundane weapons can harm me, my lady. The Wardens have knowledge and resources like no other magical organization of this world. I hope you will use this opportunity to learn more about the world of magic."

She nodded. "But what are you going to do here, Master?" she asked, her fingers fidgeting with the buttons of her shirt as she buttoned it up all the way to her neck, concealing the necklace and pendant. "The city is on fire and there are thousands of Napoleon's soldiers looting the houses."

A dark smile spread over his face. "I'm going to help the Board of Destiny unravel its path and finish what the Russian partisans started," he said coldly. "I will help the fire devour this city. Now, off you go, my lady. Ride day and night and do not stop until you find the Wardens. Remember what you're carrying with you."

"Godspeed, Master. Be safe." Countess Demidova bowed to the Master of Power and walked out of the house.

Mrak Delar opened his Sight and followed the soft glow of the Countess' magical energy until he saw her walking outside the city walls. She was a young and inexperienced witch who just finished her training with the Guardians and he wasn't sure that she was the right person for such an important job. However, the Destiny Keeper insisted that Countess Demidova was the one to do it and the young Master of Power didn't think it was his place to argue the decision of the Destiny Council.

He watched her mounting the horse and quickly disappeared from the area his Sight could cover. Once he was sure that she was gone, he snapped his fingers and teleported to the Red Square, materializing in front of the Kremlin. With remorse he observed the Kremlin and St. Basil's Cathedral, his heart aching at the idea of destroying such beautiful ancient buildings.

"This square is called red," he mumbled, "let's give the name the proper meaning."

Originally, Red Square got its name from the old Russian word *"krasnaya"* which meant beautiful and had nothing to do with the color. But right now, the color red seemed to be more appropriate for the name of the square with all the fires that were surrounding it.

He channeled the elemental power, thinking how hard it was to connect with the power in this world. In his own realm, Kendral, the Original Power surrounded the world and channeling it was easy. Here, all the magic and elemental powers were well hidden in four magical nexuses and outside these nexuses, the only way to channel the power was from nature itself.

His eyes got flooded with darkness as he let the power of Air take him over. He gathered the winds between his raised arms and unleashed a windstorm on the mostly deserted city. Supported by the wind, the fire spread through the city like a hungry beast, devouring one wooden building after another.

Mrak Delar turned the windstorm to the west, adding more power into it. He allowed the wind to pick up huge pieces of burning wood and debris and carry them through the air, unleashing the fiery rain on the city.

The dark swirling clouds of smoke rose high in the air and a few minutes later, most of the city was consumed by the blazing inferno.

1

~ ZANE BURNS, A.K.A GUNZ ~

Modern day. Key West, Florida

The evening was warm and humid. The street lights and neon gleam of the storefronts were promoting a festive and slightly mysterious atmosphere. The street was overflowing with people. The unsuspecting crowd of tourists was promenading along Duval Street, completely unaware of everything that was going on right before their noses. Carefree, they were chatting, eating, and gaping at the colorful shops' displays.

Gunz quickly crossed Duval and walked into a shadowy alley between two stores. As soon as he escaped the crowded street, diving into the muggy darkness of a small narrow alley, he reached into his pocket and pulled his Swiss army knife out. Holding the knife in his hand, he switched to a light run. His Salamander senses were heightened to the maximum revealing the presence of dark vampiric energy all around him. The vampires realized that he wasn't human, and they didn't like it. They were in front of him and behind him, surrounding him, creeping up closer and closer, following his every step.

A light breeze brought a much-needed freshness infused

with the light scent of the ocean. Gunz smirked. He was almost there. Not too far from the shore, there was an old semi-demolished house. This house was his final destination, marked by the Scarlet Queen.

A few months ago, a large group of rogue vampires settled there, using it as their nest. The vampire queen Akira Ida approached them, but they refused to accept her as their queen and comply with her rules. The Scarlet Queen wasn't the type to accept rejection easily. And since Gunz needed some practice using his newly improved sword skills in real-life situations, she decided that sending the young Fire Salamander to deal with the rebels was the right thing to do. Gunz had no doubt that it was a win-win situation for the queen—her student would get some practice and the rebellious faction of vampires would be vanquished, serving as a lesson to others who dared to disobey her.

Akira had been giving Gunz swordsmanship lessons since he got back from Kendral and she was happy with his general progress. She expressed her complete confidence in his skills, stating that he would be able to deal with the situation at hand without any problems.

Before Gunz opened his fire portal to Key West, Akira didn't forget to remind him that the point of this exercise was to destroy all the rogue vampires without using his magic or the Salamander fire power, only his sword. What she neglected to mention was how many vampires were in this nest. Right now, he could count at least ten vampires around him, if not more. And he had no idea how many of them were inside the house.

"Come out to Key West, get yourself a little vampire action, have a few laughs…" muttered Gunz, channeling John McClain as he kept running toward the ocean.

Two vampires materialized in front of him and he skidded to a screeching halt. Teleporting wasn't one of the vampire powers, but they moved so fast and soundless that it looked like they just popped up out of nowhere. The first vampire threw a punch. As a Fire Salamander, Gunz wasn't as fast as the vampires, but he was fast enough to see it coming. He took a tiny step back, turning his head to the side and watched the vampire's fist sailing less than an inch away from his face, missing him.

The force with which the punch was thrown, pulled the vampire forward, and all Gunz had to do was use his opponent's momentum to send him rolling to the ground. As the infuriated vampire scrambled to his knees growling, Gunz whispered a short spell, turning his knife into a long medieval sword. Before the dumbfounded vamp could get back to his feet, he swung his sword, decapitating the kneeling monster in one swift motion.

The dead body disintegrated in a matter of seconds, leaving nothing but a pile of dirty ashes behind. The second vampire roared as he launched at Gunz, his lips curled in a wolfish snarl. Gunz caught him in the air, his fingers firmly wrapping around the vampire's neck and threw him down. Before the vampire could get up, Gunz's sword whistled through the air and cleanly cut his head off.

He didn't wait for the beheaded corps to turn into ashes and continued on his path to the vampires' nest. As he approached the house, at least ten vampires who were guarding the entrance separated from the shadows and leisurely paced toward him, the cold grins on their faces exposing their dangerous fangs. All of them were tall and looked strong enough to stop a rhino with their bare hands even without the use of their vampire's strength. Gunz didn't slow down, a grim uneven smirk playing on his lips.

The vamps didn't wait for him to reach them. Baring their sharp fangs, all of them attacked at the same time. Gunz rolled on his shoulder, avoiding their grabby hands and long hooked claws. As he came out of the roll with one knee down, his sword hissed through the air, cutting through the muscles and ligaments of their legs.

Cursing furiously, they pulled back for a moment. The vampires were healing fast, but the damage Gunz inflicted gave him the opportunity he needed to regroup. He hopped to his feet just in time to see the growling mass of monsters closing up on him again. He spun around, his sword finding its victims as he moved in a circle with the unexpected speed that could rival the velocity of any vampire.

A few minutes later, only ten piles of gray ashes remained on the ground. It seemed that all the vampires were gone. At least on the outside. Gunz looked down at his bloodied sword, breathing hard. His clothes were torn in a few places and hot streams of blood were running down his arms, chest and back, where the vampires managed to catch him with their claws. One of them was quick enough to sink his teeth into his shoulder, leaving behind a gaping hole filled with dark blood. He touched his wounded shoulder and winced in pain.

Gunz probed the house with his Salamander senses and grunted, frustrated. The house was filled with the undead, their dark energy fused into a heavy venomous cloud. He couldn't even count how many of them were there. The house was dark, and nothing was moving inside. But it didn't mean that the vamps inside weren't alert and ready to spring into action as soon as he opened the door.

Gunz carefully moved his left arm, checking the mobility of his damaged shoulder. *No good, I have no strength in my left arm. It's useless,* thought Gunz, but slowly moved toward the door of the dark house.

"If I survive this, I swear, I'm going to give Akira a piece of my mind," he mumbled, walking up the steps, ready to kick the door open.

"Why don't you give it to me now."

Akira's soft voice filled with authority sounded behind his

back. Gunz lowered his sword and turned around. He bowed to her awkwardly as his torn shoulder responded with sharp twinges of agony to his every move. She approached him and unceremoniously pulled his shredded shirt off his shoulder, wiping a few drops of his blood off the edge of his ripped flesh with her finger. For a moment her eyes lit up with a hungry scarlet glow, but she pulled his shirt back up and took a deep breath, wiping the blood off her fingers on her pants.

"Do you want me to heal you?" asked the Scarlet Queen, her voice calm and even, like she wasn't ready to sink her fangs into his neck just a moment ago. "You know that vampire's blood has some healing properties."

"Thank you, Akira, but no," replied Gunz. "I don't want your blood circulating through my system, giving you some kind of control over me."

She shrugged her narrow shoulders indifferently. "I don't know if this so-called control would work on a Fire Salamander," she said, raising her eyebrows at him. "Zane, are you seriously considering fighting a giant vampire nest one-handed?"

Gunz shrugged and cringed, clasping his shoulder. "Unless you have a better idea, I'm going in," he said dryly. "I can't leave so many rogue vampires running around a tourist destination."

Akira shook her head. "I do have a better idea," she said with a sigh. "I was watching you fighting... How many vampires did you vanquish alone?"

"Twelve, I think. Why?"

"Because, it's enough for one day of training. We're going to go in together and you're going to use your magic, not your sword."

He nodded, a tiny lopsided smile making an appearance as he kicked the door with his leg. The door flew open hitting the wall with a loud bang but remained on its hinges. A couple of vampires that were standing close to the entrance staggered backward, stumbling into the dark mass of other vamps. The house was so dark inside that Gunz still couldn't count how many monsters he was dealing with. It seemed like the chain of glowing red eyes was endless.

"*Ventius*," he whispered, extending his right hand forward. A powerful blast of wind rushed toward the vampires, blowing them off their feet and throwing their bodies against the wall.

Akira slipped inside, touching his arm on the way in. "Give me a second," she whispered.

She approached the squirming mass of vampires who were still struggling to untangle their limbs, staring down at them from her formidable height of five feet. The undead shuffled around and a few of them got up to their feet, silently glowering at the Scarlet Queen, gnashing their fangs.

"This is your last chance. I will not ask again," said the queen calmly. "Bend your knee and pledge your fealty to me and I will let you live."

A large vampire that looked like a biker with his leather jacket and long greasy hair stepped forward. He tongued his cheek and spit on the floor aiming at her feet. "Never," he hissed, fury making his eyes glow bright red. "You work with a hunter. Against your own kind. You are not fit to be our queen."

"A hunter?" asked Akira. "Hardly. He is so much more than that. And he's not my employee. He is my student."

"Whatever he is, he's killing our kind!" yelled the vampire, scowling at the queen with freezing contempt. "We will never accept your rule."

"As you wish," said Akira indifferently and turned around. As she passed Gunz, she touched his arm again and whispered into his ear, "Fire Salamander, make this house burn hotter than hell. Kill them all." She walked out of the house and closed the door, leaving Gunz alone.

As quiet as the Scarlet Queen spoke, the vampires heard her. They all screamed at the same time, some hurdled toward Gunz, some tried to break out through the boarded windows of the house.

"*Ignius Amplio*," hissed Gunz, entwining his magic with his elemental power.

The fiery inferno unfolded before him, swallowing the house and its inhabitants within a few seconds. Guns walked out of the house when the roof caved in and the last screams of the burning monsters died out. He found Akira standing a few feet away from the burning house, her sharply angled eyes squinting at the brightness of the flames. All around her, the ground was covered in ashes. It was everything that remained of the vampires who somehow escaped from the smoldering trap that Gunz created.

Her eyes shifted to Gunz and the corners of her small mouth quirked up. For a moment, she looked like a cat who was watching a canary. He glanced down and grunted. His shirt that was already shredded before the fire, completely fell apart and his pants were torn in a few places, too.

"Well, my student, you presented yourself nicely," she said, attempting to sound serious. "I'm talking about your fighting skills, of course."

"But of course you are," muttered Gunz, shaking his head.

Akira giggled, pressing her hand to her mouth. Gunz rolled his eyes, wondering how an ancient vampire who killed more people than anyone cared to count, could still have the laughter of a little girl.

"I'll see you next week, Zane." Akira waved her hand and was gone before he could say anything else to her.

Gunz sighed and turned back to the house. It was still burning, smoldering flames rising high, the dark clouds of smoke disappearing into the night sky. He waved his hand, silently commanding the fire to cease. He was positive that by now all the vampires were dead and leaving the fire burning would just attract the attention of humans. It wasn't necessary.

As he was watching the fire gradually die down, he felt a light vibration in his pocket and reached for his phone. Good news—his phone survived the massive fight with the vampires. Bad news—his boss, Agent Andrews, was calling him at one o'clock in the morning.

"Hello," Gunz answered the phone, expecting problems.

"Gunz, did I wake you up?" Jim didn't sound sleepy. Most likely he was still in his office.

"No. What's going on, Jim?"

"I need you to come in," said Jim calmly. "There is something we need to discuss as soon as possible."

"I'll come in first thing in the morning. 8 AM sharp," replied Gunz, knowing ahead of time what would follow.

"No, I need you to come in immediately," objected Jim, notes of aggravation breaking through his calm front. "It can't wait until morning."

"Jim, it's going to have to wait until tomorrow," said Gunz with a sigh. "I'm in Key West. Just finished cleaning a giant vampires' nest. One of the vamps managed to bite a chunk off my shoulder. I'm bleeding, and my clothes are half-gone. I have to go home and heal myself, Jim. I'm in the world of pain. Sorry."

Jim grunted and Gunz heard him slamming his fist on his desk. "Bad timing, Gunz. Very bad timing. I'm sure it was the Scarlet Queen who sent you to clean up her mess."

"Yes, sir," confirmed Gunz. "But what did you want me to do? Leave a huge population of rogue vampires hunting the tourists around the Keys? It's been over a month since I came back from Kendral and I'm swimming up to my eyeballs in supernatural bullshit! It's worse than it's ever been here. I don't understand what's going on."

"I don't know," replied Jim dryly. "Your buddy Aidan is saying the same thing. Him and his team don't have a minute of peace. Anyway, I need you in my office stat. Just open your portal into my office as soon as you are ready."

"Jim—," started Gunz, but Jim interrupted him.

"Go home, heal yourself and come to my office right away. Not in the morning. Right away! Do you understand me?"

"Yes, sir. I'll see you in an hour."

Gunz hung up the phone, putting it back in his jean back pocket. Then he turned his sword back into the Swiss army knife and put it away.

"Fire Salamander—go," he muttered to himself and waved his hand, opening the fire curtain of his portal.

2

~ ZANE BURNS, A.K.A. GUNZ ~

Almost two months passed since Gunz returned from Kendral. The six months he spent in the magical realm were nonstop training. His mentor Kal—the Fire Elemental, and the Master of Power Mrak Delar were relentless. They put him through hell, teaching him how to use his fire power and magic. And if that wasn't enough, every day after the exhausting training, they were sending him to the Riders' library.

Surrounded by dusty ancient scrolls, he had to study the Dragon tongue. After all, the Dragon tongue was the original language of magic. Spells, enchantments and incantations—everything was written in this complicated, tongue-twisting language that painfully reminded him of Latin. For creation or for combat, if he wanted to use his magic effectively, he had to know the Dragon tongue and understand the laws and rules that were driving everything in the world of magic.

For a full six months he had no time to breathe, hardly getting a few hours of sleep a day. When Kal decided that he had enough of training and opened the portal for him to go back to his home-world, Gunz couldn't help but feel relieved. As usual, he was going to miss Kal and Mrak Delar with his endless sarcasm. And of course, he was going to miss all his friends in Kendral. But he desperately needed to get some rest and at least a short break from the world of magic. Just a touch of normality. Was it too much to ask?

Besides, he was concerned with the situation in his world. From an occasional message he got from Aidan, he knew that the Scarlet Queen's prediction came true. The air demon Eve left a supernatural turmoil in her wake. Eve was gone, but the chaos was still there, scarier and messier than ever before.

And now that he was finally home, he still had no peace, no break from the supernatural, not even a moment of normality that he desperately longed for.

No rest for the wicked?

* * *

GUNZ CAME out from the shower and quickly got dressed. He healed his wounds as soon as he crossed the threshold of his house, but his whole body was still aching with exhaustion. The clock was showing past two in the morning and all he wanted to do was sleep. *Jim, why are you doing this to me?* he thought grumpily, making sure that his Swiss army knife was in his pocket, and waved his hand opening the fire portal into Jim's office.

He walked through the portal and stepped out in the middle of Jim's office on the eighth floor of the FBI building. The office was semi-dark, lit only by a desk lamp that was sitting next to a computer monitor. Jim was standing next to the window with his arms folded over his chest, leaning against the wall. The yellow rays of electric light reflected on his face, throwing deep shadows around his eyes, making him look grim and worn out.

A woman was sitting in front of Jim's desk. As soon as Gunz manifested in the office, she got up and turned around. Her pale blue eyes drilled into him with unconcealed interest, but she was showing no signs of being shocked by his less-than-normal way of entering. He carefully scanned her with his senses but found no magical energy in her. Seemingly, she was human. By now he learned not to rely blindly only on his magical senses. There were quite a few powerful magical beings who could suppress and conceal their magical energy, making it undetectable to the others with magic.

The woman was dressed in a pantsuit and stood tall and erect, with her hands crossed behind her back in a military manner. All her appearance was exuding toughness, mental and physical, and the kind of authority that no one in their right mind would ever dare to challenge. Her brown hair was slicked back and twisted into a tight bun on the back of her head, and her pale face had no traces of any makeup. She wasn't ugly, but there was nothing feminine about this woman.

Jim stepped forward, gesturing toward Gunz. "Agent Zvereva, allow me to introduce my consultant, Mr. Zane Burns." Jim turned to Gunz and continued, his voice unusually raspy, "Zane, Agent Zvereva is an Interpol agent and she is here because she needs your assistance. I received a direct order to provide Agent Zvereva with anything she asks for. Anything at all. She asked for you."

Gunz eyes widened. He wasn't used to people knowing that he was working for the FBI as Jim always kept it under wraps. Outside Jim's team, no one knew about his position with the FBI. But even the members of the team didn't know what he truly was.

"Thank you for the introduction, Agent Andrews," said Agent Zvereva, her voice deep and clear.

She extended her hand to Gunz. He took her hand, feeling her icy fingers forcefully crushing his and met her cold, penetrating gaze. Without thinking twice, he applied some pressure to her hand, returning the favor. There was something unsettling about this woman, but he couldn't figure out what it was.

"Nice to meet you, ma'am," said Gunz. "What can I do for you?"

Her lips formed a thin smile, and she pointed at an empty chair in front of Jim's desk. "Sit down, Mr. Burns," she offered, taking the other chair, "we need to talk."

Agent Zvereva commandeered Jim's office, behaving like he wasn't even there. Gunz threw a quick glance at Jim, but he just gave him a hardly visible nod and didn't move. His face was slightly strained, his dark eyebrows pulled over his eyes in a frown. He behaved like a person who knew something he didn't like but was resolved to keep his mouth shut. Gunz suppressed a sigh and sat down.

"What can I do for you, Agent Zvereva," he repeated his question.

"Three days ago, a priceless artifact was stolen from a private collector in Moscow," said Agent Zvereva calmly. "I need your help to recover it and return it to the rightful owner."

Gunz leaned back in his chair, crossing his legs. "This statement doesn't tell me anything," he said. "A private collector? Why is Interpol involved in a simple robbery case? And why do you need me? I'm sure that between Russian Militsiya and their Criminal Investigation Department, they can find someone who is qualified to solve a robbery case."

She stared at him without blinking for a few seconds like he was some kind of general nuisance and when she finally replied, notes of aggravation broke through in her even voice.

"If Russian Militsiya could solve this case, they wouldn't bother contacting me. And the reason I'm here, in this office, is because you're the only person who is qualified to recover the stolen artifact. You have special talents that are quite unique, Mr. Burns. I need them."

Gunz shuddered inwardly. She obviously was implying that she needed the Fire Salamander. How could she know about his so-called special talents? How did she find out and who else knew about him? Something wasn't right. If this woman was human, how could she know all this?

"Zane," said Jim quietly without changing his position, "the order from above was loud and clear—we must cooperate."

The same thin smile cut across Agent Zvereva's face at Jim's words. "Yes, Mr. Burns. With your military background, surely you understand what an order to cooperate means, don't you?"

"Yes, ma'am," replied Gunz dryly. "I know what it means. But since you seem to know everything about me, surely you realize that I'm no longer in the military and I'm not an official FBI agent either. So, if you want my cooperation and assistance, you need to answer my questions, or you'll be watching me walk away. Let's start with how you found out about my *special talents*."

"Zane, please!" Jim shook his head, taking a step forward. There was something in Jim's voice and the way he moved that sent chills down Gunz's spine.

"It's okay, Agent Andrews," said Agent Zvereva, raising her hand up to stop him, "I'll answer his questions. At least those that I can answer." She turned to Gunz. "You are the Fire Salamander, Mr. Burns. The only Fire Salamander in our world." She checked her watch and glanced at the office door. "Just like Agent Andrews, I have my own informant. She should arrive here in a few minutes. She'll explain how I learned about you. Please, be patient—"

A soft knock interrupted her speech.

"Come in," she yelled, turning toward the door and a derisive smirk appeared on her face.

The door opened up slowly and a woman in her late twenties walked inside. Gunz gasped and jumped to his feet, knocking his chair down. A wave of rage seared through him setting his whole body ablaze as he partially lost control of his fire power. His mind was overwhelmed by anger and he couldn't think clearly. One second he was standing, his hands clenched into tight fists as he fruitlessly tried to get in control, the next second he was by the door, pinning the young woman to the wall, his flaming hand wrapped around her neck. She gasped, struggling to breathe, her pupils dilated from the pain of burns.

"You!" roared Gunz. "I warned you! I told you that if I ever see you again, I will kill you! Treacherous bitch!"

"Zane, stop!" Gunz felt someone seizing his shoulders and ripping his hand off the young woman. "Zane, please..." Somewhere in the back of his murky mind he recognized Jim's voice and let go, allowing Jim to pull him away from the woman.

"What's going on, Zane?" asked Jim, staring down at the blisters of burns on his palms. "Who is this woman and what did she do? I've never seen you so furious." Jim turned to Agent Zvereva and her informant, gesturing at the door. "Agent, may I have the room, please? I need a few minutes with Zane alone."

Agent Zvereva smirked and shook her head no.

"Anything you need to say to him, you can say in front of me, Agent Andrews. From this moment on, Mr. Burns is part of my investigation and, as such, he reports to me. If you wish to know why Mr. Burns is a little hot under the collar, I can explain."

She pointed toward the young woman who was crying silent tears, clutching her burnt neck with both hands. Zvereva's cold eyes took in her appearance and an expression of distaste distorted her features.

"Allow me to introduce Lera Volkov. She is the only daughter of the late Belarusian gangster Viktor Volkov. A couple of years ago, Lera betrayed Captain Oleg Svetlov who was Mr. Burns' commanding officer and his best friend, I believe. As a result of her actions, Mr. Burns and two of his friends almost lost their lives during the rescue operation they ran to save Captain Svetlov. So, I can understand his smoldering hate toward Lera, but he will need to curb his emotions because Lera is an integral part of this operation."

"I will never work with her," growled Gunz. He finally got in control of his fire power, but his eyes were still glowing red. "I'm done here."

He made a move toward the door, but Jim seized his arm above his elbow and whispered into his ear. "Zane, please stop. I can't order you to work with them, the only thing I can do is ask... I'm in a bad situation, man... If you don't cooperate, I'll lose everything I worked for. My career will be over. My whole life..." His whisper trailed into silence, his fingers nervously digging into Gunz's arm.

"Jim, I don't understand. What's going on? Why?" Gunz asked quietly.

Jim started to say something, but Agent Zvereva approached them, interrupting their conversation.

"Enough with the whispering," she said in a no-nonsense tone. "Mr. Burns, do we have an understanding?"

Gunz met Jim's haunted eyes and nodded. "Yes, ma'am," he replied quietly. "I'll work with you. What do you need me to do?"

She smiled icily and grabbed his left hand, checking his watch with interest. "Standard FBI issue watch, I assume? GPS tracker?" she asked, throwing a wry look at Jim. He nodded. "Leave this watch here, Mr. Burns. You won't need it where we're going."

"The watch stays," objected Gunz firmly.

Agent Zvereva shrugged but didn't argue. "Fine, you can keep your toy. Now say goodbye to Agent Andrews because we're leaving immediately."

Gunz nodded and turned toward Jim. He didn't like the situation in the slightest, but there was nothing he could do at this moment in fear of hurting his friend.

"Take care, Jim," he said, as he squeezed his hand in a firm handshake. "I don't know how long this operation will take, but if you need any help while I am gone, call Aidan. Do you understand me?" Jim nodded silently, his lips pressed in a grim straight line.

Gunz turned around and followed Agent Zvereva and Lera out of the office. They walked out of the FBI building and she led him toward a black SUV with tinted windows that was parked in front of the building. She unlocked the door and pointed at the front passenger seat.

"Sit down and put your seatbelt on," she ordered.

He shrugged but climbed into the SUV and locked the seatbelt. In the meantime, Agent Zvereva walked around and got behind the wheel, waiting for Lera to get in the back seat. Once Lera was ready, she started the car and turned to Gunz.

"Are you comfortable?" she asked with a crooked smile on her face. Gunz raised his eyes at her, surprised by her question and nodded. "Perfect! Now, it's time to sleep, Fire Salamander."

A powerful wave of magical energy expanded around her. Gunz gasped, his Salamander's senses overwhelmed by the sheer strength of her magical presence. He reached for his magic, but it was blocked. She touched his forehead with her two fingers muttering a short spell and everything around him went dark.

3

~ ZANE BURNS, A.K.A. GUNZ ~

A glass of icy water thrown in his face wasn't Gunz's favorite way to wake up, by far. To him, touching cold water felt like how submerging a hand into a pot of boiling water would feel to a human. But it wasn't only his face, every inch of his skin was affected by the contact with frosty water. His wet clothes clinging to his body added to his overall discomfort.

Gunz opened his eyes and slowly sat up, supporting himself with his arms. Agent Zvereva was towering over him with an empty glass in her hand and a contemptuous smile on her face. Lera was standing behind her, peeking over her shoulder. She was wrapped in a thick wool cape and still shivered from cold.

"I hope you had a nice rest because it's time to get to work," said Zvereva.

"You couldn't find a nicer way to wake me up than throwing the cold water in my face?" asked Gunz, wiping his face with his hand.

"Be grateful that the glass didn't follow," huffed Zvereva throwing the empty glass on the ground next to him. "Well, at least you didn't revert into your natural state. I was a little worried that waking you up in such an abrupt manner could cost my dear Lera her life, so I blocked your magic and your elemental power." She cackled, winking at a half-frozen Lera.

"I never revert unless I want to do it," muttered Gunz, surveying his surroundings.

The darkness of the night wrapped around him like a soft blanket. The sky deprived of sunlight was sparkling with a myriad of stars. The winter sky and the low temperatures added some brightness to the stars and extra crispiness into the frosty air.

He was sitting in the middle of nowhere. As far as he could see, on his left and on his right, a snow-veiled field was stretched for miles around. The snow around him melted into a frosty puddle from the heat of his body and his clothes were soaked with cold water. As the Fire Salamander, he didn't feel the cold, but he didn't enjoy the touch of wet fabric against his body.

A dark naked forest was looming a few yards away from him. A low dirty fog was swirling over the snow, slithering between leafless trees. A frosty winter breeze rushed through the woods lifting the fog up and carrying it forward, but the branches and shrubbery didn't move, remaining still and soundless. The forest looked dead and ghostly.

A tall iron post was erected on the border between the dead forest and the empty field. A thick iron chain was wrapped around the post. On the ground, all around the post, a pile of dry branches was scattered like someone was getting ready to set the post on fire.

This place was eerie and odd. But the strangest aspect of this place was the overwhelming sensation of magic and power flowing all around him. Gunz remembered the way he felt the presence of the Original Power in Kendral and what he was experiencing right now was tenfold more intense. Even with his magic blocked by Agent Zvereva, he felt intoxicated by the energy of this place. This couldn't be his world.

"Where are we?" he asked, getting up, squeezing as much water out of his pants as he could.

"I thought you'd never ask," said Agent Zvereva, shaking her head. "Don't you feel it? I'm sure even with your magic blocked, you can still feel the presence of magical energy all around you."

"I do," replied Gunz calmly. "So, where are we?"

She chuckled. "We're in the Land of Dreams, Fire Salamander. One of four magical nexuses on Earth. I hope your mentor taught you at least some history of magic."

"Why did you bring me here?" asked Gunz through clenched teeth, slowly losing his patience. She was toying with him and he felt helpless with his magic blocked and Jim's future on the line. "What do you want from me?"

Agent Zvereva pursed her lips. "Mr. Burns, you have more power and magic than you can imagine, yet your knowledge of magic is skin-deep. To be able to really use the magic, you need to understand the forces that drive it, the history behind..."

Her voice melted into nothing. Gunz stared at her lips moving but didn't hear a word she was saying, his mind far away. Everything she was saying sounded so familiar. He learned a lot about magic during the last six months. There was still a lot he didn't know, but he was far from ignorant. In his mind, he went back to the moment he saw this woman for the first time and he remembered how he couldn't sense any magical energy in her. To block a Fire Salamander's access to his elemental power, she had to be an extremely powerful witch. And the way she was shadowing her own power was like—

"Are you daydreaming?"

Zvereva's shrilling voice made him flinch. He raised his eyes at her, as understanding flashed over him.

"Are you a Guardian witch?"

"A witch? You're insulting me, Mr. Burns," she huffed. "I'm a

Guardian mage. A seventh level Guardian mage. In case you didn't know, the seventh level is the highest level a Guardian mage can achieve."

"Then why didn't you present yourself as such? Why all these lies? Why threaten Agent Andrews and pressure me? If your organization needed my help, all they had to do was ask!"

"Guardians do not disclose their true nature in front of humans, Mr. Burns," objected Zvereva coldly.

"So, what do you need me to do?"

"I already told you. I need you to retrieve a magical artifact that was stolen," started Zvereva, shoving her hands into the pockets of her jacket. "What I didn't tell you was where I needed you to go and what this artifact was."

"I assume you're going to tell me all that sooner or later," muttered Gunz.

"Yes, Mr. Burns, as soon as you take down a notch on your sarcasm," replied Zvereva, dryly. "Being disrespectful to a person who just rendered you powerless is not a very smart move."

Gunz raised his hands up, an uneven grin on his face. "Sorry. I'm all ears."

She checked her wristwatch and smirked, satisfied. "It's almost midnight. In a few minutes, I'm going to open the gates to the Nav. And you are going to walk through these gates—"

"The Nav? As in the Dark Nav? The World of spirits and demons?" hissed Gunz, staggering back a few steps. "Are you out of your goddamn mind? Right now, we are in the Yav, the world of living. No one can walk between Yav and Nav! There is only one god in the whole Slavic pantheon who can do it. And there is a good reason why no one can travel between these realms!"

"I'm pleased to see that you know the ancient Slavic mythology." Zvereva slowly clapped her hands together, applauding him. "You are not as ignorant as I thought you were. But look around, Salamander. You are standing right on the border between two worlds. I can, and I will open the gate. And when I do, you will play your part. You're an immortal Child of Fire. Besides one major Slavic deity, you are the only living being who can walk through these gates and have a chance to come back in one piece. As you put it, most of the gods can't do it, I can't do it either, so it has to be you."

Gunz gaped at her silently. The danger of this quest and all the risks involved were enormous. He wasn't afraid to die. Being the immortal Fire Salamander, death wasn't an issue. However, the idea of being lost in the World of spirits and demons didn't sound appealing. The realm of Nav was ruled by Chernobog, the god of Destruction and his wife Morena, the goddess of Winter and Death. He didn't think Chernobog would appreciate him breaking into his realm uninvited and very much alive. Only dead and things that shouldn't be alive in Yav belonged in the grim realm of Chernobog.

Zvereva took in his state of bewilderment and tapped her masculine boot on the ground, impatience in her every move.

"I have no time to deal with your fears, Mr. Burns. Remember what's at stake here. Besides the wellbeing of your boss and friend, Agent Andrews, there is also a general concern about the balance of power in this world. This artifact is extremely powerful and leaving it in the hands of Chernobog is tilting the balance of power toward the darkness. So, you will do as you are commanded. The artifact you need to recover and bring to me is a pendant that looks like a double-edged axe, decorated with gold inlays. Remember, once you go through the gates, I will be the only person who can bring you back."

Holy shit! She wants me to steal a magical pendant from Chernobog? The ancient Russian god of Destruction versus a newborn Fire Salamander. She is out of her friggin' mind!

Gunz shook his head, raising his hand up. "Hold on. I can't go into the fight with the god of Destruction on a whim. I won't be able to even come close to him. You need to give me some time, Agent Zvereva. I have to think this operation through, get some kind of a plan—"

Her cracked dry laughter interrupted him in mid-sentence, and he fell silent.

"I'm opening the gates in a few minutes, Mr. Burns, and I can't give you any time for preparations. Deal with it," she said, shoving her hands into her pants pockets. "And honestly, you shouldn't be worried about how you are going to fight with Chernobog just yet. The only question you should be asking is how you are going to get in touch with me once you complete your mission. In case you missed it, let me repeat—I'm the only person in this world who can bring you back from the Nav."

"Okay... Fine," said Gunz, swallowing hard. "How am I going to communicate with you?"

She approached him and tugged on his shirt. "Take your shirt off," she ordered, checking her watch again. "We are running out of time. Do it fast."

"Excuse me?" asked Gunz, taking a step back.

"What don't you understand?" she barked, closing the distance between them, invading his personal space. "I said, take off your goddamn shirt or I swear to God, I'll rip it off you! Move it!"

Gunz unbuttoned his shirt and took it off, holding it in his hand. Zvereva seized his left shoulder with one hand, her fingers digging into his skin, and pressed the palm of her other hand to his chest. She muttered a short spell under her breath and immediately, a searing pain jolted through his body.

Gunz cried out, fighting her grip. She let him go and cocked her head, observing her handy work. A glowing red rune was decorating his chest. Its shine was slowly dimming down as the pain was subsiding. Gunz looked down at the rune on his chest and gently probed it with his finger. It was still sore.

"How does it work?" he exhaled, the ability to speak slowly returning to him. "How can I speak with you through it?"

"You won't be able to speak with me. Once you walk through the gates, you are on your own. When you acquire the artifact and are ready to go back, press your palm to the rune and send some of your fire magic through it. I'll feel it and pull you out of the Nav. Any other questions, Mr. Burns?"

"No, ma'am," replied Gunz quietly, putting his shirt back on.

"Perfect," she muttered, turning around sharply. Zvereva grabbed Lera by her hand and pulled her forward toward the dead forest. "Now, darling, it's time for you to play your part in this operation."

Zvereva pushed Lera, and she staggered forward, wrapping her arms around the post to prevent herself from falling. Zvereva muttered another spell and thick ropes erupted from her hands, wrapping around Lera and tying her to the iron post. Lera screamed, tears streaming down her pale face, distorted by fear. But no matter how much she pushed against the magical restraints, she couldn't break free.

"What are you doing?" yelled Gunz, making a move toward Lera, but he was too late.

"Ignius Amplio!" shouted Agent Zvereva, pointing her hand at the pile of dry branches next to Lera's feet.

A wall of scorching fire surrounded the iron post, Lera's bone-chilling screams of pain breaking through the crackling of the smoldering flames.

"Cease!" yelled Gunz, but his magic and power were blocked. His own element couldn't hear him.

The magically powered fire was burning a lot hotter than a normal fire would and a few seconds later, it was all over. The flames slowly died down. The stench of burnt human flesh mixed with thick black clouds of smoke were still rising high into the night sky. There was nothing left of Lera, not even ashes.

"What did you do?" whispered Gunz, unable to take his eyes off the iron post.

Zvereva shrugged her shoulders indifferently.

"I did what I had to do to open the gates to the other side," she said coldly. There was no regret, no sympathy, no human emotions of any kind in her voice. "To open the gates to the Dark Nav, someone must die an unnatural death. Don't play innocent, soldier. I'm sure you killed your fair share during your military tours. What is one life compared to the future of this whole world, Mr. Burns? And correct me if I am wrong... Weren't you going to strangle her just a few hours ago? As far as I'm concerned, by killing her, I did you a favor."

Gunz couldn't deny that he hated Lera for her betrayal. After what she did to his friend Oleg, he could never forgive her. Just the sound of her name was making him boil with fury. But as angry with her as he was, he never wished her to die. Especially not this way. He cringed inwardly, disgust making his stomach churn.

"Why did you choose her for your sacrifice?" asked Gunz.

"Does it really matter?" Zvereva answered his question with a question.

Her eyes lingered on something behind the post and a slow predacious smile spread through her hard face. Gunz followed the direction of her gaze and everything inside him stilled. Behind the post, a black square abyss was slowly growing in size, consuming the light of the stars.

"Time to go." Zvereva gestured toward the obsidian emptiness. "This is your door to the Dark Nav. Get moving. It's not going to stay open forever."

Barely moving his unbending legs, Gunz walked toward the gaping square hole that seemed to lead into nowhere. Fear was coiling in him like a tight spring, ready to break free. He wanted to run away, but he was still walking forward.

He was almost at the edge of the gates when he heard a

commotion behind him and felt a welcome wave of fire energy enveloping him with the warmth of hope. Gunz spun around and his mouth fell open.

A man, riding on a large black stallion with a long golden mane, was approaching them at full speed. In his hand, he was holding a flaming sword, and the ground was burning behind him. His eyes were two flaming forges. His long red hair flowed over his back and shoulders like a flaming river. The amount of fire energy this man was emitting exceeded the energy of the Great Salamander himself. His fire power was so overwhelming that even with suppressed magic, Gunz could feel it.

"Stop!" shouted the man, jumping off the horse. His deep voice echoed through the dead forest and the ground trembled at the touch of his boots.

"If you're here to protect your elemental brother, you're too late, Semargl." Agent Zvereva seized Gunz's shirt sharply and pushed him through the gates.

Gunz yelped, struggling to keep his balance but he couldn't. In the last moment, he saw Semargl rushing toward Zvereva, but she whispered something and turned into a dark mist, disappearing into the night sky.

The gates to the Dark Nav closed above him and he started to fall into a swirling, mushy nothingness.

4

~ AIDAN ~

Aidan walked into his office at the Elements Martial Arts and closed the door. It was six in the afternoon and he had thirty minutes before the beginning of his next martial arts lesson. He sat down in his chair, folding his arms, stretching his legs in front of him.

Lately, there wasn't a quiet night where he didn't have to walk the streets, patrolling the city. The amount of strange and supernatural activity grew to unusual heights, and the combined efforts of his team, the FBI team and Zane with his fire power, didn't seem to be enough to keep everything under control and people safe. Even though he was a god of the Otherworld, in this world he still had a physical body and he required food and rest. And with everything that was going on, he was getting neither. Sleepless nights and constant physical exertion were taking their toll.

Aidan closed his eyes and relaxed, feeling his mind drifting away. A loud knock on his door made him jolt upright in his chair. He grunted, rubbing his face with his hands.

"Come in," he said, his voice hoarse and cleared his throat.

Agent Jim Andrews walked into his office, closely followed

by Angelique and stopped in front of his desk. Aidan observed Jim's drained face and Angelique's red glassy eyes and frowned.

"Agent Andrews," he said instead of hello. "Angelique."

"Aidan," said Jim, his voice strained and fell silent. "Aidan, I think Gunz... Zane is in trouble and it's all my—" He squeezed the bridge of his nose with his fingers, closing his eyes for a moment and sighed. "Something is wrong, and he said to call you."

"Please explain," said Aidan, rising. Jim wouldn't come to his place of business without calling first. And the fact that Jim was standing in his office, worried and upset, was giving away how serious the situation was, making him feel uneasy.

"Aidan, Zane is no longer in this world," whispered Angelique, answering his question before Jim could say anything. Tears ran down her colorless cheeks and she quickly wiped them with her fingers, averting her eyes.

"What do you mean?" asked Aidan, slightly leaning forward. "Did Kal summon him back to Kendral? You know that Zane is a Fire Salamander. He can't die. The only way the Fire Salamander can end his life is by dissolving into his own element and Zane is too young to make such an extreme decision."

Angelique shook her head no and her lips trembled. "He is no longer in the realm of the living," she said without meeting his eyes. "Since Zane came back from Kendral, I reestablished my psychic connection with him. About an hour ago, our connection was severed. I can't find him anywhere. I don't sense his life force or his magical energy."

The door opened again, and Angel nearly ran into the office. He was half-transformed into his true form, wearing his long trench coat. His hair, now black and long, was windblown, and he was breathing hard, like he just ran a half-marathon.

"Aidan, Zane crossed the veil into one of the realms of the dead," exhaled Angel, panting. "About an hour ago. When it happened, I sensed it right away. But now, I can't detect his presence in any of Death's domains."

Aidan channeled his power and a bright white glow surrounded him. His eyes shone with a brilliant white light and for a few minutes he stared into space, like he was scanning something visible to him only.

"He is not in the Otherworld," he murmured after a few minutes.

With his finger, he drew a complicated rune in the air and infused it with the brilliant glow of his power. Then he touched the rune with his finger and whispered a summoning spell. The air in front of him shimmered with a soft golden light and Uri materialized in the middle of the office, with his body engulfed in golden flames and his mighty wings opened behind his back. As soon as he noticed Jim and Angelique in the office, he grunted and quickly transformed into his human form, throwing a guilty look at Aidan.

"What are you?" mumbled Jim, awestricken, but then shook his head. "Never mind. I am not sure I want to know."

"Uri, Angel and Angelique are both saying that Zane is no longer among the living," said Aidan. "Can you sense him anywhere?"

For a moment Uri closed his eyes and stilled, slightly rising up and levitating a few inches above the floor, cold golden flames softly wrapping around him. Then he lowered himself back down and shook his head. "I can't sense him anywhere."

For a moment, complete silence enveloped the office. Angelique sat down, hiding her face in her hands. Angel and Uri exchanged a troubled look but didn't say anything.

"Jim, can you tell us anything else?" asked Aidan. "I think you're right. Zane is in the realm of the dead. If anyone would know that, it's Angel. So, let's trace it back. When did you see Zane the last time and why did you think he was in trouble because of you?"

Jim quickly recounted everything that happened last night, giving them as many details of his meeting with Agent Zvereva and Lera Volkov as he could. He also mentioned that since Zane left with Agent Zvereva, the GPS in his watch stopped working and his phone went dead too. He didn't hide the fact that Agent Zvereva pressured Zane into working with her, giving him an ultimatum—either he works with her or it would be the end of Jim's career at the FBI.

"Aidan, do you know how to summon Kal?" asked Angelique, notes of desperation in her voice. "Please, Aidan, you're a god... Do something."

"Anyone can summon Kal," said Aidan, furrowing his brow. "Anyone who isn't human, that is. Jim will have to leave."

"Do what you need to do," said Jim, turning around and halted, his eyebrows slowly climbing up, toward his hairline.

A fire curtain unfolded outside the office door and a man walked through it. He was so tall that he had to bend down slightly to pass through the doorway of the office. His body was emitting scorching heat and his eyes were glowing bright red. He quickly observed everyone in the office and his igneous gaze stopped on Aidan. He greeted him with a light nod and a tiny smile touched his lips.

"Aodh mac Lir," he said, and his deep voice with roaring R's seemed to fill the entire space of the office, "I apologize for the intrusion. There is no need to summon Kalidus. The great Fire Elemental cannot help you. I am Semargl, the Fire god of the Slavic pantheon and I can tell you what happened to the young Fire Salamander."

"Hello, Semargl," said Aidan cautiously. He wasn't sure how to take the presence of the fierce Slavic deity in his office. Semargl was a god-protector of the human realms and he wasn't sure how he could know about Zane's disappearance or that Aidan was looking for him. After all, the realms of the dead were closed to all elemental gods. "May I ask how you knew that I was searching for the young Fire Salamander?"

Semargl smirked, the flames rising in his deep eyes. "You are watchful, god of the Otherworld. But the answer you seek is simple. I am the Fire. I am everywhere, and I know everything."

"Without you, we, humans, can't even light a match…" mumbled Angelique. "This is what Kal usually says."

Semargl glanced down at her and his smile got warmer. "Yes, my lady," he replied slightly inclining his head. "Kalidus and I possess many of the same powers. And just like my old friend, the mighty Fire Elemental, I can sense when one of the Children of Fire is in distress. We all dwell in the same element." Then he switched his attention back to Aidan. "I assure you, Aodh, I am here to help."

"I apologize for my mistrust, Semargl. In my line of work, I must stay vigilant at all times," said Aidan with a light bow. "Please tell us everything you know."

"The young Fire Salamander was forced to cross the veil and enter the realm of spirits and demons," said Semargl with a sigh. "I do not know why the mage wanted him to go to the kingdom of Chernobog, but this is where he is now. In the Dark Nav."

"Then why can't I sense him there?" asked Angel. "All realms of the dead are opened to my sight."

Semargl frowned, his hand landing on the pommel of his impressively large sword as he turned to Angel. "That mage must be extremely powerful, if she can conceal the energy of a Fire Salamander from Death himself."

"A mage?" asked Jim. "Zane left my office with an Interpol Agent, not a mage. She was human."

"I forgive you your ignorance," said Semargl throwing a heavy stare in Jim's direction. "You are but a human and the ways of magic are veiled from you. Zane was with a woman who was dressed like a man and had an appearance of a man, despite her sizable bosom. She was harsh and pitiless, willing to do whatever it took to achieve her purpose. Was that the woman he left with?"

Jim nodded, cold sweat glistening on his forehead.

"She was a mage," confirmed Semargl, switching his attention back to Angel. "I assure you, Grim Horseman, your friend is in one of your domains. He is in the Dark Nav and you need to get him out of there before my brother Chernobog will discover him."

"Chernobog is not a hospitable type," mumbled Angel, shivering like from a winter blizzard. "It's not easy to enter his domain, even for me. How was a mage able to send the Fire Salamander in? The veil of the Dark Nav is well protected and hard to breach."

"That mage is clever. She possesses great knowledge that most do not have," replied Semargl. "When a person dies an unnatural death, Chernobog opens the gates into his realm to accept the soul. If a living person has a deep emotional connection with the departed, he has but a few moments to follow the soul through the gates. But there are only a few places in this world where a living person can see the gates into the Dark Nav.

"The mage knew all that. She took your Salamander into the Land of Dreams, to the border between Yav and Nav and she sacrificed someone he probably loved dearly. A young woman perished in flames a few seconds before I arrived. I could feel my element devouring her flesh while her soul was pleading her God for salvation. I was too late to help her and to stop the mage."

"A young woman," echoed Jim and shook his head. "A woman in her late twenties, slim and blond?" Semargl inclined his head. "It was Lera Volkov. Zane loathed her. He hated her so deeply that he almost killed her himself in my office, when Agent Zvereva first introduced her. Zane didn't love her, so he wouldn't be able to follow her through the gates."

Semargl rolled his eyes. "Humans," he said. "I did not say that only love connection can reveal the gate to the Dark Nav to a living. I said a deep emotional connection. Love and Hate—the two sides of a double-edge sword. These are two of the most powerful emotions human beings can share. And the mage knew it."

"I'll go to the Dark Nav and find Zane," said Angel. He transformed into his magical form, unfolding his heavy black wings.

"Do not rush, Grim Horseman," said Semargl, carefully touching Angel's wing. "Even though the Dark Nav belongs to your domain, you do not know it. You will get lost there and my brother Chernobog will find you first. You need someone who can help you. And among all the gods of Slavic pantheon, besides Chernobog himself, there is only one who has the power inside the Dark Nav. Seek Veles, the god of the Three Realms. You will need his help."

"Fine," said Angel, waving his hand irritably. "Summon Veles. Let's have a chat with him."

"Summon Veles?" repeated Semargl and burst out laughing, bright sparks surrounding his massive body. "No one summons the great Veles. If you need his assistance, you should seek him in the Prav, the Slavic realm of the gods."

"Ahh, why does it have to be so complicated?" muttered Angel, throwing his hands in the air. "Fine. Can you take me to the Prav?"

"No, I cannot," replied Semargl, the last sparks of humor gone from his flaming eyes. "The gates of Prav are locked for me just as tight as they're locked for you, Horseman. But there is someone in your midst who has the power to enter the Prav. I still can feel the traces of his magical energy in this room." Semargl moved his hand over Aidan's desk and gently touched the tender petals of the orchid.

"Of course. Svyatobor," muttered Aidan.

He drew another rune in the air, infusing it with his power

and said the summoning spell. The air shimmered with green sparks and Sven materialized in the office. He looked around, visibly surprised by the assembly. Then he noticed Semargl and stiffened. His large eyes grew even bigger, glowing with bright phosphoric light.

"My lord," said Svyatobor kneeling before Semargl, lowering his head down respectfully.

"Please rise, little kinsman," said Semargl, a soft smile hiding under his rich flaming-red mustache. "I'm glad to see you. I wish it was under better circumstances. We need your help."

Svyatobor got up and glanced at Aidan quizzically.

"Zane is missing," explained Aidan. "Semargl said that he was forced to cross over to the Dark Nav."

"Why?" asked Svyatobor. "Zane is just a little Fire Gecko. Why would someone send him to the Dark Nav? He's not very powerful in the realm of the living and in the Nav, he'll be less than what he was here. Chernobog will squash him like a bug."

"We don't know," replied Aidan, "but a powerful mage chose him for this mission and went through a lot of trouble to get him into the Dark Nav. There has to be a reason for that. In any case, we can't leave him there alone."

"I can't travel to Nav, Aidan. I don't have such power—," started Svyatobor.

"We know that, little kinsman," said Semargl, interrupting him. "I need you to accompany the Grim Horseman to the Prav. I believe you can travel into the realm of gods, can you not?"

"Yes, my lord," replied Svyatobor. "I have the power over the forests of Prav. I can do it."

"That is all we need. You have to cross to the Prav and find Veles. He is the only god who can help your friend," said Semargl. "Yet Veles is not easy to find, my young kinsman, and if you will travel your usual way, you stand no chance of finding him.

"Now, hear me well, Svyatobor, as I am not going to repeat

myself twice. You will take the Horseman with you and travel to the Land of Dreams. In the middle of the southernmost sea of the Land of Dreams, there is a small isle. Isle Buyan. In the center of this isle, the ancient oak-tree is growing. This oak-tree is so big and old, that its crown is hiding in the heavenly clouds and its deep roots are disappearing into the Nav. And only its powerful trunk is visible in the realm of the living.

"This oak-tree is the World Tree that is balancing the three realms—Prav, Yav and Nav. Nine heavens are resting upon the crown of this tree. On the seventh heaven of the World Tree, you will find the godly realm of Prav and this is where you are going to enter it. Only this way you can find the great Veles, the god of the Three Realms. Do what you have to do but convince Veles to help you. The Child of Fire should not remain in the World of Darkness for long, especially since we do not know his purpose. Even though Veles can freely move between all the three realms, he cannot let you pass to the Dark Nav, but he can help the Grim Horseman to get there and find your friend. Go at once; you must not waste any time. Do you understand me well, Svyatobor?"

"Yes, my lord, we'll leave right away," replied Svyatobor with a bow and glanced at Aidan silently asking for his permission to leave. Aidan nodded to him and Svyatobor approached Angel, placing his hand on his shoulder. He snapped his fingers and both Angel and Svyatobor vanished in a fountain of green sparks.

As soon as Svyatobor and Angel were gone, Semargl turned to Aidan. "Aodh mac Lir, I believe I did everything I could," he said with a light bow. "It is time for me to bid my farewell."

"Thank you, Semargl. I appreciate you coming here to help us," said Aidan, returning the respectful bow. "How can I summon you, in case I need your help?"

"The same way you would summon Kalidus," replied Semargl, the corners of his lips quirking up a little. "After all,

Kalidus and I are brothers in element." He waved his hand and vanished behind the wall of fire.

After Semargl was gone, Aidan sat down in his chair, rubbing his face tiredly. It wasn't enough to find Zane. He had to understand why the mage sent him to the Dark Nav. Jim mentioned that she wanted him to recover and bring back to her some kind of important artifact. What was this artifact and why did she need it?

Her reasons for choosing Zane Burns to do her bidding were more or less clear to him. As the Fire Salamander, Zane was immortal. It meant that he could walk the world of the dead without fear of dying and assuming that no one held him down, he could return to the realm of the living. But what was she looking for in the kingdom of Chernobog and why?

Another thing that was bothering Aidan was that Angel, Death himself, couldn't sense Zane's presence in the realm of the dead. The only explanation that came to his mind was that this mage was so powerful that she could shadow the energy signature of the Fire Salamander even from a different realm. This realization chilled him to the bone.

"Uri," said Aidan rising, "I am leaving, and I don't know for how long I'll be away. Can you manage the school and be our center of communications while I'm gone?"

"I have no problem running the school, but may I ask where you are going, Aidan?" asked Uri.

"I need to find out who this mage is and understand her motives," replied Aidan. "She is powerful enough to be a part of the Guardians Order. If she is a Guardian and acting upon their request, then there has to be a good reason for what she's doing, and we need to assist her. If she is not—we must stop her. I'm going to start by visiting the local Wardens at the Church by the Sea. If they know nothing of this woman, I will go to Chicago. From what I remember, this is where the Guardians HQ is located in the United States."

"You're right. We need to understand what's going on. Don't worry, I'll take care of the school." Uri turned to Jim and Angelique. "Agent Andrews, if your team needs my help while Zane and Aidan are gone, do not hesitate to summon me. I'll be your on-call freelance supernatural assistant. Angelique, I hope you know how to summon an Archangel?"

"An Archangel?" mumbled Angelique, staring at him in awe.

"Yes, ma'am," replied Uri assuming his angelic form, cold flames enveloping him with a soft golden glow. "Archangel Uriel. At your service."

For a few seconds, Angelique just stared at him speechless, but then nodded and said, "Yes, I know how to summon you. Thank you. With the situation in the city, I'm sure we'll need your assistance sooner or later."

Jim and Angelique walked toward the door, ready to leave, but at the door, Jim stopped and threw one more look full of worry at Aidan.

"Aidan…"

"I know, Jim," said Aidan, giving him a tired stare. "I'll do everything I can. I betrayed Zane once. I would never do it again. You can trust me."

"Bring him back, Aidan," said Jim, shaking his head. "You're the only person I trust to do it."

Aidan nodded and vanished from the office.

5

~ AIDAN ~

Aidan materialized on the steps of an ancient church. Even though the building was small, it had all the architectural attributes and elements of any medieval cathedral, including the two terrifying gargoyles that were nestled above the entrance. He reached for the door, but immediately pulled his hand back. The protective wards were armed, and he could see the red glow of the protection magic flowing around the church.

Aidan heard a low growl and looked up. Both gargoyles craned their thick necks, staring down at him with their round, unblinking eyes.

"Come on," mumbled Aidan, glaring at the marble beasts, "let me through. Please."

The gargoyles exchanged a look and snarled, displaying a set of giant fangs. Aidan explored the space around the church with his magical sight just to make sure that all the wards were still armed. He heard the gargoyles' soft whisper in his head and frowned.

"Yes, I'm a god of the Otherworld," he replied to gargoyles' question, aggravation making him speak through clenched teeth. "Just because I'm from the realm of the spirits, it doesn't mean I'm harboring an evil intent."

Aidan folded his arms, watching the gargoyles shifting closer together and lowering their ugly heads down. He listened to their next question and threw his hands in the air.

"No, I am not a fae... Dammit! Just be good boys and let me enter the church! I swear I'm not evil. I just need to talk to Father Beaumont and Father Collins. I need their help."

The gargoyles put their stone heads together, conversing and then stared down at Aidan. He could swear that the beasts were tittering. Their whispers sounded in his head again, and Aidan almost jumped in place.

"Are you kidding me?" he yelled, but then fell silent listening to the monsters again. "You're not joking—Fine... But you have to give me your word that if I bring you what you asked for, you'll take down the wards and let me pass—Fine... I'll be right back."

Aidan vanished from the church and materialized in the empty alley on the back of the PetSmart. He was so frustrated with the delay and so worried about Zane that he didn't care if any humans would notice him teleporting. Quickly he ran around the building and walked inside the store. It didn't take him long to find what he was looking for. He picked up a pack of Pedigree dental dog treats and rushed to the cash register. At the register, he gave the cashier a twenty-dollar bill and ran out of the store without waiting for the change.

Aidan reappeared back on the steps of the church and shook the bag with the treats. The gargoyles greeted him with happy growls.

"Here are your goddamn dental treats. Now, disarm the wards and let me through," he said, extending his hand with the bag up toward the gargoyles.

One of the marble beasts lowered his paw down and hooked the bag with his claws, snatching it out of his hands. Aidan stilled for a moment, listening to their growls in his mind and anger slowly started to boil up in him.

"You know my name—aw, you knew who I was all along… and that I wasn't evil—goddammit! Then why were you wasting my time? — Oh, you care about your dental hygiene, do you now? Remove these wards and open the door!" he shouted, his eyes blazing with the energy of his magic. "Or I swear to gods, I'll diminish you both to stone dust! Dammit! I don't have time for this!"

The gargoyles snickered but disarmed the wards and protection spells, opening the entrance door for Aidan. He threw another scorching gaze at the beasts and walked inside the church. The coolness of the air-conditioned space and the light scent of freshly cut grass enfolded him and he inhaled deeply to calm down.

At the far end of the church, he noticed a priest who was reading something out of a thick book and headed toward him. The priest was so engrossed in his work that he didn't notice Aidan approaching. Dressed in all black, like any Catholic priest, he was tall and fit. The thick mane of his dark hair fell forward obscuring his face as he leaned lower toward the book he was reading.

"Excuse me," said Aidan to attract his attention.

The priest flinched and raised his head. He looked young, no more than twenty-five, but in the world of magic looks could be illusive. Magic kept people from aging at a normal pace. His sky-blue eyes drilled into Aidan for a moment, but then he smiled and inclined his head in a light bow. His bow was perfectly measured, just enough to show his respect, but not enough to give Aidan any idea of superiority.

"Monsieur McGrath," he said with a heavy French accent, "or shall I call you Aodh mac Lir?"

"Aidan is fine," replied Aidan, "no need for formalities, Father—"

"Beaumont. Father Raoul de Beaumont," the priest introduced himself. "To what do we owe the pleasure of your visit? It's not every day a Celtic deity stops by our modest church."

"I was hoping to speak with you and Father Collins," said Aidan. "I need your help."

"Father Collins is unavailable at this time. Can I assist you… Aidan?"

Aidan wasn't sure that the young Warden would have all the information he needed, but he had no time. Beggars can't be choosers. He needed to learn as much as he could about this mage and understand why she forced Zane into the world of spirits and demons. And he had to do it fast. The longer Zane spent in the realm of the dead, the weaker he would become. He couldn't die, but it didn't mean he wouldn't suffer. And he couldn't allow that.

"We can start, and Father Collins will join us later," suggested Father Beaumont, noticing Aidan's hesitation. "I'll do my best to help you."

"My friend disappeared," started Aidan. "He was forced to cross the veil into the Slavic realm of spirits and demons. I know that it was a mage who opened the gates into the Dark Nav, and I was wondering if she was a member of the Guardians Order. To help my friend, I need to understand why she did it."

Father Beaumont shook his head, gazing at Aidan with sympathy. "If your friend crossed over to the Dark Nav, he's dead most likely. No living person can ever escape the realm of Chernobog. Even as a god of the Otherworld, there is nothing you can do to help him. I'm sorry for your loss."

"I assure you he's alive, Father," objected Aidan with a sigh. "I know that for a fact because—"

"Because your friend is the Fire Salamander and he can't die."

Aidan heard a deep voice behind him and spun around. An

older man with thick silver-gray hair and a gray beard was standing in front of him. Just like Father Beaumont, he was dressed all in black and wore a clerical collar. He was short and stout, and a kind smile was curving his lips, hiding under his thick gray mustache. But his soft and kind disposition didn't deceive Aidan. He knew that he was looking at a fierce warrior, and an ugly scar that was cutting across the old priest's face was living proof of it. Aidan had no doubt that this scar was left by a sword.

"Aidan McGrath, I'm Father Collins," said the old priest, extending his hand for a handshake. "Let's sit down. Tell me what happened to Mr. Burns. We'll do everything in our power to help you."

There was so much calm reassurance in the old priest's voice that Aidan couldn't help but feel some relief. They sat down, and he told both Wardens everything he learned from Jim and from Semargl. After he finished, Father Collins didn't talk for a while, silently staring at his hands, crossed by slithering blue veins.

"Nothing of what you just told me makes any sense," he said finally, raising his eyes at Aidan. "I don't think the Guardians would send one of their own to force the Fire Salamander do their bidding under duress. It's not the Guardians' style."

"Are you saying that if the Destiny Council ordered them, the Guardians wouldn't do *whatever* it took to complete their mission?" asked Aidan, unable to hide his sarcasm. "From what I've heard, if the Destiny Council says jump, the Guardians ask how high. No resources or lives spared. The purpose justifies the means, so to speak."

The young priest hopped to his feet, furious, obviously offended by Aidan's words or his tone. His hand automatically lowered to his hip like he was ready to unsheathe his sword, but Father Collins frowned at him and slightly shook his head no, pointing back at the bench. Father Beaumont sat down, his cheeks still flushed with irritation.

"I can understand your skepticism when it comes to the Destiny Council and their ways, Aidan," said Father Collins with his warm smile that seemed to have a calming and reassuring effect on Aidan. "I believe, Gwyn ap Nudd was your mentor, and he was never fond of them. Nevertheless, he has good reason to dislike the Council. But I'm positive that this mage wasn't acting upon the order from the Guardians or the Destiny Council. Since the Fire Salamander resides in my area, I would be notified if an order like this was issued."

Aidan got up, trying his best not to show his disappointment to Father Collins. "I guess there is nothing you can do for me then, Father. Well, thank you for your time, anyway."

"Whoa... Hold on, young man," said Father Collins rising. Then he chuckled and shook his head. "I'm sorry, Aidan, you look so young that I keep forgetting that you're almost twenty-five hundred years old."

"That's okay, Father. I prefer not to look my age," mumbled Aidan, not sure why the Priest stopped him.

"Can you humor me before you leave? Let's assume for a moment, that the mage in question indeed was a member of the Guardians," said Father Collins, walking toward the altar, gesturing at Aidan to follow him. "We, Wardens, keep a complete list of all Guardians who have served or still are serving the Order. Let's see if we can find your mage."

The old priest passed the altar and headed toward a barely visible wooden door on the right. He unlocked the door and let Aidan and Father Beaumont through. Inside, the room was small and windowless, but there was not a trace of dust and everything was kept neatly.

A small desk was sitting in the middle of the room. The rest of the space was taken by floor-to-ceiling bookshelves, stuffed with all sorts of old books, manuscripts and scrolls. Some of the books were locked inside glass cases, secured with small golden locks. There were also a few iron boxes that looked like roughly cut medieval-style safes. There were no doors. The iron boxes were seamlessly sealed.

On top of the desk there was a large book in thick leather binding. Father Collins opened the book and to his shock, Aidan noticed that the pages of the book were completely blank. They were yellow and cracked in places like old parchment, yet absolutely free of any ink.

"Aidan, do you know the name of the mage in question?" asked Father Collins.

"She introduced herself as Agent Zvereva," replied Aidan. "She didn't give her first name."

"Zvereva... Zvereva... hmm. Doesn't ring a bell. Well, let's check it out." He touched the page of the book and whispered, "*Latentius Revelare.*"

As soon as the priest said the spell, the ink manifested on the page slowly forming into sentences. But the writing wasn't static—the words were moving and shifting, scrolling up and down the page.

"Zvereva," repeated Father Collins, touching the book again, "find a Guardian mage of this surname."

The words and the sentences started to scroll faster, soon blending into one continuous blur. A few seconds later, the writing stopped moving and then vanished, leaving the page blank again.

"What does it mean?" asked Aidan, observing the book with curiosity.

"It means that the Guardian mage with this name was never recorded," explained Father Collins. "She is not in our records. But it still doesn't mean that she is not one of the Guardians. Perhaps she didn't give you her real name. So, let's try something else. Can you describe her?"

Aidan shrugged. "Only from Semargl's and Jim's words. I had never met her in person."

"Just do your best, young man," mumbled the old Warden absentmindedly. He said another spell and arched his eyebrow at Aidan, gesturing at him to proceed.

Aidan started describing Agent Zvereva. As he was talking, the pictures started to manifest on the page of the book. One after another, they were flashing in front of his eyes, getting into focus for a moment and vanishing again. All of a sudden, a bright red light overlaid the page. It disappeared quickly, replaced by the flood of images, but Father Collins noticed it.

"Cease!" he yelled, touching the book again. "Back!"

The images started to flash again, moving backward. And again, the red light colored the page.

"Stop," ordered Father Collins, touching the page and leaned over the book. "It can't be... it's impossible..." His voice trailed off as he stared at the book, his hands shaking.

"What is impossible?" asked Aidan, hairs rising on the back of his neck. "What's going on?"

The Warden raised his eyes, meeting Aidan's troubled gaze and frowned. "The page from the Book of Words is missing. It's impossible."

"Why is it impossible?" asked Aidan, throwing a quick glance at Father Beaumont, who was as pale as any vampire. The young Warden looked even more troubled than Father Collins.

"It's impossible because the book you see here doesn't really exist," he explained. "It's nothing but a reflection of the real Book of Words. There are only three books like this in our world. The rest of them are just a reflected manifestation of the original records. One of the true books is located in Chicago, in the Guardians Headquarters. The other one is in Paris, kept at the Wardens Headquarters, and the last book is guarded by the Destiny Council themselves. The physical location of the last book is unknown. My book is linked with the Book of Words that is located in Chicago and the page in this book is missing."

He closed the book and sat down, leaning heavily against the back of his chair.

"What does it mean, Father?" asked Aidan. The anxiety of both Wardens starting to affect him.

"I don't have to tell you that there are no coincidences, Mr. McGrath. Every move on the Board of Destiny is well placed and calculated," said Father Collins quietly. "An unknown powerful mage showed up here, abducted the Fire Salamander and forced him to cross the veil. At the same time, the page in our Book of Words has gone missing. Coincidence? I think not! There was something on this page she didn't want anyone to find."

"What do I need to do to recover this page?" asked Aidan calmly.

"You need to go to Chicago at once," replied Father Collins. He took a piece of paper and quickly wrote a note, offering it to Father Beaumont. "Raoul will accompany you."

"He will slow me down," objected Aidan and turned to the young Warden, a guilty smile on his face. "No offense, Father Beaumont."

"I will slow you down?" huffed Father Beaumont, shoving his hands into the pockets of his pants, his French accent heavier than ever. "Without me, you will never find the Guardians. God or not, they will never let you cross the threshold of the Guardians Headquarters! You're arrogant—"

"Father Beaumont, try to remember," hissed Father Collins. "You are talking to an ancient god! Don't say something you'll deeply regret later."

Aidan raised his hand up, stopping Father Collins and then turned toward Raoul. "I'm sorry, Father Beaumont, you're right. It was disrespectful of me to talk like that. I came here not as a god, but as a man in need of assistance. So, I would be honored if you would accompany me to the Guardians Headquarters."

Raoul nodded, hardly meeting Aidan's eyes, his shoulders square. "We shall leave at once, if you want to save *ton ami*—your immortal friend, I mean."

"Father Collins, thank you for your help," said Aidan. "I'll keep you posted on everything I learn in Chicago."

He placed his hand on Raoul's shoulder and snapped his fingers, teleporting both of them out of the church.

6

~ ZANE BURNS, A.K.A. GUNZ ~

Gunz didn't know how long he was falling. Complete darkness surrounded him. The blackness was so condensed, it was physically pressing on his eyes and on his nerves. He felt blinded and helpless, unable to break his fall. The darkness drained the hope out of his soul, leaving him in despair and anguish with the realization that he would never see the light of day again. He was doomed to spend eternity surrounded by darkness, blind and alone.

He screamed, a desperate sound that was immediately swallowed by the density of the nothingness that surrounded him. He felt like he was in a soundproof room with soundproof headphones over his ears. Gunz struggled to get in control of his body, to see something, to hear something, to feel anything at all—even if it was pain. At this moment, he would welcome real physical pain. He would welcome anything that would give him proof that he was still alive.

The more he struggled, the weaker he felt. Soon, he had no energy left in him. Gunz sighed and gave up, relinquishing his will to whatever was coming. Slowly he submitted to the fact that there was nothing he could do to control the situation he was in. He had to yield and stop struggling. He closed his eyes and let go.

The feeling of firm ground under his back was completely unexpected. Gunz carefully opened his eyes, expecting to see nothing. It was still dark, but the darkness wasn't overwhelming, and he could make out some of his surroundings. Above him there was the dark sky. At least he assumed it was the sky. There were no stars or moon and whatever it was above him, looked distant and hollow.

Slowly, Gunz turned his head from left to right. He was lying down on a small clearing, bare ground without any grass. From every direction, he was surrounded by a dark forest. However, describing his surroundings as a forest was a bit of a stretch. Dead, leafless trunks with hardly any branches, were stretching up into the void of the sky, disappearing there. Nothing around him was moving. There wasn't even the slightest breeze. The silence felt eerie, infused with an unknown danger.

His Salamander senses woke up, screaming that he needed to get up and find his way out of this place. But he felt weak and despondent and he didn't want to move. He was tired and broken. The thought of the tiniest move was painful and unwelcome. He just wanted to keep lying down. If he was going to die —so be it. Whatever will be, will be. He closed his eyes and remained motionless, submitting to his fate.

A slap in the face made Gunz gasp, and he opened his eyes. Mishka, the wyvern, was hovering above him. The wyvern seemed a little different. The golden glow was gone from his wings and his eyes weren't shining red. Mishka lowered himself down on Gunz's chest and slapped him with his wing again.

"Mishka—," whispered Gunz, hardly able to move his lips. The wyvern slapped him one more time and Gunz's head jerked to the side, but he had neither strength nor desire to move. "Mishka, stop slapping me... please... I'm awake."

"He's awake. Hallelujah!" muttered Mishka, glaring down at

him. "So, why are you lying down here, like you're a little princess in some fairytale castle? Move your fireless ass! You're going to die if you stay here. Oh wait, you can't die. Even better —you're going to get dismembered, piece by piece, while you are alive and awake. Does that sound good to you, boss?"

"Mishka, I can't," whispered Gunz. "I'm too drained and frankly, I don't care..."

"He doesn't care," parroted Mishka, and slapped him again. "Fire Almighty! Get your ass up and run! They know you are here, and they are coming for you."

Gunz groaned as his eyes watered. The last slap somehow seemed to be more annoying than the others. "Mishka, who is coming? And why are you so... persistent. Just leave me be. If you feel you need to run, then go for it. Leave me the hell alone..."

Mishka screamed and attacked Gunz, slapping him mercilessly with both wings and scratching him with his sharp claws.

"Dammit!" yelled Gunz, adding a few more choice words in Russian. "Stop it!" As anger restored some strength in his drained body, he pushed himself up on his elbows. This minuscule effort took out of him whatever the burst of anger provided, and he fell back down, closing his eyes with a soft moan.

Mishka lowered himself down to the ground by Gunz's head and switched his tactics. "Boss, please don't close your eyes," he pleaded peacefully, whispering into his ear. "Look up... look in the sky, boss. Tell me what you see."

Gunz sighed and opened his eyes, staring into the hollow sky. Somewhere far away, in the darkness, he noticed something darker than the darkness of this endless night. Whatever it was, it was moving down in a spiral motion, like a giant funnel cloud. It was soundless and sinister. The dark demonic energy washed over him like muddy waters, and he gasped. His mouth fell open as he kept gasping for air, unable to breathe in the sinister energy that polluted everything around him.

"What do you see, Gunz?" asked Mishka softly, for the first time using his nickname.

"Death... I see death," replied Gunz. He was staring at the approaching horror, not willing to make a move to save himself. "I don't care... let it take me, Mishka... I give up... I have no will to fight anymore. I'm done. Save yourself. Run..."

"No... no... no..." Mishka seized his shirt with his claws, pulling Gunz up, but he was too heavy. Mishka didn't let go even after the shirt got ripped. "You do not submit to this place. You do not let it break you. Remember who you are, Gunz!" He stopped pulling and embraced Gunz, wrapping his wings around his shoulders and pressing his hot scaly head against Gunz's cheek. "You are not human. You are a Great Fire Salamander! Suppress the human soul in you. This place is feeding on your humanity. Relinquish yourself to the Almighty Fire. Don't yield to this place! Gunz! Get up!"

Gunz screamed, trying to achieve his natural state. There was no fire. Fire as an elemental power was so diminished here that it wasn't enough for him to revert. He tried to reach his magic and felt its weak presence somewhere deep inside. With the last crumbs of his remaining strength, he raised his arm up and whispered, "*Ignius...*"

A few weak flames flickered dimly, wrapping around his fingers. Even this insignificant presence of his element made him feel a little better. The indifference and complacency slowly gave up their hold and the instincts of the Fire Salamander replaced them. Gunz let the Fire Salamander take over and forced himself to get up. He stood, swaying. The fire flickered and died, but he was up, on his feet.

"Now, let's leave this clearing," said Mishka, gently pulling him toward the dead woods.

Gunz walk toward the woods, slowly forcing himself to

move one foot after the other. Once in a while he was checking the sky, just to see the darkness ascending, getting closer by the second. And the closer it was getting, the weaker he felt. Mishka was right—this place was feeding on his humanity like some bloodthirsty vamp.

At the border with the woods, he fell to his knees, breathing laboriously like he ran a few miles, even though he walked just a few steps. He grabbed the thick trunk next to him and forced himself up. For a moment, he just stood, hugging the dead tree, dealing with the dizziness that assailed him.

"You can't just stand still, Gunz," said Mishka, gently pulling on his torn shirt. "We need to find a place to hide. Can you walk? Would be nice if you could run, just a little."

Gunz pushed himself off the tree and took his first step forward when something cold swept by him, grazing his cheek. He gasped, touching his face and felt something warm and sticky under his fingers. He didn't need to look—it was blood. Gunz glanced over his shoulder and his eyes widened. For the first time, since that mage pushed him through the gates, he felt something other than emptiness. Fear—it made his skin crawl and the small hairs rose on the back of his neck.

A dark, swirling mass was hurtling toward him, like a giant bee swarm from hell. Most of the mass was still far away, but a few shadows separated, speeding forward faster than the rest. They had large dark wings, but Gunz knew that whatever these creatures were, they weren't birds. Each of them was a size of an eagle. Their bodies were covered in feathers, yet they seemed to be translucent to a degree, like ghosts. They had long, massive beaks and sharp claws. Gunz froze, thinking that if these creatures weren't ghostly, these beaks could do some serious damage.

One of the ghostly "birds" reached him and without slowing down, flew straight through him. As it passed through his body, he felt a hot pain expanding in his chest, his heart almost stopping. He cried out, clasping his hands to his chest. The monster turned around and launched at him again. Gunz quickly realized that its beak and claws were very much material as the claws easily shredded through his shirt, and its beak tore a piece of flesh out of his chest.

Gunz yelped, trying to seize the creature that attached itself to his chest, but his fingers were sliding through its incorporeal body. The monster's head was right in front of his face as it was aiming to hit his eyes with its bloodstained beak. For a moment, Gunz stared at the terrible creature, with horror realizing that it had human eyes.

Another creature reached them and also flew through his body. The agonizing pain sent him down to his knees. Mishka shouted something and threw his small body at the monsters. He had no fire, but he was fighting tooth and nail.

"*Ignius*," Gunz cried out reaching for his magic. Maybe it was the pain or the fear, or the desperate desire to survive that finally woke up in him, but the fire magic worked. His arms went up in flames, blazing like two torches.

The ghostly monsters screeched and shied away from the fire, cowering back into the shadows of the dead forest. Gunz didn't wait for them to recover. Gathering whatever strength he had left, he ran forward, followed by the wyvern. The silence of the dead woods was deafening, and he couldn't hear anything except the blood rushing through his head and his pulse beating desperately in his ears. It was dark, and he couldn't see where he was going. But he didn't really care. As long as he was away from the ghostly terror.

As he ran, he glanced over his shoulder. The swirling mass was catching up with him. They were no longer swirling but spread as far as he could see on both sides, soundlessly drifting through the motionless woods. Gunz knew that it was only a matter of time before the deadly flock would reach him and tear him apart.

A few feet ahead, he noticed some tall shrubbery that was blocking his way, but he didn't stop. His fire was already gone, and he had nothing to protect himself. At full speed, he ran into the shrubbery. Ignoring the sharp thorns, he tore through the bushes, striving to reach the other side. He felt agonizing jolts of pain as the thorns dug into his skin, tearing his clothes to shreds.

Gunz cried out in pain but didn't stop. As he emerged on the other side of the thorn bushes, his foot caught on something and he tripped. He stumbled a few steps forward when the ground trembled and slowly dissolved under his feet. He fell through, in the last moment grabbing something with his hands.

It was a large branch that was covered in sharp thorns, just like the shrubbery he ran through. The thorns pierced his skin, but he didn't let go. The branch broke his fall and he stilled, trying to calm down and assess his situation. He was in a swamp and his body was half-submerged into the thick muddy substance. As he moved his legs, he felt a pull. The swamp was sucking him down. And the more he struggled, the faster he was going down. The air above the shrubbery got darker as the menacing swarm of ghostly monsters flew over it.

Mesmerized, he was watching the approach of the deadly monsters, their dark, venomous energy suffocating him. He couldn't move, and his magic was exhausted. Besides, he felt so drained physically, that he couldn't fight even if he could move.

"Mishka," he whispered to his wyvern, "please leave, my friend. I don't want you to share my fate..."

Gunz looked around but couldn't see Mishka anywhere. He sighed with relief—at least his little friend was safe.

The swarm attacked him all at once. He couldn't say what they were doing to him or how many ghostly creatures passed through him. They were clawing at his body, shredding his flesh with their beaks. The nonstop agony tormented him, and he wanted to die, but for whatever reason he couldn't pass out.

Gunz let go of the branch that was holding him on top of the swamp and stopped struggling. The swamp was slowly pulling him in, but he didn't care. The only thing he was hoping for was that the monsters couldn't follow him down into the muddy death.

He was down to his chest and his consciousness finally started to gradually slip away. With surprise he realized that nothing was hurting anymore. The muddy waters of the swamp snuggled his body with a cold embrace. It wasn't pleasant, but it wasn't painful either. The ghostly creatures were gone. The pain was gone. Maybe because this place had such little presence of elemental powers, he could die here. He was fine with death.

As his vision started to blur, he caught sight of a small light moving toward him. He squinted his eyes but couldn't focus his vision. The light flickered on and off, as he finally passed out.

7

~ ZANE BURNS, A.K.A. GUNZ ~

Gunz blinked a few times adjusting his vision, staring straight up at a low wooden ceiling. He felt firm ground under his back, and he knew that he was no longer dying in the swamp, attacked by the ghostly monsters. He carefully turned his head to the side. He was lying down on a narrow hard bed, inside of a small, semi-dark room.

He stirred a little, but as a sharp pain pierced him, Gunz quickly changed his mind and stilled. His whole body felt like a dark abyss filled with liquid agony. Besides the pain, every square inch of skin was itching. It was burning like someone dunked him into the water of a frozen lake. He wanted to scratch, but he couldn't feel his arms. Actually, he felt like he didn't have any arms at all.

Gunz gasped and looked to the side where his right arm was supposed to be. It was in place, moved above his head. He tilted his head backward and saw that his hands were tied up to the bed. Gunz tried to pull against his restraints, but quickly gave up this idea as every move produced a considerable amount of pain accompanied by a burning itch.

Carefully he looked down and grunted. He was completely

naked. All his clothes were gone, and only a piece of rag was wrapped around his hips. His ankles were also attached to the bed. For a moment, he thought he saw Mishka hovering over him, but when he looked up, there was no one there.

Gunz gently probed the area with his Salamander senses, noticing how weak the Fire Salamander in him was. The energy of Fire was almost nonexistent here. He checked the magic and felt its presence within him. It was burning weakly like a flickering small flame on a dying candle. He moaned softly, feeling broken and helpless.

The door opened, and a woman walked inside. Gunz stiffened, not sure what to expect. She looked young, in her mid-twenties. Her hair, bright red and long, was braided and two thick braids were running down her chest. She was dressed in a short flowery dress and tall rubber boots, and her whole appearance seemed to be out of place in the gloomy darkness of this realm. Her bright green eyes moved up and down his unobstructed body and the corners of her full lips quirked up.

"You're awake," she stated in a deep, slightly raspy voice. Her voice didn't seem to go well with her appearance either.

"Where am I?" asked Gunz. His lips moved, but no sound came out from his dry throat.

"Thirsty?" she asked, approaching a small table that was positioned next to the bed. Gunz heard her pouring some water in a glass. Then she gently lifted his head and pressed the glass with water to his lips. She let him take a few gulps of water and put the glass back on the table.

"Where am I?" asked Gunz, his voice just a whisper.

"You're enjoying the hospitality of my five-star establishment, where luxury is not a choice but a way of life," she announced, a one-sided grin on her face, "continental breakfast is included."

"Untie me... please."

"No can do," she sang, landing on the edge of the bed next to him.

"Why?"

"If I untie you right now, you'll scratch your skin off all the way to your bones," she explained as she readjusted the rag that was covering his hips. "Besides, I'm enjoying the view too much."

She shrugged her shoulders nonchalantly and got up, moving something on the table. When she turned back to him, in her hands she was holding his Swiss army knife with one of the blades extended and tweezers. Gunz stiffened and his eyes widened. She noticed his reaction and chuckled.

"Relax, dude," she said, sitting back down next to him. "Who do you think I am? I'm not going to torture you. Well... not true. I'm going to torture you. But not for the pleasure of it, I promise."

"Well, that's a relief," mumbled Gunz.

"You dragged yourself through the thorny forest yesterday, you thundertwat. What were you thinking? Now I have to remove all the thorns that stuck to your body. Otherwise your wounds will never heal, and you'll be itching like a dog full of fleas. So, yeah... I am going to torture you, but only to help you. Got it?"

"Uh-huh..."

"Do you want to come up with a safe word?" she asked snidely, an innocent smile plastered on her face.

Gunz wisely decided not to respond. She touched his arm, her fingers quickly exploring his skin.

"Sometimes you can't see all the thorns because the smaller ones are stuck under your skin... Jeez, you're like a giant pincushion." She found what she was looking for and took the knife. "Now, do you want to bite on something before I cut?"

"Just go on already," he muttered, turning away.

"Can't tolerate the sight of your own blood?" she asked, snickering. "Don't faint on me, my mighty warrior."

With a quick, precise move, she made a deep cut on his skin and took the tweezers. Gunz grunted as she moved the tweezers inside the incision, searching for a thorn. Finally, she found it and pulled it out. The pain was a lot worse than he expected. He suppressed a scream, pulling against the ropes.

"What the hell was that?" he yelled as soon as he was able to speak, breathing laboriously. "Why is removing a thorn hurting so much."

"You're just a regular everyday genius, aren't you?" she asked. If the sarcasm wasn't obvious enough in her words, her bright eyes were flooded with it.

Still holding the thorn with her tweezers, she moved it closer to his face, so he could see it. The thorn looked like an arrowhead with jagged edges and multiple sharp hooks.

"Holy shit," he muttered. "Are you ripping chunks of my muscles out as you're removing those?"

"Something like that," she agreed. "This is why I do the cut first, to minimize the damage. But it's still going to hurt like hell. And you're covered with these thorns from head to toe on your front. Well, ready for the next one?"

An hour later, Gunz was drenched in cold sweat and blood. He wasn't trying to suppress his screams. He was screaming, cursing and begging her to stop, but she stubbornly kept going.

"Please," he begged, panting, "stop... for a few minutes... Please... I can't breathe."

She stopped what she was doing for a moment, staring down at him with no sympathy in her green eyes.

"Luckily, your most precious place is free of thorns and your back is clean too. Most of the thorns were in your arms and chest with just a few in your legs, so I'm almost done," she said dryly. "If you can't take it anymore, I can punch you out. But I am not going to stop right now just to comfort you and wipe your tears with a lacy handkerchief. Don't worry, I'm not going to charge extra for punching you out. That comes free of charge."

An hour later she was done. She put away her instruments of torture and left the room. She came back a few minutes later with a bucket of water and a cloth in her hands. Without saying anything, she leaned over him and started wiping the blood and sweat off his body.

"You're stronger than I thought," she mumbled. "You'll be all right, little man." She pulled the rag off his hips and proceeded with her sponge bath. Gunz blushed and turned away. "Aw, are you shy? Don't worry, I'm not planning to ravage you, taking advantage of your vulnerable state. As tempting as it sounds, it's been years since I've been with your kind. Driving a stick hasn't been my preference for a long time."

She finished taking care of him and squeezed the bloodied cloth into the bucket with dirty water. After that, she grabbed a thin blanket and covered him, pulling it up to his chin.

"Untie me… please…"

"Not today, sweetheart." She laughed and headed toward the door.

"At least tell me your name."

She stopped at the door, one hand on the door handle and turned to him. "Maybe tomorrow. If you behave like a good boy, that is." She laughed and left the room.

GUNZ HARDLY SLEPT, his body tormented by the constant nagging pain of multiple cuts. Besides, he wasn't comfortable tied up to the bed, and his arms and shoulders were numb. He made an effort, trying to fall asleep, but as soon as he closed his eyes, all sorts of thoughts were crowding his mind.

He didn't know how much time passed. The room he was in

hadn't changed, remaining semi-dark and gloomy. The only reason he knew that it was the morning of the next day was because the door opened up and the same young woman that was taking care of him yesterday, walked inside.

"Good morning," she announced cheerfully, as she headed toward him.

"Depends who you ask," muttered Gunz. "Please, untie me already."

She didn't say anything but took the blanket off him and proceeded to check his wounds. "Well, you're healing nicely. Faster than I expected. Are you still itching?"

"No," he growled, anger slowly rising within him. He pulled at the ropes and barked at her, "Untie me, now!"

She chuckled, patting his cheek. "Aw, you look so cute when you're angry. Big strong man, shouting at a little lady and all. Do it again, would you?"

"Besides the point that I'm too weak to run, I don't even know where I am," said Gunz quietly. "And I would never hurt a woman. Please... my arms are about to fall off. I can't stay in this position another minute."

She stared down at him, frowning, and took the Swiss army knife off the table. Gunz thought she was going to cut the ropes off, but she didn't. Instead, she touched his knife and whispered a short spell, turning it into the long medieval sword. She put the blade to Gunz's neck, pushing his head up slightly. Gunz gasped, gaping at her flabbergasted. She was a witch, and if she knew how to turn his knife into a sword, she wasn't new to the world of magic.

"Now, we're going to talk, sorcerer," she said icily, "and if you want to live, you're going to tell me nothing but the truth. Am I clear?"

"Yes," said Gunz, calmly. "What do you want to know?"

"Let's start with your name."

"Zane Burns."

"This sword is made of *Ardenium* steal. Where did you get it? This type of alloy doesn't exist in our world."

"It exists only in Kendral," confirmed Gunz. "My mentor gifted it to me a while ago. In Kendral. And I'm not a sorcerer."

"Oh, really?" she swung her arm and backhanded him.

Gunz grunted, feeling the coppery taste of blood in his mouth. "Why? I told you the truth…"

"Do not lie to me, asshole. You are saying that you are not a sorcerer, yet your chest is decorated by a rune that shadows your magical energy and your sword is enchanted."

"I swear on my power, I am telling you the truth," growled Gunz, his head still buzzing after the slap. "I'm not a sorcerer. I am a Fire Salamander. And the rune on my chest was forced on me by some crazy mage. I didn't know it was shadowing my power. She didn't tell me that. She said that I need to use this rune to communicate with her when I am ready to leave the Dark Nav."

"If you're not lying, then your mentor is—"

"Kal, the Fire Elemental," said Gunz.

"Oh my God…" she whispered. "Milana was right…"

"Who is Milana and what was she right about?"

"Milana is my girlfriend. She has the gift of sight. She predicted that one day the Fire Salamander would come to the Dark Nav. I didn't believe her. First of all, I didn't know that besides Kal, there was another Fire Salamander. Second, Fire Salamanders are immortal, and to cross the veil one must die. And last, there are no elemental powers in the Dark Nav. Everything here is dead. The elemental powers are the base of life itself and they can't exist here. This is why the elemental gods are not allowed in this realm either…"

The woman stopped talking and got up, moving the blade away from his neck. In one move, she cut the ropes that were binding his wrists and then freed his ankles. Gunz exhaled with relief, but he couldn't move his arms down. She helped him lower his arms and started gently massaging his shoulders.

Gunz moaned softly as the pins and needles in his shoulders began to fade away.

"Am I pleasuring you well, my lord and commander?" she asked, giggling and threw a suggestive glance toward the rag that was wrapped around his hips. "Anything else you'd like me to massage for you?"

For a moment Gunz blushed taken aback by her forwardness, but then he smirked and retorted, "I thought you weren't driving a stick anymore."

"I'm not… But you know how it is… old habits die hard," she murmured, exuding innocence and shyness. But then she clapped her hands together and started laughing. "Just kidding. Not in your lifetime, firetwat."

"Firetwat, eh?" muttered Gunz. He tried to sit down but was too weak and gave up on that idea. "Now that you know who I am, do you want to tell me your name?"

"Sure, why not?" She chuckled, pulling a stool closer to his bed and sat down. "I'm Karma."

"Karma," repeated Gunz in disbelief. "You're kidding, right?"

"Do I look like I'm kidding?" she replied, folding her arms over her chest. "That's what people call me."

"Oh wow. I'm sure your mother didn't curse you with this name," he said, an uneven smile making an appearance before he could stifle it. "So, why do people call you that? Wait, don't tell me… You kick ass! Right?"

"Ha-ha, very funny. What are you? A lie-down comedian?" she replied, narrowing her eyes at him. "Don't I look like I can kick ass?"

Gunz took in her appearance. She was still wearing a light short dress with pink flowers on it. Today she didn't have her rubber boots on. Instead, her feet were hiding in fluffy house slippers that looked like two pink bunnies, long ears and all. Before he could stop himself, he shook his head no.

"Men and their deadly stereotypes."

She rolled her eyes and muttered something under her breath. As she completed her spell, her appearance started to change. The light dress got replaced by a black leather jacket. Tight leather slacks wrapped around her long, toned legs. The bunny-slippers were gone, replaced by heavy motorcycle boots. Even her breasts seemed to get fuller, temptingly peeking through the half-opened zipper of her jacket. A short sword was strapped behind her back and a gun holster with a sizable Glock was attached to her hip. Her long red hair was flowing in rich waves and layers down her shoulders and her green eyes were shining with cold humor as she stared down at Gunz.

"So, now, in your manly opinion, do I look like I can kick some serious ass? Or should I manifest a *Harley* here to complete the visual?"

Gunz raised his hands up, shaking his head with a smile. "That wasn't necessary. At least not on my account," he said, chuckling. "I learned a long time ago that appearances could be deceiving. Especially in the world of magic. I'm sorry if I offended you, but I just wanted to know what truly lies behind your name. Why Karma of all things?"

"Because I don't mind doing the dirty work and I always get the payback," replied Karma coldly and walked out of the room, leaving him alone.

8

~ TESSA ~

"Dear Diary... Oh, man... I hate these words. I hate this diary. And I hate writing it. But Missi insists that I do this. She keeps telling me that every Guardian Witch must have her diary and document everything for historical reasons. Or for future generations. Whatever... Well, my mom used to do it, so I'll do it too.

How long has it been, since Missi and I left South Florida? I think almost eight months now. I can't believe how fast time flies when you're having so much fun. Fun? Yeah, right. Perhaps not everything is fun. Kicking some serious supernatural ass is always fun, of course. But it's no fun when the supernatural assholes are kicking yours instead.

Or when Missi keeps nagging about the importance of learning magic and how to use my powers. That's no fun either. Who would think magic needs learning and practicing, like math or something?

After all this time, we still don't know who my parents are. And I kinda don't care about it anymore. So, I know that one of my parents was a Reaper, and that explains my wonderful power that allows me to see the dead spirits and talk to them. Woohoo! Big friggin' deal. My second parent is the real enigma though. I would really like to know who he or she was. Controlling the lightning and thunderstorms—that's the coolest power ever.

But Missi manages to suck all the fun out of using this power. She keeps telling me that until I know the origins of it, I should not use it. Unless it's a true emergency, of course. So, after seven months, I decided to cut the search and do what Missi said. Learn. (Can you see me rolling my eyes, btw?) I hated high school and the idea of coming back to learning was giving me a bad taste in my mouth. Anyway, Missi gave her recommendations to the Guardians Council and helped me pass their admission test. About a month ago, the Guardians had accepted me as an Apprentice.

I must admit that learning magic with the Guardians is not that bad. Except for the chores. I hate doing chores. I even hate this word—chores. But since I am still at the bottom of the food chain of the Guardians Order, I have to do whatever they command, including scrubbing floors and washing dishes.

Missi told me that my mom was a Guardian Mage, seventh level, which is the highest level you can achieve as a member of the Guardians Order. In the whole history of the Guardians, there were only five witches who achieved this level. I wonder how much time it took my mom to get there? Or was she so talented that she skipped a few levels?

Just in case someone who is not a Guardian reads my diary, I better explain. There are three different stages of being a Guardian—Apprentice, Witch, and Mage. And there are seven levels in each stage. Can you believe it? It'll take me forever to become a Mage. Or even a Witch. After one full month of torture, I'm still just an Apprentice, first level. Come on! It's been a full month. Shouldn't I be a Witch already? And I have the coolest power ever. None of the other apprentices have that. Sigh...

Anyway, I'm complaining too much. I better stop writing for today. Catch ya'll on the flip side.

T.D.

P.S. Hey Aidan... I hope you will never read this diary, because I *would never tell something like this to you in person. I miss you, old man. I still can't forgive what you did. But despite it, I miss you. Painfully. Every single day..."*

* * *

TESSA CROUCHED behind a dumpster in a dark alley. Carefully, she peeked from behind the dumpster to observe two men, who were standing right on the edge of a parking lot on the back of a small bikers' bar. At least twenty motorcycles were parked there, and the small bar was packed to the limit. The men didn't notice that Tessa was watching them, and they were getting louder and more animated by the minute. She didn't doubt that in a few minutes, fists would become their main way of communication, and they would start pounding each other.

Someone touched her shoulder. Tessa flinched and snapped around, suppressing a scream. Missi was crouching behind her. In the darkness of the midnight alley, in her black outfit, Missi was almost invisible. Only her bright gray eyes were standing out on her dark face. And they were heavily drilling Tessa, promising nothing good.

"What are you doing here, Tessa," hissed Missi in her ear. "There is a demonic assembly of two opposing factions inside this bar."

"Exactly, two birds—one stone," murmured Tessa, getting back to watching the two men. She wasn't planning on going inside the bar. She just wanted to observe the bar and see what the demons were up to. Maybe get rid of one or two once the assembly was over and most of the demons were gone... In the meantime, the men stopped arguing and now were talking quietly, looking down at something one of them held in his hands.

"Are you out of your goddamn mind?" Missi squeezed her shoulder, leaning closer to Tessa's ear. Tessa could feel her warm breath touching her skin. "First of all, you shouldn't be here because it's too dangerous. You can get hurt or killed. Second, if you are stupid enough to even come close to a demonic assembly of two powerful demonic factions, you shouldn't be doing it alone! And the last but not least, you are a member of the Guardians now. You shouldn't be doing anything without notifying them first! Do you want to get expelled?"

Tessa looked at Missi over her shoulder, her eyes round. "You're not gonna tell them, Missi!"

Missi rolled her eyes. "Fine, I'm not going to tell them, but this is the last time I'm covering for you. You have to understand—the Guardians are like a military organization. There is a chain of command and you need to respect it and follow their rules."

"I hate rules," muttered Tessa.

"Then why did you beg me to introduce you to the Order? I told you that you'll have to abide by their rules," growled Missi, squeezing her shoulder harder. "And Tessa, didn't they start teaching you how to shadow your own magical energy yet? I could feel your presence from a mile away."

"Yeah, Professor Montgomery started to teach us last week. I hate her... such a... ugh... stick in a mud," muttered Tessa.

"Ah, Tessa, you're behaving like a child! You must learn! You have an extremely strong magical energy signature. You must know how to hide yourself," replied Missi, throwing her hands in the air, frustrated. But then stilled for a moment looking somewhere over Tessa's shoulder and added, "I'll deal with you later. If we survive, that is."

Tessa followed Missi's gaze and her heart pounded. The men she was observing earlier were no longer at the edge of the parking lot. They were standing right in front of them, staring down at them with malicious smirks on their faces. The reek of their demonic energy invaded her senses and her stomach churned.

"Well, well, well," sneered one of the demons, "what are two nice ladies like yourselves doing in a dark alley, hiding behind the garbage, eh?"

"I lost something here. We were just looking..." mumbled Tessa, lamely.

The second demon snickered and seized Tessa's arm, pulling her up to her feet. "Let's see if we can help you find whatever you lost. Let's go, both of you."

A loud group of demons came out to the parking lot. A few demons noticed their friends standing in the alley and headed toward them. Tessa felt chills running down her spine. Only the two of them and at least ten demons. The odds definitely weren't in their favor.

Escorted by the two demons, Missi and Tessa walked toward the bar. The demons opened the door for them and pushed them through. As soon as they crossed the threshold, the heavy stench of alcohol and cigarette smoke hit them like a sledgehammer. Tessa coughed, cleared her throat and checked the bar.

It was relatively dark, and a thick curtain of smoke was hanging under the ceiling like a dirty gray cloud. It was hard to say exactly how many bodies were crammed into the limited space of the bar, but from the first observation, it looked like there were at least twenty demons there if not more. The nauseating stench of sweat mixed in with marijuana smoke made her stomach heave, and she swallowed hard.

The demons led them through the crowd toward a man and a woman that were sitting at a far table, discussing something. The woman was in her late fifties with long gray hair that was braided in a few greasy braids. The man was probably half her age, with a thick mane of dark hair and penetrating dark eyes. As soon as Tessa and Missi approached the table, both demons fell silent, observing them with their icy eyes.

"We found these two in the alley behind the bar," started one of the demons. "They were hiding behind the dumpster, watching me and Ricardo, I bet." He waved at the second demon. "They're probably just some stupid human bitches. I didn't feel any magical energy about them. But still... better safe than sorry."

The woman got up and slowly walked around Tessa and Missi. She made a full circle and stopped a foot away from them, placing her hands on her oversized hips. The woman was a little overweight, but she didn't feel shy to squeeze herself into extremely tight leather pants that were at least two sizes too small and put on a shirt that was barely reaching down to her bellybutton exposing her aging skin with a web of stretch marks. The leather vest with the gang name on it wasn't helping to avoid the overall fashion disaster.

The young man also got up but remained standing behind the table. In his looks, he was the complete opposite of the woman. He was also dressed all in leather, but every article of his clothing was well matched and fitted for his athletic body. He looked like one of those "untamed" bikers from the covers of romance novels.

"Humans?" asked the woman and without waiting for anyone's response, she hooted laughing, displaying her yellow teeth stained by coffee and nicotine. "I don't think so. Guardian Bitches—that's what they are. I'm glad you brought them here, Samuel." She glanced at the young demon over her shoulder and he gave her a light nod. "Samuel, Riccardo, take them behind the bar and kill them." She thought for a moment and added, "Take a couple more men with you."

Tessa felt demons seizing her arms, twisting them behind her back and pushing her forward, through the hooting crowd of demons. At this moment, she wasn't really scared. The adrenalin was pumping through her system in expectation of a fight and her cheeks were flushed with excitement. She glanced at Missi, waiting for a signal to get things rolling. Missi shook her head no and gave her a warning stare. It was obvious that she didn't want to start a confrontation in the confined space of the bar, surrounded by multiple demons.

As they were walking, the demons were groping and pinching them, throwing lustful glances at them and exchanging dirty jokes. Tessa was on the verge of blowing up. *If I feel another hand on my—*

"Hey sweetheart, it's a shame to dispose of such a beautiful ass without having a taste first," screeched one of the demons and slapped Missi on her ass. "Let's play, sweet cheeks, I'll show you the real magic."

All this time Missi was gritting her teeth, doing everything to keep her cool, but that slap did it. Her reaction was explosive. She let go of any control and her body shimmered with the blue glow of her magic. She hissed something, and a powerful blue ray of magical energy erupted from the open palms of her hands, burning through the demon that had the stupidity to slap her. The demon screamed, his eyes bulging in terror, his body surrounded by the blue light of her magic. He made an attempt to abandon his body, but Missi's magic locked him in. In a heartbeat, the body and the demon disintegrated into a pile of dirty dust on the floor.

"Ignius!" roared Missi, spraying the demons with a fire blast. As a couple of demons shimmered out of their burning bodies, Missi turned to Tessa and yelled, "Tessa, why are you standing, girl. Do your thing!"

"I thought you would never ask," muttered Tessa and raised her arm up in the air, channeling her power.

The lightning broke through the ceiling connecting with Tessa's hands and a mighty thunder made the walls of the bar tremble. She redirected the flow of the electricity, forking it into a few lightning bolts and hit three demons at the same time. The demons convulsed, their bodies twisted by the electric charge. A moment later, they were gone, both the body and the demonic essence destroyed by the lightning.

All the remaining demons shouted at the same time and sprang into action, charging Tessa and Missi from every direction. Missi hissed some kind of spell and a shimmering blue shield conjured by her magic surrounded them. The demons hit the shield and bounced back, unable to break through.

"Let me pass!"

Tessa recognized the young demon that was talking to the older woman when they were first brought in. The crowd separated, allowing him to come through. He touched Missi's shield and his lips stretched into a semblance of a smile that could be better described as a menacing snarl. He put his hands on the shield and closed his eyes, focusing on the dark magic he was wielding. Darkness started to spread around his hands, slowly devouring Missi's shield.

Missi moaned quietly as it was becoming too hard for her to keep the shield up. She threw a desperate glance at Tessa, her face strained with the effort of fighting the dark spell. Tessa had no illusions. As soon as Missi's shield would crumble, all the demons would attack them at once. The sheer mass of their combined weight would push them to the ground immobilizing them. They wouldn't be able to channel their magic or do anything, as the demonic energy would poison and suffocate them. The demons would beat them, bite them, and tear them apart, mercilessly crushing their bones. And once they were helpless, sprawled on the floor in a pool of their own blood, they would kill them in the most sadistic way.

Tears gathered in Tessa's eyes, but she pushed them back. She wasn't going to give up without a fight. She connected to her power. Without really knowing what she was doing, she collected as much power as she could in her body. The air around her was thick with electric discharges. Her hair, charged with static electricity, rose, surrounding her face like a dark halo and lightning zig-zagged in the depth of her brown eyes.

"Missi, drop the shield," said Tessa, and she didn't recognize her voice, there was so much strength and self-assurance in it. "Drop it now!"

Missi looked at her and her mouth shaped into the letter "O". "Now!" barked Tessa. Missi nodded letting go of her magic.

It happened exactly as Tessa expected. As soon as Missi's shield was gone, all the demons pounced on them. But Tessa was ready. She wasn't sure why she was doing it, but somehow she knew that it was the right thing to do. She dropped on one knee, firmly planting her right hand on the floor, and extended the left hand up. The thunderstorm rolled over the bar as the bright lightning connected with her hand. At the same time, the roaring waves of an earthquake spread around.

The ground quaked as a horrifying lightning storm ravaged the bar. The bolts of electricity forked and zig-zagged, striking through every single demon who was still inside. Tessa screamed, throwing her head back as she allowed her power to take her over completely. She rose in the air, levitating under the ceiling, her body surrounded by the crackling white glow of electricity. The earthquake grew stronger and a deep dark fracture slithered through the wall and then through the ceiling.

A few minutes later everything was over. Not one demon survived the storm. Tessa let go of her power and lowered herself to the floor covered in dirty shreds and ashes—all that remained of the leaders of the two powerful demonic factions. The earthquake ceased, and the thunderstorm was gone. Feeling drained, Tessa sat down on the dirty floor, propping her elbows atop of her knees and sighed.

Missi dropped on the floor next to Tessa, staring at her like she'd never seen her before. "How did you do that?" she asked, her voice hoarse.

"I don't know. I had no idea that I could do all that… I knew that I could kind of control electricity, but an earthquake?" Tessa sighed, feeling too tired to talk. "I have all these scary powers and I have no idea where they come from or how to wield them properly. I am so stupid, Missi... There is nothing I can do right. You were right. I need to take magical education more seriously..."

Missi got up and offered Tessa her hand to help her up. They walked out of the half-demolished bar together. October in Chicago was pretty cold, and Tessa shivered in her thin jacket.

"I wish I could tell you that you will have a chance to learn more, but something tells me I won't be able to cover your complete lack of discipline and disregard to the Guardians' rules this time," said Missi with a sigh. "Most likely, they will expel you and demote me into a Witch. I just recently passed the test and was qualified as a Mage, first level. They're definitely going to demote me after this mess."

"But how will they find out?" asked Tessa, her chest tightening with anxiety. "I'm not going to tell them anything. And it's also in your interest to keep your mouth shut."

Missi laughed mirthlessly. "Tessa, you really need to listen during your lessons. We don't have to tell them anything. They already know. By the time we reach headquarters, they will have a welcome party ready for us."

"But how?"

"Any time you use your magic or elemental power, you release magical energy. The more powerful your magic, the stronger the magical energy spike is. Between the two of us, the energy spike was so strong that it was probably felt in Australia..." Missi sighed. "Besides, a thunderstorm in October and an earthquake in Chicago? Trust me, they know."

"But we didn't do anything bad, Missi. It's opposite—they should be grateful to us. We destroyed two influential demonic factions. We wiped them all out of existence in one hour!"

"First, we didn't destroy two demonic factions. We just killed a few of their leaders. The demons that belonged to these two factions are still out there. Now they will join the other factions, making them stronger. So, in reality, we did more damage than good. Second, we both broke some major rules and like I was explaining earlier, Guardians are a military Order and they don't take disobedience and disregard to rules lightly."

Tessa fell silent and Missi didn't insist on talking either. They approached a small house that was hidden among taller buildings and stopped. The house wasn't the actual Headquarters building. It was just a gateway connected by a bridge to the Guardians' base. There were a few of these gateways in different parts of the city, but only Guardians knew where to look for them and how to use them.

Missi reached for the key. Attached to a keychain, there was a small round medallion that looked like a cheap, made-in-china trinket. No human would ever give it a second look. Missi took the medallion and touched the door lock with it, whispering an opening spell. For a moment, the medallion lit up with a soft golden light and the door swung open.

As soon as they walked through the gateway, Tessa realized that Missi was right. Two armed guards stood in the middle of the main hall and the Head Mage of the Guardians Council stood behind them, her hands on her hips, her eyes gleaming with fury.

"Please escort these two to the confinement chambers," she ordered the guards, her voice shaking with fury. "The Council will deal with them at the morning assembly. 8 AM sharp."

Tessa threw a terrified look at Missi as they both followed the guards.

9

~ AIDAN ~

Aidan walked outside the hotel and shivered. It was seven forty-five in the morning. The air was crispy cold and a chilly breeze from the lake wasn't helping the situation. Aidan was wearing just a short-sleeve cotton shirt, and he regretted that he teleported straight to Chicago from the Church by the Sea. He should have stopped at home first to pick up some warmer clothes. Raoul's grumpy state of mind didn't help either.

"You teleported us straight to Chicago," nagged Raoul, shivering in his black priest's attire. "You didn't even care if any humans would see you materializing out of the clear blue! You are reckless, Monsieur McGrath."

"Monsieur?" repeated Aidan, slightly unnerved. "Yes, we're in Chicago, since yesterday, in case you didn't notice. And you decided to yell at me for that just now, Raoul? Where did you want to go, anyway?"

"To my sleeping quarters, at the Church," muttered the Warden under his breath, glaring at Aidan. "At least I could get some money if not warmer clothes. I don't have money to buy food. And we need to rent a car. You're not going to be teleporting all over the city in the middle of the day."

"Well, you are a wizard, aren't you?" asked Aidan, giving Raoul an arched stare, a suggestive smirk on his face. "Do something about it. Get yourself some money."

"I will do no such thing!" stated Raoul indignantly. His temper was rising quickly, and his French accent was getting heavier with every word. "Magic should not be used in vain, for mundane tasks or personal gain. Didn't you learn anything in your twenty-five-hundred years of life?"

"Sure, I did," replied Aidan, a wide grin splitting his face. "I learned a lot of things and practiced all sorts of magic." He crossed the street and stopped in front of a Bank of America ATM machine. He pulled his bank card out of his wallet and swiped it, navigating the touch screen. "I learned a new kind of magic too—it's called ATM and Credit Cards. You should try it sometime. Very effective in getting money when you need it."

Aidan took two one-hundred-dollar bills out of the ATM and folded them into his wallet.

"Aidan, I didn't have my wallet or my cell phone on me when you teleported us," said Raoul with a sigh. "I'm sorry. I've been bitching all morning. Usually I'm not such a pain in the ass."

"Don't worry, Raoul. I'll take care of all the expenses. After all, you are here only to help me," said Aidan, giving him a quick tap on his shoulder. "But something tells me that your bitching is not over. Now, we'll be walking in this cold for about fifteen minutes to the car rental. I placed the car reservation yesterday, but we still need to pick it up."

FOLLOWING RAOUL'S DIRECTIONS, Aidan drove to the secluded area in the depths of Deerfield. They passed through the forest.

Even though it was early October, the trees were painted in gold and yellow. Living for so many years in South Florida, Aidan already forgot the breathtaking colors and the delicate scent of autumn. He lowered the driver's window and inhaled deeply, ignoring the chilly wind. As the year was slowly approaching the turning point, there was something so sad and nostalgic about the fading nature.

They stopped in front of a large iron gate. As far as Aidan could see, a tall stone wall was running in both directions away from the gate. There were no guards or intercom system.

"Now what?" asked Aidan, looking at Raoul.

"Allow me." Raoul smiled and got out of the car. He took the chain with the cross off his neck and touched the gate, whispering an enchantment. The cross in his hand lit up with a soft golden light, something clicked, and the gate opened with a loud screeching noise.

"I shall tell Madam Bonneville that the gate needs to be tended," he muttered, climbing back into the car. "Come on, Aidan. Why are we standing? There is still a ten-minute drive through the park, before we reach the building."

After a few minutes' drive, Aidan parked the car on the spacious circular motor court in front of a large building. He got out and halted observing the enormous French chateau-style mansion. The word mansion wouldn't give the Guardians Headquarters justice. It looked more like a palace. But in reality, any existing royal palace of this world would pale in comparison to this magnificent building.

Raoul didn't give him any time to enjoy the view. He grabbed Aidan's arm and pulled him up the steps toward the large double-door. He was about to use his cross to open the doors when they swung open. A tall man in a business suit greeted them with a smile that was colder than the weather outside and bent down in a formal bow.

"Father Raoul de Beaumont," he said as a form of greeting, "Ms. Bonneville instructed me to escort you"—he threw a quick appraising stare in Aidan's direction that was infused with arrogance beyond any measure— "and your friend to the Assembly Hall. Please follow me." The man turned around and walked away without giving them a second look.

Aidan sighed but followed him through the large main hall. The arrogance of this man rubbed him wrong and he would truly like to teach him a lesson in humility, but right now he needed the Guardians' assistance, so teaching any kind of lessons was out of the question.

As soon as they walked into the Assembly Hall, Raoul stopped and pulled on Aidan's arm.

"I don't know what's going on, Aidan," he said in a quick whisper. "This is the Guardians Council. All of them... That can't be good."

The Assembly Hall was a spacious room with at least thirty-foot high ceilings. Large chandeliers decorated by hundreds of crystal pendants, were hanging from the ceiling illuminating the hall. At the far end, there was a tall desk. Two women and a man were sitting behind this desk. Two smaller tables were positioned on either side of the desk and three people were sitting at each of the side tables.

The older woman that was residing in the center behind the main desk got up and gestured at them to approach. Raoul halted a few feet away from the desk and bowed. Aidan decided to err on the side of caution and inclined his head in a light bow to show his respect for the Guardians Council.

"Father Raoul de Beaumont," said the woman, a frown seemed to be permanently glued to her face. "Your visit is quite unexpected. Please explain why you are here and what moved you to bring a god of the Celtic Otherworld into our secret facility."

"I apologize, Madam Bonneville," mumbled Raoul, bowing again. He reached into his pocket and produced the letter from Father Collins. "Please read this letter, Madam Head Mage. It should explain everything."

He approached the table and with trembling hands offered the envelope to the Head Mage. She took the envelope and quickly read Father Collins' letter. Still holding the letter in her hands, she looked at Aidan and a semblance of a smile appeared on her face.

"Mr. McGrath, this letter is from the Master Warden, Father Collins. It tells me you are in need of our assistance," said the Mage. "Is that correct?"

"Yes, ma'am," replied Aidan, calmly meeting her heavy stare.

"Father Collins didn't provide any details in his letter," continued Ms. Bonneville. "The only thing he said was that we need to treat with utmost importance everything you tell us and assist you in any way we can."

"I would appreciate any help you can provide," said Aidan.

"Fine. I would like to hear you out, but in private, Mr. McGrath. Until I know what you need, there is no necessity to get the whole Council involved," said the Head Mage, sitting back down. "However, the Guardians Council has a small matter that needs to be addressed immediately. You and Father Beaumont are welcome to wait. You can sit down on the bench by the wall. It shouldn't take long. Once we're done, we'll discuss your case right away."

Aidan and Raoul walked to the bench and sat down.

"That's unusual," whispered Raoul, leaning closer to Aidan. "Normally, no one outside the Council can be present at the Council's assembly meeting."

In the meantime, the Head Mage waved at the guards and commanded, "Please bring them in. We're ready now."

The guards walked out of the Assembly Hall and came back

a minute later, escorting two women. Aidan threw one glance at them and his heart stopped, pain squeezing his chest in its iron claws. It was Tessa. His Tessa... Her clothes were covered in dust, stains of dried blood and some other unrecognizable substance. Her long black hair was in disarray and her beautiful brown eyes were red and puffy from crying. Missi didn't look much better. They didn't notice Aidan and kept walking.

The guards escorted them both to the main desk and made them stop there. The Head Mage rose, glowering down at the young women with severity.

"Therasia Raegan Donovan, First Level Apprentice and Melissa Ember Clark, First Level Mage. You stand accused of reckless behavior that endangered your own lives and that of others. You broke the rules of the Guardians Order and created chaos in the demonic organization that undoubtedly will result in more bloodshed in the future. You risked the exposure of our organization and the safety of humans in that area."

"But Ms. Bonneville, no one recognized us as—," started Tessa.

"Silence!" shouted the Head Mage. "You need to learn respect, Therasia."

Tessa fell silent, dropping her head to her chest. She looked so little and so miserable that Aidan's heart skipped a beat again. Involuntarily he started to rise, but Raoul pulled him down.

"Aidan, do not get involved," he hissed into his ear, applying pressure on his shoulder. "Tessa chose to be a part of the Guardians Order, otherwise she wouldn't be here. It was her choice and now she will have to pay the consequences for whatever she did wrong."

Aidan grunted but sat down. He wondered what Tessa and Missi did to deserve all this, but the Head Mage proceeded without giving any details of what happened.

"After a long deliberation, the Guardians Council has

decided that a transgression of this severity cannot go unpunished," she declared, turning to Missi first. "Melissa Amber Clark, you will be demoted to a Witch, First Level."

"First Level?" gasped Missi. "That's hardly above an Apprentice..." Her voice trailed away, and she fell silent under the heavy stare of the Head Mage.

"Therasia Raegan Donovan, you are an Apprentice of the First Level, which is the lowest level in our organization. As such, there is no place for demotion. You will be expelled from the Guardians Order. However, you have powers of unknown origin that you're still not in control of. We cannot leave such a dangerous weapon in the hands of an inexperienced, undisciplined youth and let you out into the mundane world. You'll be confined to the Guardians Headquarters until we decide otherwise or for the rest of your life. Whichever comes first."

"Ms. Head Mage, please!" begged Tessa, tears sliding down her ashen face. "Please. I learned my lesson. That will never happen again."

The Head Mage ignored her, waving at the guards. "Take them away. Please return Ms. Donovan back to the confinement chamber. Miss Clark is free to go to relocate to the Witches' section."

Ignoring Raoul's warning Aidan got up, blocking the guards' way. He approached Tessa, gazing down at her. More than anything, he wanted to hug her right there, hold her in his arms and tell her that everything was going to be all right. But he knew that it wasn't the right time for that.

"Aidan..." whispered Tessa, stretching her hand to him.

He smiled down at her and switched his attention to the Head Mage.

"Ms. Bonneville, if I may," he started. She nodded, and Aidan continued, "I know Ms. Donovan since she was sixteen. And I would like to speak on her behalf as a character witness."

THE BURNS WAR

"Well, that's quite unusual," said Ms. Bonneville. "But since you, Mr. McGrath, are our guest today, I will allow it."

"Tessa is young and inexperienced, but her heart is in the right place," said Aidan. "I saw her magic in action, and I agree with you, ma'am, her magic is as dangerous as it is powerful. So, instead of wasting her abilities by keeping her imprisoned, you should continue teaching her. Teach her not only how to use her magic but also how to be a useful member of the Guardians Order. I'm sure, the Order can do with a powerful witch like Tessa, once she's trained properly."

All the members of the Guardians Council fell silent, staring at the Head Mage. Tessa and Missi turned around, hope gleaming in their eyes. Raoul approached Aidan and stopped by his side.

"Oh, Aidan," he whispered, sadness shadowing his handsome features, "you're a god, but a hot human heart is still beating in your chest. Possibly, you saved the woman you love, but it'll cost you…"

"I'll pay gladly," replied Aidan quietly.

"Aidan McGrath, please come closer," called the Head Mage. Aidan approached the desk, halting a few feet away. "I'm inclined to follow your suggestion, but Ms. Donovan's pardon would be conditional upon her completing a year trial period. First, Ms. Donovan must respect and follow all the rules of our organization. One step left or right from the rules and the original sentence will apply. Am I clear, Ms. Donovan?" She looked at Tessa over Aidan's head.

"Yes, Ms. Head Mage," said Tessa, pressing her hands to her chest. "I will never break any rules again. I swear. Thank you."

"Second, since you spoke for Ms. Donovan," said the Head Mage, staring down at Aidan, "I would like you to support your belief in her worthiness by your actions, Mr. McGrath."

"What would you like me to do, ma'am?"

"For this trial period of one year, I would like you, Aodh mac

Lir, to swear your fealty to the Order and serve our purpose as we deem it necessary. One year only."

Aidan glanced at Tessa over his shoulder. Her large brown eyes were gazing at him pleadingly, still gleaming with leftover tears. She had this very same look on her face any time she wanted something, and he remembered it since she was a child. It was because of this look, these giant velvety eyes, that he could never say no to her. Or maybe, it was because he loved her so deeply that he would do anything to see her happy.

Aidan whispered an enchantment and a long sword manifested in his hand, glistening like ice. He heard Raoul's gasp, but he ignored him.

"I agree to your conditions, ma'am," said Aidan. "But before I swear my fealty, I also have a couple of my own demands."

"What are your conditions, Mr. McGrath?" asked the Head Mage, frowning.

"First, you must also restore Missi to her former rank of First Level Mage."

"Done," said the Head Mage.

"Second, I came here because I needed your help," continued Aidan. "You must provide me with your assistance and allow me to complete my original mission."

"That goes without saying," agreed the Head Mage. "I accept both of your conditions."

Aidan placed his sword, tip on the floor, and went down to one knee before the Guardians Order.

"I, Aodh mac Lir, a god of the Celtic Otherworld, pledge my fealty to the Guardians Order. From this day to the same day next year, I will serve and obey your command as a loyal member of this organization. For the greater good of this realm, protecting humans and guarding the secrecy of the World of Magic."

The Head Mage walked around the desk and stopped in front of Aidan. She touched his chest and a silver chain materialized around his neck. It looked like regular jewelry with a round silver pendant attached to it. Aidan glanced down at the necklace and with surprise noticed that the pendant had a Celtic Triskele surrounded by a delicate knotwork engraved on it.

"I thought that you'd like it," said the Head Mage. "Please rise."

"I do," replied Aidan, getting up. "But what is it? I am sure it's not a plain piece of jewelry."

"No, it's not," agreed the Head Mage. "This pendant is our communication device. Also, it will open the door of any of the Guardians' gateways or locations anywhere in this realm. Father Beaumont will teach you how to use it. For the full year of your service, you can never take this pendant off. If you take it off, we'll know, and we'll consider it a breach of your oath."

"I understand," replied Aidan, his fingers crushing the pommel of his sword.

"After we discuss your case and you complete your original mission, you're free to go back home and live your life as usual. However, you cannot leave this realm without notifying us first. It includes your visits to the Otherworld. If the Guardians Order will be in need of your services, we'll summon you."

"That's fine," said Aidan quietly.

The Head Mage got back to her desk and clapped her hands together three times. "The assembly meeting of the Guardians Council is now adjourned. You all are free to leave. Mr. McGrath and Father Beaumont, please stay behind so we can discuss your mission."

As everyone was slowly leaving the Assembly Hall, Aidan approached Tessa. He stood in front of her, not daring to put his arms around her, sadness tearing through his chest.

"Aidan, what did you do?" whispered Tessa. She wrapped her arms around his waist and pressed her cheek against his chest. "I missed you so much."

Aidan exhaled, his breath coming out almost like a hushed moan, and finally encircled her shoulders with his arms, pulling her closer. "I love you, Tessa," he whispered, gently kissing her hair. "I would die before I let anything happen to you."

Tessa hid her face in his chest and her shoulders shuddered in quiet sobs.

10

~ AIDAN ~

"Tessa, please go back to your room and get cleaned up. After that, you need to attend your lessons. Since you're still our Apprentice, you have a lot to learn and your chores are not going to do themselves," said the Head Mage dryly, approaching Tessa and Aidan. "Mr. McGrath and I need to have a grown-up conversation."

Aidan cringed inwardly at the way the old Mage addressed Tessa. Grown-up conversation? She was treating her like a silly little child. But Tessa didn't object. She glanced one more time at Aidan, squeezing his hand for a quick moment. Then she bowed to the Head Mage and walked out of the Assembly Hall.

Ms. Bonneville followed Tessa with her eyes until she walked out and shut the door. Then she turned to Aidan and smiled. Since he met her this morning, this was the first time that her face wasn't scrunched up into a frown. Her smile was relaxed and there was something possessive in the way she observed him. She patted him on his shoulder like she was his best friend.

"No need to look so sad, Mr. McGrath. The lessons are over at three in the afternoon. You can meet with Therasia then. I'm sure you have a few things to... um... discuss," she said, her mouth twitching in a sarcastic half-smile. "Now, let's get to business, shall we?"

She walked to the side table on her left and sat down. Aidan and Raoul exchanged a quick look and joined her.

"Well, Mr. McGrath, tell me what brought you here and what I can do to help," said Ms. Bonneville, now serious.

Aidan explained to her in detail everything that he knew about Gunz's disappearance in the Dark Nav and about the mage that was behind it. After that Father Raoul filled in the details about the missing page in their Book of Words. Once they finished, the Head Mage touched a pendant on her necklace and whispered a short spell.

The table shimmered with a soft golden light and a thick book materialized before their eyes. The book looked exactly like the Book of Words that Father Collins had in his church. The mage touched the book with her fingers and the book opened up on its own. She held both hands over the blank pages. With a soft noise, the pages started flipping over. After a few seconds, the Head Mage gasped and got up sharply.

"Cease," she ordered, and the pages stop, leaving the book opened in the middle. "Father Collins was right. The page is missing."

"I need this page," said Aidan, his hands squeezing the edge of the table, almost breaking it off. "I'm sure it was Agent Zvereva who stole the page. There was something in the book she didn't want us to find."

"Obviously," grumbled Ms. Bonneville, shaking her head. "Please stop breaking my furniture, Mr. McGrath. Crushing a few tables in the facility is not going to solve the problem."

Aidan raised his hands up and leaned back in his chair.

"Madam Bonneville, are you planning to send someone to Paris?" asked Raoul.

"Yes, Father Beaumont, I will dispatch one of the mages to

Paris immediately. We need to restore this page in the Book of Words and find out who this mage is and what she is hiding."

She touched the pendant on her chest again, sending a small amount of her magic through it. A few minutes later, the door into the Assembly Hall opened up and Missi walked in. She looked her normal self now that she got a chance to clean up and the fears and worries were behind her. Missi bowed to the Head Mage and smiled to Aidan and Raoul.

"Melissa, I have a very important assignment for you," said Ms. Bonneville. "And I'm sure that Mr. McGrath would be happy that it's you who is going to take care of this assignment and not someone else."

"What do you need me to do, Ms. Bonneville?" asked Missi, throwing a curious gaze at Aidan.

"Please be advised that anything we are going to say right now, must stay in this room. No one can know about it. Not even Tessa. Am I clear, Melissa?" asked the Head Mage severely.

"Yes, ma'am," replied Missi.

"A page from the Book of Words has been stolen," said the Head Mage. "I need you to travel to the Wardens Headquarters in Paris and see if they can restore our missing page. I can't stress enough how important this mission is. The life of a good man depends on it and possibly a lot more than just that..."

The old mage fell silent, her face somber. She got up and softly touched Missi's hand. "I don't want to voice my fears until I know for sure. Please be careful in Paris, Melissa, and remember—complete secrecy is a must. You can't speak to anyone about this except the Grand Master of the Wardens himself. I have no idea who this mage is, but she was obviously powerful enough to walk into our facility unnoticed, retrieve the book and mutilate it. Somehow she bypassed our guards and didn't trigger our wards and protection spells or modern security devices."

"Missi, Ms. Bonneville is right. I'm glad it's you who is

working with us on this mission and not someone else," said Aidan. "It's Zane's life on the line. Some crazy mage forced him to cross the veil into the Slavic realm of the dead. Something is not right about all this, Missi, and I can't figure out what's going on."

"I will leave immediately," said Missi, her fingers squeezing the pendant attached to her keychain. "Ms. Bonneville, can I use the gateway to Paris? It will be faster."

"Yes, use the gateway," replied the Head Mage. "It will be safer that way too, but it's still a long drive to the Paris gateway."

"If everything goes as planned, I should be back within forty-eight hours," said Missi. She turned around, ready to leave, but then came back and hugged Aidan. "I'll do everything in my power... Just find Zane and bring him back."

She gave Aidan a quick kiss on his unshaved cheek, and for a moment her eyes lingered on the pendant on his chest. A shadow of sadness crossed her face but quickly disappeared. She turned away and left the Assembly Hall.

"Father Beaumont," said the Head Mage as soon as Missi was gone, "I trust you remember where your old sleeping quarters are located?"

"Yes, Madam Bonneville," replied Raoul, getting up.

"Your old roommate is no longer here, so you can share your room with Mr. McGrath." She turned to Aidan, giving him an arched stare. "I hope it's not a problem for you, Mr. McGrath? Wardens are a warrior order and their accommodations are quite plain."

"No problem," said Aidan, his thoughts far away, "just let us know as soon as Missi is back."

"And Mr. McGrath, you can meet with Ms. Donovan in the Main Hall at three. She'll be there, waiting for you," said the mage on her way out of the Assembly Hall.

Aidan glanced at his watch and sat back down. It was a long wait until three, but he didn't feel like going into the Wardens' wing of the building. He didn't feel like going anywhere. He picked up the pendant, running his fingers over the knotwork and then dropped it back on his chest.

"You made a giant mistake, *mon ami*," said Raoul, gazing at him with sympathy. "You signed your life off to the Guardians. And being an immortal god, your life is very long."

"I did what I had to do to protect Tessa. And I didn't sign off my life, Raoul, just one year."

"Please, tell me that at your ripe age of twenty-five hundred years, you're not this naïve!" Raoul slammed his hand on the table. "Do you seriously think that after the Guardians will have a god at their beck and call, they would ever let you go?" He seized the chain with the pendant and pulled it a few times. "At least I chose this life willingly, many years ago. You sold yours. Look at this chain, Aidan. This is your brand-new collar and a leash. And don't even doubt, they won't feel shy to yank this leash around. So, say woof-woof, Aodh mac Lir!"

"Raoul, I had no choice," said Aidan quietly. "I couldn't let them do it to Tessa—"

"*Imbécile!*" exclaimed Raoul, making a three hundred sixty degree turn in place. "I can bet you anything, they knew about your feelings for Tessa and they manipulated you into submission! A life of servitude! And what do you think your true master and mentor would say when he finds out that you signed your life off to the Destiny Council? We both know how he feels about the Destiny Council and anyone who works for them, including the Guardians and the Wardens."

Aidan bowed his head to his chest and didn't answer. His demolished look took the wind out of Raoul's sails. He sighed and sat back down next to Aidan.

"I'm sorry," he said quietly. "When the time comes, we'll figure something out. I promise."

* * *

EVEN THOUGH AIDAN'S watch was showing ten to three, the Main Hall was filled with people. Guards were spread around the perimeter of the room, as young apprentices, witches and wizards were leaving their classes, heading back to their rooms. Aidan spun around, trying to find Tessa in the constantly moving crowd of people that were dressed alike.

Someone tugged on his arm and Aidan flinched, turning around. Tessa was standing next to him, a happy smile on her face. She looked a lot better than she did in the morning when he first saw her. She was dressed in an Apprentice uniform with a black leather jacket over it. Her long hair was pulled into a neat ponytail on the back of her head and she finally cut her bangs a little shorter, allowing the world to see her beautiful eyes.

"Let's get out of here," she proposed, taking Aidan's hand and pulling him toward the main entrance door.

"I thought you can't leave headquarters without their permission," said Aidan warningly.

"And I'm not planning to leave," replied Tessa with a half-shrug. "The gardens are available to us at any time. Trust me, you'll like it there."

Tessa led him through the entrance door outside and then circled around the building toward the gardens. Even at this time of the year, the gardens of the Guardians Headquarters looked magnificent. The trees didn't lose their leaves yet and were creating a rich canopy over the trail, colored in gold and orange. Tessa found a small pavilion in the heart of the gardens and led Aidan inside. She sat down on the bench and tapped it with her hand, inviting him to join her. For a few seconds, he stilled and just stood in front of her, enjoying the fact that she was so close, and she wasn't ignoring him or giving him the cold shoulder.

"Aidan, sit down," she said impatiently, pulling him down to the bench next to her. As he sat down, her fingers softly brushed his arm and she gasped. "You're freezing! All in goosebumps."

She took her leather jacket off and draped it over his shoulders, trying to cover him the best she could. Aidan chuckled and took her jacket off, returning it to her.

"Thank you," he said. He took her hand into his and planted a soft kiss on the open palm of her hand. "Don't you think I should be giving you my jacket to warm you up? Not the other way around?"

Tessa gave him an appraising stare and a mischievous smile lit up her face. "Sure, you can take your shirt off and give it to me. I don't mind taking a peek under the hood."

Aidan snorted, shaking his head. "What else don't you mind seeing?" he asked, but then caught her gaze sliding down below his waist and laughed. "No, better don't answer that question. I'm not sure I am ready to hear you say that."

Tessa got up and walked closer to Aidan, stepping between his legs and leaning into his chest. Even with him sitting and her standing, she was just a little taller than him. She cupped his face with her cold hands and tilted his head back gently. Aidan met her gaze and held his breath for a moment.

"Tessa, do you still hate me?" he asked finally. "The way you left eight months ago, I thought I'd never see you again. I was dying inside…"

She didn't answer right away. Slowly she moved her fingers through his thick blond hair and then over his cheek.

"Your hair got so much longer, it's almost down to your shoulders. And how many days didn't you shave?" she asked, sounding a little distant, and he crumbled inside. She didn't answer his question… She didn't forgive him.

"Tessa," he whispered, all the pain he felt breaking to the surface in his hoarse voice.

"I don't hate you, Aidan." She caressed his face, running her fingers over the rough stubble on his cheeks. "I don't think I ever did. I was upset with what you did, and I didn't bother to try to understand why you did it..." She fell silent biting her lip. "I was stupid and — Zane was right... I was rude, ignorant and close-minded. It took me eight months and a few thousand miles to realize it."

"Tessa—"

"Please, let me finish, Aidan," she interrupted him, tears gathering in her eyes. "I hurt you. I know I did. When you told me the truth about who you were, and you told me that you loved me. What I said back to you was—" She closed her eyes for a quick moment and swallowed her tears. "I'm sorry, Aidan. I am so, so sorry. You didn't deserve any of that. And what you did for me today. I can never repay you."

She found the silver chain under his shirt and pulled it out, slowly tracing with her finger the shape of the Triskele on the pendant. Then she dropped the pendant back to his chest and embraced him, burying her face into the golden mane of his hair. Aidan was hardly breathing, enjoying the unexpected moment of tenderness. Coming from Tessa, it was quite unusual. He was terrified to lift his arms to hug her back, or to make the tiniest move. He was afraid that if he would do anything at all, she would push him away again.

After a moment, Tessa unlocked her arms and caught his gaze again, a hardly noticeable sad smile playing on her lips. Then she leaned forward and gently kissed his cheek. The touch of her cold lips to his skin sent a wave of warmth through his body. His lips parted slightly, and his breath quickened, as he was fighting the urge to take her into his arms and kiss her, and to never let her go.

She moved back slightly, taking in his reaction and her eyes widened. "Oh my God," she whispered. "You still love me, don't you? After all, I did to you... You still love me." She didn't wait for him to reply. Instead, she leaned lower and kissed him.

Something snapped and broke inside him. He groaned,

taking over the kiss and lifted her off the ground, carefully placing her on his lap. She didn't pull away, didn't object, didn't do anything, allowing him to take the lead now.

Aidan pulled away ever so slightly and brushed his lips over her flushed cheek. "I can never stop loving you," he said, his lips almost touching hers.

He got up, holding her in his arms, his eyes and his body glowing with the brilliant white light of his magic. She moved her hand over his hair and down over his shoulder, trying to touch his magical aura and smiled.

"You're the most beautiful ancient god I've ever seen," she whispered, gazing at him in awe. "And the best-preserved old man, I've ever met."

Aidan laughed, happiness sparkling inside him just as brightly as his magical aura was shining on the outside.

"My Tessa," he whispered, crushing her lips with his. He felt her responding to his kiss, her arms wrapping around his neck tighter.

Aidan pushed off the ground and flew high in the air, carefully holding his precious cargo in his arms, feeling her heart beating with his.

"I love you, my Tessa. Always and forever."

11

~ ZANE BURNS, A.K.A. GUNZ ~

The Dark Nav was always cold. It wasn't the freezing cold of a winter. It felt more like a late autumn, when the trees dropped all the leaves and bone-chilling winds were whistling through their twisted naked arms. There was no light and there was no energy of life in this place. It was chilly, gloomy, and unfriendly.

Gunz shivered, wrapping his oversized shirt tighter and tucking it inside his pants that were held up by a rope. His own clothes were torn beyond repair and Karma brought him this shirt and pants that were at least three sizes too big. He didn't know where she got them, and he didn't want to ask.

Three days passed since Karma pulled him out of the swamp in the thorny forest. Now he knew that it was Mishka who found her by pure coincidence and brought her over to help him. Now Mishka was sleeping in his room, curled under a skimpy blanket. Gunz's cuts and wounds healed, but the front of his body was covered in hundreds of ugly scars. He felt better, his physical strength almost restored, and he didn't care about that. All he had to do to get rid of the scars was to revert to his natural state.

Nevertheless, that would have to wait until he was back in his own realm. The Dark Nav was deprived of all elemental powers, including the Fire, and reverting into the natural state of the Fire Salamander wasn't possible here. Even his magic was weak and feeble here. Every time he tried to cast the simplest of spells, he felt so drained after, that he decided that using magic here wasn't worth it. Gunz watched Karma using her magic many times, and he didn't think the Dark Nav had the same draining effect on her.

When he asked Karma about it, she just shrugged her shoulders. She wasn't sure why the Dark Nav was feeding on Gunz more than on her, but one thing she knew for sure—the life energy of nature didn't exist here. So, anytime he tried to use magic, he had to support it with his own life energy. This is why he felt so drained and exhausted after.

Little by little, his thoughts went back to the original reason he was sent here. He needed to locate that axe-looking magical artifact. To do that, he had to find his way into Chernobog's castle. Gunz cringed inwardly. The thought about facing the Slavic god of Destruction didn't appeal to him. He never told Karma any details of his mission and so far, she didn't ask, but he had no doubt that sooner or later that talk would have to happen. Either she would demand an answer, or he would have to tell her everything and ask her for help.

Gunz walked around Karma's small hut to the backyard. A pile of logs was mounted in the middle of the backyard. Usually Karma used her magic to split these logs into firewood. Dark Nav was always cold and burning firewood was the only way to keep the house at least a few degrees warmer. But even burning wood couldn't help much. Since there was no real fire here, Karma had to conjure flames, and sustaining them with her magic for as long as possible.

Gunz pulled an axe out of a large tree stump and checked the tool, probing its cutting edge with his finger. The axe was old and rusted in a few places but seemed to be sturdy and sharp enough to do the job. He grabbed one of the logs and placed it on top of the stump. Then he swung the axe over his shoulder, forcefully swinging it down through the log. With a loud crack, the log split, letting the axe slide all the way through, and fell apart on either side of the stump.

Gunz smiled, enjoying the simplicity of the physical work and the feeling of his restored strength. He knew that he didn't have to do it since Karma could take care of it magically, but he needed to clear his mind and physical work always helped. Gunz picked up the next log, placing it on top of the stump, and swung his axe again.

An hour later, he was drenched in sweat, his shirt clinging to his body, his wet hair plastered over his forehead. For the first time since he was pushed into the Dark Nav, he didn't feel cold. Gunz pulled his wet shirt out of his pants and was about to take it off when he heard a soft giggle. He spun around and found Karma and Milana sitting next to the house, watching him. He lowered his shirt, tucking it back into his overly loose pants.

"Aw, no, don't stop now," whined Karma, sounding exaggeratedly disappointed. She wrapped her arm around her girlfriend's shoulders. "We're enjoying the show too much. And please, be a good boy and take that ugly shirt off."

Gunz grunted, shaking his head and swung the axe, sticking it back into the tree stump. "Tell me, Karma, do you love objectifying all men or is it just me who is so lucky?"

"It's you," replied Karma right away with a sunshiny smile on her face. "Normally, I don't pay attention to your kind at all. I prefer to look at something more delicate, exquisite..."

She turned to gaze at her girlfriend. Gently holding her chin with her fingers, she lifted Milana's face up and kissed her. Milana leaned into her, putting her arms around Karma's waist. Gunz looked away and wiped his forehead with the back of his hand.

"Aw, sweetie, are you really so innocent?" murmured Karma as soon as she came up for breath, waving her hand at Gunz. "You don't need to look away. You're welcome to watch." She burst out laughing.

Gunz threw his hands in the air and headed back into the hut, followed by a wave of wild giggles. He walked into the house and slammed the door closed with a loud bang. Then he pulled a chair out and dropped into it, resting his elbows on the table, hiding his face in his hands.

Mishka flew over and attempted to land on his shoulder, but his paws slipped on Gunz's wet shirt. The wyvern yelped and hopped to the table, shaking his paws like a house cat that stepped into a puddle.

"You're wet!" he exclaimed indignantly. "Did you go for a swim in the swamp again?"

"I'm sweating," muttered Gunz, his thoughts elsewhere.

"Why?"

"I was working."

"Why?"

"I was chopping wood, so we could get some fire and warm up the house."

"Why? Karma could use her magic to do that."

"It helps me think…"

"You? Think? It could be hazardous to your health and for the wellbeing of those around you."

Gunz finally raised his eyes at the wyvern and chuckled. The little winged monster had enough sarcasm for a fully grown dragon.

"Mishka, we need to talk to Karma," said Gunz, slowly stroking the wyvern's wings. "I don't know what to do next. Where is this goddamn castle and how can I get inside? I need her help. And how can we steal a magical artifact from a god without getting caught."

"That's okay, boss. It's all going to work out one way or the other," said Mishka, touching his hand with his paw, a picture-perfect supportive friend. But the moment was gone quickly and Mishka snickered, his acidy self making an appearance. "What am I talking about? I'm working with an ignoramus. If I depend on you, I'm going to die in the Dark Nav." He flew toward the door screaming at the top of his tiny lungs, "Karma! Kaaar-maaa!"

The door opened and Karma walked inside, holding Milana's hand in hers. Mishka squealed in delight and landed on her shoulder.

"Prrr," he purred happily, snuggling into Karma's red hair, "you're so warm and you're not wet like this dork." He waved his wing in Gunz's direction. Gunz pointed his finger at his watch, arching his eyebrow at the wyvern. Mishka sighed and muttering something under his breath, melted into the watch.

"Not wet?" asked Karma and laughed, throwing her head back. She pulled an empty chair out, helping her girlfriend to sit down and then sat down next to Gunz, patting his shoulder. "Sweetie, why did you leave? You're our only source of entertainment here, you know?"

"Karma, we need to talk," started Gunz ignoring her last statement.

"We're already talking," said Karma with a half-shrug.

"No, Karma, I'm serious," grumbled Gunz, frustration igniting somewhere deep within him. "I need to tell you something and it's important."

Karma stared at him for a moment. "Fine, what's going on?" she asked, her gaze becoming heavier by the moment.

"Karma, I need to get inside Chernobog's castle, and I need your help," said Gunz. All this time he was thinking of a better way to tell her and ask her for her help, but now instead of being careful and diplomatic, he just blurted it out to her face, his aggravation and impatience getting the best of him. He held his breath waiting for her reaction.

Milana gasped. Karma's mouth opened up as she stared at him, a chain of emotions changing on her face—shock, disbelief, mockery.

"You think it's funny?" she asked dryly.

"Not for me," replied Gunz quietly, holding her furious gaze. "Do you think I chose to be here? Do you think I wanted it? I was thrown here against my will, forced into this place that is feeding on my life force, killing me a slow and torturous death. And the only way I can get out of here is if I do what I was ordered to do." He slammed his hand on the table, rising, anger bubbling up inside him.

"Sit down!" shouted Karma, her fist landing on the table an inch away from his hand. She was back in her interrogation mode, and her icy voice was promising nothing good for Gunz. "Do you think breaking into Chernobog's castle will be a walk in the park? Do you know what he'll do to you if he catches you? What do you need there, anyway? Answer my question and if you know what's best for you, don't try to hide anything."

"I need to locate some powerful magical artifact that looks like a small double-edged axe decorated with gold inlays," replied Gunz with a sigh, lowering himself back into his chair. "Karma, why would I lie or hide anything from you when I'm asking for your help? A little trust would be nice."

"Trust? What kind of beastie is that?" hissed Karma, her eyes scanning his insides, distaste curving her lips. "In my line of business, I trust no one. Not even people I know well. So, why would I trust *a man* I know nothing about? Say thank you I pulled you out of that swamp and didn't let the phantoms drain your life. Or didn't kill you myself when—"

"Zane, how are you planning to leave the Dark Nav? There is no way out of here," said Milana interrupting Karma, her voice soft and sympathetic.

Neither Milana nor Karma was pure-blood human. Karma was a witch and Milana was a seer. He wasn't sure how strong her gift of sight was or if she had any other magical talents. After three days that he spent with these women, he knew pretty much nothing about either of them, including how they ended up in the Dark Nav in the first place.

Gunz pulled his shirt apart, showing her the rune on his chest. "When I complete this mission, through this rune, I will contact the mage that sent me here. She will pull me out."

Milana extended her hand and placed it on his chest over the rune. Her eyes became milky white and her head tilted back slightly. She was staring into space with her unnerving white eyes, saying nothing. After a few seconds, her eyes got back to normal, and she removed her hand from Gunz's chest.

"Karma," she whispered, her voice suddenly weak and trembling. "You can trust him, my love. He's telling you the truth…" Her voice trailed off, and she lowered her head, resting her forehead on the rough surface of the table.

Karma rushed to her side and gently embraced her, kissing the top of her head. "What else did you see, darling?" she asked, her fingers playing with Milana's soft hair.

Milana straightened up, leaning back into Karma's embrace. "We must help him, Karma. He will lead us out of this deadly prison… He's the Fire Salamander I told you about, our salvation… I would do anything just to see my own world again…" She smiled tiredly at Gunz. "I'm sorry, Zane… Here, in Dark Nav, every vision I have, takes a lot of my energy. I'm just tired…"

She got up, leaning heavily on Karma's shoulder. Karma walked her toward the door of their bedroom. At the doorway, she turned back to Gunz, staring at him sternly.

"I'm going to help Milana lie down and I'll be right back." She threw him a dry look. "Don't go anywhere."

She came back a few minutes later and sat down in the chair next to Gunz, her face grim and determined.

"Now, Fire Salamander, you're going to tell me everything

that happened from the moment you met that mage," said Karma, her eyes lighting up with a green light and Gunz could feel the energy of her magic expanding around her. "You need to tell me the smallest details without hiding anything. ANYTHING!" The last word she growled through clenched teeth. "If I'm going to risk my life to help you, you better not hide anything from me, or I swear, you'll find out why my name is Karma."

"I have never lied to you, Karma," objected Gunz calmly.

"Then start talking, boy. I don't have a full day to wait for you," said Karma.

Gunz didn't object and gave her a full version of everything that happened to him from the moment he walked into Jim's office in the middle of the night.

"Fine, I'll help you," said Karma after she processed everything he just told her. "We're going to leave tomorrow morning. So, I suggest, you pray to all the gods you know that we find a way to sneak inside that castle. I tell you, it's damn close to impossible."

"How do you know?" asked Gunz, narrowing his eyes at her.

"You don't get to question me," hissed Karma angrily, but quickly ran out of steam, sighed and sat down. "I already tried. We've heard from someone that the only way to get out of the Dark Nav is through some backdoor that Chernobog built for his beloved wife." She rolled her eyes. Obviously, the healthy marital relationship between the god of Destruction and the goddess of Death didn't impress her.

"And?"

"And Chernobog's guards caught us before we got anywhere close to the castle. We're lucky to be alive and free. Chernobog doesn't tolerate any presence of life inside his domain. Nothing that's alive should be in the kingdom of death. Nothing that is dead should be in the realm of the living. That's his job description, so to speak."

Karma sighed again, turning away from Gunz for a moment. When she turned back to him, she had this pained expression on her face that set a warning flag in his mind. *How long had they spent here?* Gunz wandered as he watched her squirming a little under his steady gaze. *And how did they get here in the first place?*

"She believes in you, you know? Milana... She had one of her premonitions or visions a few days before you showed up." Karma shook her head, staring down at her hands. "She thinks you are the only one who can get us inside the castle and to that backdoor."

Gunz rubbed his eyes tiredly, his fingers sliding down over his unshaved chin. "Karma... I can't promise anything. I know nothing about Chernobog and his castle. I'm asking you to help me, and you are telling me I am your only hope." He laughed mirthlessly.

"Well, little man, my lover believes in you. And I believe in her. She's my life and I would do anything to see her happy. Just a friendly warning—you better don't disappoint her." She got up and walked away into her bedroom.

"We're all going to die," peeped Mishka from the watch.

12

~ ZANE BURNS, A.K.A. GUNZ ~

As Karma promised, they left the house early in the morning. Both Karma and Milana traveled light, confident that it was their last passage through the Dark Nav. Gunz didn't know what to hope for. He had no idea what to expect and Karma's appearance didn't match the troubling picture she painted for him yesterday. She was dressed in blue jeans and a pink t-shirt that had "Kick Like a Girl" printed on the front and a picture of a little girl kicking on the back. To complete her attire, she was wearing bedazzled pink sneakers with white shoelaces and a small pink backpack over her shoulder.

Real badass, thought Gunz suppressing the desire to roll his eyes. *And where the hell is she getting all these fluffy outfits?* He thought back to the time when he met Karma and the way she changed her appearance in front of him. Most likely, all these outfits were just illusions she created.

Milana, on the other hand, looked more the part. She was dressed in black pants and a shirt, and her tender face wore an expression of cold determination. As they followed a hardly visible trail, Gunz was thinking that Milana was placing too much faith in him and he had no idea why. He understood that she had some kind of vision, but it wasn't enough to convince him that there was nothing else behind her blind beliefs.

All around them there was nothing but darkness. The thorny forest was left far behind and it seemed like they were walking into an infinite nothingness. Except for a swirling gray fog, there was nothing else before them. However, Karma seemed to be relaxed like a person who knew where she was going.

After about an hour of walking, the scenery still didn't change. Nothing was ahead of them and nothing was behind. Once in a while, Gunz looked up to check the dark void of the sky to make sure that the flying monsters weren't coming. Karma noticed him doing it and smirked.

"If you are searching for the phantoms, I don't think you'll find them here, in this area of the Dark Nav," she pointed out. "They usually hang around the thorny forest and a few other places similar to that."

"What other places?" asked Gunz.

"You know... Closer to the gateways that Chernobog opens to pull in the souls of the dead," explained Karma with a light shrug.

"What are those things anyway?" asked Gunz.

Milana stopped for a moment and turned to face him. "You don't know?" A sincere surprise sounded in her voice. Gunz shook his head.

"They are the phantoms," explained Milana, her soft voice sounding light and breezy. "That's what becomes of human spirits here... if they die an unnatural death and their souls weren't put to rest. Nothing that's dead should exist in the world of the living. Chernobog takes these unrested spirits into his domain. They become these blood-thirsty monsters made of nightmares..." Milana fell silent and kept walking forward.

"This is why they hang around the gateways," Karma took over. "They are feeding on the newly arrived souls and trying to escape the Dark Nav in the few seconds when the gateway is open."

Gunz shivered, thinking what could happen if these monsters would escape into Yav, the realm of the living. "Do they ever escape?" he asked.

"You don't know much about the Nav," said Karma, giving him a disapproving stare.

"No, I don't," confirmed Gunz. "Sorry. This trip was a spur-of-the-moment kinda thing. Didn't have time to get ready."

"They do escape sometimes. Rarely," explained Karma with a sigh. "Chernobog is always in control, but sometimes it happens. In the realm of the living, they fly in the stormy nights, feeding on the weak, mostly kids. Luckily, Chernobog always knows when it happens, and he doesn't let them roam around for too long. He finds them and pulls them back into the Dark Nav."

"Sounds like this Chernobog is an upstanding citizen of Slavic pantheon," muttered Gunz. "Lord Protector of all human and punisher of all undead."

Karma halted and raised her hand, signaling for Gunz and Milana to stop. She stilled, and by the way her magical energy spiked around her, Gunz knew she was using some kind of spell to check the area. He sharpened his Salamander's senses and noticed a small disturbance in the space in front of him. He could actually see it. It looked like a blob of absolute blackness with the slithering tendrils spreading around it.

"What is it?" he asked, staring at the dark blob with suspicion.

She glanced at him, a light grin splitting her face. "This is our transportation," she replied. "Do you feel it? There are a few places in the Dark Nav where the fabric of reality is getting slightly warped. Those who know these places can use them to travel to Chernobog's castle, faster and safer. All we have to do is step through this… Hmm, I don't even know what to call it. A wormhole, I guess. Anyway, ready?" She took a step forward and made a circle with her hand, outlining where the wormhole was located.

"Wait," said Gunz, grabbing her arm. "Have you ever used this one? Where are we going to walk out? Inside the castle walls?"

Milana and Karma exchanged a look and dissolved into a burst of wild giggles. "No, oh bright one. Of course not. Do you think it would be that easy to get inside the castle?" asked Karma through the laughter. "We are going to walk out a few miles away from the castle. And trust me—you want it this way. Chernobog can sense the living, and we want to make sure we cover our presence the best we can. You don't want to meet the god of Destruction face to face on his turf."

Gunz held his hand up, a lopsided smirk on his face. "Yeah, I know, I'm your only source of entertainment here." He walked closer to Karma and jerked his chin toward the wormhole. "Ready?"

Karma didn't answer. She took Milana's hand, and they both melted into the darkness of the wormhole. Gunz sighed, wondering what was awaiting him on the other side and followed them.

In a way, traveling through the warped fabric of reality reminded him of teleporting, and he hated every moment of it. Just like during teleporting, he felt like his body was taken apart, cell by cell, and then thrown carelessly back together. His stomach was sitting somewhere in his throat and his head was swimming on the waves of dizziness.

The process of traveling through the wormhole was a lot longer than teleporting. By the time Gunz surfaced on the other side, he couldn't keep his balance and fell forward on all fours. Fighting nausea and lightheadedness, he dropped his head down to the ground and wrapped his hands over it, breathing with his mouth.

"Come on, my strong, virile hero," said Karma mockingly, offering him her hand. "We can't stay here long. We must keep moving."

Gunz raised his head just in time to catch a taunting smirk on her face. Slowly he got up, ignoring her hand. "This is why... I hate teleporting," he muttered, still fighting to catch his breath. "I miss my portals."

"The Fire Salamander portals!" exclaimed Milana, suddenly excited like a little girl. "I always wanted to see one. I've heard they are absolutely fascinating. Like a wall of a liquid fire."

"More like a curtain of fire," replied Gunz. "I don't think I can open one here. I need to use elemental power for that."

"Don't even try," warned Karma. She grabbed Milana's hand, pulling her forward. "For some reason Dark Nav is feeding on you more than on anyone I've ever met here. Forget about using any elemental powers. Even if you try to use just your magic, you'll be wiped out in a heartbeat. And I'm not going to carry your sorry ass."

After a half-hour of brisk walking, Gunz noticed a weak yellow light ahead of him. Any kind of light was unusual in the Dark Nav, and this light was also flickering as if it was produced by a candle flame. He added to his pace and caught up with Karma and Milana.

"You noticed it, didn't you?" asked Karma, giving him a quick once-over.

Gunz nodded. "Hard to miss. Light in the Dark."

"This is where we're going," said Karma, adding some speed into her already fast pace. "This is a sort of tavern. We supposed to meet there with someone who will help us sneak behind the castle walls. He's like a Coyote, for a lack of a better word. He can smuggle us inside unnoticed."

The "tavern" ended up being a tiny hut, roughly put together out of old, warped logs. The door was half-open, hanging on rusted hinges. Karma stopped next to the door, her hand on the door handle, and pursed her lips.

"Listen, Zane," she started, vibe of unease permeating around her, "when we're inside, don't look at anyone. No eye contact whatsoever. Keep your eyes down at all times. And don't talk. Let me do all the talking."

"Fine," replied Gunz.

"Don't eat anything and don't take a drink from anyone," continued Karma, sternly.

"Yes, Mom," said Gunz with a smirk, "I promise. I'm not going to talk to strangers, and I am not going to take any candy from them."

"Don't joke about it, Zane." She seized his shirt, pulling him closer, her green eyes shining inches away from his. "You're new here. Use your brain! Dark Nav—the place of unrested spirits and demons! With a capital letter 'D'. Most of the visitors of this place are pure-blood demons, not humans possessed by demonic essence. Do you understand? They may look like humans on the outside, but on the inside—"

"Karma, relax," said Gunz peacefully. "I promise, I'll behave."

She nodded and finally let go of his shirt. "Keep an eye on Milana for me, would you?"

Karma pushed the door open and walked inside the tavern. Gunz and Milana followed her. Inside, the tavern seemed to be even smaller than on the outside. All windows were covered with dirty gray film. It was understandable—there was nothing to look at outside except the blinding darkness.

There were six wooden tables on the floor. On top of each table there was a jar with a shimmering orange light inside. At first, Gunz thought that the orange light was a magically conjured flame, but when he walked closer to the table, he realized that it wasn't fire. The light was a tiny energy ball.

The tavern was filled with the kind of crowd that anyone in their right mind would do anything to avoid. Dressed in disheveled rags, the men were filthy, and the stench of unwashed bodies mixed in with the revolting odor of sulphur seemed to be permanently embedded into everything.

Despite the amount of people—most likely demons—that were stuffed into the tiny space, the room was relatively quiet. Everyone was speaking in hushed voices, practically whispering into each other's ears. No one talked aloud, and soft waves of whispers were floating over the tables.

Karma walked all the way through the room and stopped in front of the last table. There was only one man sitting at this table. He was short and the absence of hair on his head was well compensated by the amount of hair on his thick arms and chest. His raggedy shirt was pulled apart on his fat belly that was pushing against the edge of the table.

Karma didn't say anything. She silently stared down at the man. He raised his eyes and glanced at her briefly, quickly averting his gaze. As Karma didn't move, he got up, his stomach giggling like jelly.

"The table is yours, witch," he hissed, shifting away from her, his eyes gleaming with dark demonic energy. As he was walking away, he kept muttering and swearing quietly under his breath but didn't try to fight her.

Karma took a flimsy chair and gestured at Gunz and Milana to join her. Milana sat down right away, shifting closer to her lover. Gunz quickly observed the tavern, registering every visitor in the room, then he sat down next to Milana, folding his hands on his lap.

A few minutes later, one of the tavern visitors got up and walked up to their table. The man was tall and everything about him was dark—his hair, his eyes, his ebony skin, his worn-out clothes. Gunz carefully scanned him with his Salamander's senses just to confirm that the man was a demon. Just like Karma warned him, this man was a demon in his pure form and only a well-crafted illusion was making him look like a human.

The demon stared down at Karma calmly without saying a word. She nodded and opened her backpack. She pulled a small box out of her backpack and placed it on top of the table. The demon sat down and opened the box. It was empty inside. With a cold smirk, Karma put her hand over it and whispered one word. A soft light enveloped her hand and when she lifted it, the box was filled with the shimmering glow of her magical energy.

The demon's lips stretched into a snarl that was supposed to be a smile as he gaped at the shimmering energy. He closed the box and pocketed it. Then he nodded at Karma and got up, gesturing to the door.

Karma gave Gunz an arched stare, raising her eyebrow at him. She obviously wanted him to get up and follow the demon. Gunz got up slowly and stopped. Coyote or not, he couldn't trust a demon. It just didn't feel right. His Salamander's intuition was screaming in the back of his mind, begging him to reconsider.

In the meantime, the coyote-demon reached the door and stopped there as he noticed that they weren't following him. He turned around and frowned, waving his hand at Karma urgently.

"Let's go, Zane," hissed Karma, "he's not going to wait for us."

"Karma, something is not right," he whispered, seizing her arm above her elbow to stop her from going.

"No, Zane, that's the way it is. This is the only way you can get into the castle." She jerked her arm out of his hold and walked forward.

"I want to go back home, to my world. Please, Zane, just do what Karma said and everything is going to be all right," whispered Milana as she passed him, following her girlfriend.

Gunz shook his head, biting his lip and looked at the coyote-demon who was still standing in the doorway. Their eyes met and Gunz froze in place, barely able to breathe. Undiluted evil was staring back at him with malice. The demon's sunken eyes lit up with a carnivorous yellow light as he gnashed his teeth.

He seized Karma's shoulder, without breaking his eye contact with Gunz. "Who did you bring here, little witch?" he hissed into her ear, but Gunz had no problem hearing his every word. "Do you know who he is? What a great favor you did for me, sweetheart."

"Let me go!" growled Karma, jerking her arm, but the coyote-demon was a lot stronger.

"Let her go!" yelled Milana, forgetting about the quietness of this place. She jumped on the coyote-demon's back showering him with a downpour of punches that he could barely feel.

The demon ripped Milana off his back, throwing her down on the floor at his feet. She hit the floor hard and lost her breath, tears flooding her wide-open eyes. Then he quickly pulled Karma closer, wrapping his brawny arms around her neck. She elbowed him in his ribs and struggled to twist out of his deadly grip. The coyote-demon groaned but managed to hold her down.

"Hold this man!" he shouted, jerking his chin toward Gunz.

Every single man in the tavern got up. Like a dark wall, they silently took a step, shifting toward Gunz, all at the same time. He knew that even if he had his power and magic, he would have a hard time getting out in one piece. And now he was just a human—even the smallest use of his magic would bring him down to his knees. He couldn't fight all these demons.

The demon, still holding Karma in the chokehold, approached Gunz. "You are a Child of Fire," he said, his yellow eyes drilling into Gunz. His venomous demonic aura enveloped Gunz, suffocating him. "Chernobog is not going to be pleased to know that a fire-freak is roaming his domain, but he will pay me handsomely for disclosing your location. Even more, if I deliver you into his dungeons myself."

"Let the girls go," said Gunz quietly.

"And why would I do that?" asked the demon. His appearance was slowly changing, getting less and less human. While he was still shaped like a man, his eyes were getting deeper into his skull, glowing with a yellow light. His nose almost disappeared, and his cheeks became hollow. His whole face looked like a skull with dark, scaly skin stretched over it.

For a split-second, Karma caught Gunz's attention and gave him a pointed stare. Obviously, she wanted him to keep the demon's attention.

"I will go with you without a fight. Let the girls go and I'm yours," said Gunz to the coyote-demon, with a barely visible nod in Karma's direction.

The coyote-demon guffawed, staring down at Gunz, amusement in his toxic eyes. "You can't fight here, Child of Fire. There are no elemental powers in Chernobog's domain. So, I will take you and your sweethearts to Chernobog and you are not going to fight me, because you're not an idiot. You know that without your power, you're nothing."

Using the opportunity, Karma slammed her elbow into the demon's ribs again. The demon groaned, bending forward and his hold weakened just a little. That was enough for Karma. She elbowed him again and thrust her heel into the demon's foot. Then she twisted in his arms, channeling her magic, and blasted him with a high-voltage energy ball. The energy ball burnt through the coyote-demon's chest, obliterating him in place.

"Karma, what did you do?" yelped Milana who was back on her feet, her features contorted by fear. "Not only did you use your magic here, in the open, you killed our guide!"

Gunz didn't wait to see what would happen next. He punched the demon closest to him and grabbed Milana's hand, pulling her toward the door. The demons roared, their anger enhancing their demonic power like a catalyst. The silence was torn into shreds by the earsplitting shrieks of the demons as they rushed toward them.

"Take Milana out," shouted Karma, "I'll cover you!"

She turned around and channeled more of her magic, sending one energy ball after another flying at the attackers. A short demon in a long filthy coat was fumbling with the door lock, blocking their way out. Without stopping, Gunz swung his arm and connected his fist with the demon's ugly head. The demon yelped and swayed but didn't move.

"My turn, little fire-worm," he hissed, turning to face Gunz. In a heartbeat, the illusion that was giving him more or less a human appearance dissipated. A giant monster with six arms that looked like the slithering tentacles of an octopus was blocking his way. All six arms shot forward, wrapping around Gunz's neck and Milana's waist.

Instead of trying to fight the demonic noose, Gunz reached into his pocket and pulled the Swiss army knife out. He didn't want to use his magic to transform it into the sword, but it was still a knife with multiple sharp blades. Quickly unfolding the bigger blade, he slashed the tentacle that was strangling him. Thick black goo seeped from the wound. The demon pulled his arms back and cursed, slapping Gunz in the face with one of his free tentacles. Gunz's head jerked to the side, and he almost dropped his knife.

He staggered a step away from the octopus-demon and glanced over his shoulder, quickly assessing the situation. It didn't look good. Karma was still fighting, but she was getting weaker with every energy ball she conjured. Milana was so scared, she could hardly move. The demons were getting closer and closer, pushing them toward the door that now was locked.

It was a now or never situation. Gunz put his knife back into his pocket and channeled his magic, tapping into his own energy. "*Ignius Orbus*," he shouted. A large fireball materialized between his blazing hands. He propelled the fireball at the door, putting all his remaining strength into it. The fireball ripped the door off its hinges, setting it on fire.

"Karma, Milana," shouted Gunz, "time to leave!"

He took a step, crossing the threshold of the tavern into the darkness of the Nav and swayed. Drained by the use of magic, he dropped to his knees on the verge of fainting. Everything around him was swimming. He sat back on his heels, forcing himself to stay conscious, and glanced back over his shoulder. Karma and Milana were out, but for some reason the demons weren't following them. They stood quiet and motionless inside the building. Huddled close together, they were staring at something outside. There was no mistake. They looked terrified, practically frozen by fear.

Slowly, Gunz turned around. This motion made him sick and a crippling weakness took hold of him. He moaned and fell to his side awkwardly. Before he passed out, he saw a man on a horse emerging from the darkness. He was clad in black armor and was riding a large black stallion, soundless like a shadow. A black raven was sitting on his shoulder. If not for his eyes, blazing with the brilliant energy of magic, it would be impossible to see him in the surrounding darkness. And his blazing eyes were staring at Gunz with wrath.

The man extended his hand toward the tavern and the entire building disappeared, together with the demons, like it was never there. His eyes darted back down to Gunz, sprawled helplessly on the ground and then to Milana and Karma. Frowning, he pointed at them, shaking his head and snapped his fingers.

When Gunz was falling through the gateway into the Dark Nav, he thought the blackness couldn't be blacker, and the darkness couldn't be darker.

Now he knew how wrong he was.

It could…

13

~ AIDAN ~

Aidan turned from his side to his back, throwing his arm across his face to shield his eyes from the sunlight. It was mid-afternoon, and he was lying fully dressed on the uncomfortable bed of the Wardens sleeping chambers.

When Ms. Bonneville said the Wardens' accommodations were plain, it was an understatement. The room was a tiny bare matchbox with two narrow hard beds and a small closet. The dark gray paint on the walls was partially pealed, revealing a darker shade of gray paint beneath. The windows—two narrow slits in the thick concrete wall—had no window treatment of any kind. The whole room reminded him of a medieval monastery, sans crucifixes on the walls.

Aidan didn't feel like getting up or doing anything. Stressed to the limit, he didn't know what to do next and had a hard time restraining his frustration. It had been a few days since Svyatobor and Angel left and none of them got in touch with him. He had no idea if Svyatobor was able to find Veles or if Veles agreed to take Angel to the Dark Nav.

More than forty-eight hours had passed since Missi went to Paris. Aidan asked Ms. Bonneville if she had heard from Missi a few times, but every time she just tapped him on his shoulder in an annoyingly patronizing manner and told him to sit tight and wait. He knew nothing, and it was driving him crazy. Raoul noticed his state and mentioned that news traveled fast through the Guardians channels and if something had happened to Missi, the Head Mage would know it by now.

He talked to Uri a few times every day. Everything was going fine at the school, but Uri also had no news about Gunz, or Angel and Svyatobor. The only time he was allowing himself to relax and forget about all the problems was when he was with Tessa. In the short time he spent at the Guardians Headquarters, they didn't get a chance to spend a lot of time together, but he enjoyed every minute they had. Tessa changed. At least with everything to do with him. She seemed to sincerely regret the way she treated him back in Florida and now was doing everything to make it up to him.

"Aidan, wake up."

He felt a light touch to his shoulder and lowered his arm. The bright light cut his eyes, and he squinted to see Raoul standing above him. Slowly he sat up and rubbed his face with his hands like a person who just woke up from a terrible nightmare.

"Aidan, you need to clean up, so we can—"

"We can do what? Go down to the Assembly Hall and meet with the Head Mage, so she can patronize me like I'm another apprentice in her school?" asked Aidan, his voice a dangerous growl.

"You did it to yourself, Aidan, when you swore your allegiance and it's just the beginning," replied Raoul. "But, yes, we need to go down to the Assembly Hall. The Head Mage sent me to fetch you. Missi is back."

Aidan was on his feet in a heartbeat, his melancholic state gone. A few minutes later, he followed Raoul inside the Assembly Hall, his heart beating with hope to finally have some questions answered. But as soon as he crossed into the Hall and saw Missi, all his hopes were gone.

Missi looked like she just walked in, her clothes covered in dust and her face ashen with exhaustion. As soon as she saw Aidan, she rushed to him and hugged him. He was a little surprised. Missi didn't know him that well and she didn't seem like a hugging type. He decided to play along and returned her hug.

Gripping him tighter, she quickly whispered into his ear, "Aidan, it's worse than I thought. Agree with everything. Read it with Raoul only when you're back in Florida."

Read what? Why is Missi speaking in riddles? Aidan kissed her softly on her cheek, unlocking his arms. As she stepped away, he felt Missi slipping her hand into his shirt pocket. "I'm glad to see you back safe, Missi," he said with a sad smile. "Were you able to find the missing page in the Wardens' Book of Words?"

"No—," Missi started to say, but the Head Mage raised her hand up, interrupting her.

"Let's sit down and talk," she said, pointing at the table with a few chairs around. "I have a feeling this conversation may take a while."

She threw a wry look at Missi and headed to the table where she sat down, crossing her legs at her knees and folding her arms.

Agree with everything? What the hell did she mean by that? Missi's words flashed in his mind as he picked a chair across the table from the Head Mage and also sat down.

These words as well as Missi's uncharacteristic behavior left him uneasy and he had to work hard not to show it. Through the thin fabric of his shirt, he could feel the small piece of paper. Missi put it in there, making sure that no one except him knew about it. And the fact that she was trying to hide something from everyone in this room was sending chills down his spine. Whatever she learned while she was in Paris made her wary about the organization she devoted her whole life to.

"Melissa," said the Head Mage. She uncrossed her legs and leaned forward, drumming her fingers on the table impatiently. "You insisted that Mr. McGrath and Father Beaumont were here for your report. They're here. Care to start?"

"Yes, ma'am, of course," said Missi, clearing her throat. "I'm not going to take much of your time. Unfortunately, my report will be brief." She threw a quick look at Aidan and continued, "I brought bad news. I met with the Grand Master Warden and their Book of Words is also missing a page. The exact same page our book is missing."

"Did Grand Master Warden run an investigation?" asked the Head Mage, her irritation seemed to start boiling over.

"Yes, he did," said Missi meeting Ms. Bonneville's furious gaze with a deadpan expression. "He found nothing. Just like here, someone sneaked inside the Wardens HQ, bypassing all the wards and protective spells. The security cameras and motion detectors didn't detect this person either. So, the page is gone from both books and there is no way to restore it. And no one knows what was on this page."

Ms. Bonneville leaned back in her chair, covering her face with her hands. "It's not happening," she whispered, "not happening."

"What's not happening?" asked Aidan.

Ms. Bonneville lowered her hands and gaped at Aidan like he was some kind of nuisance. Then she gathered her thoughts and pursed her lips.

"Mr. McGrath," she said in a no-nonsense voice, "since the page you were looking for was stolen from both books available to us, there is nothing else we can do to help you with your mission. None of us know or recognize the mage you described. There is a chance, she wasn't one of ours. I want you to return to Florida and stay there until further notice. As of now, the case of mutilated Books of Words and the person who did it is an internal issue of the Guardians Order. We're going to deal with it on our own."

"Excuse me," hissed Aidan rising, his eyes glowing with the white light of his magic. "You're not going to order me around like I'm some little apprentice in your school."

"You're forgetting something, Mr. McGrath," objected Ms. Bonneville.

She snapped her fingers and the silver chain wrapped tightly around Aidan's neck. Aidan grasped at his neck. The chain was too delicate to cut off his air, but it was burning through his skin.

"You're certainly not one of my students, Mr. McGrath. You're a god of the Otherworld and your powers are mightier than mine," continued the Head Mage, observing his reaction calmly. "But you swore your loyalty to us for one year. So, no matter how powerful you are, you can't go against your oath. And you know it. Besides, little Ms. Donovan's future also depends on how well you behave and your ability to comply with our orders. So, yes, I can, and I will tell you what to do next and when to do it."

She snapped her fingers again, releasing Aidan's neck and letting the chain drop back to his chest. Aidan fell back into his chair, massaging his neck with his fingers. She was right. He swore his life to the Guardians for one year and now he had to deal with the consequences of his decision.

"Before I swore my loyalty to the Guardians, you said that you'll let me take care of my business first," reminded Aidan. "You promised to assist me with my mission."

"And I did," said the mage. Then she sighed and shook her head, correcting her last statement, "I still do. I'm not trying to manipulate you, Mr. McGrath. I did everything I could, and if I learn anything that can help you, I'll let you know at once. But if the same page is missing in both Books of Words in this realm, there is no way to restore it. Trust me, if there was any other way to help you, I would do it without a moment's hesitation."

"But you're forgetting something, Ms. Bonneville," replied Aidan through his teeth.

"What's that?"

"There is one more Book of Words," said Aidan, crossing his arms.

"I didn't forget that, Mr. McGrath," said the Head Mage. She got up and stepped behind Missi, putting her hand on her shoulder. "The third Book of Words is with the Destiny Council. There is no way to get it."

"What do you mean?" asked Aidan. He had never met with the Destiny Council in person, but he was aware that they were residing in some other dimension outside the human world. Nevertheless, he thought that the Guardians and Wardens had a way to get in touch with them. "I thought the Guardians Order works for the Destiny Council. You should be able to contact them."

"Yes, the Guardians Order reports to the Destiny Council, but we do not summon them. They summon us. They communicate their orders through the Destiny Keeper and there is no way to summon him. He comes here when the Destiny Council deems it necessary."

Aidan was about to start arguing, but he caught sight of Missi and stopped himself. She mouthed the word "no", making big eyes at him.

"Fine," said Aidan and got up. "I'll go back home and look for some other ways to help my friend."

"Good choice, Mr. McGrath," agreed the Head Mage with a blinding paper-white smile. "Melissa and I will continue working on the issue with the missing page. If we learn anything that can help you, we'll contact you. Father Beaumont will return to Florida with you. I want him to stay by your side. In case you need his assistance."

"Fine," said Aidan again. At this point, he stopped caring about what Ms. Bonneville had to say and he just wanted to be out of here. "I want to say my goodbyes to Tessa and after that Raoul and I will leave."

"Mr. McGrath," said Ms. Bonneville, putting her well-manicured hand on Aidan's shoulder. "I hope you realize how young Tessa is. Her current state is extremely vulnerable. You shouldn't say anything to her that may affect her current situation. She needs to remain here and learn to control her power and magic."

"I know that," said Aidan coldly, his gaze slipped down to the mage's hand on his shoulder and she quickly pulled it off. "Don't worry, I'm not going to say anything that could make her question her decision to be a part of the Guardians Order."

He turned around and slowly strolled toward the exit door. Raoul got up, bowed to the Head Mage and walked after him.

"Mr. McGrath," called Ms. Bonneville after him.

He already put his hand on the door handle ready to walk out but stopped and threw a tired glance at her.

"I just wanted to remind you that you cannot leave this realm without notifying me first," she said, her fingers fumbling with the pendant on her own chain.

Aidan smirked. His hand wrapped around the door handle tighter, warping the thick metal. "Just because you can't help me, it doesn't mean I will give up on my original mission. I will never leave my friends unprotected when they need me. So, I may have to travel to the Land of Dreams. Do I need to have your permission for that?"

"I didn't expect anything less of you, Mr. McGrath, and I'm not asking you to betray your friends," replied the Head Mage. "The Land of Dreams is one of four magical nexuses that are located in our realm. As long as you stay in our world, you don't need my permission. But if you wish to visit your Celtic Otherworld or Slavic Nav or Prav, you can't do it without notifying me first. Did I make myself clear, Mr. McGrath?"

"Crystal clear," muttered Aidan. He swung the door open and walked out without looking back at the old mage.

* * *

AIDAN SAT on the cold bench inside a small pavilion located in the heart of the beautiful gardens. This was the place he was meeting with Tessa. He checked his wristwatch. It was showing three thirty. Tessa was a little late, and it was making him nervous. He kept asking himself if his last conversation with the Head Mage somehow affected Tessa's situation with the Guardians Order.

When he finally felt a soft touch to his shoulders, he gave a little start. Tessa giggled at his reaction, her cold hands sliding under his shirt, and softly kissed his hair. He craned his neck, tilting his head backward so he could see her. She was standing behind him, gazing down, her eyes twinkling with mischief.

"Tessa, you have no idea how glad I am to see you," he whispered, holding her gaze. And he meant every word of it. After the conversation with the Head Mage, he required a few minutes where he didn't need to be on constant alert, measuring every word that was said to him.

She laughed softly, her voice sounding like delicate silver bells, and bent down. He felt the soft touch of her lips to his. It was an awkward, upside down kiss, but it electrified his body. Desire took over as a heat wave spread through him. A moment later, she pulled away, leaving him breathless.

"Tessa," he exhaled. His voice sounded like a moan and he lowered his head, trying to cool off, forcing his longing for her to simmer down so he could think clearly again.

She walked around the bench and stopped in front of him. He stared down at her boots, afraid to raise his eyes. He was sure that if he would look up and meet the warm gaze of her brown eyes, there would be no power in this world that could stop him from taking her into his arms and teleporting both of them back to his Ft. Lauderdale penthouse.

Tessa caressed his hair and when he still didn't raise his face, she took one knee, lowering herself on the ground between his legs and looked up into his eyes, fogged with desire.

"My handsome ancient god," she murmured playfully as she pressed her palm against his flushed cheek, "what did I do to offend your mightiness? What kind of sacrifice do I need to make to get back in your graces?"

Aidan finally met her eyes. She was more beautiful, more desirable than he could ever imagine. Before he could stop himself, he seized her shoulders and pulled her up. His lips hungrily crushed hers and a growl, hungry and feral, rumbled in his throat. She responded with a soft moan as she leaned into him.

He let her go a moment later and lowered his head again. She sat down on his lap, draping her arm around his shoulders. Aidan took a few deep breaths before starting the conversation.

"Tessa, there is something I need to tell you," he said quietly.

She probably recognized the seriousness in his voice, because she got off his lap and sat down on the bench next to him.

"What's up, Aidan?" she demanded, sounding like the Tessa he used to know back in Florida. "Spit it out already."

"I'm leaving," he replied, "and I have no idea when I'll be back to visit you here."

"What do you mean?" asked Tessa with ringing notes of nervousness in her voice. "You swore your fealty to the Guardians. I'm sure the Head Mage will call upon you sooner or later. Most likely sooner…"

Aidan nodded. He didn't need this reminder, but Tessa was right. "I'm sure, she will," he agreed with a sigh, "but not before I take care of my original mission. And because of this, I must leave, my love."

"What is this mission?" asked Tessa. She put her hand on his cheek, forcing him to look at her. "You never told me. If it's something dangerous, I want to go with you. I have some serious powers and I want to be there to protect—um, help you."

Aidan cupped her hand with his and closed his eyes for a brief moment, enjoying her touch. "I'm sorry. I can't tell you," he replied quietly. "You need to stay here, my love. You must follow the rules of the Order. You're on your probation period and you can't do anything that would trigger your original judgment. I'll be fine. After all, I am a god, right? Immortal? I'll come to see you once all this is over. I promise."

She sighed and placed her head on his shoulder, her arm encircling his waist. Aidan embraced her, lowering his head atop of hers and stilled. There was nothing else to say. It was a goodbye.

At least for now.

14

~ AIDAN ~

"Aidan, where are we?" Raoul spun around, taking in his surroundings.

"Elements Martial Arts. My martial arts school," explained Aidan absentmindedly. He sat down on the chair behind the desk and gestured at Raoul to join him. It was late, and all the students and instructors were gone. The school was dark and empty.

"Why?" asked Raoul but pulled a chair out and sat down. "I thought you were going to take me back to the Church by the Sea. I have to bring Father Collins up to date with everything that's going on."

"And you will. I promise to take you back to the Church. But first we need to read this," said Aidan. He reached into his pocket and pulled out the piece of paper Missi passed him earlier. "Missi brought this letter from Paris and it's addressed to you. But she said that we need to read it together when we got back to Florida."

Raoul took the paper from Aidan's hand carefully, like he was afraid that it would explode with his touch.

"*To Raoul le Bel,*" read Raoul and raised his eyes at Aidan. His hands shook, and he dropped the paper on the table, staring at it like it was a scorpion, ready to sting.

"Read it, Raoul," said Aidan, pushing the piece of paper closer to him.

The Warden unfolded the paper and read aloud, *"Remember Friday the 13th."*

"What the hell?" Aidan frowned—the note made no sense. "Whoever wrote it wants you to watch the horror movie? I hope you know what it means, Raoul, because I have no idea."

"Yes, yes," mumbled Raoul. His face lost all its color and his fingers were trembling. "Of course, I know what it means." He peered into the piece of paper he was holding, his eyes darting from left to right as he was re-reading it over and over.

"Raoul, I need to know," demanded Aidan slightly inclining forward. "Who is this letter from?"

"This letter is from my old friend. Luc de la Crosse. We were accepted into the Wardens Order at the same time," explained Father Beaumont, putting the note on the table. "He was the only person who used to call me Raoul *le Bel*. This note is a warning."

"Raoul the Fair?" muttered Aidan. He glanced at the young Warden and smirked. "Seems to be appropriate. But why *'Friday the 13th'*?"

"*Friday the 13th* is a warning," repeated Raoul. "Luc is trying to warn me not to trust"—he bit his lip and shook his head—"not to trust anyone in our Order. This was the codeword we came up with many cen—years ago. In case our organization was compromised."

A codeword? Aidan rubbed the bridge of his nose, trying to process the few words that Raoul managed to deliver.

"I always thought that all Wardens were deeply devoted to their organization and loyal to the Destiny Council," he muttered, shaking his head. "Why would you and your friend need to come up with a codeword to notify each other about a betrayal in your ranks?"

Raoul leaned forward, resting his elbows on the table and searched Aidan's face for a moment. "Because it's happened before. The Wardens Order was corrupt. The Wardens were betrayed and hunted like wild animals all over the world, imprisoned, tortured and burned at the stake. Many died, a few managed to escape with their lives... The Order was practically destroyed. Only with the involvement of the Destiny Keeper, did we manage to save all the scrolls and books of the Wardens' Archive." His voice faltered, and he reclined back in his chair.

"So, your friend is trying to tell us that history is repeating itself? The Wardens Order was compromised again?" asked Aidan. "That would explain how two Books of Words were mutilated, and no one noticed an intruder."

"Yes," agreed Raoul, "Wardens and most likely Guardians too. We can't trust anyone. That's what my friend is trying to warn us about."

"Friday the 13th," mumbled Aidan, twirling a pen between his fingers. "The Wardens Order was betrayed and nearly all members were destroyed..." Aidan dropped the pen and stared at Raoul with intensity in his blue eyes. "How old are you, Raoul de Beaumont?"

"Aidan, don't," pleaded Raoul, hardly meeting his eyes. "Don't press me. Don't try to guess—"

"Raoul, how old are you?"

"Younger than you are."

"Not by a lot, I think," retorted Aidan, scanning the Warden with his magic. "A few centuries, give or take. What year were you born in, Raoul le Bel?"

"Aidan, please, as a Warden I can't disclose my true identity. My past life was wiped out when I accepted the mantle of a Warden—"

"Raoul, I thought you learned to trust me in the last few

days," said Aidan with reproach. "I swear, I'll keep your secret. You don't need to give me any details. Just tell me the year of your birth."

Raoul dropped his head to his chest and whispered, "I was born in the year 1282 of our Lord—"

"Oh God, Raoul, you were—," started to say Aidan but cut himself off. "I'm sorry, I am not going to say anything else. Except — do you think the Destiny Council was compromised too?"

"I hope not," replied Raoul. "Their Book of Words is our last chance to find that missing page and find out what's going on. But I don't know how to contact them. As much as I hate to say it, the Head Mage told you the truth. There is no way to contact the Destiny Council."

"There is a way," objected Aidan quietly, rising. "But I need to do it on my own. I hope you can understand."

Raoul got up, a sad smile curving his lips. "I do, *mon ami*, I understand. You're going to contact your mentor and ask him for help. I'm not sure I want to be here for that. Can you take me back to the Church?"

Aidan put his hand on Raoul's shoulder and snapped his fingers, instantly teleporting them to the Church by the Sea.

AIDAN LEFT Raoul on the steps of the Church and teleported back to his office in the martial arts school. He sat down in his chair, stretching his long legs under the desk. For a while, he was sitting quietly, thinking, his fingers playing with the pendant on his chain. He wanted to summon his mentor. He missed him and loved him like his own father, but the thought of telling him that he swore his loyalty to the Guardians was terrifying him.

His mentor hated the Destiny Council, and he had good

reason for that. *Sooner or later, Gwyn will learn the truth, anyway. It would be better if he finds out from me.* Aidan got up and walked out of the office. Slowly, he opened the door into the dojang and stepped on the soft matts. He crossed the floor and sat down in front of the mirrored wall, crossing his legs.

Except for one night every year, Gwyn ap Nudd never left the Otherworld. Usually, when Aidan needed to see his mentor, he traveled to the Otherworld himself. But Ms. Bonneville made it clear to him that for the full year that he committed to the Guardians Order, he cannot travel to the Otherworld without her permission.

After the warning that Missi gave him and the troubling note from Raoul's friend, Aidan thought it would be better if the Head Mage of the Guardians didn't know about his intentions. He leaned forward and touched the mirror with his fingers, drawing a complex rune. When the drawing was completed, he touched it, infusing it with his magic.

"Gwyn ap Nudd, I summon thee," he whispered, watching an oval communication window slowly opening in the mirror.

For a while, the window in the mirror remained dark. Aidan started to get nervous when a brilliant white light, flooded the window. When the light dimmed down, Aidan saw a tall, muscular man standing behind the mirror. Besides jeans that were torn on his knees, he had nothing else on. His cat-like eyes were glowing with the white light of his magic from under his thick dark eyebrows. His full lips were pressed into a straight line and he looked troubled. The man threw his long black hair off his face, exposing his slightly pointed ear and folded his arms, gazing down at Aidan with concern.

"Aidan, my boy," said Gwyn ap Nudd, frowning, "what's going on? You're summoning me instead of visiting?"

"Gwyn, I can't travel to the Otherworld," said Aidan, averting his eyes. "For one year, I'm bound to this realm by my oath. For now, this will be the only way we can communicate. I summoned you because I need your help."

"You can't leave that realm?" repeated Gwyn ap Nudd, his arms dropping to his sides powerlessly.

His eyes narrowed into sharply angled slits as his gaze stopped on the chain around Aidan's neck. He gaped at the chain for a moment, shaking his head in disbelief. Aidan braced himself for his mentor's wrath.

"I had to... I'm sorry—"

"You bet your goddamn ass, you need my help!" shouted Gwyn ap Nudd and slammed both his hands on the surface of the window. But it wasn't anger that was reflected in his white eyes, it was undiluted agony and despair.

"Gwyn, please allow me to explain."

"What did you do, Aodh mac Lir?" Gwyn ap Nudd hissed, the anguish in his voice hit Aidan with a spike of guilt. "What did you do? Did you sign your life off to these assholes at the Destiny Council?" He stopped talking, his wide chest rising and falling with rapid breaths. Then he pressed his hand to his eyes for a moment and took a deep breath to calm down. "You made a mistake. It's okay, my boy, I will find a way to get you out of the mess you put yourself in."

"It wasn't a mistake, Gwyn," objected Aidan. He approached the mirror, placing his hand against Gwyn's. "I'm sorry, but I did what I had to."

"Tell me everything," said Gwyn ap Nudd, the white light extinguished in his sad eyes.

Aidan sighed and sat down on the mats. He took his time telling his mentor everything that happened from the moment Jim walked into his office with the news of Gunz. When he explained why he had to swear his fealty to the Guardians Order, Gwyn just shook his head but didn't interrupt him. He finished his story with telling his mentor about the note from Luc de la Crosse.

Gwyn ap Nudd leaned forward, resting his forehead against

the surface of the window, his hands buried into the mass of his obsidian hair. For a moment he stood silent with his eyes closed. Then he opened his eyes and they shone with a silvery-white light.

"I assume you need me to get in touch with these jackasses from the Destiny Council," he muttered, pushing himself off the window. "You need to see this missing page from the Book of Words."

"Yes," confirmed Aidan, feeling slightly relieved that his mentor was back to his normal calm disposition. "I need to restore this page in the Book of Words. That crazy mage that abducted Gunz went through a lot of trouble to erase this page from existence in both Books in this realm. My hope is that by reading this page I might find out who she is and what her intentions are."

Gwyn ap Nudd nodded. "Fine. As much as I hate to see anyone from the Destiny Council, I'll do it." He laughed but there was no humor in his laughter. "They are not going to be pleased that I left the Otherworld, breaking their friggin' rules. But screw them and their rules. Pompous assholes. Having said that, I'm not going to restore the missing page. I don't think I should."

"Why?" asked Aidan, lost. Didn't he explain clearly enough that he needed to read this page and why he needed to do it?

"I'm not going to restore the missing page, but I will copy its contents," continued Gwyn ap Nudd, giving Aidan a pointed stare. "You said it yourself that possibly both Orders—Guardians and Wardens—were infiltrated. Who knows what kind of information this page could provide to the traitors. I say, we keep it to ourselves for now."

"Agreed," said Aidan, rising, and approached the window.

"Good. Now, you are going to do everything I tell you to do," said Gwyn ap Nudd firmly. "Let's start with summoning Kalidus. Do it right now, while I'm here, my son."

"Kal? But why?" asked Aidan. Gunz never wanted to get his mentor involved in his business. He preferred to clean up his own messes, knowing that Kal didn't love getting involved into the affairs of human realms.

"Because I said so," said Gwyn ap Nudd impassively. "Gunz is the Child of Fire and Kalidus has the right to know what's going on. Just like I wish you told me what was going on before you went and swore your fealty to the Guardians. Trust me, I could have gotten your girl out of this mess without you giving up your life."

"I'm sorry, Gwyn—"

"Enough with apologies already, Aodh. Summon Kalidus," demanded Gwyn ap Nudd, drumming on the surface of the window with his fingers. "I haven't got all day, um, night."

Aidan sighed but extended his hand up and whispered, *"Ignius."* A small flame ignited in the palm of his hand. He lowered his face closer to the flame and whispered Kal's name.

A smoldering fire curtain unfolded in the middle of the dojang and a giant blacksmith, hammer included, walked through it. Kal was wearing a leather apron that was hardly covering his bare torso and his flaming-red hair was tied up with a leather ribbon in a thick messy ponytail on the back of his head. He wiped sweat off his forehead with the back of his hand and turned to Aidan. His eyes fell on the pendant on Aidan's chest and bright flames went up in his igneous eyes. He crossed the distance separating them in one long-legged stride and seized the chain, pushing Aidan back and pinning him against the wall.

"What the hell, boy!" growled the Great Salamander, flames running up and down his giant arms. "Gwyn will skin you alive if he sees it."

Aidan silently pointed to the side, not sure that he wanted to argue with the Fire Elemental. Kal looked to the side and saw

Gwyn ap Nudd. He let go of Aidan and put his hand on the surface of the window.

"Gwyn, my old friend, I'm pleased to see you," said Kal, extinguishing his fire. "Would you like me to put this dimwitted son of yours across my knee and give him a nice beating for what he did?"

Gwyn ap Nudd laughed openheartedly, throwing his head back. "That was my exact desire when I saw that chain." He sobered up quickly and added, "But the boy is in love. He did it to save the woman he loves. If anyone can relate to that, it's you, Kalidus."

"The boy is almost twenty-five hundred years old, Gwyn. He's all grown up and should have known better," replied Kal grouchy and turned to Aidan. "Why didn't you summon me before you willingly subjugated yourself to the Destiny Council?"

Aidan bowed his head, avoiding Kal's reproachful gaze.

"Kal, forget about it for now," said Gwyn, knocking on the window to attract his friend's attention. "I think we have a much bigger problem on our hands. I'll let Aidan fill you in on all the details later, but first let me tell you—I feel fluctuations of power in the underworldly realms. Not only in the Otherworld. It's everywhere. Something big is coming, and it's tipping the balance toward the darkness. I could feel it for a while already, but I can't figure out what it is. Something tells me that everything that Aidan is going to tell you somehow is connected to that big-bad that is slowly rising from beneath."

"Understood," said Kal, "I'll look into it."

"Kalidus, be careful, my brother," said Gwyn ap Nudd, his face hardened, his hands clenched into tight fists. "I wish I could be there and stand by your side, but I can't leave the Otherworld until the night of Samhain. Destiny Council be damned with their screwed-up rules. Please, help Aidan and your own child, Gunz. They're way over their heads with this one."

"Don't worry, brother. From this moment on, I'm not going to let Aidan leave my sight," promised Kal, throwing a heavy glance in Aidan's direction.

Oh, wonder-friggin-bar, thought Aidan, cringing, *Daddy thinks I need a babysitter.*

"Good," said Gwyn ap Nudd with a sigh of relief. "Now I have to go. I'm sure Aidan is getting tired holding this window open. Keep me updated on everything that's going on."

"Gwyn—," Aidan started to say, stepping closer to the window.

"I know, you're sorry," said Gwyn ap Nudd, a sad smile hiding under his black mustache. "As soon as I'm done with the Destiny Council, I'll call upon you and Kalidus. Be careful, my boy. See you soon."

Gwyn stepped backward, silently submerging into the darkness. Aidan waved his hand, closing the window, and turned to Kal. The Great Salamander stared at him for a moment, then seized his chain, wringing it around his massive fist, and pulled Aidan toward the office.

"Let's go, boy. You have a lot of talking to do."

15

~ ZANE BURNS, A.K.A. GUNZ ~

Gunz felt a gentle touch to his cheek. "Angie," he murmured without opening his eyes. The touch turned into a rough jerk on his shirt and when he didn't react, someone slapped him on the face. Gunz gasped and opened his eyes.

"You're alive. Thank God!"

He recognized Karma's voice but could see only a dark fuzzy silhouette. He blinked a few times and wanted to bring his hands down to rub his eyes but couldn't. Something was holding his arms pinned above his head. His wrists were agonizingly sore and every muscle in his body was aching.

Slowly his vision came into focus and he saw Karma's face right in front of him. He tilted his head back and looked up. *Ah, not again...* His wrists were shackled to the wall above his head with heavy iron chains. The roughly crafted rusted manacles were painfully biting into his skin. A few thin streams of blood were trickling down his arms from under the manacles.

"Goddamnit! Medieval freaks," he mumbled, lowering his head. "Why does it always have to be the chains and creepy dungeons?"

He glanced around, carefully studying his surroundings.

They were inside a small concrete cell with thick iron bars in the front. There were no windows and the only weak light was coming in from somewhere outside the cell. Karma was sitting on the floor. Her eyes were red and swollen and her face was beyond pale. Her cheeks were covered in dust and dirt, and a few clear paths left by tears were running from her eyes down to her chin. She wasn't crying anymore, but her cheeks were still wet, and her nose was suspiciously red.

"Did they hurt you?" asked Gunz with a sigh.

"No," replied Karma.

"How long have I been out?"

"Not sure," said Karma, wrapping her arms around her bent legs. "It's hard to say without a watch and yours is broken. But my guess, we're here at least twelve hours if not more."

"Where is Milana?"

Karma averted her gaze and sniffled. "I don't know," she mumbled, hardly audible. "When Chernobog teleported us to his castle, we got separated. They brought me here right away. A few hours later, the guards brought you in and shackled you to the wall. You were unconscious. But Milana..." She sniffled again, tears gathering in her eyes. She wiped her wet cheeks with her hands, smearing the dirt all over her face, and added, sounding calm now, "They never brought Milana in. I have no idea where she is."

"Who are *they*?" asked Gunz. "Do you know where we are?"

"I thought you would guess by now," muttered Karma somberly.

"I think I did, but I don't like guesses and assumptions," objected Gunz dryly. His head was ringing as if someone had kicked him a few times and his body was so sore, he was sure that someone actually did beat him up while he was unconscious.

"*They* are Chernobog's personal guards," said Karma with a sigh. "And we're in his dungeons."

Gunz nodded. Every tiny move was sending a jolt of agony through his body. He tried to readjust his position, just to realize that he was so weak that he could hardly move. But worst of all was that he had no desire to move. Just like when he fell through the gates, he felt broken and resigned. He didn't want to fight; he was ready to give in to whatever was coming.

Nevertheless, his situation was different now. He wasn't alone. He had two young women with him, and for whatever crazy reason, they believed that he could lead them out of this hell-realm. Feeling responsible for their safety, he couldn't leave them without his support.

"Do you know of any way to escape this prison?" he asked, closing his eyes for a moment to deal with the nagging pain. "And why am I so sore? The last thing I remember is fighting the demons in the tavern and then that giant man in black on a black horse... Was he...?"

"That was Chernobog himself and there is no escaping from this place. Get it out of your head, Zane," replied Karma. "There is no fighting against the god of Destruction. He rules the Nav. He is the Nav, and it responds to his every whim. He can reshape it, change the flow of time, and warp the space as he pleases. To make a long story short—we're screwed. I just hope Milana is okay..."

She stopped talking, staring down at her skinned knuckles. Karma looked just as broken and resigned as he felt. Her usual humor and sass were gone. It seemed that even the rougher side of her personality was wiped out. The woman sitting in front of him was tired and indifferent to everything. She stopped her illusion spell and now he could see the gray oversized rags that were covering her body.

"And yeah... You're sore because the guards weren't very gentle with you while you were out," she added quietly. "I don't know what they were doing with you for those few hours before they brought you into this cell."

She leaned forward and lifted his shirt up, gently probing his ribs with her fingers. Gunz grunted. Even the lightest touch to his body was agonizing. She carefully moved him to his side and checked his back. Her eyes widened for a split-second, and she cringed as she let him sit back down and lowered his shirt.

"Wow... judging by the bruises and welts on your skin, they beat you up a bit. With a... a..."—she raised her eyes and swallowed—"with a whip? No, most likely with a belt or something like that. It's not too bad. Give it a couple of days and you'll be like new."

Gunz chuckled humorlessly. "Medieval assholes," he muttered, shaking his head. "Now I can tell my friends in Kendral that I also know how it feels to be flogged."

"You find it amusing?" asked Karma, arching her eyebrows.

"It hurts like hell," replied Gunz, moving his shoulders tentatively, "but I just don't care. I don't care what they do to me. Since the moment I fell through the gate into this hellhole, I can't care about anything. And it's not really like me, you know. Normally, I don't give up without a good fight."

"It's the way the Dark Nav works." Karma crawled closer and sat down next to Gunz, leaning her back against the wall. "Until it breaks your spirit, bending you into submission, it's not going to let you through. How long were you falling?"

"Seemed like forever... I don't know for sure."

"You weren't falling at all, Zane," said Karma, staring straight forward. "You were suspended in midair, in complete darkness and the Dark Nav was feeding on you, applying pressure on your psyche to subdue your spirit. Tell me, as soon as you gave in, you found yourself on the hard ground, correct?"

"Yes..."

"This is why you're so calm and indifferent now. This dungeon works by the same principle. It takes away your spirit, your will to fight, to live... It kills you before you even die." Karma sighed. "Besides the point that it also suppresses all the magic in you and weakens you physically. I know I have to fight it. If not for myself, then for Milana. But I can't... The fact that I don't know what happened with Milana kills me, but I still have no desire in me to do anything about it..."

"How did you and Milana end up here in the first place?"

"Because of my stupidity," muttered Karma. "You know, Milana is a seer, but as a witch she is nothing compared to me. She wanted to see the World Tree, but she didn't know how to get to the Isle Buyan. Like an idiot, I agreed to show it to her. I had business I needed to take care of in the Land of Dreams, so I took her with me. You know that the World Tree connects the three main realms—Prav, Yav, and Nav, right?" Gunz nodded. "I knew it was dangerous, and I have no idea what moved me to bring her to the Isle Buyan. I'm always so careful and never do anything rash... Anyway, I don't know how it happened, but as soon as we touched the Tree, we just fell through."

She covered her face with her hands.

"Zane, it's all my fault... us, falling into the Dark Nav. And now she is missing... Why did I listen to her?" She folded her arms atop her knees and lowered her head, her shoulders shuddering in rugged sobs. "I love her so much, Zane. I'll never forgive myself if something would happen to her."

Gunz bit his lip, lowering his head to his chest. "I wish my hands were free," he muttered.

Karma stopped sobbing and raised her head. "Why? Did you want to hug me? Comfort me?" she asked snidely, suddenly her former self awakened. "Do I look like a little girl who needs to be comforted and reassured? I don't need my mommy and I certainly don't need a man to tell me that everything is going to be all right."

Gunz chuckled. "No, Karma, you certainly don't need anyone's support and reassurance," he said icily, without looking at her. "You misunderstood me, darling. I'm not here to wipe your tears with a lacy handkerchief. I wanted to have my hands free, so I could kick your sorry ass! The woman you love is missing and all you can do is cry the blues! How long have you and Milana spent in the Dark Nav that you're so damn broken?"

"I don't know. It's hard to count time when there is no difference between day and night. Seems like a few months at least. Enough time to find out that the only way out of here is through Chernobog's backdoor," she mumbled, staring at him. But then she clapped her hands a few times and burst out laughing. "Wait, Zane... Please, tell me that you didn't just turn the tables on me. You are not here to wipe *my* tears? Is that what you said?"

"You damn right, I did. Someone needs to kick your ass and remind you of who you are. Might as well be me," growled Gunz, staring at her. "I need the Karma that kept me tied up to a bed and had no hesitation in using a knife, even when I begged her to stop. She did it because it was the right thing to do and she saved me. The badass Karma, who almost summoned a *Harley Davidson* into the room. Can you bring her back?"

"I'm starting to respect you," she said, looking at him, the sincerity of her words reflecting on her face. "You're the one who's beat up and restrained, and yet you're the one who is pushing me to be stronger."

"Better late than never," muttered Gunz with a half shrug and winced from the pain.

"Yeah, I can bring that Karma back, sans the crazy outfits. No magic—no outfits." She laughed and got up, twirling in place. Her rags wrapped around her legs, sending clouds of dust in the air. "I do look sexy in this, don't I?"

"Extremely," he replied, closing his eyes. The conversation and all the movement took his remaining strength. Somehow, the pain in his sore body was getting sharper, not better. "Remember, you told me that punching me out would be free of charge? Can I call on that favor now?"

Karma squatted in front of him, searching his face with concern. "That bad?" she asked.

"Getting worse," murmured Gunz, hardly able to move his lips. "I feel like... something is draining me... and the pain is becoming more than I can handle... ahh... knock me out. I'm serious."

She kneeled and carefully lifted his shirt up. "I don't understand," she whispered, hardly touching his skin with her fingers. "The welts on your body that weren't bleeding before are bleeding now. And the bruising around your ribs is getting worse, like the blood is still spilling below the skin surface." She lowered his shirt and looked up at his shackled wrists. "And your wrists are bleeding again. I don't understand how —"

"It is happening to him because the mighty Chernobog wishes for it to happen, witch." A loud voice boomed behind them.

Karma jolted up and spun around. Gunz flinched and right away regretted as the pain almost doubled. A man whose body was covered in black chainmail, with a longsword at his belt, was standing by the bars, staring down at them with icy indifference.

"Witch," ordered the man, waving his hand at Karma, "come closer."

Karma glanced at Gunz and he gave her a short nod. She approached the bars and stopped in front of the man.

"What do you want?"

"I want you to put your hands through the bars, so I can shackle you." He showed her the chains. "I'll be taking both of you to see the Lord of the Nav."

Karma folded her arms over her chest and cocked her head. "Not a chance. I'm not going to let you touch me without a fight."

The man laughed, and the sound of his cold laughter reverberated from the walls of the dungeon. Then he pointed at Gunz, the chains in his hand jingling at his every move.

"What's going on with your friend, witch?" he asked frostily. "He is not feeling well, is he? If you will disobey my orders, I shall make sure that he feels a lot worse." He pointed at the leather belt with metal spikes that he was wearing. "Trust me, my arm does not get tired easily. I can beat him for hours without breaking a sweat."

Karma glanced at Gunz, all color drained off her face.

"Karma, we need to see Chernobog and talk to him sooner or later. Perhaps you can find out what happened to Milana," he said with a sigh and gave her an encouraging nod.

Karma turned back to the man and pushed her hands through the bars, allowing him to shackle her. "Please, don't hurt him," she said quietly. "I'll do what you want."

The man didn't laugh, remaining cold and serious. He pulled out a bunch of keys on a large ring and found an old rusty one. He gestured to Karma to step aside and unlocked the door into the cell. Then he walked to Gunz and disconnected his chains from the ring on the wall.

Until this moment, Gunz didn't realize how truly weak he was. As soon as the man let go of his chains, he knew that the only thing that was keeping him in the upright position were his restraints. His tormented body refused to obey him. Slowly he slid down and fell to his side. The pain around his ribs and his back became more than he could take. He moaned and closed his eyes, hoping to pass out.

Gunz felt the man's hands on his arms, pulling him up. "Stop. Please," he cried out, as every move intensified his pain. To his surprise, he felt the man stop moving him, carefully lowering him back to the floor, and heard him sigh.

"You will have to endure the pain for a short while."

Gunz heard the man talking and opened his eyes. The man

was on one knee next to him. His face was cold and emotionless.

"I will lift and carry you, and you are not going to enjoy the process. Mighty Chernobog ordered me to deliver both of you to his throne room, and this is exactly what I am going to do. If you want to scream, do not feel ashamed. It'll help you deal with the pain."

With these words, he easily lifted Gunz up and put him over his shoulder. Gunz grunted, clenching his teeth to stop himself from screaming. As the man made his first few steps, Gunz prayed that the walk from the dungeons to Chernobog's throne room wasn't too long. Every step the man took was radiating with an unbearable agony in his broken body.

He saw Karma falling into step with the man and six more guards joining them, surrounding them in a circle. When the man reached the stairway and started walking up, the pain became more than he could handle.

But no amount of pain could make him pass out, so he did what the man said. He let go of his control and screamed.

16

~ ZANE BURNS, A.K.A. GUNZ ~

Gunz wasn't sure why, but he expected Chernobog's throne room to be dark and musty like a cave. The room he was in looked nothing like a cave. It was more like a gothic cathedral or the Main Hall of the Castle in the City of Kendral, with a tall vaulted ceiling and giant columns, positioned along both walls. There were a few large windows on either side of the room, but they were purely decorative as there was nothing to see outside the castle walls. The windows were draped with heavy black panels. Each panel had the same golden symbol embroidered on them.

At the far end of the room, there was a massive throne. It was crafted out of dark wood and its legs were fading into a pile of animal skulls. The skulls didn't appear to be thrown carelessly. They were part of the chair's morbid design. The tall back of the throne and its seat were upholstered with black leather. A black bird that looked like an oversized raven, skillfully carved out of a solid piece of a dark wood, was sitting on top of the chair-back.

Next to the main throne there was a second one, a little smaller. It was fashioned in a similar manner, but instead of animal skulls, the smaller throne was surrounded by human skulls. A large scythe was positioned next to it, leaning against its back.

Gunz sighed. It had been a while since Chernobog's man brought him here and his pain subsided a little. But sitting for a prolonged time in the kneeling position wasn't helping. His chains were attached to the ring that was embedded into the marble floor, limiting his movements. It's not like he wanted to move, but it would be nice to know that he could if he wanted.

Karma was kneeling next to him. She wasn't shackled to the floor, but she remained motionless and quiet, with her head bowed down to her chest. Six guards were surrounding them, with their swords drawn. The man who escorted them here was gone. Undoubtedly, he went to report to his master that the prisoners were ready.

Gunz leaned forward to try to readjust his position slightly. As he was doing that, he caught his reflection in the polished black marble floor and shuddered. The dirty rags that were covering his body were stiff with dried out blood and torn on his chest. His face, drained of life, was covered in dirt and brown stains. The only thing that seemed to be alive on his face were his eyes and they were glowing red, as if all his remaining elemental fire power was redirected into his eyes. He tried to extinguish the red glow, but he couldn't.

"Karma," he whispered horrified, "when did my eyes start glowing red?"

"When we came to the tavern," replied Karma quietly, without looking at him. "That's how the coyote-demon knew that you were a Child of Fire. Your rune is also glowing, by the way."

"Why didn't you say anything to —"

"Silence!" roared one of the guards, striking Gunz on his back with the flat side of his blade. "You speak only when spoken to!"

A torturous growl escaped Gunz's lips as he fell forward on the cold floor, pain crippling him. It took some serious effort just to get back on all fours. Karma didn't dare to move to help him. And the guards were gawking at his struggles with amused expressions on their faces.

He felt someone's hands grabbing his shoulders and helping him up into the kneeling position. Gunz raised his eyes and saw the man who carried him here. He was staring at the guard who struck him, frowning.

"This man is half-dead. You did not have to add to his suffering," he scolded the guard sternly.

"Thank you," said Gunz, taken aback by this unexpected display of kindness.

"I do not take pleasure in pointless suffering of others. But do not thank me yet, for nothing good is coming your way," said the man, shaking his head. "Now, both of you, behold your King, the Lord of the Nav, mighty god of Destruction, Chernobog."

Gunz raised his eyes and held his breath. He got used to the height of his mentor Kal who was six-feet-eight, but the man who was standing in front of the throne was at least seven feet tall. He had obsidian black hair and deep black eyes and if Gunz didn't know who he was, he would think that he was a Master of Power. The elemental powers were giving all the Masters of Power this coloring.

He looked like he was in his late thirties, but Gunz knew better. The man in front of him was an ancient Slavic deity, thousands of years old. He was one of the first gods of the Slavic pantheon. In his own way he was handsome, with his large black eyes, straight eyebrows that were meeting in a frown over his eyes. He had full lips, partially concealed by his well-groomed facial hair. But his expression was hard and cold, and the curve of his lips was betraying natural pride bordering with arrogance and proclivity to cruelty and ferocity.

The overwhelming energy of Chernobog's magic and godly power surrounded him with a dark glow. He was dressed in a long caftan that was held on his waist by a wide leather belt. Black leather armor was fastened over his caftan and an enormous sword in a scabbard decorated with black onyx was attached to his belt.

Chernobog took his long black cape off and threw it over the back of his throne. Then he nodded to his man and sat down on the throne. Relaxing, he leaned against the back of the chair and peered at Gunz, his black eyes narrowed.

"A Child of Fire and a witch," he boomed. His deep voice wasn't loud, but somehow it managed to reach even the farthest corners of the throne room.

Gunz glanced at Karma. She was frozen in fear. Her head bowed down low, she was trying to take as little space as possible under Chernobog's furious gaze.

"My lord," said Gunz calmly, inclining his head in a bow. He caught Karma's petrified gaze in the corner of his eye. She was probably thinking he was a nutcase, talking to the god of Destruction.

Chernobog lips twitched in a smirk as his obsidian eyes drilled deeper into Gunz's chest. Gunz cringed inwardly, feeling Chernobog's magic scanning him.

"What are you doing in my realm?" demanded the god of Destruction. "None of you belong here. And you, Child of Fire, you're immortal. You have no business in the realm of the dead."

It was pointless to lie to a god. *The truth it is,* decided Gunz.

"My lord," said Gunz, meeting the god's heavy gaze, "I was forced to cross into your domain against my will. And Karma and her girlfriend Milana fell into the Dark Nav accidentally when they approached the World Tree."

"Accidentally?" repeated Chernobog and barked laughing, throwing his head back. "There is no such thing. You cannot accidentally fall into the Dark Nav. One of them had an intent to come here, and she was privy to the knowledge available to a chosen few. When they touched the Tree, one of them was powerful enough to wield magic that opened the path into the Nav. The World Tree connects the three realms, but also it has a passage that allows those with knowledge to open the gates into the Nav or to the Prav. Not everyone can do it. Not even all gods…"

"I don't understand…" mumbled Karma. She threw a desperate glance at Gunz. "It's not possible. I didn't even know that it was possible to get into the Dark Nav and Milana… She's just a lowly seer. Her magic is so insignificant that she can't even cast some basic spells."

"Interesting," said Chernobog, rising. He walked up to them and stopped just a foot away. "So, where is your girlfriend now? Let's ask her."

Karma's eyes widened as she craned her neck to look up at Chernobog. "She is not in your dungeons?" she whispered. "All three of us were taken at the same time. You were there, my lord."

"Yes, I was there, but I do not recall her," muttered Chernobog, rubbing his forehead. He turned around and walked back to his throne. He sat down and then waved his hand at his man. "Voron, can you please ask my wife to join us?"

The man, Voron, rushed out of the throne room and returned a few minutes later, followed by a young woman. She walked inside, the vibe of authority preceding her. Her face, while breathtakingly beautiful, had an imprint of unyielding strength and her walk had a bounce of irritation that every mortal woman had when she wasn't happy with her significant other. She stopped in front of her husband, placing her hands on her curvy hips and frowned at him, tapping her foot.

"You called?" she asked icily. "What do you want now?"

"Morena, darling," said Chernobog, rising, a peaceful smile on his face. "I need your help, my love." He approached his wife, attempting to hug her, but she twirled away from him and sat down on her throne, crossing her legs.

"Sweetheart, I seem to have misplaced one of my prisoners," said Chernobog, sounding apologetical. "I was wondering if you knew—"

"What do I care about your prisoners," huffed the goddess of Winter and Death rising. "I know nothing, and I do not care—"

She cut herself in mid-sentence as her gaze stopped on Gunz's face. Morena got up and slowly approached him. She grabbed a handful of his hair, jerking his head backward and bent over slightly, staring into his eyes. He knew exactly what the goddess saw in his eyes—the dancing flames, the energy of the Fire in its purest form.

Still holding his hair in her grip, she ran her nail over his cheek. A path of frost stained his skin and Gunz cried out, pulling at his chains. For a Fire Salamander, the touch of ice was worse than the touch of cold water.

"Oh, my darling," purred Morena, turning to her husband, "you got yourself a little fire-pet here. Why didn't you tell me, sweetie? What are your plans for him?"

Chernobog walked to his wife and put his arm around her shoulders. She stiffened for a moment but didn't object to his touch this time.

"I don't know yet, my love," he replied, gently taking her hands away from Gunz. "I'm still trying to interrogate them and find out what they are doing in our realm."

"Let's hear then," said Morena. She turned around and headed to her throne, holding her husband's hand in hers. They both sat down and Morena waved at Chernobog. "Please continue. Why did you need me? You said you lost one of your prisoners?"

"My love, yesterday I captured the Fire Salamander and two witches. One of them is here, but the other one is missing," said Chernobog. "Do you know anything about her whereabouts?"

"Me?" asked Morena, fluttering her long white eyelashes at her husband. "Why would I know anything about her? I didn't even know you had any new prisoners. Just ask Voron. He's the one you share everything with, not me. Sometimes I wonder if he's the one who's sharing your bed instead of your wife."

"Morena, my love, what are you saying?" hissed Chernobog. "That's completely inappropriate and untrue. There is no one I love more than you."

"You've yet to prove your words with your actions," muttered Morena, her eyes darting from her husband back to Gunz.

"Aw, Morena... Let's leave this discussion for the privacy of my chambers." Chernobog sighed. "Voron, tell me what happened yesterday. Where is one more witch?"

"My lord, I remember that I brought two people into your dungeons," replied Voron with a bow. "I locked the witch into the cell and then went to the interrogation chamber where your guards were taking care of this man." He pointed at Gunz. "There was never a third person as far as I recall. I swear, my lord, I'm telling you the truth."

Gunz glanced at Karma. She wrapped her chained arms around herself and was slowly rocking back and forth, tears running down her ashen face. Then she raised her eyes at Voron and pointed her trembling hand at him.

"You killed her," she whispered. She jumped to her feet and before anyone could stop her, she launched herself at him. "You killed the woman I loved. You killed her!"

Karma swung her shackled arms and smashed them into the side of Voron's head. The man collapsed, blood spilling from the fresh wound, coloring the side of his face scarlet. Morena hooted laughing, clapping her hands. Chernobog jumped to his feet, quickly covering the distance separating him and his right-hand man. Gunz was worried that the angered god would kill

Karma in place, but there was nothing he could do to help. He was drained and chained to the floor.

Chernobog just touched Karma's head, and she fell to the floor, unconscious but still alive. The Lord of the Dark Nav kneeled next to Voron and quickly checked him, making sure that he was alive. Then he touched his forehead, whispering something, and the man stirred in his hands. Chernobog sighed with relief and rose, helping Voron to his feet.

While all this was going on, Morena got up and walked back to Gunz. She squatted in front of him, observing his face with interest. He had no doubt that if Morena decided to decapitate him right now, no one would stop her.

"So, boy," she said, her glacial eyes shining with freezing contempt, "now you are going to tell me the truth."

"What would you like to know, my lady?" asked Gunz, bowing to her.

"Do not bow your head, Child of Fire. I want to see your flaming eyes when you're trying to lie to me."

She grasped his chin with her fingers and jerked his head up. Gunz met her icy gaze and shuddered. In her eyes, he read his own judgment. It didn't matter if he told her the truth or lied to her. She would torture him anyway, for the pleasure of hearing his screams.

"Tell me why you are here, in my husband's domain," she said.

"I was forced to cross the veil, my lady—," repeated Gunz, but she didn't let him finish.

Slowly and deliberately she moved her long fingernail across his face, leaving a trail of frost and ice on his skin. Gunz moaned, her touch sending him into the dark pool of agony.

"I didn't lie, my lady, please," he hissed, his jaws locked.

"Why did you come here? What do you want in my husband's domain?" she repeated her questions.

"It wasn't my choice. I was sent here against my will," he repeated.

She let go of his chin and ripped the shirt on his chest, exposing the glowing rune. Then she backhanded him, sending him flying to the floor. Gunz didn't even try to get up. He was lying on his side, blood slowly trickling down from the corner of his mouth to the polished black tiles.

Morena got up and put her high-heeled boot on his chest, turning him to his back and pressing the sharp heel between his ribs.

"Husband!" she yelled, pouting like a little girl who was ready to throw a tantrum. "Your pet is lying to me. He disrespects me and refuses to tell me why he is here."

Chernobog turned around and frowned at his wintry wife. Then he sighed and kneeled next to Gunz. Gently he lifted his wife's foot off Gunz's chest and probed the rune with his fingers.

"Curious," he said. "Child of Fire, now I believe that you were forced to come here. No one in their right mind would choose to have this rune burnt into his own chest."

"Why?" whispered Gunz, choking on his own blood.

"A few reasons," explained the god of Destruction. "This particular rune has multiple qualities and powers. For one, it is hiding your fiery presence, shadowing your elemental fire power. I would assume that this effect was desired. But did you know that it also drains you? So, you have to feel weakened and sick all the time. My realm feeds on your life energy and this rune is feeding on your magic. Whoever placed this curse on you, didn't wish you well, Child of Fire."

"I figured as much," muttered Gunz, wiping the blood with the side of his hand. "Like I was trying to tell your wife, I was thrown here by some insane mage."

"Let's assume for a moment that I am actually stupid enough to believe you," hissed Morena, stamping her high-heeled boot.

"What did this crazy mage want you to do? I'm sure she didn't go through all the troubles of opening the gate into the Dark Nav, just to send you for an evening walk."

Gunz tried to get up but had no strength and fell back. Chernobog seized his shoulders and yanked him up into a kneeling position. Gunz swayed as everything spun around him and pulled on the chains to stop himself from falling back.

"She wanted me to…" His voice trailed off as he realized that he was about to admit that he was here to steal something from the god.

"What did she want you to do?" asked Chernobog, his voice almost sympathetic. "Tell me the truth, Child of Fire, don't be frightened."

Are they playing a "good cop, bad cop" routine on me? Gunz glanced at Morena and then back at Chernobog.

"She wanted me to steal a magical artifact from you, my lord," Gunz blurted out in one breath and fell silent, bracing himself for more pain.

Chernobog and Morena exchanged a quick look, and both started laughing.

"Do you know how many powerful magical artifacts I have in my possession?" asked Chernobog when he finally was able to speak again. "Which one did she want? The name of it, please?"

"I don't know the name," said Gunz. "She said that it's a pendant that looks like a double-edged axe decorated with gold inlays."

The silence that enveloped the throne room sounded like his death sentence. Neither Chernobog nor Morena said anything, but Chernobog's hand automatically went up to his neck. He reached under his leather armor and pulled out a gold chain.

At the end of the chain where the pendant was supposed to be, there was nothing.

17

~ ZANE BURNS, A.K.A. GUNZ ~

The silence was deafening. No one said a word. Karma was still unconscious, spread on the floor. Chernobog was staring at his chain that was missing the most important element—the magical pendant. Voron's face fell, like he just lost something precious to him. But for some reason he was staring at Gunz, not at the chain in Chernobog's hand. And the haunted expression in Voron's eyes wasn't giving Gunz a warm and fuzzy feeling.

A heartbeat later, the silence got shattered into thousands of shards, exploding like a broken windshield. Morena filled her lungs with oxygen to the maximum and emitted an ear-piercing shriek.

"You!" she squealed, pointing at Gunz. "You and your girlfriends. You stole it! You stole it and gave it to your witch-girlfriend. And then you two stayed behind to cover up her escape!"

It makes no sense. Gunz raised his hand up, shaking his head no, his heart beating desperately against his ribcage.

She didn't pay attention. Reaching Gunz in one long jump, she punched him, driving her fist infused with her deadly winter power into the bridge of his nose. The bone broke with a sickening crack and a blinding white light exploded in his head. Gunz fell on his side, sliding on the floor as far as his chain allowed him. He didn't scream, there was neither strength nor desire for that.

He lay motionless on the cold marble tiles, sprawled in an awkward position, helplessly watching Morena pulling her foot back and slamming it into his stomach. At the moment of the impact, the frost spread over his skin, penetrating his body. Gunz coughed, splattering the blood all over the beautifully polished black floor and moaned. The pain was excruciating, but he couldn't make a sound, his vocal cords frozen and locked.

Morena grabbed his shirt, yanking him up and pulled her other hand back, determined to strike him again. Gunz closed his eyes, ready for the next punch. But nothing happened. He cracked his eyes open and saw Voron, holding Morena's wrist.

"My lady, I am begging you, do not strike an innocent man," said Voron calmly.

Morena gasped and let go of Gunz's shirt. He dropped back on the floor into the puddle of his own blood.

"How dare you touch me, you worthless maggot," hissed Morena. Voron released her wrist and dropped to his knees, bowing his head low. She stood, breathing hard, her glacial eyes burning with wrath. She extended her hand, and the scythe vanished from her throne, materializing in her hand. She brought the scythe above her shoulder, ready to swing it.

Chernobog stepped between his wife and his right-hand man, raising his hands up. "My love, please do not do something you surely will regret later," he said as peacefully as he could muster. "Voron did nothing wrong. He was trying to prevent you from making a mistake."

Morena gaped at her husband, her true desires written all over her snowy face. Then she took a few deep breaths and smirked. Her eyes darted from Chernobog to Voron and then to

Gunz. Her smirk stretched wider. Malignant and predacious as a feral snarl of a wolf, it exposed her small sharp teeth.

"Fine, darling," she seethed, "you're right. If I smite your loyal servant, you probably would make me regret it at some point. But I will not regret killing these unworthy thieves. So, my love, I spare your servant, if you give me what I want."

"What do you want?" moaned Chernobog, dropping his arms to his sides. "Ask and see it done."

Morena cackled, patting her godly husband on his shoulder. "I want these two executed. And I want it done immediately."

Chernobog threw his hands in the air, gazing heavenwards. "Sweetie, please be reasonable," he mumbled with a sigh. "I can't just execute them—"

"And why not?" asked Morena furiously, taking a step closer to Chernobog and pushing him in his chest with her finger. "Aren't you the Lord of this realm?"

"Yes, I am, but—"

"Aren't you the god of Destruction?"

"I am, my love, but—"

"Then do your job and destruct! Um... I mean destroy."

"Morena!" yelled Chernobog, his eyes flooded with darkness. "Be reasonable. I can't execute a Fire Salamander because he is an immortal Child of Fire! Immortal! Means he cannot be killed. Not even by the god of Destruction!"

"Fine!" yelled Morena, twirling in place, aggravation pouring from her every move. It started to snow inside the throne room. "Execute her"—she jerked her thumb at Karma—"and give the Salamander to me. I will put him to torture that would make him wish he was dead. I will find out where he is hiding your magical axe and then I will continue tormenting him until he will choose to die on his own volition."

"Sweetheart, it's inhumane—," mumbled Chernobog, burying his hands into his long black hair.

"Do I look like a filthy human to you? It's either them or

Voron," seethed Morena. A heavy blizzard rushed through the throne room. "Your choice... darling." Quick as a winter storm, she swooshed her scythe through the air, stopping it an inch away from Voron's neck. Voron shut his eyes, clenching his jaws, but didn't move a muscle.

"Fine! Fine! Stop!" yelled Chernobog, perspiration covering his forehead despite the freezing temperature in the throne room. "You can have them. Do what you want. Damn, woman! You always manage to get anything you wish out of me!"

"Now, sweetie, it wasn't that hard, was it?" Morena snickered, patting her husband's cheek.

Chernobog grunted, shaking his head. "At least tell me what you are intending to do with these two."

Morena kneeled next to Gunz, carefully making sure not to stain her silvery gown in his blood. She turned his head to the side, so she could see his face and glowered down at him, gloating over the sight of his defenselessness.

"Tell me, boy," she said frostily, "who is your true Lord and master? Is it Kalidus, the Great Salamander?"

Gunz tried to speak, but no sound came out from his swollen lips. He nodded, calmly holding his torturer's deadly stare. Morena glanced at her husband, arching her eyebrow and got up.

"No, Morena," whispered Chernobog, his face turning sickly green. "Please tell me, you are not planning to do what I think you are planning to do... Have a heart, woman..."

Morena laughed, a cold venomous sound that spread through the throne room, repeated over and over by the hollow echo.

"Yes, my dear husband, this is exactly what I am planning to do," she hissed. "It's only right that the son should follow in the steps of his father. I'm planning to do to him what was done to the Great Salamander centuries ago. And I will make this little bitchy-witch watch him suffer. I will make sure that she can't sleep and can't pass out and the only thing she can do is watch his pain, hear his screams and understand that there is not much she can do to help him. And the only way she can stop all this is by telling me where the stolen pendant is.

"And after she finally tells me where her little friend with your magical axe is, I will execute her. I will burn her at the stake. After all, *thou shalt not suffer a witch to live*. Isn't that what you, humans, say, boy?"

She poked Gunz in his ribs with her shoe. He moaned and tried to say something but couldn't. Gunz knew exactly what the goddess of Winter and Death was planning to do to him. Kal told him the story of how he was tortured for years, locked in some cave in the Land of Dreams by his crazy ex-girlfriend.

But that wasn't what scared him. He didn't want Karma to watch and the thought of her dying in fire was hurting him more than the prospect of the terrible torture. He was sure that Karma didn't have Chernobog's magical axe, and neither did Milana.

"Please," he croaked, "spare her... do what you wish with me..." Gunz didn't think that she could hear him, but she did.

"I have to give it to him. He is valiant, your fire-pet," huffed Morena, winking at her husband. Both Chernobog and Voron stood stupefied by her cruelty, unable to speak.

"Morena, my beautiful goddess, I don't want to argue with you. I love you and every argument we have pains me greatly," said Chernobog pleadingly. "Listen to me, sweetheart. I'm sure these two witches or this young Salamander couldn't steal a pendant that was attached to the necklace which I never take off my neck. It was someone a lot more powerful. These two are only guilty of being at the wrong place at the wrong time. Please, I am begging you to reconsider. Have a heart, my love..."

"A heart?" Morena laughed, pressing her hand to her chest above the heart. "I'm the goddess of Winter and Death. What heart are you talking about? Ice!"

She snapped her fingers, teleporting everyone from the throne room into the dungeons. Gunz recognized the same cell him and Karma were locked in before. Morena whispered another spell, erecting a tall iron pole that was running from the low ceiling to the floor of the cell. Rough iron manacles were attached to the top of the pole, dangling on a long thick chain.

"Voron, do your duty," she said coldly, pointing at Gunz and then at the pole. "You know what to do."

Voron glanced at his master, but Chernobog just nodded to him, ordering to proceed. Voron carefully lifted Gunz and locked his wrist into the manacles. He pulled him all the way up and locked the chains.

"I'm truly sorry," he whispered into Gunz's ear, leaving him strung up at the pole.

Morena approached Gunz and ripped the leftovers of his shirt off. She drew a circle of ice on the floor around him and locked it with her spell. Then she touched the circle and a thin icy wall rose up, surrounding the pole and encapsulating it all the way from the floor to the ceiling in a cylindrical glass-like contraption.

After that she touched Karma's forehead waking her up. Karma sat up and looked around, horror reflecting on her face. She tried to say something, but Morena snapped her fingers removing her ability to speak.

"Witch," she said coldly, "I want the axe back. Tell me now where your little girlfriend is, and I'll spare you both a lot of pain." She snapped her fingers again, allowing Karma to speak.

"My lady, I swear, neither I nor Milana touched the axe. I've never even seen it! Please have mercy, let him go," Karma begged, kneeling in front of the goddess.

"I gave you a chance," growled Morena, staring down at Karma severely, "you chose not to take it. And now you both will suffer the consequences."

She approached the icy cylinder and muttered a spell. At

once, the water slowly started to fill the cylinder, rising higher and higher with every moment. The water was frosty cold, filled with icicles. Gunz grasped at the chains as the pain ripped through him and his body arched like from an electric shock.

Karma gasped, an expression of horror frozen on her face, and crawled to the cylinder, wrapping her arms around the ice. "Please, my lady," she cried, tears running down her colorless face, "don't do it to him... I would tell you where the axe was if I knew. I swear, I have no idea! Please!"

Morena ignored her. She waited until the freezing water reached Gunz's shoulders and stopped it. She drummed some complicated rhythm on the glass-like surface of the cylinder and smiled.

"You're not screaming, my sweet pet," she said airily. "But you will, in a moment. You're about to experience firsthand what your Lord and master went through centuries ago. Are you ready, boy?"

She cackled and tapped the ice. At her touch the water inside the cylinder froze, turning into a solid chunk of ice. For a moment, Gunz thought his heart blew up, leaving a bloody mess inside his chest and if that was the truth, he would accept the death with gratitude. But it wasn't possible. He couldn't die.

The unbearable anguish unlike anything he experienced before, split his whole universe into billions of pieces, crushing him into nothing, and dunking whatever was left of him into a sea of torment. He didn't scream. The sound that escaped his lips didn't resemble the voice of a human being. It wasn't a howl of a wounded animal either. It was something bone-chilling, indescribable and Gunz couldn't believe that it was his voice cords that produced this awful, inhuman sound.

He saw Karma, squirming at his feet, pleading for his release. He even heard Chernobog, asking his wife to stop it. Voron was on his knees, begging to take his life and stop the despicable torture. But nothing would make the Winter goddess change her mind.

Gunz could see everything but his feverish brain wasn't processing what he saw. Besides the unbearable agony his body was tormented by, the images of his past were flashing in front of his eyes, overlaying everything that was going on in the present, making it impossible for him to focus on anything.

As the pain intensified, Gunz screamed again. Focusing on his physical pain allowed him to suppress the mental anguish the flashbacks were inflicting upon his mind. Like through the red distorted glass he saw a blinding light exploding in the middle of the cell and felt the ground trembling beneath his icy prison. Two men walked through the light and stopped in front of him.

One of the men stood as tall as Chernobog. He had long silver hair that was falling down to his waist. His face, hardened by time and experience, was partially concealed by his thick gray mustache and beard. In his hand, he held a tall staff. The runes on the staff were glowing with the red energy of his magic. As soon as Morena saw this man, she blanched and vanished from the room.

The man frowned at Chernobog and shook his head disapprovingly. Then he touched the cylinder and all the ice shattered into tiny sparkling cubes with an ear-splitting bang of a broken glass, releasing Gunz from his frozen prison. Gunz moaned as the pain slowly started to subside. He couldn't stand on his own, hanging powerlessly in his restraints.

The second man approached the pole and carefully freed Gunz's wrists, gently lowering him to the floor. Gunz moaned and relaxed in the man's arms. He blinked a few times, trying to focus his vision, still distorted and blurry.

"I'm sorry it took me so long, my friend," muttered the man. His voice sounded so familiar, but Gunz couldn't organize his thoughts enough to recall where he heard this voice before. The man pulled his trench coat off and covered Gunz's shivering body with it.

This trench coat... I remember... Gunz looked up, finally recognizing the man.

"Angel... Am I glad... to see you..." whispered Gunz, his teeth still chattering.

"Yeah, not too many people say that when they see me, my young friend," said Angel chuckling.

In the meantime, the other man approached Chernobog and put his hand on his shoulder.

"Hello, brother," he said in a deep clear voice. "I see you still let your wife run your life..."

18

~ AIDAN ~

Kal paced the limited space of Aidan's office, muttering something under his breath. With his massive shoulders and his height of six-feet-eight he was making the room look tiny. Aidan kept following him with his eyes, wondering how he managed to turn around, forget about pacing.

Finally, Kal stopped in front of Aidan and leaned forward, planting both his fists on to the desk. Aidan silently waved at the chair for the hundredth time, inviting the Great Salamander to sit down.

"What are we waiting for?" asked Kal, his voice low and heavy.

Kal wasn't happy with Aidan and the fire within him kept breaking through, setting his long hair ablaze and igniting furious flames on the bottom of his deeply set eyes. His body was emitting an unbearable heat like any industrial oven, and the air conditioner in the office couldn't keep it cool.

"I'm waiting for Uri to get back to me," explained Aidan calmly, taking a Kleenex from the box on his desk and wiping perspiration off his forehead. "He is trying to get in touch with Angel and Svyatobor. I want to know if there are any new developments before we jump headfirst into the Land of Dreams."

"Why, Aidan?" asked Kal but didn't sit down. "No matter what Uri will say, we should go to the Isle Buyan and see what we can do to help Gunz..." His voice trailed away, and he shook his head. "Agh... I wish both of you were a bit smarter and knew when it was time to be asking for help and when you should clean up your own mess... I'm sure Gwyn agreed with me."

The air shimmered with a soft golden glow, and before Aidan could say anything, Uri materialized in the office next to Kal. Uri glanced up at the Great Salamander and his mouth opened slightly. Taking a step back, away from Kal's heat, Uri bowed to him.

"Great Salamander," he said, quickly hiding his surprise. "It's nice to see you after so many years. Since the moment the young Fire Salamander crossed the threshold of this dojang, I suspected that I'd see you sooner or later."

"Archangel Uriel," replied Kal, inclining his head. "It's been a while since I had the pleasure of talking with one of your kind."

"Any news, Uri?" asked Aidan, breaking into their conversation.

"I've heard from Svyatobor," said Uri. "He is waiting for you at the World Tree. He found Veles, and Veles agreed to take Angel to the Dark Nav."

"Oh, good," said Aidan, feeling relieved. After all this time, as inconclusive as it was, it was the first message from Svyatobor. At least now he knew that Angel and Veles were on their way to help Gunz. "Thank you, Uri. Kal and I will be leaving at once."

"Finally," growled Kal. He waved his hand unfolding his fire-portal and gave a sarcastic stare to Aidan. "I believe you have some fire in you, boy. My portal shouldn't be a problem for you, eh?"

Aidan threw a reproachful gaze at Kal and passed through the fire. He walked out of the portal and halted, awestruck. The energy of magic and elemental powers flooded him, intoxicating him. He drew in a sharp breath, pressing his hand to his chest and his eyes ignited with the brilliant light of his magic. Kal closed his portal and stood with his arms crossed, observing him with an uneven smirk.

"I thought in your long godly life, you experienced the effects of the magical nexus," he said, patting Aidan on his shoulder.

"I did," replied Aidan, his voice hoarse. "I've been to a few of them. But it's been a while, and I already forgot how it felt to be surrounded by the undiluted energy of magic. The initial effect is quite jarring."

"Well, breathe in and out." Kal chuckled and pointed forward. "This is where we need to go. It's a short walk to the World Tree."

Aidan turned around, taking in his surroundings. They were standing on a narrow strip of land, soft dark waves rushing on and off. Ahead of them, the land was getting wider, while still staying completely flat. Farther on the horizon, he saw a giant tree. It was so tall that he couldn't see its crown as it was disappearing into the sky, leaving just a few massive branches visible. Its trunk was so wide that a dozen people wouldn't be able to encircle it, holding their hands together. The World Tree was surrounded by green shrubbery and thickets that were obscuring the bottom of the trunk.

It was scorching hot. Aidan looked up, noticing that the sun was high above their head, blasting from the east side of the World Tree. On the west side of the World Tree, the sky was darker, resembling late evening, and the silver disk of the moon was shining through the thick green leaves of the Tree.

Kal didn't seem to be affected by the heat. On the contrary, he seemed to enjoy it. Giving another quick tap on Aidan's shoulder, Kal headed toward the Tree. A few minutes later, they passed through the shrubbery and wound up on a large clearing. Tall lush grass bedazzled with colorful wild flowers covered the land. The light warm breeze was blowing through the grass, its soft whispering sound peaceful and lulling.

The air was filled with the thin buzzing of busy bees that were zooming in and out of the World Tree, exploring the flowers. Now that they didn't have the thickets and shrubbery obscuring their view, Aidan saw a massive stone located in the center of the meadow. The World Tree's powerful root system was wrapped around the rock and disappeared under the ground.

"Alatyr Stone," said Kal, pointing at the rock. "This is the center of the Slavic Realms. It has some healing properties and magic of its own, by the way."

"Thank you for the guided tour, but I know that," murmured Aidan, searching around. "What I don't know is where Svyatobor is. He was supposed to meet us here."

"I guess you didn't instill discipline and the fear of a tiny god of the Celtic Otherworld in your team," said Kal snidely.

"Ah, Kal, give me a break," muttered Aidan, rubbing his forehead. "I just want to know that Svyatobor is okay. It's enough that Gunz is missing. I don't need any added worries."

He heard a loud rustling noise, coming somewhere from above and raised his eyes. Right above his head, on the sunny side of the World Tree, he saw a large bird. Aidan stepped back and placed his hand above his eyes to shield them from the bright sunlight.

The creature that was sitting on the lowest branch of the World Tree was a bird, but it wasn't. As large as an ostrich, the bird had a rich white plumage. Its tail was as long as the tail of a peacock, decorated by silvery-white feathers and its wide wings were spread open. But instead of a bird's head with a beak, the creature had the head of a young, beautiful woman. She had large blue eyes, framed in thick black lashes and pink full lips. The bird looked down at them and smiled, exuding happiness and cheerfulness with its disposition.

"Don't worry, Aodh. You'll find your friend," she sang. Her voice was pleasant and mesmerizing and Aidan couldn't take his eyes off her.

"Sure, you'll find your friend. I just don't know if you'll find him alive."

Aidan heard another voice and snapped his head to the right. A second creature—a cross between a large bird and a young woman—was sitting on the moon-side of the World Tree. The second creature looked like she could have been the twin sister of the first bird. But her plumage was dark, black and electric blue feathers were decorating its chest and long tail. Her amazing aquamarine eyes were flooded with sadness and clear tears were sliding down her tender cheeks without stop.

"Don't listen to her, handsome young god," sang the first bird with a happy smile. "My sister is a pessimist. Her glass is always half-empty."

"I'm not a pessimist! Glass half-empty," huffed the dark bird, rolling her deep blue eyes, spilling more tears. "I'm a realist and as opposed to my happy-go-lucky sister, I think things through before jumping into conclusions."

Aidan glanced at Kal but found nothing but a wide grin on the face of the Great Salamander.

"Did any of you see Svyatobor?" asked Aidan with a sigh. "He was supposed to meet us here."

"Svyatobor? That cute god of nature?" asked the white bird and her bright smile grew wider. "Of course I saw him. He's not the kind of man you can forget easily."

"Of course she saw him," parroted the dark bird, rolling her sad eyes. "How many centuries ago?"

Kal clapped a few times and burst out laughing. Aidan threw his hands in the air and turned away from both birds. It was obvious that he couldn't get a clear answer from them.

"Aw, we got the handsome young god upset, sister," said the white bird, her cheerful voice not wavering even for a moment.

"He was like this when he got here," replied the dark bird, folding its wings.

"Aidan, stop talking to them. It's useless. This is the Bird Alkonost and her sister, Bird Sirin. Alkonost is always singing happy, cheerful songs and Sirin is her opposite. She sings of sadness and prophesies troubles. To get the true answers from them, you need to know how to ask."

Aidan heard Svyatobor's voice and spun around. The Slavic god of nature was sitting at the evening side of the World Tree, his large eyes glowing with a phosphoric light.

"Aw, darling, thank you for your kind words," said Alkonost, gazing down at Svyatobor, her eyes filled with admiration.

"What did he say so sweet that got you melting away?" huffed Sirin, staring at her sister with disdain. "Let me translate for you his words, sister. He said that you're a euphoric idiot and I am clinically depressed. And he also said that no one should ask us any questions because we're deceiving bitches."

Kal snickered, shaking his head and sat down on the ground, resting his back at the Alatyr Stone. "One thing I can say—these two beauties are always entertaining."

"The Great Salamander loves us," squealed Alkonost in delight, hopping up and down on her branch.

"Ugh, what are you talking about? He thinks we're dimwitted clowns, here to entertain him," replied Sirin bursting into tears.

"Ahh..." exhaled Svyatobor. "Shoo! Both of you. Go away! I'll summon you if I need you!"

Both bird-women gasped indignantly and flew up, migrating to one of the top branches of the tree, disappearing into the sky. Kal burst out laughing. "Finally, the first smart move from you, old bear," he told Svyatobor through the laughter. He wiped his eyes, getting serious. "What did you find out about my Salamander?"

"Nothing," said Svyatobor. "I don't know anything new. Veles took Angel to the Dark Nav and he asked us to wait here and do nothing."

"Do nothing?" asked Kal, suddenly on his feet. He wasn't laughing, his face tensed, small flames circling around his arms.

"What is it, Kal?" asked Aidan, troubled by such an abrupt change in Kal's behavior and disposition.

Kal didn't reply. He turned around and put both of his hands on the roots of the World Tree. Then he closed his eyes and stilled like a person listening to something only he could hear. His face hardened, and his massive muscles tensed, wrapping around his arms and back like thick ropes.

"No," he whispered. "God, please, no... Not this... not to my boy..."

Which god is he praying to? Chernobog? Veles? There was so much pain in Kal's voice that Aidan took a step forward and carefully touched his shoulder.

"Kal—," Aidan started to say but cut himself off as the Great Salamander turned around and stared at him with unseeing eyes.

Kal looked terrifying. His eyes were filled with angry flames and his whole body was ablaze with scorching fire. For a moment he stood, staring into nowhere. Then he threw his head back and screamed, burying his hands into his hair. His power, fueled by agony and despair, ran wild and a sweeping wave of pure energy of fire spread around him like a blast wave of an atomic bomb.

Kal turned around and hissed a few words in Dragon Tongue, striking the Alatyr Stone with the palm of his hand. A dark swirling void of a portal opened up at the foot of the stone. It wasn't the usual portal of a Fire Salamander and it was breathing with the dark demonic energy and the presence of death.

"Kal, what are you doing?" yelled Aidan, grabbing his arm to stop him.

Kal glared at him over his shoulder and twisted his arm, throwing Aidan's hand off. As he was ready to jump into the portal, Aidan felt that the energy of Fire that was ravaging the Isle Buyan somehow doubled. A curtain of Fire opened up right next to Kal and Semargl, the fiery Slavic deity, walked out of it. His glowing igneous eyes stopped on the dark void of the portal and he rushed forward, wrapping his arms around Kal and pulled him back, away from the darkness.

"You cannot go there, brother," he yelled, struggling to keep Kal locked in his arms. "There are no elemental powers in the Dark Nav. You'll be nothing but a weak human there, broken and lost in the darkness."

"I must!" growled Kal, fighting Semargl's bearhug. "I can't leave my child alone and unprotected! Do you know what they're doing to him?"

"I know. I can feel his pain. This is why I had to come here, my brother. But if you jump into the Dark Nav, you won't be able to help him," hissed Semargl. He was slowly losing his fight. Holding on to the Great Salamander with all his might, he turned to Aidan and shouted, "Don't just stand there, boy. Don't you see. I can't hold him much longer. Summon a Master of Power!"

Semargl's voice ripped Aidan out of shock. Quickly, he drew a glowing rune in the air, filling it with the light of his magic and touched it, summoning Mrak Delar, the Ancient Master of Power.

Mrak Delar responded to the summons right away. Before Aidan completed the last word of the summoning spell, the Master of Power materialized next to him. He quickly observed the situation and his eyes flooded with the red color of the fire energy. He extended his arm toward Kal and said one word, "Cease."

A shimmering red hoop of his power wrapped around Kal's arms and chest, rendering him motionless. Kal grunted and dropped his head to his chest. He didn't fight Mrak Delar's control and Semargl let him go.

"Great Salamander, I'm sorry. I know that I have no right to control you, but I had to do it," said Mrak Delar. He waved his hand, muttering a spell and closed the portal to the Dark Nav. "Be patient. We're all here to help."

"You can release me, Mrak," whispered Kal. He lifted his head. A single tear, a drop of liquid fire, escaped his flaming eyes.

Mrak Delar hesitated for a moment, but then let go of his power and the shimmering red hoop slowly dissipated. Kal sighed and almost dropped to the ground, leaning his back against the stone.

"You have no idea what they're doing to him," he said, his voice dead and hollow.

"I know, Kalidus. Your young Salamander is in a lot of pain," said Semargl. "I can feel his suffering. But there is nothing you or I can do to help him. It is up to the Grim Horseman and Veles to save him now."

Kal shook his head, a cold smirk on his face. "It's not only the physical pain that he is tortured with. This particular torture also brings forth all the painful memories and experiences, even those that he went through as a child and doesn't recall now... And I know that, because centuries ago, Morgan La Fey put me through the exact same torture."

19

~ ZANE BURNS, A.K.A. GUNZ ~

The sensation of teleportation made his stomach churn. The nausea was magnified tenfold by the nagging pain and non-stop flashbacks that were playing in his mind. Gunz grunted and swallowed, suppressing the nausea. Luckily, it passed quick. A split-second later, he felt something hard and steady under his back. Then Angel's hands grabbed his shoulders, gently trying to lift him up. He wanted to tell Angel to leave him alone, but he couldn't put the words together.

"Do you have the Fire here?"

Gunz heard Angel's question and shook his head. There was no fire in the Dark Nav.

"Any Fire? Elemental or Fire magic?" Angel asked again. He obviously didn't see him shaking his head no.

"There are no elemental powers in the Dark Nav," replied Chernobog. Gunz shuddered at the sound of his voice.

"He needs to revert into the natural state of the Fire Salamander. This is the only way he can heal his body and clear his mind from the effects of the torture your wife put him through." Angel's voice sounded angry, almost like a growl.

Angel, didn't you hear anything? There is no Fire here.

"I'm sorry, Grim Horseman." Chernobog sounded awkward, even remorseful. "You will have to take him to the Yav. That's the only way."

"That's not true, brother."

Gunz recognized the voice of the other man that came with Angel. By now his face was so swollen that he couldn't open his eyes all the way. He cracked his eyelids open as much as he could and tried to focus his blurred vision. He could see the fuzzy silhouette of a giant man standing next to Chernobog, but he couldn't make out his features.

"I surely don't understand what you mean, Veles," said Chernobog dryly.

Veles? The Slavic god of the Three Realms? What is he doing here? And did he come here with Angel?

"Can I take your place, Horseman?" Veles spoke again, stepping closer to Gunz.

Angel, don't leave! I don't trust any of these Russian gods!

Angel got up and the floor under Gunz's back shook slightly, making him realize that he was lying on a low sofa, not on the floor. Veles sat down on the edge of the sofa next to him and its springs moaned, bending down under the weight of his colossal body. For a moment, Veles stared at Gunz, then sighed and patted Gunz's shoulder gently.

"What's your name, Child of Fire?" asked Veles.

My name is Zane... I'm sorry, I don't think I can speak...

"Zane Burns," Angel replied instead of him. "His name is Zane Burns and I don't think he can speak right now."

"Chernobog, brother, you shouldn't let your wife run your life," said Veles, scrutinizing his brother with a disapproving glance. "She is as cold as her powers and no matter what you do, she'll never return your love. I don't think she's capable of such strong feelings."

"In all fairness, it's not her fault," said Chernobog quietly, dropping his head to his chest. "We don't know what happened to her when Zmey held her captive—"

"It happened a long time ago, brother, before you married her. She made us all believe that she was fine, and that she put all that behind!" growled Veles. "Look what she did to this innocent man and this young witch."

Karma! She's alive. Please, someone tell me that she survived all that. Gunz tried to lift his head to look for Karma but couldn't.

Veles noticed his struggles and waved his hand. "Karma, come closer, so he can see that you're alive and well." A moment later, Karma came into his view. Gunz exhaled and closed his eyes, relaxing.

"Okay, Zane," said Veles and Gunz opened his eyes again. "Here is the deal, child. I can't heal you, but I can make you feel a little better. At least, you'll be able to communicate and keep your eyes open. Do you understand me?"

I understand you just fine, thought Gunz. *Too bad I can't tell you that.* He blinked once, hoping that Veles could understand him.

"Listen, Zane, I'm going to use my magic to help you. Like I said, it's not going to heal you, but it'll give you a temporary boost of energy," continued Veles. "You're not going to like it, but it'll hurt just for a moment. Okay? Ready?"

Gunz blinked once, bracing himself for more pain. Veles pushed his massive arm under his back, lifting his chest up slightly. He extended his other hand and whispered, *"Ignisio Orbus."* A small fire ball manifested in the palm of his hand.

Fire... Yessss....

Just being in close proximity to his element was making him feel better.

"Now," said Veles and thrusted the fireball through Gunz's chest.

The heat surged through him, igniting every cell in his body, making his eyes glow brighter with the dancing flames. The initial pain was insignificant compared to the way the fire made him feel, restoring his strength and killing the pain. Veles was right. This small fireball wasn't enough to completely heal him, but at least now the pain wasn't as unbearable as it was before, the flashbacks stopped, and he could finally speak.

"Oh, God..." exhaled Gunz, panting. "Thank you... I can... it stopped... thank you."

Veles smiled, his eyes squinting beneath his bushy gray eyebrows. He gently lowered Gunz back on the sofa and got up, offering his place to Angel.

"Alive?" asked Angel, helping Gunz to sit up.

"Barely," muttered Gunz. The small infusion of fire took the edge off the pain and stopped the flashbacks, but he was still weak and sore all over.

"Let's get to business," said Veles. He walked past Chernobog and sat down into a massive chair that looked more like a throne. "This boost is not going to keep Zane up forever and I need to ask a few questions while he still can talk."

"What would you like me to tell you, my lord," said Gunz, bringing forth all the medieval manners Kal taught him in Kendral and hoping that he was sounding respectful enough. After all, he was in the presence of two ancient Slavic deities, two of the first and most powerful gods of Slavic pantheon. Ancient gods weren't known for their patience and forgiveness. And these two were at the top of the list—the god of Destruction and the god of the Three Realms.

Veles was the only god of Slavic pantheon who could freely move between all three realms—the Nav, the Yav and the Prav. He was as powerful in the Dark Nav as he was in the realm of gods—Prav. Even though some of the northern Slovenians considered Veles to be the god of Wisdom and Magic, he wasn't famous for keeping his cool or for a kind disposition. So, in the company of these two, being humble and respectful sounded like the right thing to do.

"I've heard your story from Svyatobor and from the Horseman," said Veles, slightly inclining his head, "and I have no reason to doubt their words. However, I would like to hear it again in your words. How did you get here and what was your purpose?"

Gunz quickly recounted everything that happened to him since the moment he met Agent Zvereva, to the moment Morena locked him up in the icy prison. He didn't hold anything back and the further he proceeded with his story, the grimmer Veles looked.

When he finished, Veles turned to Chernobog, who was standing next to his chair. "Brother, which pendant was he sent to steal from you?"

Chernobog silently pulled the chain out from under his leather armor and showed it to Veles. At the sight of the missing pendant, Veles blanched. His eyes widened, and his hands gripped harder at the arms of the chair.

"I thought you were never taking this chain off, Chernobog. It was your duty to protect it!" Veles wasn't shouting, but his voice filled all the space of the small room, pressing on Gunz's ears, making him feel like he was deep underwater without any scuba equipment.

"I never took it off, brother. I swear," replied Chernobog, his dark energy spiking around him. "Not even when I sleep."

"Then how did it go missing?" hissed Veles, throwing his hands in the air. "I don't believe for a second that this little witch and the Fire Salamander could steal it from you."

"Neither do I," agreed Chernobog, "but Morena is of a different opinion."

"I don't give a damn about her opinion," growled Veles. "But I would really like to know why she was so bent on killing them both."

Veles got up and approached Gunz again, staring down at him heavily. Gunz recoiled, pressing into the back of the sofa. The ancient god seized his chin, lifting his face up, staring directly into his eyes. Veles' magic enveloped him, penetrating the deepest corners of his soul. Gunz flinched in his hands but couldn't break eye contact. After a moment Veles let him go and repeated the procedure with Karma.

After he was done, he went back to his chair and sat down, shaking his head.

"This man is a warrior," he said to Chernobog. "It wasn't his will that brought him to this place and he's definitely not a petty thief. The woman is a different story. Her ways are a lot darker. But I'm sure, in the case of the missing pendant, she is innocent."

Both gods stopped talking and silence enveloped the small room. Veles closed his eyes and for a while he appeared to be sleeping. However, no one, including his brother, was brave enough to bother him. After a few minutes, Veles opened his eyes and waved his hand at Gunz.

"Zane, this glowing rune on your chest. Did you say that you were supposed to activate it when you completed your mission and ready to leave the Dark Nav?"

"Yes, my lord," replied Gunz, his hand involuntarily moving up to his chest.

"I want you to activate it," demanded Veles.

"My lord, if I do it, the mage will pull me out of the Nav," said Gunz quietly. He wasn't ready to leave. The powerful magical artifact was truly missing. Milana was MIA. And he didn't want to leave neither Karma nor Angel behind.

Veles and Chernobog exchanged a quick look, and both laughed.

"You still think this boy is capable of stealing anything from you?" asked Veles, still chuckling. "Like I said—he's innocent in all this. Your cold-hearted wife was wrong."

Chernobog nodded and his eyes stopped on Gunz. A smile curved his lips as he stared at him.

"The mage lied to you, Child of Fire," explained Chernobog.

"No one can pull you out of the Dark Nav. It's impossible. There are no doors in or out of here, except the gates that only I can open. Veles and I are the only two gods who can let you out of here. Well, my wife can also move between Yav and Nav, of course. Anyway, you can safely activate this rune—trust me, nothing will happen to you."

"No doors?" mumbled Karma. This was the first time she had spoken since Chernobog teleported them into this room. "I thought there was some kind of backdoor to Yav, that you built for your wife..."

"Backdoor?" repeated Chernobog, shaking his head. "There is no such thing."

Karma looked at Gunz, her eyes wide with worry. "Then where is Milana? She was sure that there was a backdoor in your palace that led to the outside world."

"I assure you, witch," replied Chernobog coldly, "if there was such a door, I would know. Nothing can be hidden from me in my realm. And as far as your girlfriend, Milana, I can also guarantee that she is no longer in the Dark Nav."

Karma's eyes swam with tears and she silently averted her gaze. Gunz sighed. He had no choice but to trust Veles and Chernobog. And the only way to see if they were right was to activate the rune and see what would happen.

Like in response to Gunz's thoughts, Angel softly touched his shoulder and said, "Zane, activate the rune. Let's see if this mage lied to you."

Gunz held out his hand. *"Ignius,"* he whispered, and right away weak flickering flames wrapped around his fingers. Gently he pressed his hand over the rune and send the fire through it.

At first, nothing happened. A few seconds later, blinding pain erupted in his brain. He wrapped his arms around his head, bending forward. Everything went black and Agent Zvereva's face emerged from the darkness.

"Why are you using the rune, Salamander?" she asked frostily, her mouth twisted with arrogance and distaste. "I'm positive you don't have the artifact."

"I thought you... couldn't... communicate..." Gunz managed to say.

The mage laughed, and his anguish increased. "I can do many things," she seethed. "I can do things you can't even comprehend with your primitive mind."

"Can you... get me out of the Dark Nav?" moaned Gunz.

"Well, that's one thing I can't do." Zvereva cackled. "I was never planning to get you out of the Nav. Just like I always knew that you were not capable of getting the artifact back from Chernobog."

Her answer was so unexpected that for a moment Gunz forgot about the pain. His arms dropped and his eyes, blinded by the darkness, widened.

"Then why?" he whispered, fear twisting his guts. "Why did you need to blackmail Agent Andrews? Why did you kill Lera? Why do all these things if you knew that I couldn't do what was needed to be done?"

"Isn't it obvious?" asked Zvereva, her face hardened. "You were just a decoy, boy. You kept Chernobog and his guards busy. This rune was never supposed to pull you out of the Nav. It was suppressing your fiery presence, hiding you from Chernobog in the beginning. And when I needed him to find you, I made it glow, sending some fire through it into your eyes. Decoy—that was your only purpose. And now that I have the artifact, I need to bid my farewell. Goodbye, Child of Fire. Enjoy eternity in Chernobog's dungeons."

Zvereva's face dissolved into the darkness. The headache stopped and Gunz was able to see again. However, the use of his magic and the pain Zvereva inflicted on him took away the effect of Veles's healing. The world spun around him and he fell back on the sofa. Cold sweat covered his forehead, and he started to shiver violently. The flashbacks returned with menace and he could hardly make the difference between what was real and what was the manifestations from his past.

He felt Angel's hands squeezing his shoulders. Like through a cotton wall, he heard his voice.

"Zane!" shouted Angel and shook him slightly. "Zane, can you hear me?"

"Angel," said Gunz, "please stop… don't shake me. Hurts…"

"Zane, you must tell us everything Zvereva told you. Please, man, put yourself together for one more minute."

"Angel, Veles was right," Gunz managed to say. "She was never planning to bring me back. I was just a decoy… keeping Chernobog busy… She has the pendant…" He closed his eyes. The mingled reality was becoming too much for him to handle.

"Veles, we need to take him to the Yav," said Angel urgently. Gunz felt Angel's arm supporting his back, as he tried to pull him into the upright position. "We need to do it now. I can't have him tormented like this for another moment."

"The Horseman is right." Chernobog's voice sounded somewhere far away in Gunz's murky mind. "My apologies, Child of Fire. I knew that you were innocent, yet I let my wife put you through this terrible ordeal."

"Karma…" whispered Gunz without opening his eyes.

"I'm coming with you, Zane. I'm here." He felt Karma's cold fingers finding his hand.

"Brace yourselves," said Veles. "I'm going to take all of you to the Land of Dreams. We'll use the World Tree passage and the voyage might be a little bumpy. Brother, I'll see you soon. We need to get ready. A deadly war is coming."

Gunz felt Angel pulling him to his feet, providing him the support of his shoulder and Karma holding him from his other side. Veles snapped his fingers, and the ground disappeared from under his feet.

20

~ ZANE BURNS, A.K.A. GUNZ ~

After the constant darkness of the Dark Nav, the sunlight was jarring, unexpected, almost painful. It was hurting his eyes even through the closed eyelids. The elemental powers and magical energy rushed through him and Gunz squeezed Angel's shoulder, asking him to stop.

"Angel, where are we?" he whispered. "Fire... there is fire here... I need to—"

"You are in the magical nexus, the Land of Dreams," explained Angel. "You can revert now. There is more Fire here than anywhere on Earth. I know your face is swollen and you can't really see, but we are standing right next to the World Tree."

"You and Karma need to let go of me and move away," said Gunz quietly. "I'm sure you and Veles will be fine, but Karma still may get hurt by the fire—"

He didn't finish talking as the energy of fire he felt just a moment ago, suddenly tripled. His breath caught, and he cracked his swollen eyes open just a little. He could hardly see, but he didn't need his vision to recognize the Fire Elemental, his mentor, his friend and the only person in his life he had ever called *Father*.

"Father," he moaned, letting go of Angel's shoulder and stretching his hand toward Kal, "you're here... How did you know?"

"Of course, I'm here," mumbled Kal, putting his hand on Gunz's shoulder. "I came as soon as Aidan told me what happened. You didn't think I would leave you alone when you needed my help?"

Angel lowered him down to the ground. Kal squatted down next to him and placed his hand on his forehead, gently channeling the energy of Fire through him. He relaxed, feeling his strength slowly getting restored, and the fog of the flashbacks cleared from his mind. After a few minutes, Kal let go and got up.

Gunz finally was able to open his eyes and see clearly. He was lying on a wide clearing covered in tall, soft grass and wild flowers. Right above him, he saw a giant tree. Its massive root system wrapped around a solid piece of rock, disappearing into the ground. He had never seen a tree so large before. Svyatobor, Mrak Delar, Aidan and a tall man in ancient Russian armor were standing next to the rock. He stared at the man, recognizing the presence of elemental fire power in him, but he was sure that he had never met him before.

"I would suggest for everyone to move at least a few yards away and give the Salamander some space," said Kal rising. "Master Mrak Delar, even though this young lady is a witch, you should shield her."

Mrak Delar nodded and turned to Karma. "My lady," he said with a light bow, "I'm going to erect a power shield around you. It may slightly restrict your movements. Don't get alarmed. I shall keep you safe."

Karma shrugged and pursed her lips. Gunz knew exactly what she was thinking. *"Lady? How dare this master-of-whatever even think that I need the protection of a man? I don't need his goddamn shield!*" But Karma probably realized that insulting a Master of Power wasn't the smartest thing to do and she just nodded at him. Mrak Delar snapped his fingers and a dense layer of his power shield wrapped around Karma.

Svyatobor chuckled. "He's just a little Fire Gecko. He's completely harmless when it comes to us, gods. And his natural state is nothing I haven't seen before."

Kal gave him a sarcastic gaze and his thin lips stretched into a wide grin. "Sure, then stay as close to him as you possibly can," he said, waving his hand dismissively. "And the next time you're in Florida, also cross the street on a red light and play with matches. I'm sure as a tiny god of Nature, you'll be absolutely safe."

Mrak Delar chuckled, stepping back to the Alatyr Stone and leaning his back against it for support. Everyone backed away, giving Gunz some space. Even Veles respectfully stepped aside. But Svyatobor stubbornly crossed his arms and remained standing next to Kal.

"Suit yourself," muttered Kal in Svyatobor's direction and turned to Gunz. "Now revert, my boy. Let go completely, like you never did before. The dark magic you were tortured with inflicted some serious damage on your body and your mind. You need to burn it out of your system. To do it, you must let the Fire Salamander take you over completely. Don't worry, you're not going to lose your humanity."

Gunz nodded to Kal and channeled the elemental Fire. The power came immediately and easy, wrapping around him like a tender embrace of a lover, penetrating his body and soul, taking him over. Following his mentor's advice, he let go completely, surrendering to his element. As the healing energy of the Fire flooded him, exultation coursed through him. His fingers dug into the ground as every muscle in his body tensed and he screamed.

A powerful surge of fire energy spread around him, rushing through the Isle Buyan for miles. The blast was so strong that it knocked Svyatobor who was standing next to him off his feet and propelled him a few feet away. Svyatobor hit the rock with his back and lost his breath for a moment, his phosphoric eyes tearing.

A wall of fire erupted in the place where Gunz was lying down just a moment ago and when the fire subsided, a giant Fire Salamander, a golden lizard with red stripes and spots along its back, was levitating a few feet above the ground. The lizard's eyes were filled with scorching fire and small flames were running along the length of its back, all the way to the tip of its long tail.

"I can't believe it..." Veles pointed at Gunz, his glowing eyes darted from Kal and then back to Gunz. "This young man is the Great Fire Salamander. Kalidus, did you know... Never mind. Of course you knew that."

Kal approached Gunz and brushed his fingers over his flaming back. "Come back to me, my son," he said with a soft smile.

Gunz let go of the power, slowly assuming his human appearance. He felt strong and recharged like he never felt after reverting into his natural state before. Usually, he still was tired and weak, but not now. The pain was gone. The flashbacks disappeared completely. Unfortunately, his clothes were also gone, burnt by the fire. All the clothes he normally wore, were fireproofed by a spell Mrak Delar taught him a while ago. But the rags that Karma got for him in the Dark Nav was nothing but that—useless rags.

Gunz became aware of his state of undress and gasped, stepping behind Kal. Angel took his trench coat off and threw it over Gunz's shoulders, which he gratefully accepted. As he was buttoning up the coat, Gunz noticed that all the scars were gone from his body. Only in the place where Agent Zvereva placed her cursed rune were there thin white lines in the shape of that rune.

Kal touched his chest, tracing the shape of the white lines with his fingers. "Scars left by magic never disappear," he muttered and slipped a heavy gaze at Mrak Delar. "Am I right, Ancient Master?"

For a split-second, Mrak Delar's face became ashen, but he quickly collected himself and cleared his throat. "Yes, Great Salamander," he replied quietly. "That's true."

The tall man whom Gunz couldn't recognize came closer and offered his hand for a handshake.

"My name is Semargl, Great Fire Salamander," he said, giving Gunz's hand a firm shake.

"Slavic god of Fire," said Gunz, observing the man with interest. "It's an honor to meet you, sir."

"The honor is mine. It's not every day a Great Fire Salamander is born," said Semargl, a smile hiding beneath his flaming mustache. "I am glad you are all right. Dark Nav is not gentle with our kind. However, you are safe now and it is time for me to leave. If you ever need me, you know how to summon me."

Semargl waved his hand unfolding the fire curtain of his portal and walked through it, disappearing on the other side. Once Semargl was gone, Veles spoke up, pushing Kal lightly on his shoulder.

"So, your little one is the Great Fire Lizard, eh?" he said with a lopsided smirk that didn't seem to fit his overall grizzly appearance. Kal nodded and Veles continued, his face cold and serious once more, "I do not have much time. I believe war is coming and my brother Chernobog and I will need your help if we stand a chance of winning it. We'll need all of you fighting on our side."

"War?" asked Aidan. "Am I missing something?"

"Aodh mac Lir," said Veles inclining his head, "I'm glad to see you here, god of the Otherworld. I will need you to tell everything I'm going to say right now to the Lord of the Wild Hunt, Gwyn ap Nudd. And the answer to your question is yes. You are missing something. So are all your friends."

Gunz exchanged an uneasy look with Karma and Angel. But they were just as puzzled as he was. Kal frowned and put his hand on Gunz's shoulder, like he was trying to protect him from what was coming. Mrak Delar's hand moved down to the black long sword at his belt and he frowned. The energy of his elemental power spiked up around him, coloring his eyes black, betraying his true emotional state.

"What are we missing, Great Veles?" asked Aidan.

"The pendant that was stolen. Young Salamander, do you know what this pendant was?" asked Veles, raising his hand up to pet a large black bird that was nestled on his shoulder. The bird produced a screeching *kraa* and shifted closer to Veles' cheek.

"The mage never told me what this artifact was or what kind of magical properties it possessed," replied Gunz, observing the bird with interest, wondering how he didn't notice it before.

"The Axe of Perun," replied Veles. "That's what it was—"

"No!" exclaimed Mrak Delar, taking a step forward. "No, it can't be. In 1812, I personally entrusted a young Guardian witch, Countess Anastasia Demidova, with the safekeeping of the pendant. How did it end up in Chernobog's possession? She was supposed to guard it for as long as she could and then pass it to the next worthy Guardian of her choosing."

"Countess Demidova was the one who summoned Chernobog and delivered the Axe to him," explained Veles. "She believed that the location of the pendant was compromised, and that she no longer could protect it. She was an elderly woman at that time and she didn't trust anyone in the Order, including her own daughter. She strongly believed that Chernobog was the only god of Slavic pantheon who needed it the most and had the best chance of keeping it safe."

"On no, it's worse than I expected," muttered Mrak Delar. "For a few months, I was sensing some disturbance beneath. I could feel it even in Kendral. But I never thought..." His voice trailed off, and he felt silent. The storm gathered around the World Tree and lightning split the sky. Masters of Power were able to control the weather and the quickly gathering storm showed that the turmoil of Mrak Delar's emotions was affecting his control of the power.

"Gwyn ap Nudd mentioned something along those lines too —disturbance beneath, something dark rising," said Kal, frowning. "Mrak, why didn't you say something to me?"

Mrak just shook his head and didn't reply. The Ancient Master was showing signs of distress and fear. Mrak Delar went through many wars—human and magical, torture and slavery, but he never showed any fear no matter what he had to face. This behavior was so unlike him that Gunz felt chills running down his spine.

"Kal, Mrak, can someone please explain to me what's going?" asked Gunz, throwing his hands in the air.

"I can try," said Veles with a sigh. For a moment, the ancient god appeared tired and despondent. "I do not have time to spare, but you need to understand. The Axe of Perun is a powerful magical object. It is a weapon like nothing you have ever seen in your short life, young one. Perun, the god of Thunder wielded this weapon in his fight with Skiper-Zmey, the Lord of Chaos.

"It happened quite a few thousand years ago. I doubt even Kalidus is old enough to remember those dreadful days. The Lord of Chaos ruled this realm. Terrible times, indeed." Veles shook his head, his bushy eyebrows gathering above his blazing eyes in a frown. "Skiper-Zmey captured Perun and held him captive in chains for three hundred years. And when his brothers finally freed him, Perun used his Axe to fight the Lord of Chaos.

"To make a long story short, Perun defeated Skiper-Zmey. Him and his brothers confined the Lord of Chaos inside a large oak coffin, restraining him with heavy chains, sealed the coffin with cold iron, and buried it in a sacred location. I placed the enchantment on the place myself. For three hundred and three years, Skiper-Zmey remains in his enchanted sleep, dead to the world. But as a part of his punishment, every three hundred and three years Zmey awakens. He recalls his defeat and thrashes around in his coffin, unable to break his chains and free himself. After three days, he falls back into his enchanted sleep.

"Only the Axe of Perun can destroy the coffin and break the chains that hold the Lord of Chaos. This is the only weapon in this world or any other world that can set Zmey free. And now it is missing. Right at the time when the Lord of Chaos is supposed to wake up."

"I'm sorry, but it just so—," said Gunz, stopping himself from using a word that would offend the powerful Slavic deity. It wasn't news to him that all serious spells and enchantments always had some disclaimers in tiny letters attached to them. But some of the ancient enchantments were done in a way that was just inviting trouble to happen. "Why would you place an enchantment that wakes this pure evil up? Why not just destroy him. Or at least keep him in his enchanted sleep forever?"

"You are very young, Child of Fire, and I will forgive you your insolence," said Veles, pinning Gunz with his calm gaze and his icy eyes darted to Kal. "Kalidus, you must teach him our ways. Your son is extremely powerful, and he would do well to understand the balance between good and evil in this world and how it works." Then he turned back to Gunz and continued, "Besides the fact that I had to preserve the natural balance, my enchantment was the worst punishment I could inflict upon the Lord of Chaos. He is forced to wake up and remember his shameful defeat. Feeling powerless to change anything, he repeats this cycle over and over for all eternity. What can be more agonizing for an immortal being?"

"So, you believe that this mage, Zvereva, stole the Axe of Perun to free Zmey?" asked Aidan.

"Yes, Aodh, that is exactly what I am saying," replied Veles, inclining his head. "In a few days from now, the Skiper-Zmey will wake up in his coffin and I believe that the mage will attempt to bring him back, using the Axe of Perun."

"Hold on," chimed in Svyatobor, getting up. "I thought that only Perun and those of Perun's bloodline could wield this weapon and use its full power. Unless this mage is a great-great-granddaughter of Perun, she won't be able to use it. And as far as I know, Perun didn't sleep around. Definitely not with mortal women."

"You are right, but you are also wrong, Svyatobor," said Veles with a half shrug. "The full power of the Axe is available to Perun and his blood kin only, but anyone with magic can use it to a degree. So, this mage can use the Axe to break Zmey's restraints. And we cannot allow it to happen."

"Ah... I need this missing page," muttered Aidan. "We must know more about this mage."

"Yes, Aodh, anything we can learn about her will help us fight her," agreed Veles. "In the meantime, I must go back to the Dark Nav. My brother and I must get ready."

"Wait," said Gunz. "I need to know how much time we have to get ready. When is the Skiper-Zmey supposed to wake up? You said that it was supposed to happen in a few days. How many days do we have, my lord?"

Veles slowly put his left hand on the pommel of his sword, his fingers squeezing it absentmindedly. "We do not have much time, young one," he replied, moving his arm up. The black bird stepped from his shoulder to his hand. "Only ten days. It is truly unfortunate that this year Zmey is supposed to wake up on the night of All Hallows' Eve. The night where the veil between the worlds of the living and realms of Spirits and Demons is at its weakest."

"I thought All Hallows' Eve doesn't apply to Slavic pantheon," muttered Gunz. "Svyatki is the time when all the evil spirits and demons come out to roam the Slavic realm of the living. But it's in January, not in October."

Veles smirked. "Very good, young one. But what you fail to understand is that no matter what our beliefs are and which pantheon we belong to, we live in the same realm and we all are connected. So, on the night of October 31st, the Zmey will wake up and the mage will exploit the weakness of the veil to break him free."

"Samhain…" whispered Aidan, his face lit up with a grim smirk. "The only night when Gwyn ap Nudd can walk the realms of the living."

"That's right," agreed Veles. "We'll need his help." The ancient god bent down and let the bird hop to the ground. "Voron, rise."

The bird screeched and spun in place. It disappeared in a continuous blur and a heartbeat later, Voron materialized in its place. Gunz gaped at Chernobog's right hand-man with his mouth open.

"Are you a shifter?" he mumbled.

"No, I am not," replied Voron without giving any further explanation. His eyes crinkled at the corners slightly, but his lips didn't form a smile. "I am here to create a bridge between you and the Dark Nav, so all of you can communicate easily with my lords Veles and Chernobog."

"I will get in touch with you within twenty-four hours through Voron," said Veles, nodding to Gunz.

Gunz glanced around, not sure if the god of the Three Realms was addressing him. Surrounded by ancient deities of different pantheons and the Master of Power, he was the least powerful and certainly the youngest. Why would Veles address him and not Kal, Aidan or Mrak Delar?

"Yes, I am talking to you, young one," said Veles, chuckling. "It is you whom the mage chose and tried to dispose of. Something about you makes her... um... uneasy. So, try to learn everything you can about this mage and get ready. A deadly battle is coming, and we cannot afford losing it."

Veles snapped his fingers and vanished from the Isle Buyan.

21

~ ZANE BURNS, A.K.A. GUNZ ~

As soon as Veles was gone, Gunz sighed with relief. He didn't know why, but the ancient deity was making him feel uneasy. He couldn't explain it. Veles was nothing but kind and respectful to him. He saved him, releasing him from the ice prison, and protected him from Morena. Even though Voron was still here, standing right next to him, Chernobog's right-hand man wasn't giving him the same vibe as Veles.

Gunz observed his friends, his eyes shifting from face to face, stopping on Aidan. He smiled, watching Aidan, Svyatobor and Angel. Aidan was trying to tell them something, but Angel and Svyatobor were ignoring him, bickering with each other. It was such a familiar and peaceful picture that for a moment Gunz forgot why they were here and felt like he was back home in Florida.

"Thank you, guys," he said, walking up to his friends. All three of them turned around at once.

"Thank you?" repeated Svyatobor snickering. "You know that you owe me now, Fire Gecko, right? And I don't sell my services cheap."

"Aw, shut up," said Angel, chuckling. "You're not the one who had to go down to the Dark Nav and meet with the god of Destruction."

"Shut up, both of you," interrupted Aidan. "Gunz, with everything that's going on, I'm just glad to see you in one piece. No gratitude required. You would do the same and more for anyone of us."

All of a sudden, Aidan stilled and looked up, his eyes swirling with white and silver light. A moment later, a soft smile lit up his face and his eyes returned to their normal blue color.

"Gunz, I have to leave now. Are you coming home with me?" he asked, his voice still sounding a little distant.

"No," replied Gunz. "I need to talk to Kal first."

"Who was it? Gwyn?" asked Kal.

"Yes," confirmed Aidan. "Gwyn ap Nudd is back, and he is summoning me. I must go back to my school and open the window to the Otherworld. He's waiting for me. Would you like to speak with him?"

"Not yet, I still need to have a word with my son," said Kal, putting his hand on Gunz's shoulder. "Go ahead, Aidan, talk to Gwyn. I hope he was able to get that missing page. Gunz will get in touch with you as soon as he gets home."

Aidan bowed to Kal and Mrak Delar respectfully and said his goodbyes to Voron and Karma. After that he put his hands on Svyatobor's and Angel's shoulders and they vanished from the Isle. Gunz walked to the Alatyr Stone, stopping in front of the Master of Power, who was sitting on the ground, his arms resting atop his bent knees.

"Master Mrak Delar," said Gunz bowing to him, "may I ask you for a favor?"

"Yes, young Salamander," replied Mrak Delar, rising. "What can I do for you?"

"Can you please take Karma and Voron to my house in Coral Springs?" asked Gunz, sending a guilty look in Karma's direction. "I lost my keys, but you can—"

"I am a Master of Power," replied Mrak, chuckling. "Trust me, I don't need a key to open your house. I'll take them to your house and stay with them until you're back home."

"Thank you, Master," said Gunz bowing to him.

Mrak Delar approached Voron and Karma ready to teleport them out of the Isle, but Karma raised her hand, asking him to wait. She came closer to Gunz, a guilty look on her face.

"Zane, I can't go," she said quietly, taking his hand into hers. "I'm sorry, but I can't leave the Land of Dreams. I need to find Milana. She has to be somewhere in the Dark Nav. She couldn't just disappear without a trace."

Gunz bit his lip, shaking his head slightly. "Karma, Chernobog himself said that Milana is not in the Dark Nav. He would know if she was—"

"And when did you start believing Chernobog?" snapped Karma. "Was it before or after he ordered you flogged and allowed his wife to torture you? You firetwat!"

Gunz sighed. The old Karma was back, armed with sarcasm and dangerous. "Karma, you said it yourself—Chernobog is the Nav. He would know if Milana was there and I don't see a reason for him to lie to us. How about we make a deal? Let's sort out this little problem with the Lord of Chaos rising and once it is all over, I'll help you find Milana. Deal?"

Karma sighed. "I hate to admit it, but you're right... The end of the world kind of takes priority here. But once it's all over, assuming we succeed and all of us are still alive, you're my errand-boy until we find Milana. No ifs, ands or buts."

"Done," said Gunz, sealing their deal with a handshake. Then he tapped his watch with his finger, asking Mishka to come out. The wyvern burst out of the watch and expanded his wings. He was back to normal—his eyes shining with the energy of fire and his wings golden once again.

"Don't say a word, boss," said Mishka, landing on Gunz's

shoulder. "I'm going with the Master of Power and will keep your guests entertained until you come back home."

"Thank you, my friend," said Gunz, gently petting wyvern's golden wings with his fingers. He was happy to see that Mishka was alive and well, worried about what happened to the wyvern when Morena was torturing him. "I'll see you soon."

For a moment, Mishka wrapped his wings around Gunz's neck and then flew over to Mrak Delar's shoulder. Voron put his hand on Mrak's shoulder. The Master took Karma's elbow and snapped his fingers. All four of them vanished from the Isle, leaving Gunz alone with Kal.

Kal lowered himself down to the ground, resting his back against the stone. He didn't say anything, just dropped his head down. Gunz sat down next to him, staring straight forward.

"You didn't tell me," he whispered. "Why didn't you warn me, Kal?"

Kal didn't reply right away. "I didn't know," he said after a moment. "I am sorry. I had no idea that someone would use this ancient torture on you, a modern man. I could never imagine—" Gunz didn't interrupt him, but Kal abruptly stopped talking and turned away.

"It was... unbearable," said Gunz quietly. "I thought I was losing my mind. The physical pain—I could deal with it. But the flashbacks, the memories I didn't know I had... Kal, I saw my biological father dying. He was killed when I was less than two years old. And all the memories from the war, my friends being shot, blown to pieces, dying and suffering. And it wasn't just memories. It was so real... the sounds, the smells, the pain... I was reliving it all, over and over, repeating the worst moments of my life in an infinite loop. Kal, I was praying for death and it wasn't coming... You told me about the pain of this torture, but why didn't you warn me about the mental anguish of it?"

Kal didn't reply, still looking away from Gunz.

"Father! Why?" demanded Gunz louder, muscle working in his jaw.

Kal turned around and Gunz shuddered from the pained expression on his mentor's face. Tears, liquid fire, were silently sliding from his fiery eyes.

"In your short twenty-eight years of life, you saw and suffered more than some people during the course of their full life. I am sorry, my boy," said Kal, his voice hoarse. "That's all I can say. You're right. I should have told you everything. I don't know why I didn't. Maybe I was trying to protect you, spare you from the knowledge that something so awful could happen to you?"

"Father..."

"I made a mistake, and you paid for it," continued Kal, shaking his head. "I know that the torture wouldn't get any easier if you knew, but at least you would be ready for it."

"I don't know how long she tortured me—a few minutes or a few hours. But you," said Gunz, feeling numb all over, "you suffered like this for centuries? How did you survive it?"

"I don't know," replied Kal with a sigh. "In the beginning I thought that any minute she would walk in and set me free. With all our differences, I loved her more than life itself. But she never came back for me. The hate took the place of love and the only thing that kept me going was the burning desire for vengeance." Kal silenced and shook his head slightly like he was trying to get rid of those painful memories. "Anyway, this wasn't what I wanted to talk with you about."

"This was what *I* wanted to talk with you about," said Gunz, turning away from Kal. "Promise me that you will tell me everything about being the Fire Salamander. Good and bad. Swear on your power that you will never hide anything from me, Father."

"You have my word, son. I will never hide anything from you again. I'll tell you everything and I'll teach you everything I know," said Kal rising, offering him his hand. "I swear on my power."

"Thank you, Father." Gunz took Kal's hand and got up.

"Now, let's do what needs to be done," said Kal. Turning toward the World Tree, he waved his hand, sending some of his fire energy through it and shouted, "Alkonost! Sirin! Come back down, girls. I know you were listening."

The rich greenery of the World Tree parted, and two giant beautiful birds with heads of young women emerged, settling on the lowest branches of the Tree. The white one sat on the day side of the Tree and the dark one took place on the evening side, the rich feathers of her electric-blue and black tail swaying in the light breeze.

"You see? I told you! The Great Salamander loves us. He even stayed behind with his son to talk to us. He's our best friend," said the white bird happy, her fluffy feathers surrounding her tender face in a soft white cloud.

"Sure, he loves us," replied the dark bird. "Friendship of convenience. He needs something from us. This is why he is here."

"Oh, come on, Sirin," said the white bird, throwing her wings up. "Can you be positive for one minute? Look how cute they are—loving Father and Son. What can be more precious? Let's help them."

"Positive? Why not," replied Sirin, snickering. "I'm all positivity. Father and Son. Father lied to his Son and his Son almost kicked the bucket because of that. What can be cuter than that?"

Kal chuckled. "Ignore them, Gunz. They are harmless if you pay no attention to their sibling rivalry. Alkonost sees only positive in everything and Sirin always picks the negative side. But if you force them to talk together, you may get to the truth of things." He extended his hand toward the birds and whispered a spell in Dragon tongue, *"Veritatius Revelare."*

The birds came closer together, Alkonost draping her snow-white wing over Sirin's shoulder and both inclined forward slightly.

"Great Salamander," said Alkonost and Sirin in one voice, "what would you like to know?"

"I need to know what's coming," said Kal. "A great evil is stirring beneath. Tell me what to expect."

Both birds sighed, Sirin's blue eyes filled with clear tears that were sparkling in the light of the moon like small diamonds.

"The Serpent shall rise in the world beneath on the night when death and evil runs amok the human realms freely," sung both birds in unison.

"The veil shall shutter and fall apart, and the realm of the dead will collide with the realm of the living.

"The bloody shadow shall overcast the sun and the moon, and the world shall fall into chaos of darkness."

The birds fell silent and both Kal and Gunz stood frozen, horrified by the terrible prophesy. After a moment Kal cleared his throat, wiping cold sweat off his forehead with the back of his hand.

"What can we do to stop this prophesy from becoming a reality?" he asked quietly.

"Alone you can do nothing!" exclaimed both birds at the same time, opening their wide wings. "The ancient gods of different pantheons, the Master of Power, humans, and witches and the creatures of elements must come together as a united front to overthrow this prophesy.

"Only working together as one you stand a chance of taming the Serpent, sending him back into the grave he came from. Only together may you survive the battle and claim victory.

"There will be a betrayal that no one could see. And there will be a sacrifice that no one expected.

"The price will be high... Too high for some... But it must be paid..."

The birds stopped talking and separated, Alkonost returning

to the day side of the Tree and Sirin moving to the evening side. They looked at each other and without saying another word flew up and disappeared in the upper branches of the Tree.

"Kal, what the hell was that?" asked Gunz, his heart pounding somewhere in his throat. "What were they talking about? What price?"

"That was the prophesy of Skiper-Zmey rising on Samhain," replied Kal and pushed Gunz slightly on his shoulder. "Snap out of it, son. They didn't say anything Veles didn't tell us already."

"I know," said Gunz, "but somehow they sounded a lot more terrifying than Veles."

"I've heard enough prophesies and they all sound like the end of the world is coming." He scratched his head, messing up his flaming hair, sending a few bright sparks into the air. "Well, in this case, the end of world possibly is coming. Anyway, you can ask Mrak Delar. He had a prophesy written about him personally. And it also sounded like the end of the world. Yet he is still here."

"The price will be high," Gunz repeated the words of the prophesy shrugging his shoulders. "No matter how high the price will be, we have no choice but to fight this battle. We can't let that Serpent rise and take over the world."

"That's right," said Kal, chuckling. "We have a whole ten days to get ready. We should have no problem whatsoever."

Kal waved his hand, opened his fire-portal and walked through it, pulling Gunz with him.

22

~ AIDAN ~

Still feeling the soft ping of Gwyn ap Nudd's summoning call in his head, Aidan rushed through the dojang and quickly drew the rune on the mirror, infusing it with his power. The mirror opened up into the communication window immediately and this time Gwyn was ready, standing in front of the thin glass wall of the spell that separated them.

"Aidan, my boy," said Gwyn ap Nudd, placing his both hands on the window.

There was something in his voice that made Aidan's blood run cold. Immediately alert, he took in Gwyn ap Nudd's appearance. There was no doubt, his mentor was concerned, almost to the point of fear. His sharply angled cat eyes were swirling with the white light of his magic and his black eyebrows were connected above his eyes, creating a sharp crease that was cutting through his tall forehead. His lips were slightly opened, and his chest was rising and falling with heavy breaths.

"Gwyn, are you okay?" asked Aidan, placing his palm on the window against Gwyn's hand. "I can see that something troubles you. What did you find out?"

"Nothing good," replied Gwyn ap Nudd, his arms dropping

down. "I met with the Destiny Council and surprisingly they cooperated. They showed me their Book of Words and it was intact. However, they had no idea that something was going on in the realm of humans. Even the Destiny Keepers who visit your world all the time had no idea."

"Well, that's highly unusual," mumbled Aidan. "Usually they know everything."

"They thought someone was messing around with their communication channels. They started an investigation and asked me for assistance, but I said no," continued Gwyn ap Nudd. "I believe I'll be needed here more than there."

"You're right," agreed Aidan. "I'll explain everything in a minute, but first, tell me what was on that page."

Gwyn waved his hand, and a chair materialized in front of the window. He sat down, resting his elbows on his knees and leaned forward, covering his face with his hands. His long black hair fell over his eyes, but he didn't bother brushing it off. He remained silent for a moment and then raised his face.

"Everything I feared," replied Gwyn ap Nudd. "All the information that the Guardians had on this mage was on the page that was stolen. There could be no mistake—it's her, because both sides of the missing page were devoted to the same person. After I read it, I had no doubt of her intentions or why she stole this page."

"Go on," said Aidan through his clenched teeth.

"This woman was a Guardian mage, seventh level," continued Gwyn ap Nudd. "Not too many witches can reach this level of skill even by the end of their very long lives. And that makes her extremely dangerous. She is over a hundred years old. She's knowledgeable and experienced in many different branches of magic, including the forbidden branches like necromancy, conjuration and maleficium."

"Goddamnit," cursed Aidan, raking his fingers through his

hair. "Are you saying that we're dealing with a master of Dark Arts?"

"You got it."

"I thought the Guardians were the good guys," said Aidan. "How did they tolerate such a high-ranking member doing such illegal things."

"They didn't. She was playing her dirty games for a while. But you know how it is. You can't hide your true nature forever," explained Gwyn ap Nudd. "One day, she was caught with a group of followers, doing some kind of blood-sacrifice ritual. The Guardians were able to block her magic and confine her to their dungeons where she was supposed to remain, awaiting the Destiny Council trial."

Gwyn grimaced, like the words *'Destiny Council Trial'* were giving him a bad taste in his mouth.

"Let me guess," said Aidan. Suddenly feeling worn out, he sat down on the mats in front of the window. "The trial never happened."

"Good guess," replied Gwyn ap Nudd. "Some young witch who was never suspected in practicing Dark Arts, helped her escape. Her name wasn't mentioned in the Book of Words. Anyway, she disappeared, and no one has heard of her until now."

"Needless to say, Zvereva is not her true name," murmured Aidan, more to himself than to his mentor.

Gwyn ap Nudd arched his eyebrows. "Was there ever a doubt?" He chuckled, leaning forward slightly. "Her real name is Valeria Demidova."

"Dammit!" Aidan slammed his hand on the soft mat. "That's the name Mrak Delar mentioned. He said something about Countess Demidova being the guardian of the Axe of Perun. I don't understand."

"You don't understand because you don't know everything yet," explained Gwyn ap Nudd. "Valeria Demidova was the only daughter of Countess Demidova of whom Mrak Delar was speaking. Come closer, Aidan. There is something you need to see."

Aidan got up and approached the window. Silently he watched Gwyn ap Nudd disappearing into the darkness for a moment. He returned a few seconds later and held out his hand. A crystal orb was resting in the palm of his hand. The orb was filled with silvery liquid that resembled mercury. Gwyn touched the orb and whispered a short spell. The silvery liquid inside the orb swirled around and then stilled, creating a smooth reflective surface.

"Now watch," whispered Gwyn ap Nudd and touched the orb again, sending a small amount of his magic through it.

The surface inside the orb lit up with a soft silvery light and an image of a semi-dark room materialized before their eyes. An old woman was lying on a narrow bed. Her weather-beaten face was crossed by a web of wrinkles. Her eyes, surrounded by dark circles, looked too large for her face. Her thin gray hair was scattered in limp strands around her face. With her sunken cheeks and colorless lips, she looked like she was half way through the veil already.

A young woman was sitting on the edge of the bed, holding the old woman's skinny hand in hers. She leaned forward and gently removed a loose strand of hair off her face.

"Mama, why don't you allow me to heal you?" asked the young woman, true concern ringing in her voice.

"There is no more healing for me, Valeria. It's my time to go," replied the old woman, hardly moving her lips. She turned away from her daughter and sighed.

"Why, Mama? You know that I can do it. I can heal you," objected Valeria. "I have the power!"

The dying woman turned her head to her daughter and revulsion mixed in with deep disappointment reflected in her pale eyes.

"Don't you dare touch me with your—," she started to say, but a heavy cough rattled her chest and she had to stop. The coughing fit left her weaker and more exhausted than she was before. She slowly picked up a handkerchief, wiped a thin pink layer off her lips and continued, now her voice almost a whisper, "Do not touch me with your healing. Even when you're not wielding your dark magic, I can feel its presence within you. I can see the darkness within your soul, coiling like a serpent..."

"What are you talking about, Mama?" said the young woman, her fingers forming a fist. "I'm a good witch. My magic is strong—"

"You gave in to the darkness and now there is no way back." The old woman pulled her hand away from her daughter's grip. Her hand slowly traveled to her chest, her fingers moving up and down like she was searching for something.

"Mama, I don't know what darkness you see in me. If you don't want me to heal you, I understand," said the young woman quietly. "At least allow me to fulfill my duty to you and to the Guardians."

"Do not lie to yourself, child," wheezed the old woman, breathing laboriously. "Once the darkness takes hold of one's soul, there is no way to expel it. You can lie to yourself all you want. You can even deceit others with magic. But the truth is still there, no matter how much you try concealing it. I do not trust you and will not give it to you. You are not worthy..."

The last few words she pronounced slowly and clearly, with added strength in her trembling voice. The young woman rose, her face hardened, her expression changing from concern to icy arrogance.

"You're dying, Mother," she seethed. "Who is going to protect the pendant after you're dead? Give it to me! I will keep it safe!"

"The darkness will never have it..."

"You're crazy! Delusional! There is no darkness! Give it to

me at once!" yelled Valeria, her eyes glowing with the poisonous yellow energy of her dark magic.

The old woman gasped, raising her shaking hand up like she was trying to shield herself from her daughter's malignant gaze.

"It's no longer in my possession," she whispered. "Someone who's a lot more powerful than you is guarding it now. I trust that he'll protect it from the darkness and the likes of you, Valeria."

Valeria seized her dying mother's shirt, almost lifting her off her bed. "Who is he?" she shouted, her face just inches away from her mother's.

"You'll never know... I'll die before I tell you anything."

"I! AM! A GOOD! WITCH!" shouted the young woman.

She let go, dropping her mother on her bed like a worthless pile of rags and grabbed her pillow. For a moment she stared at the pillow in her hands, shaking with fury. Then she lowered the pillow down, pressing it over the face of her dying mother. The old woman thrashed feebly, struggling for the last breaths of her almost extinguished life. A couple of minutes later, she stilled, but Valeria was still holding the pillow over her face.

"I'm a good witch," she kept repeating over and over, staring down at the body of her dead mother.

Circles spread over the mercurial liquid inside the crystal orb and the image disappeared. Aidan stood silent, horrified. Over thousands of years of his life he saw evil in all sorts of shapes and forms, and yet he felt shaken to the core by everything he just witnessed.

"Is that—?" he exhaled.

"Yes," replied Gwyn ap Nudd. "That was the daughter of Countess Demidova. Valeria Demidova."

"Did she—"

"Yes, she murdered her dying mother in cold blood," said Gwyn ap Nudd. "And this woman is the mage you're dealing with. The mage you will have to face soon in battle. Your adversary."

Aidan swallowed hard, staring at his mentor. "How did you come by this... whatever this was?"

"A memory. It was someone's memory," said Gwyn ap Nudd, twirling the crystal orb in his fingers. "Someone stored it in the Destiny Council archives."

Aidan rested his forehead against the cold surface of the window and sighed. "Father, you have no idea how much I wish to be home right now." Even though he loved and respected his mentor as father, he hardly ever called him that.

"Aidan," Gwyn ap Nudd called him, a sad smile hiding under his black mustache, "are you afraid of what's coming, my boy? You can tell me, there is no shame in that. The Lord of Chaos is rising and stopping him is not going to be easy. The fight will be brutal and deadly. Not all of us will survive it. I know I'm terrified of what may happen if we lose this fight."

Aidan dropped his head. "I don't know," he said quietly. "I don't know if I'm scared or angry or tired. I don't think I feel anything at the moment. The Zmey will be rising on Samhain, Father... I was wondering if you would—"

"Wondering? You have to ask?" Gwyn ap Nudd chuckled, running his fingers over the window that separated him from his son. "Count me in. Wouldn't miss this fight for the world."

Aidan smiled, feeling a slight relief from the knowledge that Gwyn ap Nudd will support them. Suddenly, he felt that the chain on his neck got warmer. Something buzzed in his ears and the world around him spun. The persistent ping of the summoning call was giving him a headache. He grunted and seized the chain on his neck ready to yank it off.

"Aidan, stop!" yelled Gwyn ap Nudd, slamming his massive fist against the window. "You can't take this chain off! What you feel is a summoning call of the Guardians. You must go, my boy. Keep me updated on everything that's going on."

Aidan nodded and touched the mirror, closing the window. For a moment he saw his own reflection and shuddered. His face was glistening with sweat and his eyes were bloodshot from the splitting headache the summoning call was giving him.

He snapped his fingers and vanished from the dojang.

23

~ ZANE BURNS, A.K.A. GUNZ ~

Kal's portal took Gunz straight to the backyard of his Coral Springs house. Kal didn't go with him and returned to Kendral. With surprise, Gunz found Mrak Delar sitting on the steps next to the backdoor. As soon as he walked out of the portal, Mrak got up and greeted him with a tired smile.

"Your guests are asleep," said the Master of Power, opening the door and letting Gunz inside. "Karma is a handful, is she not?" He chuckled, putting a k-cup inside the coffeemaker and gesturing for Gunz to sit down.

"Thank you, Master," said Gunz, sitting down. "Yeah, she's complicated. I still don't know who she is and what she was doing in the Land of Dreams. But she did save my life. More than once. And she is a fighter. With everything that's going on, we need everyone who can wield magic and hold a sword or a gun."

Mrak Delar touched the coffeemaker to speed up the process and a moment later placed a cup with steaming coffee in front of him. Gunz closed his eyes, inhaling the bitter-sweet scent of hot coffee. His body was healed, and his mind was more or less cleared, but he felt broken down. He took a sip of coffee and smiled at Mrak Delar over the rim of his cup.

"I missed it in the Dark Nav," he said quietly. "Not only the coffee, but this"—he waved his hand around—"you know, just sitting in the kitchen and talking to a friend. Peace... as short-lived as it is. Mrak, thank you."

Mrak Delar's obsidian eyes warmed up and a light smile curved his full lips. Gunz observed his face with interest. The Ancient Master was almost three-hundred years old, but he didn't look a day over thirty. With his raven-black long hair and attentive black eyes, he was the embodiment of a fairytale prince-charming, or at least a knight of King Arthur's court.

Walking next to him on the streets of South Florida was always a challenge. People were stopping to gape openly at him. Women were turning around to do double-takes. Well, and some men too. His male-model worthy appearance was completed by a charming but complex personality and manners of a medieval knight.

Gunz always liked and respected Mrak Delar, but he never forgot how dangerous and powerful this man truly was. Smart and sometimes a little reckless, he was afraid of nothing and was ready to step into most dangerous situations if he felt it was the right thing to do. The Ancient Master had a complicated past, but one thing Gunz knew for sure—should he ever need his help, Mrak Delar would always be there for him.

"It was my pleasure to assist you, young Salamander," said Mrak Delar. He threw a quick glance to the living room. "Voron elected to sleep on your couch in the living room. He is a true warrior, you know. I don't know what happened between you and him in the Dark Nav, but he respects you deeply."

"Nothing really happened," replied Gunz with a half-shrug. "I hardly got a chance to know him. He is loyal to Chernobog, but he tried to help me when Morena was... Like you said, he's a true warrior. I have no hard feelings toward him."

"Good to know. If you don't need me, I should get going. I miss my wife." A dreamy smile flashed through his face and quickly disappeared. "And you need to take a shower and put something on. Something other than the trench coat that belongs to Death." He laughed and got up.

"Are you trying to say that I stink and am pretty much naked?" Gunz laughed, looking down at his bare feet, covered in dirt.

A wide grin split Mrak Delar's face. "I've looked worse, trust me, and had a few occasions when I had fewer clothes to cover my body than you have right now," he said, waving his hand dismissively. "Go, you need a good night's sleep. And if anything happens, call me." The Ancient Master winked at him and vanished from the room.

Gunz finished his coffee, put the empty cup in the sink and silently moved through the living room toward the stairs, hoping not to wake Voron up. But as a trained warrior, Voron was awake as soon as Gunz stepped into the room.

"Zane," he said quietly, sitting up. "That is your name, right?"

"Yes, Voron," replied Gunz, stopping with his hand on the rail. "I'm sorry I woke you up. Go back to sleep."

"My gratitude, Zane," said Voron, slightly inclining his head. "Thank you for allowing me to stay in your home. After the way I treated you, I did not expect this kindness."

"You're a soldier. You did what you were ordered to do," replied Gunz, ready to leave. "No hard feelings here. Good night, Voron. We'll talk in the morning."

"One more moment of your time," Voron called after him and Gunz turned around to face him. "I have something that belongs to you."

He outstretched his hand and Gunz saw his Swiss Army knife in his palm. He walked back to Voron and took it.

"Thank you for returning my pocket knife," he said with a lopsided grin.

"Do not insult my intelligence, young Salamander," muttered Voron, shaking his head. "It is not a pocket knife. It is a sword. A mighty blade worthy of a great warrior."

"You're right. Sorry," whispered Gunz. "It was a gift from my Father, the Great Salamander. Thank you for returning it to me."

Voron inclined his head and lay back down, closing his eyes. Gunz walked up the stairs and quietly slipped into his room. Finally, a shower with hot water and his own bed. He took Angel's trench coat off and threw it on the chair. Then he put his knife on the stand next to his bed and headed to the bathroom.

* * *

GUNZ FELT a soft touch to his shoulder and woke up with a start, his hand immediately reaching for his Swiss Army knife. Someone's hand heavily pressed against his mouth, but he wasn't going to scream. In the darkness of the room, he saw the silhouette of a man, leaning over him with one knee on the edge of his bed.

"Do not scream," whispered the man. "I mean no harm."

Gunz recognized Voron's voice and gave him a sharp nod. Voron lifted his hand, freeing him and gestured to get up. Gunz threw the blanket to the side and softly slid off the bed, soundlessly stepping on the floor. Dressed only in his pajama pants, he found his shoes and quickly put them on. Then he grabbed the first shirt that came into his hands out of the closet and pulled it on. Voron pressed his finger to his lips and waved toward the door, asking Gunz to follow him.

On the way out of the room, Gunz grabbed his cell phone and checked the time. Five o'clock in the morning. *What the hell is going on?* As soon as he walked downstairs, he didn't have to ask. The stench of dark demonic energy washed over him, and he stilled, staring at Voron with wide-open eyes.

"You sense it too," whispered Voron, unsheathing his longsword with a thin metallic sound.

Gunz nodded. It was hard to miss. He sharpened his Salamander senses and probed the area around the house. He could feel the presence of hostile demonic energy in every direction. But the energy signature wasn't pure demonic. He felt the presence of vampires mixed in with demons, which was quite unusual.

"Demons and vampires," hissed Gunz. "Unusual. But they can't come inside. I have wards and protection spells on the house."

Voron sheathed his sword and spun in place, turning into a large raven. He flew to the kitchen and landed next to the window. Gunz carefully cracked the window open, letting the bird out. Voron came back a few minutes later. He turned back into his human form, breathing laboriously and heavily leaning on the kitchen table.

"Too many... all around," he whispered between breaths and made a circular motion with his hand. "You were right, demons and vampires... together."

"They can't come inside," repeated Gunz. "And vampires can't cross the threshold uninvited."

"You are forgetting something, Salamander," whispered Voron. "Your statement about the threshold would be true if you were human or even a Wizard. You are not human. Not since you discovered the Fire. You are the creature of Elements. They can, and they will cross your threshold uninvited, and your wards won't be able to hold such a massive attack for long."

"Dammit," Gunz swore quietly, slamming his hand on the table. "You're right."

"You are a Great Fire Salamander," said Voron. "Revert and

use your elemental power. You can burn them all to ashes in a matter of a few seconds."

Gunz shook his head. "You're forgetting that you're in the realm of the living, Voron. How many humans will be killed if I revert? I can't use my elemental power."

"How many humans will die if we leave this evil herd outside?" asked Voron. As proof of his words, they heard a loud shriek coming from the street. The voice of a woman was filled with terror.

Gunz cringed and headed toward the door, but Voron seized his arm, stopping him.

"We need to go outside and fight them," hissed Gunz.

"There are only two of us," replied Voron. "We are outmanned. Severely. We cannot win this fight."

"Three, not two."

Gunz spun around and found Karma standing in the doorway. She was still wearing pink pajamas with white poodles printed all over them that belonged to Mrak Delar's wife and didn't look too threatening, but he knew better. It didn't matter how Karma looked. She was powerful, and she was dangerous. She approached Voron and tapped him on his shoulder.

"Hey, old man, can I borrow your dagger?" she asked, pointing at the blade sheathed in the leather scabbard, attached to Voron's belt. Voron pinned her with a killer-look but unsheathed his dagger and handed it to her, holding it by the blade. Karma took the dagger, checking the balance and the comfort of the grip.

"Ready?" asked Voron, putting his hand on the door handle, ready to open it.

Voron is right, thought Gunz, sensing the amount of demonic and vampiric energy outside his house walls. *If we go outside, guns blazing, we're going to get wiped out. I wonder where all these vampires came from and why they're working with demons.*

"Voron, wait. How many vampires are out there?" asked Gunz.

"I did not count the evil beasties," said Voron with a shrug. "But it seemed to me that there were more vampires and their toothy kind than pure demons."

"Perfect," muttered Gunz.

Pulling his cell phone out, he dialed a number. The dialing tone sounded like a church bell in the dead silence of the night. After five rings, a woman answered the phone with a short "speak".

"I need your help. My house. Now," said Gunz quietly and hung up the phone. "Ready now."

Voron opened the backdoor letting Gunz out first. Gunz walked out and stopped. It was still dark, and the coolness of the October night enveloped him. But it wasn't the cold air that made him hold his breath. The cloud of malignant evil energy invaded his senses, fogging his mind with its toxic presence. In the shadow of his backyard he saw at least twenty dark shapes. The vampires' eyes were glowing with the bloody-red light, betraying their presence and separating them from the demons.

Gunz channeled the fire, transforming his knife into the sword and the blade went up in bright flames. Adding more power, he allowed his fire to surface. His eyes burned with the scarlet light like two torches and flames wrapped around his arms. Karma and Voron stopped behind him, avoiding the smoldering heat his body was emitting.

His fire illuminated the backyard and now he could see that he was dealing with a lot more than twenty demons. Maybe they arrived from the front of the house. Demons could *shimmer*, stealthily teleporting from place to place, and vampires could move so fast that he wouldn't notice the movement. But possibly, he just miscalculated before, given the darkness, and if that was true, then there were more demons in the front of the house.

Gunz extended his arm with the sword forward, toward demons. "What are you doing here?" he growled.

The demons shifted, exchanging looks and snickered. One of them stepped forward. He was a tall man, dressed in jeans and a black shirt, with a massive sword in his hand. Gunz gave him a quick once-over, wondering what a demon was doing with a sword. Usually, they resorted to use of their dark magic and occasionally knives or guns.

"We're here for you, Child of Fire," shouted the demon, pointing at Gunz with his sword. "Come with us and we will let your friends leave with their lives."

Gunz chuckled, channeling more fire, now his whole body ablaze. "Do you know how many times I've heard that one, dumbass? You would think that by now your kind would come up with a new line."

"Why change something that has been working for years?" The demon shrugged, a menacing smirk spreading on his face. "You're a cocky little lizard, aren't you?" he seethed, taking a step forward. "But before you get too smart for your own good, look around." He waved, pointing with his sword above Gunz's head.

Gunz pivoted around and glanced up. At least ten vampires were standing on the roof of the house, staring down at them, carnivorous red light glowing in their eyes. More demons were arriving, grouping outside the fence. They were surrounded in a tight circle and the monsters were holding higher ground. *Shit, what do we do?*

"I hope you are not considering going with this distinguished crowd," said Voron. He calmly observed the wall of demons and then turned around to check the roof.

"Any better ideas?" hissed Gunz.

"Yes," replied Voron, pulling his sword out. "We fight!"

The air around Voron shimmered as he started the transformation. But this time he transformed only partially. He still looked like a man and was his normal height, but giant raven's wings sprung out behind his back. He pushed off the ground and flew up to the rooftop, swinging his longsword as he did it.

Who the hell is this man? A thought flashed through Gunz's mind, but he had no time to contemplate on it. "Mishka," he shouted, and the wyvern materialized in front of him. "You're with Karma. Take care of her!"

Then he grabbed Karma's arm, pushing her slightly behind as he moved toward the demons. "Stay behind me and watch your neck! Mishka will give you some fire advantage."

"I say, it's them who need to watch their necks." Karma raised Voron's dagger up and laughed coldly, her eyes blazing with the excitement of the fight. "I'm going to take this group of cuties on the left. The ugly ones on the right are all yours. Mishka, come on!"

"No, we're stronger together," shouted Gunz, but it was too late. Karma ran to the left, screaming something in Dragon tongue and jumped at the first vampire in line, cleanly cutting his head off. The wyvern followed her closely, spitting fire at the heads of the monsters.

"Ignius," shouted Gunz, spraying the first row of demons with fire.

The demons howled in pain and anger and a few dark shadows separated from the burning bodies of their hosts. The front line fell apart, shying away from the smoldering flames and Gunz used this opportunity to break deeper into their lines. He stepped into the fire, feeling refreshed by the touch of his element, and then pushed through, into the middle of the crowd. Spinning around, he swung his sword, cutting and setting on fire as many demons and vampires as he could.

His body was emitting unbearable heat and angry flames were surrounding him, protecting him from the monsters. But the more demons he obliterated and vampires he beheaded, the more were coming to stand in place of the dead monsters. They were pushing him from every direction, invading his space, ignoring the fire and the heat.

He heard Karma shouting spells and the moans of the dying monsters. That told him she was still there, fighting. Over the heads of demons that were trying to close up on him, he could see Voron dealing with the vampires on the roof.

Even though they were still holding their ground, Gunz didn't know how much longer they would be able to keep it up. Fighting at this pace was taking a lot of strength and the extensive use of magic was taking its toll. Despite the adrenalin that was surging through his body, he started to feel the signs of exhaustion. He was also sure that both Karma and Voron were getting tired too, possibly faster than he was.

Gunz felt a sharp pain in his shoulder as one of the vampires struck him with its sharp claws. He ignored the pain and swung his sword again, cleanly shaving the monster's head off his shoulders. Feeling that his sword started to get too heavy, he decided to see if he could break through the wall of monsters that surrounded him from every direction. He punched the demon on his left, and then grabbed the face of the demon in front of him with his hand, channeling the energy of the fire through him. The demon screamed and writhed but couldn't break his hold. In a heartbeat, only a steaming pile of ash was left.

Gunz saw a small opening and pushed toward it, punching and burning anyone who came across his way. As he was just a step away from freedom, something seized his legs above his ankles and pulled. He fell face-forward on the ground, losing the hold of his sword.

Ignoring the fire, another demon jumped on his back and grabbed a handful of his hair, pushing his face into the ground. Gunz grunted, struggling to regain his freedom, but it was impossible. He felt a few hands taking hold of him, twisting his arms behind his back. The demon was still holding his hair, pushing his face down, suffocating him.

He couldn't breathe and the lack of oxygen was affecting his elemental power. The fire went off in his eyes, leaving him exhausted. Somewhere on his left, he heard Karma screaming his name. He didn't know if she needed his help or she called him because she saw him falling. His lungs were burning, and he was on the verge of passing out.

Don't die... people around...

"Just take a rock and knock him out." He heard a hissing voice of a demon somewhere above his head. "Just make sure not to kill him or we are all dead."

Gunz tried to struggle again just to realize that he was completely immobilized. All of a sudden, he felt the weight on his back lighten up and he was finally able to lift his head, filling his lungs with oxygen. For a moment, the monsters abandoned him, giving him the opportunity to scramble to his knees. He found his sword and got up.

The monsters were fighting someone new, but Gunz couldn't see who it was. All he could see was the blur of bright red streaks.

24

~ ZANE BURNS, A.K.A. GUNZ ~

The army of demons trembled as the invisible fighter swept through their front lines, planting the seeds of destruction. As a majority of them turned around to face the new threat, Gunz used the opportunity to pull back and regroup. He swung his sword through the air, the heavy blade whistling softly as he did it. A few demons charged him again, and he met them, his flaming blade carrying death with every move.

A few minutes later, everything was over. While Gunz dealt with the leftover demons, his reinforcement destroyed every single vampire. Voron cleared the roof and landed next to Gunz, transforming back into his human form. His hair was drenched with sweat and his clothes were dark with blood, but as exhausted as he was, he was still standing, heavily leaning on his sword.

Karma also was done, slowly walking toward Gunz and Voron with a bloodied dagger in her hands. Mishka sat on top of her head, golden wings opened wide, winning gleam in his red eyes. Karma was covered in ashes and dirt from head to toe, her red hair in disarray. Her pink pajamas were soaked in blood, but she announced right away that the blood wasn't hers, cutting off all questions.

"Who was that?" asked Karma, searching the backyard. "Whoever it was, they were moving so fast that I couldn't see them."

"I believe it was the Scarlet Queen," answered Gunz, probing the prickling wound on his shoulder with his fingers. He turned around and shouted, "Ms. Akira Ida, show yourself. Please. Allow me to express my gratitude for your much-needed assistance."

A shadow separated from the house and Akira materialized in front of them. As usual, she was moving with lightning speed and it looked like she just popped up from thin air. She was dressed in a leather jacket and tight leather pants and was holding two of her katanas in her hands, fresh blood dripping from her blades. Unlike Gunz, Karma and Voron, she was showing no signs of tiredness. Her face was as pale as usual and not one hair was out of place on her slick ponytail.

"Thank you." Gunz bowed to her, a Japanese traditional bow as she taught him.

She touched his shoulder lightly, asking him to rise and took in his appearance. "You're hurt, Zane," she said, brushing her fingers over the wound on his shoulder. Then her eyes darted to Voron and a tiny smile lifted the corners of her lips. "Your friend is hurt too. Would you like me to heal you both?"

"As usual, thank you for your generous offer, but no," replied Gunz, shaking his head. "But allow me to introduce my friends, Karma and Voron."

Akira inclined her head in Karma's direction and her glacial eyes halted on Voron. The warrior stepped forward and kneeled before Akira, lowering his head in a courtly bow.

"Akira Ida," he said without lifting his head. "My lady, you are as breathtaking as I remember you. Time is powerless against your beauty and strength."

"And you are as charming as I remember you, Lord Voron. Please rise." Akira smiled and embraced Voron like he was her dearest friend.

Voron gently hugged her, careful not to crush her in his bearhug even though she was a vampire. "I didn't realize that the young Salamander, and you were aquatinted, my lady."

"Zane and I go way back," purred Akira, closing her angled eye in a sly wink. "He's my student. I'm teaching him swordsmanship."

"I thought some of his moves looked familiar." Voron chuckled and winced, pressing his hand to his ribs. "And where is your son, Akira? Is he still with you?"

Gunz felt a movement in the air and the presence of a vampiric energy, other than Akira's. But before he raised his sword, Akira seized his wrist, shaking her head no. A tall young man appeared next to her. His straight blond hair was falling below his shoulders and his eyes were glowing with a scarlet light, betraying his vampiric nature. His white shirt was torn on his chest and covered in dark red stains, and both his Katanas were smeared in blood.

"Mother, I took care of the filth in front of the house," he said, his voice unexpectedly soft but deep. "None of the vampires belonged to our organization."

Akira glanced at him, a mix of pride and love gleaming in her eyes just like it would in the eyes of any mother who were gazing upon her grown-up son.

"Allow me to introduce my son, Yaroslav," said Akira, putting her hand on her son's arm affectionately.

"Yaroslav?" asked Gunz, his eyebrows rising.

Akira giggled, her laughter sounding as girly as ever. "Yes, I know. The son of a Japanese vampire has an ancient Russian name. Many years ago, he was Yaroslav Potemkin, illegitimate son of Prince Potemkin. He is my only son, Zane, as I swore that

I would never create another vampire. And he is my pride and joy."

Yaroslav bent in a formal Japanese bow, his long golden hair falling over his chiseled face, but then straightened and extended his hand to Gunz. "Nice to meet you, Mr. Burns," he said, an open smile exposing his long fangs. "My mother told me a lot about you. I hope one day I'll have the honor to cross my sword with you." Then he cleared his throat uncomfortably and smiled again, his fangs retracted now. "In training, of course."

"But of course," said Gunz, squeezing his icy fingers in his hand. "I would love that, but I'm afraid that even with your mother's training, I stand no chance against you, Yaroslav."

The vampire laughed, throwing the long strands of his hair off his face and shook his head. "We'll see. And Slavik is fine. My mother loves the full name, but to me Yaroslav sounds too official."

"Slavik," repeated Gunz, thinking how inappropriate this name sounded for this old vampire, even though he looked like a twenty-year-old boy. Then he turned to Akira and waved his hand toward the house. "Akira, may I invite you and your son into my home? I think we should talk about what just happened."

"Yes," replied Akira, "we should talk."

Gunz opened the door, allowing the vampires, Voron and Karma into the house. As Karma was passing through, Mishka hopped from her head to Gunz's shoulder. The backyard was covered in dead bodies. When vampires died, they disintegrated into a pile of ashes, but demons left the dead bodies of their hosts behind.

"Mishka, my friend" said Gunz quietly, pointing at his yard that looked like a battlefield, "can you help me? I need to talk with Akira. It's important. Can you clean up my backyard for me? And check the area around the house. Yaroslav was fighting there. I hope he didn't leave any dead bodies on the street."

"Mishka the Incinerator is at your service, boss," said the wyvern, raising his wing in a salute. He flew out of the house and a moment later, Gunz saw him flying over the bodies, setting them on fire.

Gunz walked inside the living room and found Akira, sitting on the couch and discussing something with Voron. Yaroslav stood by the window, talking with Karma. She looked unusually sweet and flirty, and Gunz wondered if the vampire turned his charm on her or she actually liked him.

As soon as Akira saw him, she stopped her conversation with Voron and waved her hand at an empty chair across from the couch, inviting him to sit down. Gunz took a seat, folding his arms.

"Do you know why the demons attacked you, Zane?" asked Akira. "That was an organized attack and whoever organized it wasn't joking. They brought a bunch of demons and vampires out of state because I didn't recognize any of them."

"I am not sure," replied Gunz, "but I think someone was sending me a message. Someone knows that I escaped from the Dark Nav and wants me out of the way."

"You were in the Dark Nav?" asked Akira, her thin eyebrows climbing up. "How did you survive there? A creature of the Elements... You had to suffer greatly..." Sympathy reflected on her face, but it disappeared in a heartbeat, replaced by her usual calm and indifferent expression. "I guess, that is not important. Can you tell me what happened and how you ended up there in the first place?"

With the help of Voron and Karma, Gunz told her everything that happened in the Dark Nav and everything that Veles told them before leaving the Isle Buyan. Akira was sitting silent and motionless. Like most of the old vampires, she could remain without making the tiniest movement for a prolonged period of time. After Gunz finished talking, she glanced at her son and frowned.

"Dark times are upon us, young Salamander," she said quietly, her fingers running along the blade of her katana that was lying on the couch next to her. "I assume you and your team will attempt to stop the Lord of Chaos from rising. This is why you have Voron here. Chernobog and Veles are getting ready to defend the veil."

"Yes, ma'am," replied Gunz. "Aidan and his team, Kal and Master Mrak Delar are also with us in this fight."

Akira shook her head, narrowing her eyes into slits. "May not be enough."

"What do you mean?" asked Gunz, his chest tightened with worry.

"Whoever is behind all this... That mage, I presume. She is running a clever warfare," explained Akira. "I'm sure she will attack the city to create a diversion and split your forces. She knows you well, Zane. She's sure that you will not leave humans unprotected."

"Another thing you may want to consider is that the veil between the grave where the Zmey is chained is the weakest inside the Dark Nav," chimed in Yaroslav. "There is a chance that the mage will break the coffin in the human realm, but the Zmey will rise through the Dark Nav, tearing the veil apart. You must stop the mage before she breaks Zmey's restraints, but if you fail, you should be prepared to fight the Zmey inside the Dark Nav. You can't let him break free into the realm of the living. And you definitely can't let him destroy the veil between the two realms."

"Dammit," muttered Gunz, raking his fingers through his hair, "this attack was a test and I passed it with flying colors. Agent Zvereva wanted to see if I would revert to take care of her demons. Now she knows for sure that I wouldn't sacrifice human lives. You're right, Akira. I have to talk to Jim. He needs to be ready to defend the city on October 31st."

"Tell Agent Andrews that my son and I will patrol the city that night. He will need some supernatural reinforcement. Neither you nor Aidan McGrath with his team will be able to help him. And who knows what kind of monsters will invade the city," said Akira. "Tell him that *EverSafe Security* will stand by his side."

"Thank you, Akira," said Gunz, "I deeply appreciate it. I will talk to him later on today and fill him in on everything that's going on."

Akira got up, gathering her swords, and waved at her son to follow her.

"The sunrise is coming," said Akira airily, gazing toward the window where the first gray light of the upcoming morning was visible through the half-opened blinds. "Neither Yaroslav nor I particularly enjoy sunbathing. We must leave you now. Zane, would you kindly walk me outside?"

She bowed in her Japanese manner to Voron and Karma and headed through the kitchen toward the backdoor. Yaroslav sent one more smoldering gaze in Karma's direction but got up and followed his mother. Gunz opened the door, allowing Akira and her son to walk out into the backyard. She pulled him all the way to the other end of the backyard and stopped there.

"Zane, I know Voron for many years," she started, "and you can trust him fully. He is a man of honor. He will do the right thing, no matter the cost. However, I am not sure that you can trust Karma. She's a *Sword for Hire* and people like that are loyal only to their bank accounts."

"A Sword for Hire?" repeated Gunz incredulously.

"Yes," confirmed Akira. "You didn't know? I believe humans call people like that—an assassin. A hired gun. But in the supernatural world, we call assassins, a Sword for Hire. She is a paranormal assassin. Be careful, Zane. You cannot trust her. Swords for Hire have no honor."

Gunz grunted, rubbing his face tiredly. "No, I didn't know," he said quietly. "But so far she has not given me a reason not to trust her."

"You always see the good in people first," said Akira, shaking her head. "Innocent until proven guilty. I'm afraid, it'll be your undoing one day, my student. With the Lord of Chaos rising in ten days, you should trust no one."

Akira and Yaroslav left, but Gunz stood a few minutes, leaning against the tree, and watched the sun slowly rising, decorating the dark morning clouds with pink and yellow lining.

Trust no one...

Akira's words rang in his head and he shuddered. The war is coming, and it'll be impossible to fight it if he can't trust the people who stand by his side. Maybe Akira was right, and it would be his undoing one day.

But not today.

25

~ ZANE BURNS, A.K.A. GUNZ ~

Since Gunz had only two bathrooms in his house, he let Karma use the shower in his bedroom and went downstairs to wait for Voron to clean up, so he could take care of his wounds. Luckily, Voron's injuries weren't serious—a couple of bruised ribs and a few lacerations on his chest and back, left by vampire claws.

Karma took her sweet time and used up an unimaginable amount of hot water. By the time Gunz made it into his shower, he got drenched by water that was slightly above room temperature. He clenched his teeth, swearing up and down, and grabbed the soap from the shelf.

Halfway through his shower, he heard the doorbell. Hastily washing off shampoo from his hair, he probed the area in front of the house and smiled, recognizing Angelique's magical energy signature. Jim and Angelique were here. He quickly finished and hopped out of the shower, grabbing the towel on his way out.

He threw the wet towel on his bed, put his jeans on and pulled a shirt over his half-wet body, and then rushed downstairs. As he walked into the living room, he saw Angelique standing with her hands on her hips, fuming, and Jim who resembled a man who wanted to be a few miles away from where he was.

Karma stood by the door, dressed in nothing but a towel that was wrapped around her torso, hardly covering her shapely bottom. Voron sat on the couch, looking mildly amused.

Uh-oh. Gunz didn't have to guess why Angelique wore a murderous look. Karma's state of undress explained it all.

Cautiously, Gunz made his way to the door and stopped, catching Jim's sympathetic glance. Angelique noticed his arrival and paced toward him, throwing a killer-look at Karma as she passed her.

"Who is this woman, and what is she doing undressed in your house?" demanded Angelique, fury making her voice tremble.

"I told her I'm your friend and I have no desire to be anything more than that," replied Karma with a shrug, almost losing her towel as she did that.

Gunz turned to Karma and sighed. "Can you please get dressed, Karma? This is Agent Jim Andrews and his partner, Angelique. We need to bring them up to date on everything that's going on."

"Sure," murmured Karma, heading upstairs, "but since I don't have any clothes here, can I borrow yours?"

"Ugh!" Angelique stamped her foot, crossing her arms over her chest. "His partner? Is that what I am to you now?"

"Take anything you like in my closet," Gunz replied to Karma, wishing to become invisible this very moment.

He shook Jim's hand and introduced him to Voron. Jim proceeded inside and sat down on the couch, stretching his legs. Gunz tried to take Angelique's hand, but she jerked her hand away. He shook his head and seized her elbow, pulling her through the living room, into the kitchen and then outside, to the backyard that was freshly cleaned by Mishka.

"Angie, stop," he said attempting to hug her, but she pushed against his chest and he let her go.

"Why do you have a strange woman taking a shower in your house? Early in the morning, clothed in nothing but a towel. Your towel." She stared at him with reproach, tears gathering in her eyes.

"Angie, Karma told you the truth. She is just a friend. A friend who saved my life and who helped me survive the Dark Nav," replied Gunz quietly. "You have no reason to be jealous—"

"Me? Jealous? You think too highly of yourself, Alexander Burns!"

He chuckled, shaking his head. "This is not what I imagined our first meeting would be like," he said softly, pulling her closer, ignoring her protests. "Every moment I spent in the Dark Nav, all I could think of was coming back to you, Angie."

"I don't see a reason for you to miss me. You managed to find a suitable replacement even in the world of spirits," she replied grouchy but stopped pushing him away.

"A suitable replacement?" Gunz laughed openly. "I think not. Karma plays for the other team. She would much rather spend a night with you than with me."

Angelique flushed scarlet for a moment, but then threw her arms around his neck and fell apart, crying on his chest.

"Zane, I thought you were dead. Gone forever," she managed to say between sobs. "No one could sense you. Not even Death... I mean, Angel... And the Archangel Uriel. Not even Aidan. I thought I lost you forever..."

Gunz pulled her closer, gently stroking her hair and her back. "I'm so sorry," he whispered into her hair. "I had no way to communicate with anyone. But you know that I can't die, right? And as long as I'm alive, I'll come back to you."

He found her chin and gently lifted her wet face. Carefully he wiped her face with his fingers, covering her cheeks with kisses, feeling the salty taste of her tears on his lips.

"Don't cry, Angie. I'm here. I'm with you. Everything is going to be okay now." He lowered his face and gently kissed her.

"Everything is going to be okay? Well, that's a matter of opinion."

Gunz heard Jim's voice and unwillingly pulled away from Angelique. Jim stood in the doorway, his hands in the pockets of his pants. Karma was behind him, now dressed in Gunz's sweatpants and t-shirt.

"Besides the end of the world that's apparently coming, everything else is going to be totally fine," added Jim, with a dismissive wave of his hand. "So, you can continue with whatever it is you two were doing."

Jim pivoted on his heel and walked back inside the house. Gunz sighed and followed him, holding Angelique's hand in his. Karma giggled and winked at him as he was passing her in the doorway. Jim didn't go back to the living room but sat down at the kitchen table, slowly folding and unfolding a paper napkin.

"Voron already told me everything," said Jim as soon Gunz sat down. "I think we all have a bit of work to do."

Angelique tugged on Gunz's sleeve, raising her eyebrows.

"I'll give you all the details later," said Gunz quietly.

"No, you won't," said Jim, frowning. "I'll tell her everything she needs to know when we get back to the office. I think you need to focus on the issue at hand. From what Voron explained, you're the center of this whole operation. So, what's your plan of action, commander Burns?"

Gunz turned to Voron, throwing a surprised stare at him. "Me? Why me? Veles is the eldest, and he fought Skiper-Zmey already. Him and his brothers. He should be running the show."

"Veles said it has to be you," replied Voron, lowering himself down on a chair next to Jim. "He will get in touch with you tomorrow."

Gunz nodded. "Who am I to argue with the god of the Three Realms? Fine. I'll talk with Veles tomorrow. Also, I need to see

Aidan. He left yesterday and was supposed to meet with Gwyn ap Nudd. I haven't heard from him since then, and it's not like Aidan. He would get in touch with me whether Gwyn succeeded in restoring that missing page or not."

"Like I said, you got your hands full," noted Jim.

"You too, Jim," replied Gunz. "You need to get ready to defend the city on the night of All Hallows' Eve. I have no idea what to expect, and neither I nor Aidan is going to be here to help you. The Scarlet Queen offered her support though. At sundown, she, her son and her whole company will be patrolling the city. Make sure that your team is aware and don't hunt them."

"That's all fine and dandy, but how are we supposed to know which vampires are—I can't believe I'm saying this—which vampires are good, and which are bad. They all look the same in the dark," said Jim.

"Well, it's safe to assume that if a vampire is not trying to eat you, they are Akira's," suggested Gunz, snickering.

"Aw, a nice one, Gunz," huffed Jim, rolling his eyes. "Remember, I'm still your boss, so joke carefully."

"Is that a threat?" asked Gunz, suppressing laughter. "Don't worry, Jim. We still have nine days to get ready. I'll talk to Akira and make sure that her vamps wear something, so you can easily recognize them."

"If you told me yesterday that the day would come when I'd be relying on the Scarlet Queen's help, I would kick your ass." Jim sighed and got up, moving his chair closer to the table.

"You can trust Akira Ida," added Voron. "She is the master of her word. If she said that she will support you, rest assured—she will."

"Good to know," mumbled Jim, heading toward the exit. He stopped at the door and turned to Gunz. "Stay in touch and keep me updated." He turned to Angelique, raising his eyebrows. "Ready?"

"Jim, I'll come to the office in an hour. I want to talk to Zane," said Angelique, a vibe of discomfort lingering around her.

"Talk? Is that what you youngsters are calling it nowadays? Sorry, but you're coming with me right now," objected Jim dryly. "We all have a lot of work to do and only nine days for everything. You can *'talk'* with him all night long when all this is over."

Angelique sighed but nodded. She threw a longing gaze at Gunz and followed Jim out the door. As soon as the door closed, Gunz's phone rang. He pulled it from the back pocket of his jeans and looked at the name on the screen.

Aidan McGrath.

26

~ AIDAN ~

Aidan teleported to the Guardians HQ in Chicago. He thought he knew exactly where he was going, and he couldn't understand how he miscalculated his final destination. On arrival, he hit something hard and got thrown to the ground, face down. Between the excruciating, pounding pain in his head and the jolt of the hard fall, he blanked out for a moment.

When he regained consciousness, he found himself lying next to the main gates of the Guardians Headquarters. The ping of the summoning call was still ringing in his ears and the headache became a continuous torment. He groaned, scrambling to his feet and headed to the side of the gates, hardly able to move his legs. As he reached under his shirt to pull the pendant out, he realized that his hands were shaking.

"Please, stop the summoning call. I'm here already," hissed Aidan. He doubted that the Head Mage could hear him, but with his mind in torment, he wasn't sure that he could focus enough to use his magic and open the gate. Since there was no response to his plea, he leaned on the gate and touched it with his pendant, channeling a small amount of magic through it.

The gate screeched and moved to the side. Aidan lost his balance and dropped to the ground again. He struggled to get on all fours, when he felt someone's hands grabbing his arms and pulling him up. Two guards were standing on either side of him, holding him in the upright position.

"Stop the pain... kill the summoning call... please..."

The guards ignored his request, unceremoniously dragging him to a golf cart. By the time they reached the Assembly Hall, he was on the verge of fainting again. The guards brought him to the middle of the room and lowered him to the floor.

Aidan raised his head with an effort and saw Ms. Bonneville towering above him. She stared down at him with a cold smirk on her face.

"Welcome back, Mr. McGrath."

"Ms. Bonneville, please..." whispered Aidan, squeezing his head with his hands.

She snickered and muttered a quick spell. The relief came immediately. Slowly he got up, still feeling a little shaken and dizzy.

"I wanted your first summoning call to be special, Mr. McGrath," said the mage. She headed toward a side table, gesturing for Aidan to follow her. "You see, now you know that we're quite capable of handling insignificant old gods like yourself that still walk this world and you learned a few useful lessons—you can't ignore our summons, you can't teleport inside the Guardians Headquarters, and you can't disobey us."

Aidan dropped into the chair she offered, wiping his forehead with the back of his hand. His eyes were still watering, and his vision was slightly blurred, but he could clearly see the nasty smirk on the Head Mage's face. He knew exactly what she was doing. She wanted to make it very clear to him that even though he was a god, he was no match to her, and as long as he wore this pendant, she had him over a barrel.

"You didn't have to do it," said Aidan quietly, catching his breath. "I wasn't going to ignore your call. However, let me remind you that per our agreement, I have the right to complete my original mission first."

Ms. Bonneville tapped the table with her fingers and a small piece of paper and a pen appeared in front of her. "But of course, Mr. McGrath, that was the deal," she replied, picking the pen up. "Your original mission was to recover your missing friend, I believe. Now, correct me if I'm wrong—Mr. Zane Burns is safe in his house in South Florida. Am I right?"

"Yes, ma'am, but—"

"There are no buts, Mr. McGrath," objected the Head Mage coldly. "Your original mission has been completed. And now that we settled it, I have something I need you to do for the Guardians."

She quickly wrote something on the paper and handed it to him. Aidan took the note from her hands and peered at it. Some Buffalo Grove address was written on the paper. He raised his eyes, giving the mage a puzzled stare.

"I need you to deal with a group of rogue demons, and this is the address where I need you to go in order to find them. They settled in a highly populated residential area and that presents all sorts of problems. I need them gone," explained the mage.

"Really?" asked Aidan, crushing the paper in his fist as aggravation spiked within him. "You truly don't have a witch available that could deal with some lowlife demons? You needed to summon a god for that."

"I will attribute your rude outburst to the light headache I gave you, Mr. McGrath," drawled the Head Mage. "Let me remind you that you swore your loyalty to the Guardians Order for one year. It means that I can summon you at any time and ask you to perform any task for the Order. If I tell you I need you to clean the toilets, you do that. No questions asked. Am I clear, Mr. McGrath?"

"Yes, ma'am," said Aidan, his jaw set.

"Having said that, I didn't ask you to come here just to demonstrate my power over you," continued the Head Mage, leaning back in her chair. "Of course, I have capable witches and mages here. Any of them could deal with these demons with great success. However, I wanted *you* to take care of them because this rogue clique of demons was created as a result of your little friend Tessa's actions. It would be only right if you were the one to clean up her mess. Wouldn't you agree, Mr. McGrath?"

"Seems that you leave me no choice but to agree with you," said Aidan.

"No. No choice," confirmed the Head Mage. "Guardians, just like Wardens, are a military Order. We command, you must comply—leave your freewill outside these doors. You'll get used to it, Aidan. May I call you Aidan?"

Aidan nodded, just now realizing the full consequences of giving his oath to the Guardians. For a moment he felt slightly dizzy and disoriented, and he rubbed his eyes to clear his vision.

"I will let you take two hours of rest, Aidan," continued Ms. Bonneville. "I'm sure you're still experiencing the slight dizziness and weakness as a result of my summoning spell. It all should clear out in about an hour. You can use the room you stayed in the last time you were here. Once you feel back to normal, you should be on your way to Buffalo Grove."

Aidan got up and slowly headed toward the exit door, everything around him still flowing in a fluid sickening motion.

"And Aidan, I don't want Tessa to know that you're here," screamed the Head Mage after him. Aidan cringed and halted at the door, glaring at the mage over his shoulder. "She's been doing remarkably well, and I don't want your short visit to disrupt her progress. I hope you understand."

"I understand," said Aidan and walked out of the Assembly Hall.

He found the same small room he had been staying in with

Raoul and collapsed on the bed. Feeling demolished and slightly sick, after a few minutes, he fell asleep.

Aidan woke up an hour later and sat up on the bed. The effects of the summoning spell were gone, and he felt normal. He reached in his pocket and pulled out his phone. Quickly scrolling through his contact list, he found Zane's phone number and clicked the dial button.

"Aidan!" He heard Zane's voice and smiled, relieved.

"Zane, are you back home? Is everything okay?"

"Everything is as expected—you know, me getting attacked by an army of demons and vamps. Other than that, everything is just fine."

Aidan squeezed the bridge of his nose, processing Zane's statement. *Attacked by demons and vamps? Together?* That was highly unusual.

"Are you okay?" he asked.

"Just peachy." Zane chuckled. "And where did you disappear? You were supposed to check in as soon as you talked with Gwyn ap Nudd."

"I didn't get a chance," replied Aidan with a sigh. "The Guardians summoned me, and I couldn't ignore them. Their summoning call was blowing my brains out. I had to go right away."

"Well, now you know how I felt when you summoned me last year..."

"I did that to you?" exclaimed Aidan, horrified. "I swear I had no idea... Anyway, Zane, I can't talk. I must go and do what the Guardians ordered me to do. When I come back to Florida, I'll find you. I don't want to talk from here. These walls have ears. Since I'm surrounded by powerful witches and mages, I don't think a concealment spell would work."

He hung up his phone and walked out of the room.

* * *

AIDAN DIDN'T KNOW the area, and teleporting wasn't an option. He drove to Buffalo Grove and left the car that the Guardians gave him on a Jewel's supermarket parking lot. He followed the street through the quiet suburban neighborhood until he found the right house.

He passed the house and circled around the block to see what kind of area he was dealing with. It was past nine in the morning and most of the residents were gone to work. The street was mostly vacant with an occasional car passing through.

As a morning breeze rushed through the air, Aidan shivered, thinking that it was the second time he teleported to Chicago without any warm clothes. He also stood out, walking in the chilly October weather dressed in a short-sleeve shirt without any jacket or sweater on. Finally satisfied, he stopped in front of the house that was indicated on the Head Mage's note.

What were the supposedly rough and violent demons doing, nesting in a quiet suburban house? Aidan thought as he stood in front of the building. Usually, demons were finding housing in areas that were away from heavy human population, in industrial areas or abandoned buildings.

He pulled the note out and checked the address again. No, he didn't make a mistake. This was the house. Aidan sighed and quietly walked up to the door. As a god, he wasn't afraid of demons. Just a touch of his power would burn the demonic energy out before the demon could escape.

He scanned the house with his magical sight and found that there were at least six demons inside. He could feel clearly the presence of their demonic energy. Only six? Maybe he was missing something. He recalled the story Tessa told him. It was a meeting of two demonic factions. Missi and Tessa killed all the leaders of both factions. If the remaining demons decided to get together and create their own click, there should be a lot more than six demons there.

Aidan stood indecisively in front of the door. Something didn't add up. He glanced at his watch and sighed. He shouldn't be here now. His place was in South Florida with Gunz and his team. Dealing with the evil mage and possible rise of Skiper-Zmey seemed to be a lot more important than getting rid of six demons in suburbia.

For a moment, he was thinking about going back to HQ and telling the Head Mage about everything that was going on. After all, the Guardians were the good guys. Maybe they could assist them with that mage and her evil plans. But then he remembered Luc de la Crosse's warning and he decided against it. He had no idea who he could trust in the Guardians Order and who he couldn't. It would be a lot safer and faster if he would just clean up this nest and was on his way back home.

Aidan put his hand on the door handle and carefully turned it. The door was locked. *"Recludius,"* he whispered the opening spell and heard the soft click of the door lock. The door opened up soundlessly, and he slid inside the house.

All the blinds were tightly shut and the small area between the stairs and the living room was dark. Aidan observed the living room to make sure it was vacant. Then he opened his other sight, carefully exploring the rest of the house. He still felt the presence of only six demons and they seemed to be on the second floor.

Aidan snapped his fingers, teleporting upstairs. On the second floor, there were three bedrooms. He walked down the hallway toward the master bedroom and stopped in front of a closed door. His first thought was to knock the door out with his foot, but he changed his mind and turned the door handle. The door wasn't locked and opened easily. He walked inside the room and halted.

Six demons—two women and four men—were standing at the opposite wall, staring at him with mild surprise in their eyes. They didn't attack him at the get go and that set a red flag in Aidan's mind. *Rogue demons?* They didn't look very ferocious to him. He scanned them with his magical sight again just to confirm that the hosts of the bodies these demons were possessing were no longer there.

"You're breaking and entering," said one of the demons, stepping forward. "I already called the police."

Aidan smirked. That was a new one—demons calling police. "No, you did not," he replied calmly. "This house, just like the body you're wearing, doesn't belong to you. To either of you."

He heard a soft noise from above and glanced up. A seventh demon that he didn't register before, launched down at him. Aidan didn't get a chance to react as the demon crushed him with the weight of his body. He dropped to the floor with the demon sitting heavily on top of his chest. The demon swung his fist, punching Aidan in his jaw. The punch didn't produce the effect the monster desired. Aidan growled as anger swept through him, igniting his power with new strength.

He seized the demon's arm, pulling him down and slammed his palm over his chest, sending a stream of his power through the demon. The monster wailed and jolted up, trying to escape Aidan's grip. Aidan increased the flow of his power, burning not only through the flesh but also through the monster's demonic essence.

The remains of the demon's body flaked down, covering Aidan in ash. Aidan rose under the intense stares of the other six demons. Deliberately slow, he brushed his shirt and raked his fingers through his hair, getting rid of the ash, and a cold smirk crossed his face.

"Next," he hissed, squeezing his hands into tight fists.

The demons exchanged furious looks and screamed, charging at Aidan all at once. Aidan laughed and brought forth his godly power. His body emitted an unbearable brilliant light, igniting in the depth of his eyes. The blast of his power spread around him obliterating all the demons at once—their borrowed bodies and the demonic essence. A moment later, it was all over. The rogue demons were gone, and Aidan was standing in the middle of the room surrounded by dirty dust and ashes.

"I have no time to deal with you one at the time," muttered Aidan as he stepped over the pile of ashes.

* * *

HE DROVE like a maniac and the only thing he could think of was that he needed to be in Florida, not here. Thirty minutes later he parked his car in front of the Guardians Headquarters and ran up the stairs. The main hall in front of the entrance was empty and Aidan headed toward the door of the Assembly Hall. Two guards in front of the door crossed their spears, stopping him.

Aidan stepped back, irritation spiraling through him, but he decided that smiting these two assholes right inside the Guardians HQ wouldn't be received well and took a cleansing breath.

"Ms. Bonneville is expecting me," he said, suppressing his aggravation.

"Ms. Bonneville is attending to an urgent matter, and she is expecting you to comply with her orders, Aidan McGrath," said one of the guards dryly. "She wishes you to return to your room in the Wardens' wing and remain there until she summons you."

Aidan threw his hands in the air but turned around and headed to the Wardens' quarters. He walked inside his room and slammed the door shut. He needed to talk to Gunz and let him know everything that Gwyn ap Nudd told him, but he knew that he couldn't do it within these walls. The delay was driving him crazy. For a few minutes, he paced around the room, dealing with his aggravation.

After a while he lay down on the bed, throwing his arm over

his eyes. He tried to get some sleep, but his restless, agitated mind wouldn't let him. He was dozing on and off, waking up at the tiniest sound or movement. He got up a couple of hours later and sat down on the bed. His stomach rumbled with hunger.

Aidan thought for a moment and headed out of the room, hoping to find something to eat while he was waiting for the Head Mage to summon him. With surprise, he found a young guard standing by his door. As soon as he tried to leave the room, the guard stopped him.

"Ms. Bonneville ordered you to stay in your room," said the guard calmly. "Is there anything I can get you, Mr. McGrath?"

Aidan sighed. The Head Mage didn't trust him to obey her command, and she made sure that he wouldn't be going anywhere. The young guard looked at him, expecting him to say something.

"Could you please get me something to eat?" he asked quietly. It wasn't this young man's fault that the Head Mage confined him to this room. "I haven't eaten anything since yesterday."

"I can fetch you some food, but can I trust you not to leave this room, sir?" asked the guard gingerly.

He's probably new to all this, decided Aidan, *he's too nice and too polite.*

"You can trust me," promised Aidan with a smile that he hoped looked friendly enough, "I'm going nowhere."

The guard left, and Aidan returned inside his room, silently cursing the Head Mage and his situation. Fifteen minutes later, the young guard came back and knocked on his door. Aidan took the tray with the food out of his hands, inviting him to come in and join him. The guard smiled shyly but declined his invitation, stating that he was on duty and he'd be outside if Aidan needed anything else.

The sun was slowly shifting toward the horizon when he felt

the soft ping of the summoning call in his head and the chain with the pendant got warmer, glowing with a soft silvery light. This time the summoning call was different. It still wasn't pleasant, but it wasn't crippling.

As he opened the door, ready to walk out, he ran into his guard. The young man smiled, gesturing for him to follow. "Ms. Bonneville is expecting you in the Assembly Hall, Mr. McGrath."

The Head Mage was waiting for him, pacing irritably in the Assembly Hall. As soon as Aidan walked in, she crossed the room, halting in front of him. Aidan inclined his head slightly. It wasn't quite a bow, just a way to show his respect.

"Aidan, how many demons were in that house?" started the Head Mage without any preamble.

"Seven," replied Aidan, wondering where she was going with this question.

"Did you really have to use your full godly power to exterminate them?" she asked, aggravation breathing from her every word.

"No, I didn't have to," said Aidan, calmly meeting her furious eyes, "but it was faster than if I would fight them using my magic. If you didn't hear me the first time, Ms. Bonneville, I have a serious matter I need to attend back in Florida. I don't have time to—"

"You could have exposed us all!" she shouted, stamping her high-heeled foot. "The use of your godly powers created a huge energy spike, plus the brilliant light of your power was visible from a few blocks away!"

"If you didn't want me to fight as a god, why did you send a god for such a small task!" yelled Aidan, unwilling to stand down. "Sending me to kill seven demons who seemingly didn't bother anyone was equivalent to using a missile to shoot at a sparrow! I don't have time for this bullshit!"

Ms. Bonneville pulled her arm back and slapped Aidan

across his face. Aidan gasped and staggered back, holding his hand to his burning cheek.

"You will learn some respect, Mr. McGrath," hissed the Head Mage.

She snapped her fingers, and the chain wrapped tightly around Aidan's neck, burning his skin. He jerked his hand up to grab the chain, but stopped himself, dropping his hand back down and remained silent and motionless, a muscle twitching in his jaw.

"You will learn to show me proper respect," repeated the Head Mage, her voice shaking with fury. "You will do what I say, when I say it. And you will comply with the rules of the Order. If you disagree, you can get the hell out of here and your little girlfriend will be sent back to the dungeons, where she belongs!" She waved at the guards and shouted, "Guards, please bring Therasia Donovan here at once!"

"No! Please. I will do what you want," said Aidan, raising his hand up to stop her.

The Head Mage stopped the guards and turned back to Aidan. "Are you ready to behave like a loyal member of this Order, Mr. McGrath?"

"Yes, ma'am," replied Aidan quietly, dropping his head. "I completed your assignment. Not the way you wanted me to do it, but all the demons are dead anyway. Would you allow me to leave now?"

"You sound a lot more appropriate now," said Ms. Bonneville, raking him with an arrogant stare. "The only thing you still need to learn is to bow to me when you're greeting me and when I dismiss you."

Aidan's face lost all color, but he forced himself not to react. "Would you allow me to leave now?" he repeated his question, through gritted teeth.

"No, not yet," replied the Head Mage. She walked back to the table and grabbed an envelope. "While you were playing games with the demons, another problem has arisen. This is a more serious problem, and I need you to handle it for us."

She handed him the envelope. Aidan took it and peered inside. A single round trip ticket to Phoenix Arizona was inside the envelope.

"What is it?"

"I trust you know how to read. This is a plane ticket to Phoenix, of course," said the mage with a shrug. "We discovered a large pack of werewolves on the outskirts of Phoenix that is not regulated by any of the supernatural organizations. Seems that the local hunters have a problem dealing with them. They reported that the pack is out of control, turning humans to beef up their ranks and they requested our assistance."

"Ma'am, I'm a god. I don't need any modern transportation to travel," suggested Aidan carefully. "I know the Phoenix area well enough. I can teleport to a place where no one will see me and be done with this little werewolf problem within one hour. Wouldn't it be faster and better—"

"Mr. McGrath, what did I tell you about complying with the rules and obeying all my commands?" asked the mage sternly.

Aidan fell silent. The rage was coursing through his veins, but he clenched his teeth and said nothing.

"Very good, Aidan," said the mage, patting him on his shoulder. "I see you're learning your place. Anyway, inside this envelope you will find complete instructions on where to find the pack. Deal with them swiftly and quietly, but without using your godly powers. I don't need any unwanted attention to the Order."

"Do you want me to fight them as a man? As a hunter?" asked Aidan without raising his eyes.

"Don't be silly, of course not," replied the mage. "Use your magic all you want. You can fight them as any wizard would. Did you understand what you need to do and how you should do it, Aidan?"

"Yes, ma'am."

"Perfect. Your plane is leaving at 5 AM from O'Hare airport. I'll send one of my guards to drive you there," said Ms. Bonneville with a dismissive wave of her hand. "Now, that'll be all. Off you go."

Aidan turned around and headed toward the exit, clutching the envelope in his fist when he heard the mage clearing her throat suggestively. He stopped and turned around.

"Forgetting something, Mr. McGrath?" she asked, giving him an arched stare. Aidan frowned, not quite sure what she was talking about. "When I allow you to leave, you must bow to me before leaving."

Aidan stiffened for a moment. *Choose your battles wisely*, he ordered himself. *This is not the battle I need to fight right now.*

Feeling sick to his stomach, Aidan bent forward in a formal bow.

27

~ ZANE BURNS, A.K.A. GUNZ ~

Gunz sat in the kitchen with a bottle of water in his hands. He was alone. Karma went out to get some clothes and Voron decided to accompany her. It'd been many years since Voron visited the realm of the living and he wanted to see how the world had changed. Mishka slept in his room, curled up on his pillow, and this solitude was a welcome change for Gunz.

After his time in the Dark Nav, he craved for a few minutes of quiet, so he could think in peace. What he really wanted was a few hours somewhere at a lake with a fishing pole in his hand, surrounded by nature only, with no people around. However, at this time, it wasn't an option. Maybe after everything was over, he could allow himself a short vacation. But not yet. Not right now.

He thought about Yaroslav's words. If Zmey was going to try to break free through the Dark Nav, he couldn't fight him inside the realm of demons and spirits where there were no elemental powers. Kal, Mrak Delar and Semargl couldn't fight there either. Anyone who wielded the elements were powerless inside the Dark Nav and Agent Zvereva knew that. So, Yaroslav was right—if they failed to stop Zvereva from breaking the restraints and releasing the Lord of Chaos, the Zmey would rise within the Dark Nav, tearing the veil and invading the world of the living.

Gunz was so deep in his thoughts that when the fire curtain of Kal's portal opened next to him, he almost fell off his chair, spilling his water all over the table. Kal walked through the curtain, followed by Mrak Delar. Gunz grabbed a paper towel and wiped the water off the table. Both Kal and Mrak Delar sat down at the table, across from him.

"I've heard you had a little demon-slash-vampire mishap," said Kal, his blazing eyes crinkling with humor.

"Yeah, something like that," replied Gunz and turned to Mrak Delar. "Coffee?"

"I can never say no to that," answered the Master of Power.

"Kal, how about you? Coffee?" asked Gunz, but Kal shook his head no.

Gunz put a k-cup and a cup of water in the coffeemaker and turned back to his mentor. "Akira's son Yaroslav said something that I think we should seriously consider."

"Oh, yeah? You've met the *Russkij* blondie?" Kal chuckled. "So, what did *'GQ Undead-Style'* say that was so important?"

"You shouldn't make fun of him, Kal, just because he is prettier than you," said Gunz, sarcasm breaking to the surface. "Yaroslav is a fighter to be reckoned with. I would love to have him by my side in everything that's coming. But I think he's going to stay here with his mother, helping Jim to control the city." He recounted quickly everything that happened last night and his conversation with Akira and Yaroslav.

"Blondie was right," admitted Kal. "And this leads us to the reason for our visit."

"I suspected that you didn't come here for a cup of coffee," muttered Gunz.

"Not today," said Mrak Delar rising. "We asked Voron to

keep Karma out, so we could have a peaceful conversation with Veles, without witnesses."

"You also don't trust her?" asked Gunz, exploring Mrak's emotionless face.

"No," he replied. "Trust is not given, it's earned. And as far as I know, this young lady is a Sword for Hire. No one in their right mind can trust her kind."

"I can," murmured Gunz.

"Who said that you were in your right mind?" asked Mrak Delar with an expression of innocence on his face, but evil twinkles were shining in his eyes.

"Of course, I left it wide-open for you. I forgot who I'm dealing with," said Gunz chuckling, but then sobered up. "After everything that happened in the Dark Nav, I trust her. But Akira is in agreement with you, Mrak. So, let's do it your way."

Mrak Delar connected with his power, his black eyes becoming a pool of darkness and drew a pentagram in the air. He waved his hand over the pentagram, whispering something in Dragon tongue. A split-second later, a portal opened up in the place where the pentagram was. Usually portals looked like a swirling void, shimmering with a bright blue light. This portal was a dark hole, seemingly leading into nowhere. Mrak Delar touched the edge of the portal, sending some of his magic through it and whispered Veles' name, summoning the god of the Three Realms.

Veles emerged out of the portal right away. It was almost like he was just sitting and waiting for Mrak Delar's summoning call. In his ancient-Russian style armor and with a twisted wooden staff in his hand, he appeared bigger and grimmer than Gunz remembered him. He pressed his hand to his heart and then lowered it down with a bow.

"Goi esi, dobri molodtsi," he rumbled the Old-Russian greeting. "It's nice to see you all in good spirits."

"My lord," said Gunz, bowing to the ancient deity, noticing

Mrak Delar and Kal also returning the bow. "Please sit down." He pulled a chair out offering it to Veles.

Veles sat down, and the chair squeaked mournfully under his considerable weight. His icy eyes stopped on Mrak Delar, and he waved his hand. "If you please, Ancient Master. A concealment spell."

"*Oprimenta Amnia,*" muttered Mrak Delar with a flick of his wrist and the soft yellow light of the concealment spell flooded the room.

"Now we can talk," said Veles, turning to Gunz. "I don't want to keep your attention longer than needed. So, let's get straight to business. Chernobog, Morena and I are ready to defend the Dark Nav in case Zmey decides to break through the veil. How about you, Great Salamander?"

The god stared in Gunz's direction, and he couldn't help but throw a quick glance at Kal. No one ever addressed him in this manner and it didn't feel right.

"I'm talking to you, young Salamander," said Veles, inclining slightly toward him.

"There is only one Great Salamander here. My Father," replied Gunz. "Anyway, with everything we learned in the last couple days, I don't think the three of you would be enough. If my team fails to stop the mage from freeing Skiper-Zmey, I'm almost a hundred percent sure that he'll make a break through the Dark Nav. Actually, make it a hundred percent. From what I've learned, the Dark Nav is the only place Skiper-Zmey can regain his full power. And if it'll come to that, you'll need some help to stop him before he can tear the veil on his way out."

"None of you can fight in the Dark Nav. Without elemental powers, you'll be helpless there," said Veles with a light shrug. "What are you suggesting?"

"Agreed," replied Gunz. "But Aidan can fight in the Dark Nav and so can Gwyn ap Nudd. They both belong to the Celtic Otherworld, which is not far from the Nav. And Angel is actually stronger in the realms of the dead. So, we can send them to help you. It is the night of the Wild Hunt, so Gwyn ap Nudd can be there at sunset."

Gunz glanced at Kal and Mrak Delar. Kal nodded at him, encouraging him to proceed.

"Kal, Mrak Delar, Svyatobor, Karma and I will meet the mage in the Yav, at Mount Karasova where the Zmey was buried," continued Gunz. "Voron will probably want to stand by Chernobog's side. But I'll leave the decision up to him. And I hope that Semargl will join us."

"That's all good," agreed Veles. "Here is what you need to know though. It's not easy to break Zmey's restraints. Besides the Axe of Perun, the mage will need a blood sacrifice. If you can stop the ritual, the war is over. If she fails, we don't need to defend the Dark Nav. So, my advice—stop the ritual before it even starts. You can't fail."

"No shit," murmured Gunz. "How am I supposed to know when and where she will do that ritual? Maybe I'm not the right person to run this show…"

"You're the only person to run this show, as you put it," objected Veles, shaking his head. "Yes, the Great Salamander is a lot more powerful than you are and so is Mrak Delar. But all of them, including your friend Aidan, are ancient warriors. And you're going to fight in the modern world of the living.

"I don't know much about this woman, but she seems to be smart and resourceful. There is a reason she wanted you, young Salamander, detained in the Dark Nav. You were the one she wanted out of the picture, not any of us. Have you ever thought why that was?"

"Of course, I thought about it," replied Gunz. "But the only explanation that made any sense was the one Zvereva gave me. She said that I was the only one who could cross the veil and still live to see another day. Which is bullshit, because later on she said that I was just a decoy and she never was going to get me out."

"Here is what I think," continued Veles. "Among us, you're the only one young enough to know and understand modern warfare. And the mage knows it. This tells me that besides the demons and witches, she will have modern-day mercenaries defending her while she's performing the ritual."

"But mundane weapons can't kill any of us," noted Gunz. "What can a mercenary do against a Master of Power or a Fire Elemental?"

"They can slow us down. Significantly. Maybe not the gods like Svyatobor or Semargl. But I know bullets would present a problem for me and for you, Zane," admitted Mrak Delar quietly. "I see Veles' point. Any delay on our part will give the mage a chance to complete the ritual and raise the Zmey. Yes, bullets can't kill any of us, but they still hurt like hell and if a wound is serious enough, we have to stop what we're doing to perform healing magic. That would take not only time, but our physical strength and our magical energy."

"And what if she finds a way to block your magic?" asked Veles. "Can you fight without your combat magic? I know that you all, especially Mrak, still can wield the elements, but would that be enough?"

"Without magic, modern weapons may become a serious problem," agreed Mrak Delar.

Kal chuckled, patting Mrak Delar on his shoulder. "Who knew that the day would come when I'd see the Ancient Master worried about guns."

"Yeah, I didn't think that the day would come when a regular whip would bring me down to my knees, but it did," replied Mrak Delar dryly. "So, I prefer to expect the unexpected."

"I can't say for Semargl, but I know for a fact that Svyatobor's physical body can get hurt," added Gunz. "Nothing mundane would kill him, but as fast as he heals, he still feels pain. I made him bleed enough times during the training at Aidan's dojang."

"Ugh, this insufferable trickster," muttered Veles, slamming his hand on the table. "Remind me to have a word with him when all this is over. He is a pureblood Slavic deity. He doesn't bleed. He was just tricking you into believing that you were hurting him."

Kal laughed. "I think I like this kid already."

"How about Aidan?" asked Gunz. "I know he can get hurt physically. It wasn't a trick. His pain was real."

"Aidan? Aodh mac Lir?" asked Veles with a smirk. "Well, that I can believe. He's not a pureblood god. So, yes, he feels pain, he needs to sleep and eat. He has a human part to him, just like you, young Salamander, or the Master of Power. Nevertheless, he's extremely powerful. Almost as powerful as his mentor, Gwyn ap Nudd."

Veles stopped talking and raised his hand up in a warning gesture, like a person who was listening to something only he could hear.

"Voron just told me that Karma and he are on the way here," he explained a moment later, rising. "It is my time to bid farewell. If you need me for any reason, you can communicate with me through Voron. We are psychically connected for the time being."

Veles snapped his fingers and vanished from the room. As soon as the god was gone, Gunz turned back to Mrak Delar and Kal.

"I don't understand why Veles is so worried about modern weapons and mercenaries. Mercenaries are just humans and the Fire Salamander's natural state is deadly to them. I can revert any time I want, and Kal is always in his natural state. As soon as we come closer to their lines, we'll obliterate them."

Mrak Delar glanced at him and sighed, his index finger slowly circling the rim of his cup. "I wish it was that easy," he said with a light smirk. "There are quite a few different spells that can safely contain the fire energy or shield humans from it. Why do you think any time Kal comes here into the world of humans, he asks me to come along? I'm here to contain his natural state from harming humans. Do you have any doubts that a mage as powerful as Zvereva would realize that and would know how to protect her soldiers?"

Gunz bit his lip, frowning. "You're right, Mrak. She knows that I escaped the Dark Nav and she'll be ready. She'll expect that Kal and I will be at the Mountain Karasova to stop her. Right now, she seems to be a few steps ahead of us, manipulating the situation to her advantage. So, we have to think of something that she won't expect."

Mrak Delar and Kal got up. Mrak Delar put an empty coffee cup in the sink and turned to Gunz.

"Well, Great Salamander Junior, I guess, we'll go too. If you're in trouble, don't call me. I don't want any part of it. Ta-ta for now."

"Ta-ta for now? Where did you even learn these words?" Gunz stared at him, flabbergasted. "You are not serious, Mrak, are you?"

Mrak Delar burst out laughing. "Of course not. You should have seen your face. Of course, you can summon me any time you need me. For anything. Even if you just want someone's company to drink a cup of coffee with. And of course, I'll be right next to you when the time comes to fight. Wouldn't miss it for the world, little Salamander."

Kal unfolded the fire-curtain of his portal, letting Mrak Delar through first. "Gunz, this is one of those rare occasions when I want to know everything that's going on," he said, putting his hand on Gunz's shoulder. "You know that usually I don't get involved in the affairs of human realms and I don't like to dictate every step of your life. As I promised—you're free to make your own choices. But this time is different, so please keep me updated. I want to hear from you every day. And if you're in trouble, don't feel ashamed to call me. You understand me, my child?"

"Yes, sir," replied Gunz, troubled and touched by the notes of concern in Kal's voice. "Thank you, Father. I'll stay in touch."

The moment Kal vanished from the kitchen, Gunz heard the sound of a key opening the door. Karma peeked through the doorway into the kitchen and waved at Gunz.

"Missed me, firetwat?" she asked with a sly wink. She reached into one of the shopping bags and threw Gunz's sweatpants and shirt into his hand. "Thank you. Finally, got my own garb."

She pirouetted, demonstrating him her new outfit and headed upstairs into her bedroom. Gunz followed her with his eyes and cringed inwardly. He didn't like the idea of keeping things from Karma. Maybe she was an assassin for hire, but it didn't mean that she would betray him the first chance she's got. How could he trust her to fight by his side if he couldn't trust her enough to share all the information?

He sighed and caught Voron's heavy stare. He was standing in the doorway, leaning his shoulder at the doorframe.

"We must be sure first," he said quietly. "Chernobog didn't like the situation with her girlfriend's suspicious disappearance. He checked the Dark Nav after you left a few times and did not find her. She is not in the Dark Nav. So, tell me, Zane, you've been to the Nav and back. You know well that there is no escaping there without Chernobog's permission. How did a young seer without any notable magical power escape the Dark Nav? Someone assisted her. It was not me and it was not my lord Chernobog."

Gunz dropped his head, biting his lip. "I don't know, Voron. It makes no sense. But if you saw how heartbroken Karma was, you would know that she had no hand in Milana's disappearance."

"I guess, only time will tell," said Voron. "Did you talk to Lord Veles? Are we all on the same page now?"

"Yes, we are. Except for Aidan and his crew. He is still not back from Chicago and that troubles me." Gunz thoughts circled back to his last conversation with Aidan. Something wasn't right there. Nevertheless, Aidan was a god and he could hold his own.

"Do not worry, young Salamander," said Voron calmly with a light smirk. "Your friend will return in time."

I wish I had his nerves and his self-assurance. Gunz sighed, checking his phone.

There were no messages from Aidan.

28

~ AIDAN ~

Aidan walked out of the Phoenix airport early in the morning. It was slightly past eight, but the airport was crowded. Since he didn't have any luggage, it took him just a few minutes to go through the gates and walk outside. The cold morning air hit him, and he shivered in his thin shirt. It was a little warmer than Chicago but still too cold for the way he was dressed.

He took a shuttle to the car rental, silently cursing the Head Mage for forbidding him to use his full power or to teleport. It was slowing him down considerably and he couldn't understand why she would do it. With her magic, she had to sense the disturbance beneath, just like he did. Yet she was determined to waste his power and abilities on performing some minuscule tasks.

He needed to go back to Florida and see if there were any new developments. He had to tell Zane everything he learned from Gwyn ap Nudd, so they could get ready for what was to come. Instead, he was forced to run errands for the Guardians, traveling via mundane transportation and fighting like a human hunter.

On top of all that, he was bound to lose another twenty-four hours. His flight back to Chicago was leaving Phoenix at 8:45 PM and arriving in O'Hare airport at six in the morning with a two-hour stop in San Francisco. All this was driving Aidan crazy.

Why didn't she book a non-stop flight? Why did she get a ticket with the departure at such a late hour? Surely, she didn't think he would need twelve hours to get rid of a single pack of werewolves, no matter how large it was. He thought about it. Fighting a large pack of werewolves, especially if some of them were purebreds, could take a little time, especially if he couldn't use his full power. He also stood the chance of getting injured. Even though he could heal himself later, he didn't want to get hurt in the first place.

He was positive that Ms. Bonneville wasn't trying to save on the cost of tickets. Since the Guardians weren't tight on funds, extreme couponing wasn't her style. There was only one reasonable explanation—she was trying to keep him tied up with the Guardians, doing whatever errands she needed him to do.

Or is she trying to delay my return to Florida and keep me away from everything that is happening there?

He thought back to the warning he received from Raoul's friend. If the Guardians Order was corrupt, who could guarantee that the Head Mage was on the right side of the fence. Aidan shuddered from the mere thought.

AIDAN DROVE his car through the desert, from time to time, checking the GPS on his phone. According to the GPS, he was driving in the right direction, but the scenery remained unchanged—brownish-yellow colors of the Sonoran Desert land covered in patches of grass, occasional thorny bushes and tall spikes of Saguaro cacti.

He drove for miles without seeing any houses and he started to think that the mage sent him on a wild-goose chase, when he finally noticed white fences of a horse ranch far on the horizon. A small bi-road was branching away from the main road, leading to the left, deeper into the desert.

Aidan slowed down, battling with doubt. His intuition was telling him to take the bi-road. His GPS was insisting on following the main road.

"Intuition wins," murmured Aidan, turning left.

He drove for a while through the desert, happy that he rented an SUV. After a few miles, he noticed a small farmhouse surrounded by fences. Possibly it was a horse ranch. But if the ranch belonged to the werewolves, it would be quite unusual. Horses, sensitive by nature, could feel the supernatural element and they wouldn't be keen on obeying supernatural owners.

A mile away from the ranch house, Aidan abandoned the bi-road and drove a few yards into the desert. He stopped the car and walked out. He didn't want to drive all the way to the house. The noise of the SUV's engine would alert the pack about his presence far in advance.

He waved his hand, muttering the words of a cloaking spell and the car disappeared, becoming invisible. Then he returned to the bi-road and headed toward the ranch house. About fifteen minutes later, he stopped by the fence that surrounded the ranch. The land looked well taken care of, but he couldn't see the presence of any animals on the grounds—no horses, no dogs, not even a cat. Just a few chickens were roaming around the front yard, busy pecking at the dry patches of grass. Perhaps the mage was right—this house belonged to a pack after all.

Instead of going through the main gate, Aidan hopped over the fence and slowly circled the perimeter of the property. Behind the main house, there was another building that used to be a barn or a horse stable, but now was turned into a mechanic's shop. Judging by the equipment and the vehicles that were parked outside the shop, the owner was mostly working on agricultural machinery.

It looked like there was no one in the shop. Aidan walked around the mechanic's shop and halted behind the main house. He probed the building with his magical sight and counted five people inside. They weren't quite people. A hardly noticeable glow of supernatural energy was surrounding each one of them.

Aidan had no problem recognizing the house inhabitants as werewolves. It wasn't a full moon yet and their energy signature was feeble. That told him that these five werewolves weren't purebred. Unlike turned werewolves, purebred ones could transform at any day of the month, full moon or not, and their magical signature was always strong, easily recognizable.

Everything about what he discovered so far made him think. The house was far away from any populated area. It told him that the pack wanted to stay as far away from humans as they possibly could. They had a small business, and they took care of their land. The Head Mage described them as a vicious pack that was killing and turning humans to build up their ranks.

During the course of his long life in this world, Aidan had seen enough of werewolves and was familiar with their lifestyle. He could easily make out the difference between "vicious and dangerous" packs and people who suffered with their condition and were trying to live their life as normal as possible, doing everything to avoid harming others.

While all werewolves were short-fused, extremely strong and fast, in his full power Aidan could easily handle them. However, Ms. Bonneville had his hands tied by ordering him not to use his full power.

Aidan sighed, shaking his head. *Screw that,* he thought resolutely, heading toward the entrance of the house. *I'm not going to kill these people just because the Guardians said so. I need to see how dangerous and vicious they truly are for myself first. After all, they're not purebreds. It means they are monsters only three days a month and the rest of the time, they're normal people.*

Aidan knocked on the door and listened, probing the house with his magical sight again. He heard steps and agitated whispers, but no one opened the door. He pressed the door handle down, realizing that the door wasn't locked. He pushed it in, opening it soundlessly. A small room in front of the door was empty. On the wall, there was a hanger with a few adult-size jackets hanging. A single chair was standing on the right of the entrance door. The room led straight into a small kitchen and the doors on either side of kitchen were tightly shut.

Even though Aidan felt the presence of the werewolves in the next room, he proceeded inside. "Hello?" he said tentatively, connecting with his magic. He heard a shuffling behind the door on the right, and a young preteen boy walked into the room.

"Hello, sir, how can I help you?" he asked. His eyes were round with fear, his skinny shoulders squared.

"Are you home alone?" asked Aidan, knowing perfectly well that he wasn't. "Can I talk to your parents?"

The boy shuffled from foot to foot, but shook his head no. "I'm home alone, sir, and I can't talk to strangers. Would you like to come back in an hour?"

"If you don't mind, I'll wait for them here," said Aidan, mustering a friendly smile. He pulled a chair and sat down.

The boy got agitated. His eyes grew bigger and rounder than they were before, and his face lost all its color. "No, sir, please," he mumbled. "You're better off coming back in a while."

Aidan folded his arms over his chest and jerked his chin in the direction of the closed door. "You can tell your siblings to come out. I'm not going to bite." *No pun intended...*

"But we are." He heard a voice behind him, and the cold barrel of a gun pressed into the back of his head. The door opened and two girls and a boy, all in their teens, walked into the room, staring at him with interest. Aidan started to turn around but heard the click of a cocked weapon and stilled.

"Yeah, you better don't move, old man," said the original boy. Surrounded by his family he felt braver and stronger.

Aidan sighed, observing four teens in front of him. By the sound of the voice, the person who was holding the gun to his head was also a young man, possibly a teenager.

"I mean no harm," said Aidan peacefully, raising both hands in the air. "I just wanted to talk to someone — um — older."

"Put your hands down and behind your back," ordered the man with the gun.

Aidan decided not to argue and comply. He knew that he could easily break any mundane restraints and preferred not to take the chance of getting shot in the back of his head. He wouldn't die, but the pain would be unimaginable, and the self-healing process would take time. Also, he didn't want to fight with these kids. He would much rather talk to the adult members of the pack to see what really was going on here. He put his hands behind his back and heard the metallic click of handcuffs.

"Drew, come here," ordered the man with the gun. "Cuff him."

The older boy went around the chair. Aidan grunted as metal bit into the skin of his wrists.

"Take the duct tape on the table, right there," ordered the man with the gun again. Aidan heard Drew shuffling something on the table. "His ankles to the chair."

As soon as Drew was done restraining him, the man with the gun came forward, now pressing the barrel of the gun against Aidan's forehead. As he suspected, he was the oldest among the five. The young man was in his late teens or early twenties. He had a mop of straw-like blond hair and brown eyes, blazing with fury.

"Okay, asshole, now you're going to tell me why you are here," he drawled, pressing the gun harder.

Aidan met his stare calmly. "I already told you. I wanted to talk with your parents or someone older. Just a peaceful conversation without any violence. You should try it sometimes. Quite satisfying."

"Don't get smart with me, jackass," yelled the young man and raised his hand with the gun, ready to strike him.

Aidan turned his head to the side, bracing himself for the impact, but it didn't come. He heard voices outside and the door opened again. Since he was sitting with his back toward the entrance, he couldn't see what was going on there. With his second sight he detected at least ten people, all werewolves. And one of them was a purebred, no doubt he was the Alpha.

If these young lycanthropes still didn't detect his magic, he was positive that the purebred could feel his presence as soon as he crossed the threshold of the house. Possibly even earlier.

"What's going on here, Chris?"

The voice was deep, with an added growl and without a doubt it belonged to an older man. The man walked around the chair and halted before Aidan, studying him with the golden-yellow eyes of a predator. His skin was dark from working for hours in the open sun and a few old scars marred the left side of his face, running from his cheekbone down to his neck. He was tall and brawny, massive muscles wrapped around his arms and chest.

Unlike the rest of the pack, this man was a purebred, and the cold wasn't affecting him as much. The body temperature of purebred werewolves was slightly above that of humans and turned lycanthropes. Even in this chilly weather he wore just his cargo pants and a buttoned shirt with rolled-up sleeves. His magical energy washed over Aidan, and he drew in a sharp breath. There were no doubts—this man was the Alpha.

"This asshole was trespassing on our property, sir. I saw him jumping over the fence on the south side. So, I thought I'd give him a nice meet and greet and find out who sent him here," explained Chris proudly, returning his gun back to Aidan's forehead. "And if he is working for Simon—"

"Silence!" hissed Alpha. "And kindly stop pointing your weapon at an ancient god! You can't kill him or scare him with this useless toy. But he can smite us all in a heartbeat. He doesn't even need to move his hands."

Chris gasped, backing away from Aidan. The Alpha kneeled, bowing his head, pressing his fist to his chest. "My lord, please forgive my children's ignorance. They are still too young to recognize who you are and treat you with the proper respect."

Aidan smiled. *"Recludius,"* he muttered, and the handcuffs dropped on the floor with a loud jingle. Then he bent forward and ripped the tape off his ankles. The younger werewolves huddled closer together, gaping at Aidan with fear and curiosity in their widened eyes.

"Please, no need to kneel," said Aidan, touching the Alpha's shoulder. "I'm here because I wanted to talk to the Alpha of this pack. Since you're the only purebred here, I assume, it's you."

"Yes, my lord," replied the Alpha rising, "I'm the Alpha, the master of this pack. What can I do for you?"

"Can we talk somewhere a little more private?" asked Aidan, also getting up, massaging his wrists.

The older members of the pack shifted closer to their pack master at Aidan's request, but the Alpha raised his hand warningly and they stopped.

"Please give us the room," ordered the Alpha. "And no eavesdropping. I mean it." He narrowed his eyes at the teenage girls. They giggled and ran out of the house. The rest of the pack followed them. The Alpha closed all the doors and pointed at the kitchen. "Can I get you anything, my lord? Eat or drink?"

"The name is Aidan. You don't have to call me 'my lord' or

bow to me. And thank you for your kind offer. A glass of water would be great," he said.

His stomach clenched at the mention of food. The last time he ate was when the young guard brought him some food at the Guardians Headquarters. He followed the Alpha into the kitchen and sat down next to the table. The Alpha set a coffeemaker and turned to Aidan.

"Thank you, Aidan. I'm Hawk," he said, offering his hand to Aidan with a light smile that lit up his face, hardened by time. "It still early enough. I don't think you would say no to a cup of coffee."

Aidan squeezed his hand in a handshake, feeling Hawk's firm grip that was a little stronger than a human handshake would be. "I can never say no to coffee. Thank you."

A few minutes later, the Alpha placed two cups with hot coffee on the table and sat down across from Aidan.

"So, what can a modest werewolf do for a god?" he asked calmly, taking a sip of his coffee.

Aidan sighed. He didn't like the flow of events. Everything he saw so far told him that the mage gave him wrong information. Yes, all these people were werewolves, but they didn't come across as vicious killers.

"You can tell me about yourself and the members of your pack," said Aidan, having a hard time meeting the old Alpha's penetrating eyes. "I'll be honest with you, Hawk. I was sent here to kill you all."

The Alpha stiffened, his fingers wrapping tighter around his cup. "Then why didn't you? I can sense your power, Aidan. You could have wiped us all out of existence without breaking a sweat. What stopped you?"

"I don't kill just because someone ordered me to do so. I need to know that what I've been told is true before I comply with the order," replied Aidan. "I was told that your pack is killing humans or turning them into werewolves to build up the pack. However, when I came here and observed your property, I started to doubt the information that was given to me."

"You're a god, not a human hunter," objected Hawk, frowning. "Who can order a god?"

"The people who have the power to control me," replied Aidan through clenched teeth. "Not for much longer though."

"Oh boy," mumbled Hawk. He leaned back in his chair, shaking his head. "I know what you are, Aidan. You're a god of some underworld realm. I'm old and experienced enough to sense your origin."

"Otherworld," corrected Aidan.

"Yes, you're a god of the Celtic Otherworld. It means you have the power to hear my soul. Even though I'm a purebred, I still have a soul. Listen to it. You've been fed lies. Neither I nor the members of my pack are cold-blooded killers. The reason we live so far in the desert is to protect humans from harm. I'm the only purebred in this pack and I devoted my life to finding newly turned people and teaching them how to live more or less normal lives, how to deal with the wolf within and control him. I swear it!"

He slammed his hand on the table. There wasn't any anger in Hawk's words, but there was so much pain and desperation that Aidan cringed.

"If I do it, it's not going to be… pleasant," muttered Aidan, putting his cup on the table.

"I don't care," replied Hawk with a sigh. "Do it. I have nothing to hide. And if you find that I speak false words, you can kill me and my whole pack. No one will try to fight you."

Aidan got up, channeling his power. His eyes lit up with white light and his body got surrounded by the brilliant glow of his power.

"Sorry, Hawk," he muttered, placing his hand on the Alpha's chest. Hawk tensed and grunted as Aidan started to scan his soul, but fearlessly met his eyes. The soul of a purebred werewolf didn't feel the same as a human soul. It was a lot harder to read. The images were scrambled and out of focus in places, but Aidan still was getting a clear enough reading to know that Hawk didn't lie to him. It meant that Ms. Bonneville did. The question remained—why did she lie to him?

Slowly, he removed his hand and let go of his power. Hawk exhaled and collapsed on his chair, breathing hard.

"Whoa... When you said that it wasn't going to be pleasant, you really didn't give it justice." He chuckled, wiping perspiration off his forehead. "I felt like you were turning me inside out."

"In a way, I was," said Aidan. "I'm sorry I had to do it to you."

"Better this than all of us dead," replied the Alpha with a shrug. "I owe you, god of the Otherworld. If you ever need a loyal pack, all you need to do is call me."

"Thank you," said Aidan, meaning it. "I'll be leaving now. But Hawk, you can't relax. I don't know why, but the Guardians want you and your pack dead. I didn't do the job—they'll send someone else in my stead. Someone who's not going to care if you're good or bad. They will just fulfill their duty."

"I understand, but if it is Guardians who want us dead, there is nowhere to run." Hawk dropped his head, his hands balled into fists so tight that the slithering veins popped under his suntanned skin.

"You're right, there is nowhere to run. But it doesn't mean that you need to roll over and die," said Aidan. Then he motioned at the door. "Would you accompany me for a short walk around your property, Hawk?"

Hawk's bushy eyebrows climbed up under his high hairline that was characteristic to purebred lycanthropes, but he nodded and followed Aidan outside. Once out of the house, Aidan put his hand on Hawk's shoulder and teleported to the outside fence of his property.

He sent some of his magic toward his hand and drew a

glowing white rune on the pole of the main gate, whispering a spell in Dragon tongue. They teleported around the perimeter of the property as Aidan was placing the same rune every few hundred yards. After they made a full circle and returned to the main gate, he drew the last rune and a shimmering dome of light encapsulated the property. The dome glowed for a few seconds and dissipated.

"Hawk, I don't think there is anything else I can do for you and your family," said Aidan. "I placed powerful wards and protection spells around your land. You all should be safe inside the protective circle. It doesn't mean that the Guardian mages won't be able to break my enchantment, but at least it'll slow them down and give you a head start."

"My lord," said the Alpha, kneeling in front of him, pressing his fist to his chest, "I'm forever indebted to you for everything you've done for me and my pack."

"Don't kneel, Hawk. It doesn't suit you. Take care of your family," replied Aidan with a sad smile and vanished from the ranch.

29

~ AIDAN ~

Aidan was restless all night. He couldn't relax in the confided space of the airplane's coach seating or when he was sitting at the San Francisco airport, waiting for his next flight. In his mind he kept revisiting everything that happened from the moment Ms. Bonneville summoned him, trying to find any fact that would point toward her innocence or guilt.

When he left Hawk's property, the anger was boiling in him and his first desire was to teleport straight back home. However, he thought of Tessa and what would happen to her if he broke his oath and his anger simmered down. By not killing Hawk and his pack, he already broke the Guardians' orders and disobeyed their rules. He decided that for Tessa's sake he shouldn't aggravate the situation any further.

Using his power of a god to teleport back to Chicago or leave completely and go back home would certainly make it worse. Besides that, he wanted to give the benefit of the doubt to Ms. Bonneville and see if she was misinformed herself.

When he walked out of the airport, ready to order an Uber, he found the same young guard waiting for him next to the gate. A shy smile lit up his face as he waved at Aidan.

"Mr. McGrath, welcome back," he said as soon as Aidan approached him. "Ms. Bonneville asked me to drive you straight to the HQ. She's expecting you, sir."

"Is there a problem?" asked Aidan carefully as they walked through O'Hare airport in the direction of the parking garage.

"Not that I know of, sir," replied the guard. "But I'm just a guard and pretty new to all this, so I wouldn't know."

Aidan nodded, thinking that he was going straight into the lion's den, armed with no information whatsoever. He sat down on the front seat, even though the guard opened the back door for him. They drove in silence, Aidan focusing on controlling his emotions and taming the fury that was burning within him. When they finally parked in front of the Guardians' HQ, the only thing Aidan felt was exhaustion.

The guard led him toward the Assembly Hall and opened the door for him. Aidan walked inside and halted, surprised to see the Guardians Council in full assembly. Ms. Bonneville was sitting at the center of the main table, reviewing some documents. As soon as she saw Aidan walking in, she got up.

"I apologize," she addressed the Guardians Council, "but I need to talk with Mr. McGrath and it's urgent. This meeting is adjourned. Kindly give me and Mr. McGrath the room."

Aidan stood still next to the door, watching the Guardians walking by him, leaving the Assembly Hall. As he heard the sound of the door shut behind his back, leaving him alone with the Head Mage, for a split-second he felt helpless and vulnerable, and the anger that he was trying so hard to suppress all this time, broke through. He took a deep breath, clenching his jaw.

Ms. Bonneville stopped in front of him, looking up, and put her hands on her hips. "So, Mr. McGrath, how was your trip?" she demanded. "I need a full report. Did you clean up the area?"

"There was nothing to clean up," said Aidan calmly. "I met with the pack and I believe you were misinformed, Ms.—"

"You didn't kill them?" hissed the Head Mage, taking a step closer to him.

"No, I didn't," replied Aidan. "Like I was trying to tell you, you were misinformed. The pack is not vicious and dangerous. They are trying to live their lives away from humans, and they didn't harm anyone in the area. There was only one purebred among them. He is the Alpha, and he's a decent man."

Ms. Bonneville threw her hands in the air, fury coloring her face in a deep shade of magenta. "Did I send you there to make an assessment? No, I did not!" she hissed, slowly and deliberately spitting one word at the time. "I don't give a damn about your opinion. You disobeyed my direct order!"

She snapped her fingers and an all-consuming pain erupted in Aidan's head. The chain lit up, burning his skin. Aidan grunted and swayed, wrapping his arms around his head. As the pain intensified, he dropped to his knees and bent forward, now his forehead touching the cold tiles of the floor. The Head Mage leaned forward and pulled on his hair, lifting his head up.

"When are you going to learn, Aidan? You can't fight me. For as long as your oath stands, you must obey my orders! You have no choice! I must teach you a good lesson that you'll remember for the remaining time of your service to the Guardians." She let go of him and clapped two times. "Guards!"

Two guards rushed inside the room and stopped on either side of him, waiting for Ms. Bonneville's order.

"Guards," continued the Head Mage, pointing at Aidan, "take him to the confinement chambers. Use the special one—the one which was built to contain the power of any god. I will deal with him in a few hours. Make sure he doesn't enjoy his stay."

As Aidan heard her words, a fury like he never experienced before took hold of him. His power responded to his emotion and the floor trembled. Fighting the effects of her spell and the blinding pain in his head, he got up to his feet and let his full power of the god of the Otherworld consume him. Blinding white light filled the room as he assumed his true form. The guards gasped, shielding their eyes and backed away.

"The first person who dares to put his hand on me will die screaming," he said quietly. He waved his hand and the door into the Assembly Hall burst open, flying off its hinges with a thunderous noise. He turned back to the guards, pointing at the exit and shouted, "Out! The god of the Otherworld is here, and he has a few words to say to the Head Mage."

The guards didn't ask twice and rushed out of the Assembly Hall. Aidan turned back to the Head Mage, and she shrunk under his blazing gaze.

"Aidan—," she started.

"Silence, witch, when a god is talking to you!" yelled Aidan, and the floor shook again as the light around him shone brighter. "You thought you could bully me, torture me into submission, turning me into your mindless pawn? Think again!" His hand swept forward, and he seized her neck, forcing her head up. She shut her eyelids tightly, struggling to avoid full eye contact. "What I wish to know is, which side you're playing on. Your actions make me doubt your position in this war."

"Which war?" croaked the Head Mage.

"My lord," growled Aidan coldly, wrapping his finger tighter around her neck. "When you address an ancient god, you must bow to me and address me as 'my lord.'"

"Which war are you referring to… my lord?" asked the Head Mage, her voice breaking and spiking with fear.

Aidan laughed humorlessly. "Do not lie to me, witch. I can sense the lies. With your power, I'm sure you can feel the disturbance beneath. Something is coming and there will be a war. So, why are you trying to keep me busy with nonsense that any apprentice of yours can take care of? Why did you order me to kill innocent people? Why are you holding me here, when I should be investigating what's rising from beneath? Think well before you answer these questions. I don't feel charitable today."

"They weren't innocent, my lord. Please, I'm telling you the truth. I can show the reports I received," she begged, grabbing his wrist with both hands.

"Open your eyes," ordered Aidan. "If you're telling me the truth, you have nothing to worry about."

She cracked her eyes opened, and Aidan heard the cry of fear exuding from her soul. He scanned her with his power, and he wasn't gentle about it. The tears welled up in the Head Mage's eyes and she squirmed in his grip. Aidan channeled more power through her, ignoring her moans. Her soul wasn't cloudless, but he couldn't find anything that would tell him that she was working on the side of Chaos. After a few seconds, he unlocked his fingers, letting Ms. Bonneville drop to the floor and let go of his power.

"Ms. Bonneville," he said, staring down at her, "from now on, our relationship will change."

"Anything you wish, my lord," whispered Ms. Bonneville, coughing.

"I gave my word and I'll stand by it. As a god, I cannot break my oath," continued Aidan. "However, you will never again try to inflict any pain on me. You will summon me only by means of mundane communications. I will give you my cell phone number and you can call me at any time you need my help."

He walked to the table and grabbed a piece of paper and a pen. Quickly he wrote his phone number down and walked back to the Head Mage who was still kneeling on the floor. He threw the piece of paper into her hands.

"Yes, my lord," she said, taking the paper and putting it in her pocket.

"You will not bother me with anything that can be taken care of by a witch or a mage," continued Aidan. "If you get into a situation where you need the help of a god, you may call me. Am I clear?"

"Yes, my lord."

"Now, about Tessa," he said, crossing his arms. "She needs the Guardians' help to find out about the origins of her magic and to learn how to control it. So, you will treat her with respect, like the rest of your students here, and you'll do everything in your power to help her. Understand, you have no power to control me, and attempting to blackmail me again, dangling Tessa's life and wellbeing over my head, will get you killed. Do you understand me?"

"I understand you, my lord..."

"Now, I'm going to leave," continued Aidan. "I have a situation that is a lot more important to deal with at home. I'm not going to visit Tessa before I leave, but I hold the privilege of visiting her any time I wish. You will not attempt to stop me."

"Yes, my lord, you can visit Therasia any time you wish. But please, my lord, don't disrupt her education. You can see her after her lessons and during weekends and holidays."

"Good," exhaled Aidan. He let go of his power completely and now he felt how tired and shaken he was. "Before I leave, there is one more thing. You will leave Hawk and his pack in Arizona alone. You will not send other assassins after him."

"But, my lord," objected the mage, carefully raising her head, "aren't we in the business of killing monsters?"

"Not every creature of magic or supernatural being is a monster," replied Aidan icily. "Yes, they're werewolves, but Hawk takes care of his pack and they're not harming humans. Leave them alone! It's an order."

"Yes, my lord," hissed the mage through her clenched teeth. "Sooner or later one of them will slip and bite or kill a human. And you'll be responsible for that."

"If that happens," replied Aidan, "I'll go there and destroy the pack myself."

He turned around and headed out of the room. At the doorway he stopped and glanced over his shoulder at Ms. Bonneville who was still kneeling in the middle of the room, her shoulders slumped. He waved his hand at her, unable to suppress an uneven smirk from curving his lips. "You may rise now," he threw at her and walked out of the Assembly Hall.

The young guard was waiting for him outside, an expression of shock imprinted on his face. There was no doubt that he heard at least part of what was said in the Assembly Hall, but he didn't ask anything.

"Are you leaving, sir?" he asked carefully.

"Yes, I must go back home," answered Aidan. "You're the only person who showed me kindness here and I don't even know your name."

"Jamie," replied the guard, an openhearted smile changing his face. "I mean, James Coldwell."

"Well, Jamie, I hope you would do one more favor for me," said Aidan. "Since I can't teleport within the Guardians' land, would you be so kind and drive me to the main gate?"

The young guard took Aidan to the main gate and led him outside the gates, leaving him there. Aidan touched the pendant on his chest and smirked. His servitude to the Guardians order was over. He was still under the oath, but he seriously doubted that the Head Mage would be bothering him anytime soon. She would think twice before she called him again.

He snapped his fingers and vanished.

30

~ AIDAN ~

A while ago, Zane adjusted his wards so Aidan could come in and out any time he needed. Now Aidan teleported straight into Zane's living room, manifesting right next to him. Zane yelped and jumped aside, his sword at ready in his hands. His face was glistening with sweat, his shirt clinging to his body. He looked like he just ran a 10K.

"Dammit, Aidan, you scared me shitless," he yelled, lowering his sword. "I could've run you through. What's going on?"

"You'll find out soon enough," muttered Aidan, reaching forward. He seized Zane's arm, and both vanished from the living room.

A moment later, they manifested in front of the Church by the Sea. Aidan headed toward the door, pulling Zane with him. The gargoyles gathered above the door and lowered their heads, hissing at them.

"Whoa," mumbled Zane, fighting Aidan's pull, "what are these beasts? Do they bite?"

"Yeah, fried lizard is their favorite delicatessen," replied Aidan, snickering. His second sight detected that the protective wards were armed, and he waved at the gargoyles impatiently.

"Hey, you two, mutts! Let us through. You know perfectly well who we are, and I have no patience for your shenanigans today. Let us through, or I'll reduce you into a pile of rocks and dust. God knows, Zane could do with some fresh pebbles to decorate his front yard."

The gargoyles yelped and hopped aside, their marble eyes growing round. Aidan opened his sight and checked the wards again just to make sure that the gargoyles didn't trick him. Once he was sure, he ran up the steps and opened the door, gesturing at Zane to follow him.

They walked inside and found the church completely empty. Zane stopped, observing the stained-glass windows and tall vaulted ceiling with awe. But Aidan didn't give him time to marvel upon architectural wonders. He proceeded through the passage between the seats to the altar.

"Raoul!" he roared without slowing down. His voice bounced off the ceiling, reverberating over and over. "Raoul, I need you."

A small door, hidden behind the altar opened up and Raoul appeared in the doorway. He saw Aidan and headed to him, followed by Father Collins. Aidan turned to Zane, nudging him slightly closer to the altar.

"Allow me to introduce my friend—," he started to say, but Father Collins interrupted him, which was quite unlike the old Warden.

"Mr. Zane Burns. The young Fire Salamander," he said, extending his hand to Zane. "It's an honor to finally make your acquaintance. I'm Father Collins, the Master Warden, and this is Father Raoul de Beaumont."

Aidan watched Zane flush scarlet for a moment, as he mumbled something in response and shook both priests' hands and thought how young his friend was. He could still blush, feeling shy and awkward when someone was complimenting him.

"I hate to cut the niceties short, but there is a reason I abducted Zane from his house and brought him here," he said with a sigh. "There is a lot I need to tell you and I don't want to repeat it twice."

They sat down on the first row of seats and Aidan went over everything that Gwyn ap Nudd told him and everything that transpired since Ms. Bonneville summoned him to the Guardians HQ.

"She is an extremely powerful mage," said Aidan, shaking his head. "She brought me down to my knees with her summoning call and then again with some kind of spell which I didn't recognize. It took my full power of a god to counteract her magic."

"Are you worried about a possible confrontation with a mage?" asked Raoul, furrowing his brow. "Don't forget, if Madam Bonneville is in league with the followers of Chaos, we'll be facing two seventh level mages." He visibly cringed.

"Is there a way to find out where her loyalties lie?" asked Zane.

"Not without making certain inquiries," replied Father Collins. "But if I do it, she'll know. Aidan, you're a god of the Otherworld. Can't you listen to her soul?"

"I did, and I sensed nothing. Nothing serious," replied Aidan.

"Then why are you still worried?" asked Raoul. "I thought it was impossible to hide anything in your soul from a god of the Otherworld."

"I thought so too, Raoul, but my intuition tells me otherwise," murmured Aidan. "And after the warning your friend, Luc, sent us, I can't trust anyone among the Guardians and Wardens. No offense to present company."

They discussed the situation for a while. Zane shared his worries about the need to split the team in two, leaving Jim behind to protect the city. Aidan listed to everything Zane was telling him and doubts were crowding his mind, making him uneasy.

Aidan understood why Zane wanted to split into two teams. He was right—they had to be ready to defend both the Yav and the Nav, and anyone who wielded elemental powers was powerless in the Dark Nav. Nevertheless, he hated this idea with a passion. It was never a good choice to divide your team.

The other thing that bothered him was that Jim was the city's only hope, in case Zane was right and Zvereva was planning to open the third front by attacking the city. Should this happen, Jim, the only human on their team would be the city's last and only line of defense. A human FBI agent and a team of vampires. *Well, that doesn't sound strange at all,* thought Aidan shaking his head.

They spent most of the day polishing Zane's plan, trying to predict possible scenarios and be ready for anything that the crazed mage could throw their way. By the time Aidan and Zane walked out of the church, it was dark outside. The fresh breeze, infused with the smells of the ocean, ruffled Aidan's hair. He inhaled enjoying the freshness of the evening.

"Do you have a few minutes?" he asked, staring toward the ocean wistfully.

"You practically kidnapped me," replied Zane with his usual lopsided smirk, "I don't think a few extra minutes would make any difference."

Aidan walked toward the ocean and sat down on the soft sand of the beach. Zane sat next to him, resting his arms atop his bent knees. For a few minutes they sat in silence, listening to the soft whispering of the ocean waves.

"I love the ocean," said Aidan, staring into the horizon, where the dark waters were meeting the stormy sky. "I guess it came from my biological father... He was a god of the sea after all."

Zane didn't say anything. He lay back on the cool sand, folding his arms under his head, staring up into the shadowy clouds. "I love nature... used to love the ocean too. Now water can hurt me. Especially cold water." He chuckled.

"We have less than six days left," said Aidan quietly. "We are not ready."

"We can never be ready," replied Zane calmly. "There is no way to get ready when you don't know what to expect. Everything we discussed earlier were just our best guesses, some wild theories. And so far, this goddamn mage is ahead of us at least ten steps. So, the only thing we can do is play it by ear and fight to the death when the time comes."

"You're too smart for an infant," said Aidan, silently admiring how calm and collected his friend always was, no matter what situation he was in. He picked up a handful of sand, allowing it to trickle down through his fingers. "In a few days from now..." He didn't finish his statement and cut himself short. "I don't know about you, but if these were my last few days on Earth, I know exactly where and with whom I would want to spend them."

"Give my best to Tessa, Aidan." Zane chuckled. "Just don't get her involved in all this mess. The less you're going to tell her the safer she'll be."

"I know. Same applies to Angelique. But I'm sure, she's not going to leave Jim alone fighting for the city," replied Aidan.

Zane nodded, and they both fell silent for a few minutes. "And why are you talking about the last days on Earth, being an immortal god and all," said Zane all of a sudden, rising up on his elbows.

"You're too young, Zane—"

"Jealous, old man?"

Aidan laughed, shaking his head. "Not at all. You're too young to realize that there is nothing wrong with death. Death is not good or evil. It just is. It's natural. I believe you're on the first name basis with Death. There is nothing evil about him, don't you agree? Angel can tell you everything there is to know about dying."

"Immortal, remember?" replied Zane, lying back down.

"Immortality is not a gift, it's a curse," muttered Aidan. "Like I said, you're too young to understand some things yet. There are things in life that are a lot scarier than death."

"Well, you're in a morbid mood today," said Zane, turning his head to the side to see Aidan better. "What scares you, Aidan?"

"The loss of people I love," continued Aidan, his memory traveling back thousands of years ago. "To me it is scarier than dying myself. I survived the death of my siblings whom I loved with all my heart. Especially my twin-sister. Almost twenty-five hundred years later, I still mourn her death. Since then, I didn't open my heart to anyone. Until Tessa came into my life, that is. If something would happen to her, I don't think I could survive another loss like that."

Zane sat down sharply, locking his glowing red eyes with his. "What are you trying to tell me, Aidan? Tessa is going to remain with the Guardians in Chicago. She should be safe there. As safe as the rest of the world."

"If we lose the battle... If the Chaos will run free—"

"Then let's not lose the battle," said Zane. He hopped up, seizing Aidan's arm above his elbow and yanked him up to his feet. Aidan felt the heat of Zane's hand as the fire energy spiked up around his friend. "We both know what we need to do. So, go and spend some time with Tessa while you can, and we'll meet at my house on the morning of the day before Samhain."

"I think I'll do that," agreed Aidan. "I'll use a couple of days for all the preparations as we discussed and then travel to Chicago to spend one day with Tessa."

Zane waved his hand, unfolding the fire-curtain of his portal. "See you soon." He walked through the fire, disappearing on the other side.

Aidan sat back down, thinking about everything he still

needed to do and about his visit to Tessa. The idea of traveling back to the Guardians HQ didn't give him a pleasant vibe, but that was the only way he could see her. With everything that was going on, he wanted Tessa to remain within the highly protected walls of the Guardians Headquarters, safe and away from all the dangers of the outside world.

31

~ AIDAN ~

Aidan walked through the long driveway toward the mansion of the Guardians HQ. He teleported to the gate but decided not to summon the guards and just take a walk. It was giving him a little extra time to think and prepare himself for the meeting with Ms. Bonneville. Also, it was only two o'clock and Tessa's lessons were over at three. He had an hour to spare. This time he checked the weather and had a leather jacket over his shirt, so the long walk through the park was pleasant and relaxing.

When he finally reached the mansion and opened the front door, he wasn't surprised to find Ms. Bonneville accompanied by a few guards, meeting him. He stopped a few steps away and stared down at her, narrowing his eyes. For extra effect, he sent some of his magic toward his eyes, making them glow bright-white.

She caught his icy gaze for a brief moment and averted her eyes, greeting him with a bow. "My lord, I didn't summon you," she seethed through clenched teeth. "To what do I owe the pleasure of your visit?"

Aidan smirked at her greeting. He could sense the fear in

her, but also, he could sense the hatred and resentment. *Expected.*

"I would like to spend a few hours with Tessa," replied Aidan simply. "For a few hours, I would like to take her outside the Guardians Headquarters. As a loyal and respectful member of the Guardians Order, I'm asking you to grant Tessa a short leave for the rest of the day today." He was trying to sound sincere, but he couldn't help it and the words "loyal and respectful" were overflowing with sarcasm.

"Of course, my lord," grumbled Ms. Bonneville. "Let me send a guard to bring her over."

Aidan checked his watch. It was almost 2:30 PM. "That won't be necessary, Ms. Bonneville. Let Tessa finish her lessons. I'll wait for her here, if you don't mind."

"As you wish. But do try to bring her back before midnight. The apprentices' wing will be locked by that time... my lord."

"I will," promised Aidan, waving his hand at the Head Mage in a dismissive gesture. "That'll be all. You may go now."

"My lord," hissed Ms. Bonneville, bowing. She pivoted on her high heels and marched out of the main hall, anger radiating around her like a stormy cloud. He followed her exit with his eyes, thinking that he gained a serious enemy in her, but somehow at this moment he couldn't care less.

Aidan leaned on the wall, folding his arms over his chest. He sighed, checking his wristwatch again. He had to wait just thirty minutes, but the time was moving torturously slow. He closed his eyes, lowering his head to his chest.

It had been a long few days. They were trying to get everything ready for the possible attack on the city and go over their plan one more time with each member of their team. Even though they did everything they could and covered all possible options they could foresee, they both felt uneasy, driven by an eerie perception that there was something they didn't account for. They felt that they were missing something, but none of them could point out what it was.

Submerged under the heavy burden of his thoughts and doubts, he didn't notice how the time passed and the main hall got filled with people. He felt a soft touch to his elbow and opened his eyes. Tessa was standing in front of him. In her black apprentice's uniform, she looked slim and delicate. She was gazing up at him, her bottomless brown eyes unobstructed by her long hair. She caught his gaze and a happy smile ignited warmth in the depth of her eyes. She was so breathtakingly beautiful that for one moment Aidan forgot everything that bothered him.

"Tessa..." he exhaled, not sure that he could take his eyes off her.

She didn't say anything but took a step forward and encircled his waist with her arms, pressing her cheek to his chest. He hugged her, his fingers softly threading through the thick mane of her hair and softly kissed the top of her head.

"Aidan, why are you here?" she asked, pulling away from him. "Is everything okay?"

He smiled down at her, feeling slightly intoxicated by her gentle touch. "Why wouldn't it be? All is good," he lied, shame clenching his throat. Now he was lying to her. A while ago, she just thought that he lied to her and he almost lost her. But it was better to lose her than to endanger her life by telling her the truth.

"I don't believe you," she stated bluntly. "You're a terrible liar, Aidan McGrath."

He cupped her face with his hands and gently kissed her forehead. "Tessa, I missed you," he said, hoping that he sounded sincere enough. After all, he did miss her every moment of every day. "I had to see you. I talked to the Head Mage, and she allowed me to take you out of the Guardians' premises for an evening, so we could spend a few hours together."

"She did?" asked Tessa, narrowing her eyes at him with suspicion.

"Of course, she did," confirmed Aidan. "I would never jeopardize your position with the Guardians Order. Where would you like to go?"

She took a step back and gave him a quick once-over, disbelief still written all over her face. "Fine. Give me five minutes. I want to change into something more—um—city-appropriate." She giggled and ran away.

Aidan gazed in the direction where she disappeared, thinking about these few hours that he would get to spend with her when he felt a light touch to his arm. He snapped his head to the side and saw Jamie, the young guard who was always helpful and kind to him.

"Jamie, hi," he said, offering his hand for a handshake.

"Mr. McGrath, it's nice to see you here again," he said, shaking his hand. "Ms. Bonneville sent me here. She said to drive you and your friend anywhere you wish to go. I'm your driver and guard for the night, sir."

"Thank you, Jamie," replied Aidan. "Let's wait for Tessa and then we can go."

* * *

JAMIE OPENED the back door of his car for them, and Aidan let Tessa in first. The young guard drove the car through the main gate and stopped.

"Where would you like to go, Mr. McGrath?" he asked, looking at him in the rearview mirror.

"Jamie, I don't need a guard and I definitely don't need a driver, as I'm sure you realized after my last stay here," said Aidan, trying to sound calm and friendly.

"Yes, sir, I figured as much," replied Jamie, chuckling. "I

figured you were some powerful wizard, but it's the order I received from Ms. Bonneville. I must follow my orders."

"He's not a wizard," huffed Tessa, rolling her eyes, but Aidan put his hand on her shoulder and shook his head.

"Jamie, drive in any direction," said Aidan. "I don't care where you take us. I just want to spend time with Tessa."

"Yes, sir." Jamie turned the soft music on in the car and switched it to drive, turning right to the main road.

"Jamie, you've been honest and friendly so far and I want to repay you in kind," continued Aidan as soon as they were far enough from the Guardians HQ. He whispered a spell and a hardly noticeable wave of air rushed through the car. The radio choked and fell silent. "If this car was bugged technically or magically, it no longer is. So, we can talk openly."

"I don't think it was bugged, sir," said Jamie. Aidan noticed fear in the eyes of the young guard.

"Jamie, you don't have to fear me," he said calmly. "I swear you're absolutely safe with me. I'm not a wizard, I'm a god. And something tells me that your role today is also not a guard and a driver." Jamie shrunk behind the steering wheel, averting his gaze. "Did Ms. Bonneville send you with me to spy on me and report to her on all my moves? Please, be honest with me."

Jamie parked the car on the side of the road and turned in the driver's seat to face him. "I'm sorry, Mr. McGrath. I'm not a spy, but you're right. Ms. Bonneville ordered me to report to her on every place you visit and everything you do. I have no choice. Besides, if I refused to do it, she would send someone else."

"It's okay, Jamie. Later on, tonight, you will take Tessa back to the Guardians HQ and you can honestly report to Ms. Bonneville everything you saw and every word we said. Except for this particular conversation, of course," said Aidan peacefully. "I don't want to put your job or your life at risk."

"Thank you, sir," said Jamie, his cheeks still flushed with embarrassment of his mission. "So, where can I take you?"

Aidan threw a quick glance at Tessa and a light smile quirked up his lips. "Take us to the Chicago Botanic Garden."

"You know that it'll be closed at five and it's already past three," said Jamie starting the car.

Aidan chuckled and winked. "That doesn't bother me," he replied, relaxing in the back seat. "I've heard that the Garden is beautiful after dark, when no one is there."

* * *

JAMIE PARKED the car in the parking lot of the Chicago Botanic Garden and walked around the car to open the door for Aidan.

"What would you like me to do while you're enjoying the gardens, Mr. McGrath," he asked without raising his eyes at Aidan, fidgeting with a leather bracelet on his left wrist. "I realize that you can teleport anywhere you wish from here, so just tell me what I should say when I'm back at the Guardians HQ."

Aidan glanced at him, feeling bad for the young guard. Then he reached in his pocket, pulled out his wallet and found his credit card.

"Tessa, do me a favor," he said, giving his credit card to her. "Can you please get us the tickets while I have a word with Jamie here?"

Tessa pulled away, pursing her lips. "I don't need you to pay for my ticket, Aidan."

"This one time, Tessa, please, just indulge me," he said with a sigh. "You know I'm old school."

"Yeah, old school, alright," muttered Tessa as she turned around and marched away. "Like twenty-five hundred years old school."

"Interesting young lady," mumbled Jamie, following Tessa as she disappeared inside a building.

"You have no idea," replied Aidan, chuckling. "Just don't call her lady if you want to keep your teeth. Listen, Jamie, I don't want you to have any problems with the Head Mage, so I'm going to tell you the truth and you can do with it whatever you want."

"Thank you, Mr. McGrath," said the guard, finally raising his eyes.

"However, before I say anything else, there is something I must do and you're not going to like it. So, brace yourself," said Aidan.

Moving quickly, he seized the young guard's shoulder and pressed his right hand to his chest, locking his glowing eyes with his. Jamie gasped as Aidan's power invaded his soul. A few seconds later, Aidan released him. The young guard didn't lie to him. His soul was pure. It was a soul of an honest and loyal man. Jamie wasn't quite pureblood human. Aidan could sense traces of magical energy in him. He was a wizard, but his magic was weak and undeveloped, and Aidan had to wonder if Jamie even knew about its existence.

"What… did you do… to me?" panted Jamie, pressing his hand to his heart.

"I'm sorry, Jamie," said Aidan. "I had to be sure that you were honest. I read your soul. It's one of my powers as a god."

"I felt like you were… scanning my insides," mumbled Jamie, slowly catching his breath.

"I was and now I know that I can trust you," continued Aidan. "Anyway, the only reason I am here today is because I love Tessa and I want to spend a few hours with her alone, without any witnesses. Do you know what I mean?"

"Yes, sir, I understand."

"There are no other agendas. Just that. I want to spend time with the woman I love," added Aidan. "We're going to go inside the gardens and walk a little. Then I will teleport her anywhere she wishes to go. I promise that I'm not going to leave the great Chicago area and we'll meet you right here before midnight. You can do anything you want in the meantime."

"I have to stay here, Mr. McGrath," said Jamie. "I'm sure Ms. Bonneville is going to check the GPS in my car. So, if I'm going to tell her that you were here all this time, I have to stay here all this time."

"Okay, then I don't like it. I don't want you to sit here alone in your car. With everything that's been going on lately, it's not safe." Aidan reached in his pocket and pulled a small notebook and pen. He wrote an address of a hotel and tore a page out, giving it to Jamie. "While we're in the garden, drive to this hotel and rent two rooms—one for us and one for yourself. I'll let them know to expect you there, so they'll charge my card for everything. Leave the key for me at the front desk. Use the second room, order yourself a nice dinner and relax. I'll meet you at 11:30 PM in the lobby of the hotel."

"Thank you, sir, I'll see you later at the hotel lobby," said Jamie, taking the note and hiding it in his pocket. Aidan noticed notes of surprise in his voice and had to wonder what the Head Mage told the young guard about him.

AIDAN FOUND Tessa inside the building and they entered the gardens. For a short while they were walking in silence. Tessa wrapped her arm around his waist, leaning into his side and he draped his arm around her shoulders, enjoying their closeness. After a little while, Tessa pulled him toward one of the benches and sat down, gesturing at him to join her.

"What are we doing here, Aidan?" she asked, gazing up into his eyes. "Why did you bring me to this place? You're not telling me something and it makes me sick with worry."

"Tessa, I just wanted to spend some time with you," Aidan started to say, but she shook her head frowning.

"Aidan, I'm not a child." She leaned forward, resting her bent elbows on her knees, staring down at her boots. "Something is going on. I feel something... I don't understand and I didn't have anyone to ask because Ms. Bonneville sent Missi away on assignment. But I feel something... something evil. I don't know what it is, but it's coming." She bit her lip, turning her head to glance at Aidan. "I'm sure that this... evil thing... whatever it is, is the reason you're here today. You came to say goodbye. You're planning to fight it and you're not sure that you can win this fight. Am I right?"

"You can feel it?" asked Aidan, a cold wave of fear spreading through his body.

Tessa nodded and leaned back, resting her head on his shoulder. "Aidan, can you tell me what's going on? Please. Not knowing is a lot worse."

He pulled her closer, resting his cheek atop her head. "I can't, my love. The less you know, the safer you're going to be," he whispered, feeling her hand squeezing into a fist on his lap.

"So, I was right," she said, lifting her head, and pushed him away. "You came here because you're afraid that you're not going to survive the fight!"

He forced a laugh, trying to look relaxed, at ease. "Come on, Tess. I'm an immortal god, remember? Nothing can happen to me. I'll be back. I had a few hours, and I wanted to see you. That's all."

"Gods can be killed," Tessa said quietly. "I'm learning, Aidan. Now I know that some gods can kill gods."

She got up and halted in front of him, placing her hands on his shoulders, pinning his back to the bench. He glanced up at her, not sure what to expect next. She leaned forward and kissed him, hungrily and desperately, her hands moving up his neck, grabbing his hair. Passion ignited within him, every inch of his body craving her, and his hands gripped at the bench. The wood cracked loudly, and Tessa pulled away. She took in his appearance and chuckled.

"Can you afford a hotel room, old man?" she asked, brushing her fingers over his unshaved cheek. "I don't want you destroying public property here."

"Tessa... no..." he said, his breath quickened as her hand traveled down his chest.

A soft laugh escaped her lips. She put her knee on the bench between his legs and leaned down, wrapping her arms around his neck. She ran her lips over his cheek to his mouth, forcing his lips apart. He could hear her heart thundering in her chest, beating in unison with his.

"Tessa..." he exhaled, panting as she finally allowed him to breathe.

"You want me, Aidan, admit it. You can't fight it," she whispered into his ear and the touch of her warm breath to his skin sent his world spinning. Her hand traveled south over the tight muscles of his abdomen, stopping between his legs. Aidan grunted, covering her hand with his to stop her.

"Tessa..."

"Hotel, Aidan. Now," she ordered.

Aidan got up, lifting her in his arms. "Your wish is my command, my lady," he said, cringing inwardly at how raspy his voice sounded. He teleported from the garden and manifested a moment later in the back of the Hilton Hotel.

The key to the room was waiting for him at the front desk. He smiled, in his mind thanking Jamie for renting the room. They took the elevator to the eighth floor. As soon as the elevator door closed behind them, Aidan pushed Tessa against the mirrored wall and kissed her. Her breath caught as she responded eagerly to his kiss, and he smiled over her lips.

"I can play this game too." He smiled gazing down at her foggy dark eyes, gently tucking a loose strand of her hair behind her ear. The elevator stopped, and they made their way to their room.

The room wasn't big with a queen-size bed taking most of the space. Tessa sat down on the bed and glanced up at Aidan, a dazed smile playing on her lips. For a moment, freezing fear gripped his heart, with merciless clarity reminding him what would happen if they lost the battle with Chaos. Ruled by the Lord of Chaos, the world would never be the same. Love, happiness, kindness, everything good that existed now would be destroyed. He would never see Tessa again.

"Aidan, what's wrong?"

Tessa's voice, filled with concern, brought him back. He took a step forward, dropping to his knees before her and hid his face in her lap. His arms wrapped around her waist and he froze, hardly breathing.

"Aidan, I understand you don't want to tell me what's going on," said Tessa, her fingers slowly threading through his hair. "I can see that it's something serious—"

"Tessa, please, don't ask any questions," he pleaded, lifting his head to see her. "I don't want to talk about it. Tonight, I just want to be with you. We have but a few hours together, my love."

She nodded, her eyes like two round mirrors reflecting his torment and despair. "I'm not going to ask any questions," she whispered, leaning forward and gently kissing his forehead. She took the lapels of his jacket and pulled it off, gazing down at him. Then she slowly unbuttoned his shirt, exposing his chest. "Take your clothes off, Aidan."

"Tessa, no. You don't have to do it," he said quietly, averting his gaze. "This is not why I'm here."

"I know I don't have to do it." She shrugged. "You told me that my wish is your command, didn't you?"

"Always."

"I wish to see you, my handsome ancient god," said Tessa, caressing his face. "Take your clothes off. All of them."

He got up and slowly pulled his shirt off, dropping it on the floor. Then he unzipped his jeans, his trembling fingers fumbling with the button a touch too long.

"Your jeans, Aidan. I want to see them on the floor next to your shirt." She smiled at him, her large eyes twinkling with humor. "I command you."

He took his jeans off, dropping them on the floor and straightened up, still leaving his underwear on.

"Forgetting something?"

She hooked her finger at the waistband of his underwear and pulled them all the way down. Aidan gasped, suddenly feeling more naked than he ever felt in his whole life, instinctively crossing his hands over his groin. She giggled, catching his awkward reaction and sat back down, observing him like a piece of art. Then she reached forward and seized his wrists, forcing his hands apart.

"You're the most handsome man I've ever seen," she whispered, her eyes gliding up and down his unclothed body.

Aidan cleared his throat, not sure that he could speak. "And exactly how many naked men have you seen so far?"

"Well, that's none of your business, is it, Aidan McGrath?" she huffed. "I'm sure the list of women you've been with is a lot longer anyway, considering your age and all."

She got up, standing less than an inch away from him and stretched up on her tiptoes to give him a quick kiss. He could feel her breath on his bare skin and desire spiked in him with a new strength. He closed his eyes for a brief moment and immediately felt her hand slowly sliding down below his waist. He grabbed her wrist, ready to stop her, but she let go right away.

"Lie down, Aidan," she said, pointing at the bed. Then she thought for a moment and added, "Please."

Aidan smiled shyly at her, still feeling a little uncomfortable and exposed. Never could he imagine that he was still capable of feeling shy and vulnerable in the presence of a woman. Tessa pulled the cover and the blanket off the bed and he lay down, placing his arms under his head, wondering what she would do next.

For a moment, Tessa stood still at the foot of the bed, caressing him with her gaze, her mouth slightly opened, her eyes dark with desire. Then she averted her gaze and took her jacket off, throwing it on the floor on the heap of his clothes. Just as slowly, she pulled her t-shirt off and dropped it. She had no bra under it.

She turned to Aidan, so he could see her clearly. He knew that she was doing it for him, but he wasn't sure if he should say something or just let her do whatever she wanted. Tessa took her jeans off, leaving a thin lacy underwear on and walked to the side of the bed. At first, she sat down on the edge of the bed, gazing at Aidan, a smile, sensual and slightly drunk, curving her lips.

"You're breathtaking," whispered Aidan, without moving. More than anything, he wanted to touch her, feel her slim body against his, make her moan with pleasure. But he didn't move, afraid to ruin the moment.

Tessa smiled wider, her eyes gleaming with happiness. She climbed up on the bed and straddled his hips. Aidan sucked in a sharp breath and she chuckled, moving slightly against him. He wasn't sure how long he would be able to control his desire with her playing with his body like that.

"Tessa," he whispered, his breath caught as she leaned forward, resting her hands on his chest.

"Shh," she said, pressing her finger to her lips and then moved farther up to kiss him. Her kiss ignited him, setting his mind on fire. He felt her hand on the back of his head, holding him closer as she deepened her kiss. He was burning for her and at this moment he didn't remember feeling like this with anyone else.

Tessa pulled away ever so slightly and her lips brushed his once more. "Aidan," she whispered, moving closer to his ear, an unusual air of shyness surrounding her, "do you want me? Do you enjoy? You know... what I'm doing..."

He laughed tenderly. She was so wonderfully young and so sweet. "Tessa, you seriously have to ask? I enjoy every second of just being near to you. What you're giving me right now means so much more to me than just physical pleasure, my love. Do I want you? Yes, of course! With every cell of my body and with every fiber of my soul. I love you, my Tessa. I love you more than life itself."

She pushed herself up, her arms on either side of him, and for a long moment was gazing down at him, studying his face with her deep dark eyes. "Aidan," she said finally, and the tone of her trembling voice told him more than her words, "you are my... everything... You always were. Love me, Aidan, love me like there is no tomorrow."

A low growl rumbled deep in his throat as he seized her slim waist and gently lifted her, lowering her on the bed next to him. He rolled to his side and pulled her closer, covering her mouth with his.

Like there is no tomorrow? There is no tomorrow for me, not without you, he thought, surrendering his body and his soul to this young woman who held his heart and his life in her hands.

32

~ ZANE BURNS, A.K.A. GUNZ ~

It was late evening when Gunz knocked on the door of Angelique's apartment. The door swung open right away and Angelique stepped aside, letting him pass through. As soon as she closed the door, she threw her arms around his neck, clinging her whole body tightly to him. He hugged her, closing his eyes for a moment, her delicate scent invading his senses. For a few seconds, she was holding him close, hiding her face in his chest. He ran his hands over her sides and gently kissed the top of her head.

"Angie, hi," he said, feeling her finally pulling away.

"Tomorrow?" she asked instead of hello, her eyes searching his face. She found his hand and entwined her fingers with his.

He didn't need any additional explanation, knowing well what she was asking. "Tomorrow morning," he replied. "Both teams are going to meet in my house, and we all will leave from there."

She nodded, biting her lip and pulled him into the living room. "Are you hungry? Can I get you anything?"

"No, thank you," he objected. He didn't remember when he ate the last time, but right now he didn't feel hungry. He didn't need food. He needed a few minutes of peace, something to take his mind off everything that was coming tomorrow and on the night of All Hallows' Eve.

Angelique sat down next to him, clenching her hands on her lap, staring straight forward. Gunz took in her appearance and sighed. She was wearing her favorite silk kimono robe. Dark red silk was wrapped around her willowy figure, effectively accentuating her narrow waist. Her hair spilled over her back and chest, shining darkly against the redness of her kimono. She was as beautiful as he ever remembered her, but her pale face was wearing signs of tears, tiredness and stress.

He took her hands in his, gently squeezing her fingers. She peered at their joined hands and a single drop of water fell on the floor. She pressed her other hand to her eyes, swallowing her tears.

"Angie, it's going to be all right," he said, gently caressing the top of her hand with his thumb. "Two days and I'll be right back here, with you. Plus, I'm not going to be alone there. I'll have Kal and Mrak Delar by my side. I know that Svyatobor is also going to be with us and hopefully Semargl will join us too." She bit her lip again and turned away, hiding her newly gathering tears. "Come on, sweetheart. Two Slavic deities, Fire Elemental and a Master of Power. In their company, I'll be as safe as I can be. Plus, I'm immortal. Nothing can happen to me. I'm more worried about you here... Are you planning to stay with Jim?"

She didn't answer his question but turned back to him, her eyes swimming with tears. "How about Karma and Voron?" she asked airily.

"Karma will stay with us, but Voron decided to go with Aidan and stand by his Lord and master's side. He will return to the Dark Nav to protect Chernobog."

"I wish I could go with you," she whispered, placing her hand on top of his. "I have this feeling—"

"Angie, don't do it, please," Gunz interrupted her. "I would feel a lot better if you remained here, in the city. I'm sure Jim will need your guidance."

She laughed, a short and bitter sound. "I know. I'm just a seer—useless when it comes to combat magic. Karma is equipped a lot better for that than I am. She's an assassin after all."

"Sweetheart, you have no reason to be—"

"I am not jealous!" yelled Angelique, jumping off the couch. "But I envy her. I envy that she can stand and fight by your side. She can be there to protect you and I can't!"

Gunz got up and gathered her into his arms, pulling her closer. She pressed her hands against his chest, for a brief moment fighting his embrace, but then let go and fell apart crying.

"I know what you need," he murmured into her ear, lifting her up. He carried her into the kitchen and sat her on top of the kitchen counter. "Your favorite tea?"

She smiled through tears and nodded. Gunz filled the kettle with cold water and put it on the stove. Then he touched the kettle, channeling the fire energy through it. A moment later, the water boiled. He poured the boiling water into a cup with a tea bag and put it on the counter next to her.

The bitter-sweet aroma of herbal tea wafted through the kitchen. Angelique took honey from the cabinet next to her and added some into her cup, carefully mixing it with a spoon.

"It's handy to have you around the house, you know," she said evenly, like she wasn't crying just a moment ago. "Big savings on electricity. You can boil any amount of water within seconds."

"I hope your electric bill is not the only reason you wish to have me here," said Gunz, leaning back in his chair, folding his hands behind his head.

She stared at him thoughtfully for a moment, but then shook her head and took a sip of her tea. "No, that's the only reason I can think of," she said nonchalantly. "What? Is there anything else you're good for?"

Gunz laughed. He got up and approached her. "Allow me to prove my worth, my lady," he said, separating her legs and stepping in, closer to her.

She put the cup with the leftover tea on the counter and brushed his face with her fingers, gazing into his eyes. He pulled her a little closer and kissed her. The desire came to life within him, and his fire energy spiked up, responding to his emotions. Gunz pulled away, taking a few breaths to get his power under control.

He was getting better at controlling his power, but for Angelique's safety, he still preferred to use the bracelet that Mrak Delar made for him. The bracelet was locking his fire power within his body, allowing him to relax and let go.

Angelique wrapped her legs around his waist, pulling him closer again. He didn't object. He cupped her face and kissed her, pouring all his need into a single kiss. She moaned, her hands sliding down his shoulders, moving over his back. She found the bottom edge of his shirt and pulled it off, placing it on the counter next to her. Then she leaned forward and nuzzled his neck, sending shivers down his body.

Gunz grunted from the feeling of fire, figurative and literal, rushing through him, igniting the dancing flames in his eyes. He sighed and stepped away, his chest rising and falling with heavy breaths, small flames rushing up and down his arms. Angelique gazed at him. There was so much affection in her eyes that he felt drunk, intoxicated by her love and desire for him.

"I guess I do know how to light your fire," she murmured, not without amusement.

"Angie," he managed to say, still breathing hard, "where is my bracelet?"

"Aw, sweetie, you need a condom for your magic?" she teased him, jumping off the counter.

She approached him and blew at a small flame on his shoulder. The flame flickered and died out. He took a few deep breaths to cool down. She touched his skin carefully, like she was testing a hot iron, and jerked her hand away.

"Mpmm, I got myself a smoldering hot man." Angelique giggled and headed out of the kitchen, waving for him to follow.

He threw his hands in the air but went after her into the bedroom. She had this uncanny ability to joke in any situation, no matter how relaxed or serious they were, and he loved it about her.

The bedroom was dark, the only light coming through the doorway into the living room. Angie was standing by the side of the bed, holding his bracelet in her hand. A large red stone was gleaming dimly.

"Come here," she whispered, stretching her hand to him. The red light of the stone reflected on her face and in her deep eyes. She looked magical and mysterious.

Hypnotized by her looks, Gunz slowly approached her. She took his right hand and locked the bracelet on his wrist, gently kissing his knuckles. The bracelet suppressed his fire power, and a wave of weakness spread over him. He exhaled, swaying slightly and felt Angelique's hands gently supporting him right away.

"I hate what it does to you," she said as he eased himself to the bed.

"I'll be all right in a moment." Gunz smiled gazing up at her. "It's the only way, Angie. I need to be sure that I won't hurt you."

He pulled down on her hand, forcing her to step between his legs. The dizziness slowly cleared, and he was back to normal. He found the sash that was holding her kimono together and pulled on it. The sash fell, and the robe opened up, giving him a delectable view of her smooth stomach. He put his hands on her sides under her kimono, pulling her a little closer, and explored every inch of her satin skin with his lips.

She moaned and shuddered in his hands, throwing her head back, closing her eyes. Without stopping what he was doing, Gunz pulled her on his lap, his lips traveling up her breasts and to her neck. Her body arched toward him, electrifying him with passion. He lifted her and lowered her on the bed.

"Zane..." she whispered without opening her eyes. "I love you..."

Gunz quickly undressed and lay down on the bed, next to her, supporting himself on his bent elbow. He peered down at her tender face. Her lips were parted, and her dark hair fanned around her face, making her skin look marble white, almost glowing in the darkness of the room. Gently he lowered his face down and found her lips, his hand moving down to cup her breast.

"Angie," he whispered between kisses, "I love you too." He never said those words to anyone before, but right now it felt right. It was true. He loved her from the first moment he laid his eyes on her in Jim's office, but it took him all this time to realize it.

She opened her eyes for a moment to meet his gaze, high with desire and love, and smiled. "I thought I'd never hear it from you. Say it again... please..."

"I love you," he repeated, gently lowering his body on top of hers.

THE WALL CLOCK was showing almost five in the morning when Gunz woke up. He found Angelique sleeping in his arms, snuggled to his chest. He smiled down at her, the memory of last night still fresh, but his mind was slowly coming back to harsh reality. In this reality, he would be leaving her in less than an hour to face a dangerous and deadly adversary. The fairytale was over. He stifled a sigh, not wanting to wake her up.

"I wish we could stay like this forever," she whispered suddenly, without lifting her head.

"In a perfect world we could stay like this forever," he replied, his fingers drawing circles on her shoulder absentmindedly.

"The world *is* perfect, silly," she replied with a sad smile. "All I want is to wake up with you next to me every day. My own little perfect universe is within the circle of your arms, Zane."

She lowered her head back down. He felt her tears sliding down his chest and glanced at her, pressing her tighter to his side.

"Angie, why are you crying?" he asked, troubled.

She just shook her head and didn't answer.

"Did you have a vision last night?" he asked. "What did you see?"

"Nothing," she whispered into his chest. "I saw absolutely nothing."

"Then why are you so worried?"

She sat up, staring down at him, and frowned. "I see nothing, Zane. Nothing at all. I don't see anything past forty-eight hours from now. It's like the world is gone. You understand?"

"Are you predicting that we'll lose the battle?" asked Gunz, fear chilling him to the bone. "Are you saying that the Lord of Chaos will rule the Earth again?"

"No! I predict nothing," she replied, tracing the shape of his jaw with her fingers. "The only thing I'm saying is that I can't see the future. I can't see the battle. I don't even see if the city is going to be attacked. It's like there is no future. I've never had anything like this happen to me before."

"It's that crazy mage. Zvereva," he said reassuringly, gazing up at her. "She's so powerful. I'm sure she is blocking your sight. Don't worry, Angie. It'll be all right. No matter what, I'm coming back to you."

"You can't know that, Zane," she said shaking her head. "I'm a seer and even I can't know that. How can you be so sure?"

"It's not my first war, Angie. And if I learned anything, it's that I have to have faith," replied Gunz. "When you're facing an enemy as dangerous and as powerful as the Skiper-Zmey, you must believe that you can win. You must believe that you're on the right side of history. If you don't, you will lose."

Gunz pushed himself up and draped his arm over her shoulders. She laid her head on his shoulder and sighed. "You're probably right," she mumbled, reaching for the watch on his wrist. "Oh, Zane, did you know that your watch is broken? Not ticking…"

"Yeah, I know," he replied, waving his hand dismissively. "It broke when I crossed the veil and with everything that's going on, I forgot to ask Jim for a new one. The only reason I'm still wearing it is because it's Mishka's safe house."

Angelique giggled. "Are you saying that Mishka was with us all night?"

"Oh, God, no," replied Gunz, laughing. "I left him with Karma. She actually likes that annoying little monster."

Angelique smiled and kissed him on his cheek. Then she ran her fingers over his prickly stubble. "Last night you were shaved."

"I probably was," he replied, scratching his chin. He glanced at the wall clock and sighed. "I have to go now, Angie. I don't want Kal and Mrak waiting for me. You know how Kal is… He doesn't like to wait."

She slid off the bed and found her kimono, draping it over her shoulders. "Yes, of course. Go."

Gunz got off the bed and put his pants and shoes on. Angelique ran to the kitchen and brought his shirt. He kissed Angelique one more time, taking the shirt out of her hands, and opened his portal in the middle of her bedroom.

"Be careful, Zane," she said. "Remember, you're the one who's holding my perfect world. It doesn't exist without you."

"Stay away from trouble. If something happens here, Jim is ready. Go to him. Akira and Jim will take care of everything. And as soon as it's all over, I'll find you, Angie," he promised and walked through the portal, leaving her in the dark and empty bedroom.

* * *

HE WALKED out of the portal in the middle of the living room. Karma was sleeping, but he could hear the water running in the guest bathroom on the first floor. Voron was up and getting ready. He glanced at the watch, registering that he had about thirty minutes to take a quick shower and change.

He ran upstairs, skipping steps. As soon as he closed the door to his bedroom, he yelled, "Mishka!"

The wyvern materialized immediately, hopping up and down in front of his face.

"I'm here, boss," he reported, giving him a military-style salute with his wing.

"Mishka, I need you to do something extremely important for me," continued Gunz. "When I leave today, I want you to stay behind. You are not coming with me."

"But why, boss?" asked Mishka, horror making his red eyes glow brighter. "I'm bound to protect you. I'm bound by my true master, the Fire Elemental. I can't disobey his orders."

"Mishka, you're not going to be disobeying Kal," said Gunz with a sigh. "You're going to protect me. But instead of protecting my body, I trust you to protect my heart."

"I don't understand," mumbled Mishka, landing on his shoulder. He craned his long neck down, pressing his head to Gunz's chest. "Hmm, your heart is still in your chest. I can hear it beating. How can I protect your heart by staying behind?"

"Aw, Mishka, stop taking everything so literally," said Gunz, shaking his head. "It was a figure of speech. I need you to stay behind to protect Angelique. Do you understand me?"

"You want me abandon my duty to protect a little seer?" huffed Mishka.

"I love her," replied Gunz quietly, petting the wyvern's golden wings. "I don't know what I would do if something happened to her. I'd die…"

"Eww!" Mishka flew up in the air and made a few circles around him, singing, "Boss got a girlfriend."

"Mishka!" yelled Gunz, throwing his hands in the air. "Did I make myself clear? You are going to stay with Angelique, and you are not going to leave her even for a moment. Wherever she goes, you follow her. Until I come back, you're in charge of her safety."

"Fine," muttered Mishka, finally landing on the bed. "But if someone kills your clumsy ass, and Kal will try to blame me for that, I'm going to tell him that it was all your fault and that he should punish you."

"That's fine," agreed Gunz, suppressing his laughter. "If I die, you can send Kal to punish me. I have no problem with that. Now, go to Angelique, my friend."

Mishka threw a scorching gaze at him and vanished from the room.

33

~ ZANE BURNS, A.K.A. GUNZ ~

The street of the village was empty. Too empty for this time of day. There were neither people nor animals outside. The houses stood dark and cold, unkept, with peeling paint, caved in roofs, and broken fences.

The winds were hissing and whistling between the houses, banging with the window shutters and open gates. It seemed like the winds were blowing from every direction. Despite the season, it felt wintry.

The forest that was rising just outside the village stood lifeless, free of foliage. Low dark clouds stretched over the land, threatening to turn into a freezing downpour at any moment. Gunz glanced up at the sky and shivered. He couldn't feel the cold, but he wasn't looking forward to the icy rain.

Kal noticed his discomfort and chuckled. "Relax, Gunz," he said, his deep voice carried through the empty street by the next gust of the wind. "We're almost there. Don't forget, we have a Master of Power with us. If need be, he can control the weather."

"Aw, don't worry, sugar. I'm not going to let you melt," sang Karma, pushing her hand through the crook of Gunz's arm. "I'll protect you from the mean rain. I can always conjure an umbrella for you."

Gunz took her leather-clothed hand, shaking it off his arm. He had to admit that today Karma looked badass. No more fluffy slippers and bedazzled pink jeans. She was wearing a black leather jacket and trousers; her outfit complete with combat boots and leather gloves. With a military-style tactical sling-bag on her back and throwing knives in holders attached to her legs, she looked all business. He was sure that inside her jacket, she was also packing some kind of gun or two, but it wasn't visible on the outside and he didn't bother asking.

Mrak Delar pointed to the last house that was sitting right on the border with the forest. "The last house," he said. "Almost there. But let's not tempt fate. We have two Fire Salamanders here. A cold rain may present a problem."

He channeled the elemental power from nature and his eyes flooded with the darkness of power. Muttering something, he extended his arm up. The wind picked up, driving the rain clouds off the sky. By the time they reached the last house, the sky was clear and airy, but somehow retained its original gray shade.

Mrak Delar walked through the half-demolished fence and knocked on the door of the last house. No one answered. Mrak knocked again. After a few seconds, they heard slow steps. Someone was shuffling toward the door, hardly moving their feet. The door cracked open and an old lady stepped through the threshold. Her face was covered in a web of deep wrinkles. Her snowy hair was pulled in a tight bun on the back of her head. She looked no less than ninety-years old, but her blue eyes were bright and clear like that of a twenty-year-old girl.

"My lady," said Mrak Delar bowing to her.

She shuffled closer to him, craning her neck to look up at him. "Oh my God," she whispered, her trembling hand reaching to his face. "Master Mrak Delar. I can't believe my eyes... You didn't change at all. Just as handsome and charming as you were in 1812. All these years later. Gwyn ap Nudd said that I'll see you today, but I didn't expect to see a young man."

"I'm still a Master of Power, Countess Demidova," replied Mrak Delar, taking her hand and bringing it up to his lips. "Even though I got the title 'ancient' attached to my name now, I don't age at the same pace as humans."

"Countess Demidova?" echoed Gunz, flabbergasted. "But you should be dead. Your own daughter killed you years ago. How is it possible?"

"Oh, she killed me all right." The old lady chuckled, a smile igniting a bright twinkle in her youthful eyes. She petted Gunz on his cheek with a motherly gesture and waved at the door. "Why are we standing outside? Please come in. October is cold in Arkhangelsk. After all, it is the north of Russia."

Gunz walked inside the house and the heat enveloped him. He rolled his shoulders, relaxing, enjoying the warmth and the close presence of his element. The house was light and spacious. On the left, there was a large table with two benches on either side. The table was covered with a white tablecloth. On his right, there was a large fireplace. Bright flames were dancing inside it. He headed to it and squatted, putting his hands into the fire.

"The young one is a Child of Fire, is he not?" asked the Countess.

"Yes. He's my child," replied Kal, sounding like a proud father.

Gunz felt Kal's hand on his shoulder and got up. Mrak Delar and Karma were already sitting at the table. They joined them. The Countess sat down next to him and smiled.

"Gwyn ap Nudd said that you all need my help," she said. "He convinced Death to bring me back for two days to assist the Guardians and you all. So, what am I doing back in Arkhangelsk and what can I do to help you?"

"Do you remember that night in Moscow, September 1812?" asked Mrak Delar.

She chuckled, shaking her head. "You mean that night when you burnt the ancient city to the ground, Master?"

"Yes, my lady," replied Mrak Delar calmly, but a dark shadow flashed across his handsome face. "That night I entrusted you with a powerful magical artifact."

"I'm dead, Master, but I assure you, my memories are intact," said the Countess dryly. "I guarded that artifact as long as I deemed it safe. When I felt that there was no one I could trust with it, I summoned Chernobog. He has it now."

"He doesn't," objected Mrak Delar. "This is why we're here."

"What do you mean, he doesn't?" hissed the Countess, slowly rising. She leaned toward Mrak Delar, planting her fists on the table. "How could he lose it?"

"He didn't lose it, ma'am," explained Gunz. "It was stolen from him. I was there when it happened, and I still can't figure out who did it and how."

"To make a long story short," continued Mrak Delar, "your daughter has it now and she's planning to raise the Lord of Chaos. Tomorrow."

"That little bitch," hissed the old lady slamming her withered hand on the table. "Damned be the day when she clawed her way out of my body."

Gunz exchanged a quick look with Karma, catching a shocked expression on her face. The old Countess was swearing like a sailor. The Countess caught their exchange and smirked.

"Oh, get over yourselves, you two," she said, waving her hand at them. "You have no idea how hard it is to live a very long life, watching your only child turn into an evil abomination..." She sighed, shaking her head.

"My lady," said Mrak Delar, "you spent your life here, in this tiny village, living by Mount Karasova. Is there anything you can tell us that could help us stop your daughter tomorrow?"

"Just the four of you? That's all? None of you have any divine powers," she said, staring at them with widened eyes. "It's not a good time to be playing jokes on me."

"Svyatobor and Semargl will join us tomorrow," replied Kal. "Do you think a Master of Power, two Great Fire Salamanders, two Slavic deities and a witch, skilled in combat, wouldn't be enough to stop your daughter?"

The old lady laughed, her cracked elderly laughter sending chills down Gunz's spine.

"Not enough, not even close," she said coldly. "My daughter is not only a powerful dark mage. She's clever and resourceful. You're not going to know what hit you. And by the time you realize that you've been fooled, she'll use the Axe of Perun and the Skiper-Zmey will rule this realm again. Besides, being so close to the Lord of Chaos, she'll be channeling his dark energy and that would make her as powerful as any old god.

"Last time it took the power of Perun himself and all the brothers Svarozhich to bind Zmey into the coffin, deep underground. And after that, Stribog, the god of Air and Wind, with his four sons brought sands from the four sides of the Yav and enchanted them, creating Mount Karasova. That's a lot of divine-power, including major deities like Veles and Chernobog. What makes you think the six of you can do the same?"

"Nothing," replied Mrak Delar calmly. "But we have no choice in the matter. It has to be us. There is no one else. So, we'll fight your daughter and her followers to the death and if we fail, Chernobog will make a stand in the Dark Nav."

"Chernobog alone?" asked Countess, looking mortified.

"No, he is not going to be alone," replied Mrak Delar. "His wife Morena and Veles are with him. Gwyn ap Nudd, Aodh mac Lir and Death will help them too."

"God help us all," mumbled the old lady, shaking her head. "How did it come to this? Where is Perun?"

"He doesn't answer the summons," answered Kal. "Svyatobor searched the Yav and the Prav, but he couldn't find him."

"Without Perun, how are you planning to wield his Axe to force the Zmey back into his coffin? Only Perun or someone of his bloodline can use the Axe to its full potency. The Axe is the key to breaking the chains and freeing Zmey, so you don't need the full might of Perun's magical weapon. But to lock him back in, you'll need the full power of the Axe."

Countess Demidova got up and walked to the window. She pulled the curtain aside and peered at the empty street.

"You see this village? Every single person who lives here, devoted their lives to keeping the Lord of Chaos in his grave," she said quietly, tears gathering in her eyes. "Including yours truly. Every single person here is a skilled wizard, witch or mage. We cast and sustained a powerful 'turn-away' spell that stops anyone—human or supernatural—from approaching Mount Karasova.

"Our enchantment covers a huge territory—Mount Karasova and its surrounding area. It takes a lot of magical energy to sustain this spell. I don't know if you noticed, but there are no photographs or paintings depicting the Mount. The place is known as evil and cursed, and no one in their right mind willingly would go there.

"The Guardians were maintaining the spell for centuries. It becomes especially challenging when the Skiper-Zmey is about to wake up. It happens every three hundred and three years. And even though we are sustaining our spell, humans still notice that something is going on with the Mount. They swear that the Mount is moving and shifting as if there is a giant who is holding it on his shoulders. They say that the movement of the mountain is a bad omen, predicting something truly devastating.

"But it's not the giant that's moving the mountain. In three hundred and three years, all the evil energy that is harbored by the Lord of Chaos is getting accumulated inside his coffin. When Zmey is ready to be awakened, the evil energy breaks through the enchanted sands, carrying death and destruction to the world of the living.

"And it will happen tomorrow again. All Guardians are already stationed around the Mount, powering up the spell. Since we know of my daughter's evil plans, it's more important than ever to keep humans away from this place.

"So, the Guardians won't be able to assist you in your struggle, but they will keep the magical energy you'll be wielding within the protective circle of their spell, hence protecting the world of magic from exposure and the world of the living from harm. I will go with you to the Mount and make sure that you can safely travel through the protective circle."

"Thank you, Countess," said Mrak Delar for everyone. "We'll be leaving tomorrow at around three in the afternoon. We want to take our time, observing the area before we jump in headfirst."

"My home is your home," said the Countess, rising.

Gunz also got up and headed toward the exit door. Kal gave him an arched look, and he stopped at the door. "Just want to get some air," he said to Kal. "You know, clear my head."

Kal nodded and Gunz walked outside. The sky got lighter, but the air was still cold and crispy. He observed the empty street and slowly moved toward the forest, in the direction of Mount Karasova.

A few minutes later, something hit him between the shoulder blades, and he spun around. Karma was standing just a few feet away, laughing. She quickly caught up with him and grabbed his elbow.

"I thought I'd keep you company," she said, lightheartedly. "Make sure that no one would pull on your tail, little lizard."

"Really?" asked Gunz with a crooked smirk. "You're so worried about my safety. Why don't I believe it?"

Karma turned away for a moment, permeating discomfort around her. "You're right." She sighed. "I just don't feel comfortable around Mrak Delar. He has this heavy stare and every time I catch his black eyes on me, I feel like he is trying to dissect me. And the way he looks. His beauty is eerie... He gives me the heebie-jeebies. Plus, I've heard that he's evil to the bone. The only evil Master of Power in modern days."

"That's priceless, coming from the assassin for hire," cut Gunz sharply. Realizing that it came out too harsh, he sighed and turned to Karma. "I'm sorry. That was uncalled for."

"Why are you apologizing, Zane?" She shrugged and forced a smile, but it was obvious that his words hurt her. "I am an assassin. A gun for hire. Pay me and I don't really care what I have to do and whom I have to kill."

"I'm sorry," repeated Gunz, gently touching her shoulder. "I don't believe it to be the truth and I'm sorry my words hurt you. I'm a little on edge and what you said about Mrak pushed me over that edge, I guess."

"What? It's not true?"

"No, it's not," objected Gunz. "Mrak is not evil. He can be ruthless at times, and he's willing to do whatever it takes to protect the people he loves or to carry on his duty as the Master of Power. But he is not evil. You don't know him the way I do. He has a complicated past, but he is a knight of the old code."

"The noblest Roman of them all?" asked Karma without hiding her sarcasm.

"Yes, he is. The bravest and the noblest," replied Gunz seriously, ignoring her subtle comparison of Mrak to Brutus. "And he is madly in love with his wife. He went through hell and back to save her life and to be with her. He was stripped of his magic, enslaved, beaten and forced to his knees, but he still found his way back to her. Even Merlin himself admitted that Mrak is the strongest person he'd ever met."

"Merlin is real?" asked Karma, awestricken.

Gunz chuckled. "And here I thought you knew it all." Karma pursed her lips, punching him lightly on his shoulder. "Yeah, Merlin is real and there are a lot of other things that are real. Anyway, don't feel uncomfortable around Mrak. He's one of the best people I'm lucky to have in my life."

They reached the edge of the forest and stopped. Gunz moved his arm from left to right, like he was touching something invisible in front of him.

"Do you feel it?" he asked quietly without looking at Karma.

"Feel what?"

"The magical energy," replied Gunz, closing his eyes and sharpening his Salamander senses. "Our fight hasn't started yet, but the confrontation between the darkness and the light has begun already. Feel it. I can sense the energy of the magic the Guardians are wielding. The bursts of their magic are reaching as far as the end of the village. But if you extend your senses farther toward Mount Karasova, you'll feel the dark magic at work. I don't know if it is Agent Zvereva's magic or the evil of the Zmey that I sense, but it's dark out there... Poisonous..." He shivered like from a cold wind.

"Not all of us going to come back in one piece tomorrow," muttered Karma, shaking her head. "I just hope that I'll find Milana and see her one more time before—" She cut herself off and sighed.

Gunz pulled her closer to his side, hugging her. She didn't object, placing her head on his shoulder. "Karma, we'll find Milana. If we survive whatever comes tomorrow, I'm sure Chernobog will be inclined to help us. We'll find her, I promise. Among the six of us, you're the most fragile. So, be careful, watch your back and don't do anything crazy."

She chuckled darkly. "*Crazy* is my middle name, buddy. Deal with it."

Gunz rolled his eyes. "Could you say anything cheesier than that? You're losing your touch, Karma."

She laughed, but her eyes remained sad. "Maybe I'm losing my touch, but you're the one who's scared. I could feel the fear coiling in you since this morning."

"You're right," he agreed. "I'm afraid. It's not my first war and from experience I know that it's okay to be afraid before a battle, as long as you don't let this fear rule you. As long as you can keep it under control, it's okay to be scared. A healthy dose of fear will keep you alive."

"Perhaps you're right," she agreed. "We'll find out tomorrow."

Karma brushed his shoulder lightly with her hand and then turned around and headed back into the village. Gunz followed her, thinking that one thing she was right about—not all of them were coming back in one piece. Since his return from the Dark Nav, he couldn't shake off the feeling that something terrible was about to happen. Not just the possible rise of the Skiper-Zmey, but something else. He felt it, but he couldn't identify what it was.

Just an eerie feeling that didn't let him sleep at night.

34

~ ZANE BURNS, A.K.A. GUNZ ~

As they entered the dark forest at around three in the afternoon, following Countess Demidova, Gunz could sense the powerful magical energy flowing all around him and the closer they were getting to the protective circle around Mount Karasova, the stronger he felt the magical presence. With his heightened Salamander senses, he could easily separate the protective magic the Guardians were wielding from the other, darker energy that was polluting the area with its nauseating stench.

"Do you feel it?" asked Kal, jerking his chin in the direction of the mountain.

"Yes, it's extremely powerful," Gunz replied quietly.

Mrak Delar stopped suddenly, dropping his head low to his chest, breathing laboriously. Not expecting it, Gunz almost ran into him.

"Ancient Master, is everything okay?" asked Kal, stopping next to him.

Mrak Delar lifted his head. His lips were opened, and he was taking ragged breaths through his mouth. His eyes, widened and submerged into darkness, were blindly staring into space.

"It's dark here," he whispered.

Gunz shuddered. There was so much suppressed anger and cold in Mrak's voice that he could barely recognize it. "Mrak, what's going on?" He put his hand on his shoulder, channeling some of his purifying fire energy through his friend.

Mrak Delar took another strained breath and closed his eyes for a moment. When he opened his eyes again, they were back to normal. He looked at Gunz and a hardly visible smile touched his full lips.

"Thank you," he said, slightly uncomfortable. "There is so much dark energy here that it overwhelmed my senses for a moment. But I'm ready now. It's not going to happen again."

As they kept walking, the forest started to lose its thickness and soon Gunz noticed the dark silhouette of the mountain looming not more than a few hundred yards away. Countess Demidova stopped and moved her hand from left to right, whispering something. The air shimmered with a bluish-white light and a man materialized in front of them. He was dressed in a black Guardians' uniform. A leather scabbard with a short sword was attached to his back. His hands were glowing with the energy of the magic he was wielding.

"Jasper, what is the situation?" asked the Countess, touching his shoulder to get the man's attention.

The man turned his head and his attentive eyes, glowing with magic, quickly checked all of them. He looked like he was in his late forties or thereabouts, but he was probably a lot older. His face was strained, a thick blue vein crossing his forehead, his lips pressed together in a tight grim line. Muscles were bulging on his arms and shoulders, his chest rising with laborious breaths.

"It's hard," he hissed, his voice just as tense as his face. "Harder than I'd ever remembered... or than it was described in our historical records. There is more darkness gathered within the Mount—" He stopped talking to take a deep breath and then continued, "More than we can handle... And it's fluctuating, the amount of dark energy growing with each hour we spend here..."

"This has to be my daughter and her followers," muttered the Countess bitterly, shaking her head. "Whatever they're doing, it makes Zmey stronger."

"Jasper, what will happen when we start fighting Valeria Demidova and her followers?" asked Gunz. "Will you and your team still be able to hold your protective circle around the mountain."

Jasper glanced at him and a pained smirk cut through his face. "No," he replied bluntly. "Even right now, we're at the end of our wits, our magic is barely holding. We're all here and there is no one to replace us when our magical and physical strength will get depleted. If all of you add more magical energy into the explosive mix inside the Mount..." He shook his head. "There is no way that we can hold all this energy in the confines of our spell. Our circle will crash. The magical energy, especially the dark one, will spread around like a tidal wave for hundreds of miles... Well, you all are experienced enough to know what would happen then."

Gunz knew what Jasper was talking about. The dark energy would rush through the land, destroying every living soul in its way. Hundreds of thousands would die and the souls of those who would survive the blast would be corrupt by the darkness. He couldn't let it happen. He looked at Kal and then at Mrak Delar. They seemed to be troubled by the same thought.

Gunz used a small amount of his fire energy and drew a flaming rune in the air. Then he touched it with his hand, whispering a summoning spell. Jasper stared at him with a question in his eyes. The air shimmered with green and red sparks, and Svyatobor and Semargl materialized next to Gunz. Jasper gasped, gaping at the ancient Slavic gods in awe.

"We are ready, little brother," said Semargl.

He glanced around and his flaming eyes stopped on Jasper. He frowned and touched the air next to Jasper with his fingers. A glowing dome of light manifested at his touch, exposing the circle of protective magic that was encapsulating the huge area around the mountain and Mount Karasova itself. The dome was flickering, glowing weaker for a moment and then returning to its full strength again. The god of Fire turned to Gunz and his red eyebrows pulled lower above his burning eyes.

"I see the problem," he said, raking his fingers through the scorching mane of his hair. "Who do you wish to leave behind? Me or Svyatobor? We must make sure that this protective dome doesn't fail."

"I'll stay behind," volunteered Svyatobor. "As a fighter, Semargl is a lot more capable than I am. And this is my domain." He waved his hand around the forest. "I'm the strongest here, surrounded by forest, not inside of a magical pile of sand. I'll stay with the Guardians to enforce their protective circle."

"Thank you, Svyatobor," said Gunz, unease spreading through him. "Make sure that this protective circle doesn't fail, no matter how much magic and fire energy we'll be wielding inside. Nothing should break through it."

Gunz looked at his friend, biting his lip, doubts tearing at his soul. Leaving a Master of Power behind wouldn't be enough. Besides, Mrak Delar was a fierce experienced warrior, and he was the only one among them who had the power to heal others. Same applied to him and to Kal. The power of a Fire Elemental or a Fire Salamander wasn't enough to help the Guardians. He didn't even consider Karma. She was just a witch and adding her magic wouldn't make much difference.

To make sure that the protective spell didn't fail, he had to add the power of a god into the mix. Gunz knew that he was doing the right thing, yet it wasn't making him feel any better. Now, it was only the five of them left. Five of them against the unknown number of dark mages and the Lord of Chaos.

"Countess, before we cross inside the circle, is there anything else you can tell about Mount Karasova?" asked Gunz. "Anything that can help us?"

"Nothing can help you, boy," huffed the old lady, her voice screeching like nails on a chalkboard. "In your infinite wisdom, you are leaving a god behind. Not the smartest decision as far as I can see. And I don't understand how your master, Kalidus, is allowing this stupidity."

"He might be young, but he's not a boy. He's a Great Fire Salamander. And he made the only right decision there was in our situation," growled Mrak Delar, putting his hand on Gunz's shoulder. "I would do the same."

"I second that," said Kal quietly.

"You're idiots. All of you," yelled the Countess, tears gathering in her eyes. "Who cares if the protective circle breaks and a few hundred thousand humans die? If my daughter succeeds, we all are gonna die anyway!"

Mrak Delar seized her shoulders and shook her once. "Look at me, Countess Demidova," he said, his voice a low growl. "Did I teach you nothing back in Moscow?"

The old lady gaped up at the Master of Power, her hands trembling. Mrak Delar took her hands into his, gently squeezing them.

"I know it's hard and I know you're scared, but I promise you—the five of us are going to stop your daughter. Skiper-Zmey is not going to rise. But you and the Guardians must do your duty. Remember the oath you gave when you joined the Guardians Order. Keep the circle up. Protect the humans."

The Countess let go of Mrak Delar's hands and threw her arms around his neck. "It's hard for me. Everything that's going on is my fault," she moaned. "It's my daughter, Mrak... My own flesh and blood. And now you... and your friends are going to risk everything to undo her evil." She spoke fast, her voice breaking and faltering. "Oh, Mrak... seeing you again brought back so many memories. In 1812, you let me escape with my life. You should have killed me. And now your kindness will kill you and your men. I can't... I can't..."

"Countess, stop," said Mrak Delar, gently pulling her to his chest. "First of all, I didn't show you any kindness by letting you escape Moscow. I did what I was ordered to do, and you were chosen by the Destiny Council to protect the Axe of Perun.

"Maybe there was a reason the Destiny Council chose you as the guardian of the Axe. Think about it, Countess. You were chosen to keep the only weapon that could free the Skiper-Zmey from his prison and you're the mother of the very person who's dedicated her life to freeing him.

"You know as well as I do that every move on the Board of Destiny has a reason. Nothing is coincidental. So, please, you need to get yourself together. If there is anything else that you know about Mount Karasova, tell us. Anything would help."

Mrak Delar pulled away, bending slightly down to see the Countess' face.

"I'm sorry," she whispered, avoiding Mrak's gaze. "There is only one more thing that comes to my mind. In front of the Mount there is a small lake. Its waters look clean and inviting, but don't trust its serenity. The lake has a double bottom. You step into it and it'll suck you in faster than any swamp. Even gods can't escape its deadly grip. Stay clear of it and be safe. All of you."

Mrak Delar took her hand and kissed it. "Thank you, Anastasia."

"You know my name?" exhaled the old lady, raising her eyes at Mrak Delar.

"I always did." He chuckled. "I'll see you when it's all over."

Gunz approached Jasper. "We need to pass through your protective magic to the other side. Can you let us through?"

Jasper nodded and moved his right hand up and down. The protective dome lit up with a soft white light. Jasper said one word and an opening, just big enough for an adult man to pass through, materialized in front of them.

Gunz thanked him and stepped through the opening. Mrak Delar, Kal, Karma and Semargl followed. As they started to walk toward the edge of the forest, Gunz turned around. He saw Countess Anastasia Demidova stopping by Jasper's side and adding her magic into the mix. Svyatobor joined her. His power flowed through the protective dome, adding a soft green color to its glow. As soon Svyatobor added his power to the Guardians' magic, the dome stopped flickering and shone brighter.

It worked. Svyatobor's power will keep the area protected, Gunz thought as he watched Jasper closing the door. *Now all we have to do, is keep the Lord of Chaos in his grave. Easy...*

35

~ ZANE BURNS, A.K.A. GUNZ ~

Mount Karasova stood out in the surroundings like an unnatural sore thumb. In the forest-covered land, the Mount was the only stark rock, rising above the land like a sinister dark omen. At the foot of Mount Karasova, a small lake was glistening dimly reflecting the gray skies. At the very bottom of the mountain, there was a small dark hole, undoubtedly an entrance into a cave.

Gunz stopped at the edge of the forest and probed the mountain with his Salamander's senses. The presence of dark energy was so strong here that he could practically see it flowing through the air, wrapping around the lifeless rock. But besides the energy of Zmey, he could feel other magical energy signatures inside and outside the mountain. He could see the dark shadows of people that were crowding around the entrance into the cave.

Veles was right, he thought, probing the area in front of the Mount. *Zvereva brought some serious reinforcement, but none of them were pureblood humans. They all had magic.*

Gunz turned to Kal, pointing back at the forest. No one

asked anything. They stepped back, submerging into the shadows.

"Did you feel their presence?" he asked. Except Karma everyone nodded. She was standing at the edge of the forest, observing the area. "They all have magic, so Veles was right. Just using Kal's fire energy won't work. We'll have to fight our way through."

"There are at least a hundred of them there if not more," pointed out Mrak Delar. "We can't go through them without using our magic and power. It'll weaken us before we even get inside."

"It'll also alert Valeria Demidova to our presence, prematurely," added Semargl.

"Hey, Karma," Gunz called out in a loud whisper. She turned around, arching her eyebrow at him. "I know you're packing. What do you have in your non-magical arsenal?"

"What do you need?" she asked, a crooked smirk on her face.

"A sniper rifle," replied Gunz.

Karma pulled her sling bag off her shoulder and dropped it on the ground. She touched the bag, sending some of her magic through it. Then she opened the bag and pulled a VKS sniper rifle and a box with ammunition out of it.

"Is there anything else you want for Christmas, little boy?" she asked winking at him.

"Christmas came early this year," murmured Gunz. He took the rifle, placing it to his shoulder and checked its telescopic sight. "This will do. Do you know how to use one of these?"

"Really? Knowing my line of business, you had to ask?" Karma rolled her eyes, pulling a second rifle out of her bag.

"Do you see that hill?" Gunz pointed to his right. A small hill covered in shrubbery was rising just a few feet away. "It'll give us better visibility and the shrubbery will serve as a natural screen."

Karma sighed, shaking her head. "Too much wind here," she

whispered. "The winds seem to be blowing from all directions at the same time. As an expert sniper, you have to know that it would be impossible to make a clean shot in these conditions."

Gunz turned to Mrak Delar. The Master of Power smirked. "I can take care of the winds, Junior," he said with a nonchalant wave of his hand. "It would require just a tiny bit of my power."

"Can you also suppress the sounds of the gunshots? I don't want you to drain yourself doing that, but we should keep it under wraps for as long as possible," asked Gunz.

"No problem," replied Mrak Delar. "A small effort like that is not going to drain me."

Gunz turned to Kal and Semargl. "I know that Semargl can't get hurt. He's a god," he said, looking up at Kal. "I've never asked you this, Father. Can mundane weapons hurt you? I know that they can't kill you, but will you be in pain if you get shot?"

Kal's thin lips stretched into a smile and he shook his head no. "I'm more fire than human now," he replied, his fingers exploring the barrel of the rifle in Gunz's hands. "A gunshot is not going to be pleasant, but not painful enough to cripple me. I don't bleed red anymore. It's been centuries since I've seen my own blood. Don't worry, my boy. I'll be fine. Tell us what you want us to do."

Gunz nodded. "Karma and I will try to take down as many mercenaries as we can quietly. But once they realize that they're under attack, you need to step in. Both of you. Use your swords to bring them down for as long as you can. Try not to use your magic. Your fire energy signatures are too powerful, and it will alert that evil bitch as soon as you start using it. Keep in mind—this is not the real fight. These people are nothing but a decoy, a hurdle Demidova threw to slow us down and to make us use our magic to weaken us. So, try not overexerting yourselves. And we'll join you as soon as we can."

Mrak Delar, Karma and Gunz walked up the hill and took a position behind the shrubbery. Mrak channeled his power and with a light flick of his wrist, commanded the winds to stop. The winds ceased all at once and silence ascended upon the forest.

"Your Master of Power is amazing. Can I borrow him for my next job?" muttered Karma, staring into her scope. "Zane, do you see those few strays on the far left and right of the entrance? About ten on each side. You think they'll be missed?"

"Mrak, the sound suppression please," hissed Gunz, pressing the stock of his rifle against his shoulder.

He found his first target through the scope and held his breath, softly pressing the trigger. He felt the kickback but there was no characteristic barking sound of a gunshot. The first man silently fell with the others none the wiser. He noticed another man going down on the right side of the entrance and threw a quick glance at Karma. She was lying on the ground with her scope at her eye, searching for the next target.

They were able to take down quite a few mercenaries before the rest of them noticed that something was going on. Someone shouted something, and they all came to motion. Gunz sent a small amount of fire energy to Kal to attract his attention. Kal glanced at him and immediately vanished together with Semargl. A moment later, Gunz saw them both with flaming swords in their hands, unleashing their wrath at the mercenaries.

"I'll keep the winds down, and you keep doing whatever it is you two were doing," said Mrak Delar. "I need to help Kal and Semargl and block the entrance into the Mount. Do try not to shoot me." He snapped his fingers and vanished.

A moment later Mrak Delar materialized between Kal and Semargl with a sword in his hand. His giant silhouette prominent against the gray surface of the mountain was making a perfect target. Through his scope, Gunz noticed a man, ready to take a shot at Mrak. Gunz cringed inwardly, thinking that a bullet could bring down Mrak Delar and even though the

Ancient Master had the power to heal himself and others, he would be hurt and weakened. Gunz fixed on the man in his scope and pressed the trigger. The man yelped, throwing his arms up and fell.

Mrak Delar glanced over his shoulder in the direction of the hill and a dark smile crossed his face. The Ancient Master channeled more of his power and a magical energy field spiked around him. The mercenaries screamed as a powerful gust of wind slammed them against the mountain. A few of them managed to recover and rushed toward the entrance, but as soon as they attempted to enter the cave, they hit an invisible wall and were thrown back. Gunz didn't have to guess what happened—Mrak Delar erected a power field, blocking the entrance.

The mercenaries realized that whoever attacked them weren't just humans and resorted to their magic. Mrak Delar shouted a spell, blocking their magic and unfolded a second shield, pinning as many men as he could to the wall.

Kal and Semargl launched forward with flaming swords in their hands. More men came rushing from both sides to help those who were disabled by Mrak's magic. Gunz could see the flashes of the gunshots, but there was no sound. Mrak took care of that too. It was like watching a terrifying silent movie.

With horror, Gunz thought that the Master of Power was using too much of his magic, draining himself. At least Kal and Semargl, cutting and slashing with their giant swords left and right, weren't utilizing their full power. He saw a bullet catching Mrak Delar on his shoulder. The Master of Power staggered back but didn't fall, keeping up his spells.

Gunz pressed the scope to his eyes, checking the area. He knew that soon all this was going to be over, but he needed to make sure that no one else could shoot Mrak Delar. He saw another man aiming at the Master and he didn't give him a chance, silently taking him out.

Karma kept reloading her rifle, taking out one mercenary at the time. Kal channeled more of his elemental power, rising slightly above the ground. A powerful stream of fire erupted from his flaming sword, carrying death to anyone before him. Semargl laughed, adding his fire blast to Kal's.

A few minutes later, it was all over. The small flat area between Mount Karasova and the lake was covered in dead bodies. Some of the corps were still burning and the suffocating stench of burnt flesh was polluting the air. Kal and Semargl lowered their swords. Mrak Delar released his magic and lowered himself to his knees, clutching his hand to his bleeding shoulder.

Gunz scanned the area with his Salamander's sight and dropped his rifle on the ground. All the mercenaries were dead. They never had the opportunity to use their magic to defend themselves. Fighting against a Master of Power as wizards or even mages, they stood no chance. And with the added assault of the Fire Elemental and the god of Fire, it was all over for them before it started. The only negative side to all this was that the three of them still had to use a lot of magic and elemental powers. As much as he was trying to avoid it, Gunz was positive that Valeria Demidova knew about their arrival by now.

Gunz sighed and opened his fire portal.

"Karma, let's go," he said, watching her slowly rising.

She grabbed her sling bag, throwing it over her shoulder, but before she could come closer to the fire-curtain, Gunz stopped her. In one move he lifted her and walked through the portal with her in his arms.

They walked out next to Mrak Delar and Gunz lowered Karma carefully down. As soon as her feet touched the ground, she twisted and punched him in the shoulder. Gunz gasped and massaged his shoulder, snickering.

"Do it again and the next time—"

"And the next time you try to walk on your own through a

Fire Salamander's portal, you'll die," interjected Kal chuckling. "You should be kissing my son, girl, not punching him."

"Kissing him? Ew!" A mix of disgust and fury reflected on Karma's face. "He can dream about it! In his wet dreams!"

Mrak Delar laughed and immediately winced. "Okay, people, you need to give me a chance to heal before you can continue with this... Whatever it is..."—he twirled his hand —"amusing conversation."

He connected with the healing power of Earth, circulating it through the bleeding hole on his shoulder. A few seconds later, the bleeding stopped, and the wound closed up. Mrak Delar got up and flexed his shoulders.

"Still a little sore, but it'll do. We should get moving," he said, picking up his black sword from the ground and sheathing it in the black leather scabbard attached to his belt.

As they started to walk toward the entrance, the ground shook. Gunz stopped in his tracks, staring at the mountain in astonishment. Mount Karasova trembled and its outline became distorted, like he was looking at a photo with a computer glitch. A low rumbling sound erupted from the depth of the mountain, as if a giant beast was waking up and roaring, displeased by the intrusion of the morning light. The sound was so deep and so loud that there was no doubt, anyone could hear it within a few miles' radius.

Mount Karasova shook again and a thick cloud of sand spread around it in all directions. The winds picked up, howling and bending the trees to the ground. They carried the sand far away from the mountain, clearing the air. A few seconds later, the mountain stilled, and the winds slowed down.

"It's happening," said Semargl. "We need to hurry."

Gunz glanced at him. The mighty god of Fire looked troubled. Even more so, he could see the signs of fear on the Slavic deity's hardened face. Quietly they passed through the threshold and walked into the belly of Mount Karasova.

Inside, the darkness was absolute. Gunz rubbed his eyes, trying to readjust his vision to no avail. It reminded him of the Dark Nav, and he shuddered inwardly. Mrak Delar opened his hand and a few glowing blue orbs manifested in his palm. He threw them high in the air and a shimmering blue light filled the cave.

The cave didn't look like any caves he had ever seen before. It seemed that everything here was built out of sand, compressed by magic and time. His Salamander senses screamed, overwhelmed by the magical energy that was permeating from the walls of the cave. Gunz took a ragged breath, all of a sudden feeling weak and disoriented.

"What is all this magic?" he asked, fighting the dizziness.

"This is the magic that my brother Stribog used to create this mountain and keep anyone from entering it," Semargl explained in a hushed voice. "We should keep moving. The farther we go from the entrance, the better we all will feel."

Gunz surveyed the cave and found a single passage that was leading farther into the depth of the mountain. They followed the passage. It was just as dark as the cave and a musty smell seemed to be permanently embedded into the walls. The only light they had was produced by the shimmering orbs that Mrak conjured. As they moved farther away from the cave, the effect of Stribog's magic started to fade away.

The passage was moving down, curving slightly to the left. Soon they saw a weak gray light at the far end of it. Gunz raised his hand, asking everyone to stop. He came closer to Mrak Delar.

"We don't know what to expect," he whispered. "How are you feeling? Can you conjure a shield? At least to cover yourself and Karma."

The Ancient Master smirked. "I'm fine, Gunz. This wound was nothing to me. Don't worry, I can protect us all. Let's just keep moving." He unfolded his power shield, covering all of them.

As they were nearing the end of the passage, a soft humming reached his ears. At the beginning, it reminded him of the soft buzzing of a beehive. But soon, it became louder, and now he could clearly hear the sound of human voices. They were chanting something—one continuous stream of words he couldn't recognize.

"They started," whispered Karma. For the first time, Gunz noticed the tones of fear in her voice. "Are we too late?"

"No," replied Mrak Delar, "we're perfectly on time."

They reached the end of the passage and stopped. The passage opened up into a wide cave, generously lit by the light of torches. The cave was so tall that its ceiling seemed to be disappearing into nowhere. In the center of the cave, there was a massive stone monolith that looked like an ancient sacrificial table. Three hooded persons were standing around the monolith, chanting.

Surrounding them, there was a second circle of people, veiled by long gray cloaks from shoulders to toes. Their faces were concealed under ugly masks. Their hands were joined, and they were swaying from side to side in unison, also chanting.

One of the three cloaked figured turned around and Gunz recognized Agent Zvereva, a.k.a. Valeria Demidova. Her eyes were glowing with a poisonous yellow light. Dark veins were slithering across her cheeks and forehead, originating around her eyes.

She recognized him too and a predatory smile distorted her features, turning her face into a horrendous evil mask. She clapped her hands and at least twenty more people materialized in the cave. Their bodies were covered in strange armor that reminded him of medieval chainmail. Some of them had swords in their hands, but most of them were armed with magic. Their combined dark magical energy washed over Gunz and his stomach knotted.

Valeria Demidova cackled, the sound of her laughter more nauseating than the malignant magical energy she was exuding. She waved her hand in their direction and ordered, "You know the drill. Kill them all. Restrain those who can't be killed. They cannot interrupt my work." Then she turned around and continued chanting like nothing was going on around her.

All her men turned around at once and blasted them with their magic. Their spells impacted Mrak Delar's shield with astounding strength. Mrak grunted but withheld the attack, channeling more of his power into his shield. The muscles on his arms and shoulders tensed and a pulsing blue vein popped up on his neck.

"I like what she said," growled Gunz, pulling Kal and Semargl outside the protective shield. "Kill them all!"

All three of them connected to the elemental Fire at the same time and a wall of scorching flames rose around them. Gunz manifested his sword, channeling his power through it for better targeting. The evil army didn't have time for the next attack when the fire reached their front row. They screamed in anguish, their long robes devoured by flames. A thick gray smoke rose in the air, making it hard to see what was going on around the stone monolith.

The others didn't try to help them. They pushed screaming people aside, meeting the fire attack with their own magic. To Gunz's surprise, they weren't trying to defend themselves. Instead, they moved directly into the attack, striking them with the next set of spells.

"*Praecidio Amnia,*" shouted Gunz, raising his own shield of protective magic.

Kal laughed, the excitement of the fight setting his giant figure in flames, and a powerful wave of fire energy rushed through the cave, pushing the dark mages a few feet back. They regrouped fast, retaliating with a blast of water. Kal twirled in place, avoiding the stream of water.

"*Ventus!*" shouted Mrak Delar.

Gunz turned around to see the Master of Power standing right behind him, his eyes swirling with all the colors of the power, his obsidian hair surrounding his face like a dark cloud. A hurricane force wind slammed the rows of the dark mages, sending them flying across the cave. Gunz expected at least a few of them to hit the three hooded figures around the stone monolith, but it didn't happen. Valeria Demidova and the other two were surrounded by some kind of a powerful magical shield.

"I'll look into it," shouted Semargl. Rising in the air, he started exploring the size and the strength of the shield surrounding the monolith.

Mrak Delar pulled his sword out and attacked the men who were still recovering after his air-strike. Gunz and Kal joined him. As Gunz swung his sword, decapitating one of the men, he heard the sound of a blade swooshing through the air somewhere behind him. He spun around and saw another mage, his face twisted into an angry scowl, lowering his sword at him. He ducked, knowing perfectly well that he was bound to get hurt.

The sword lowered on his shoulder. He cried out in pain, but luckily the wound wasn't deep. In the last moment, the attacker's grip failed, and his sword dropped on the floor. Another blade penetrated the man's chest. He grabbed the blade with both hands, thick streams of blood, dripping from his mouth. He coughed, splattering the blood, and crashed forward, dead.

"I got your back, firetwat," said Karma, pulling her blade out of the dead body.

"Thanks, now watch yours," said Gunz. "I need to heal, and it's about to get really hot here."

He channeled his power allowing himself to revert into his natural state for a quick moment. Another wave of the fire energy rushed through the cave. Those mages, who managed to get back to their feet, got knocked out again and Kal, Karma and Mrak Delar finished them all.

The ground shook again, and an overwhelming surge of dark energy swept through the cave. For a moment, everything around got distorted into a computer glitch-like image. Demidova cackled and turned around, meeting Gunz's deadpan gaze. She glanced around and stamped her foot, noticing that her main army was destroyed.

"I need a few more minutes," she shouted at the men in cloaks. "Keep them busy."

She turned back and continued chanting, seemingly ignoring the mayhem that unfolded outside her protective shield, as well as Semargl's fire attacks from the air.

"I can't break this protective shield!" shouted Semargl, sending a ray of undiluted power at the shield, but it didn't budge.

The last circle of mages seemed to be a lot more powerful than the other group. Their combat magic was doing some damage. Gunz saw Karma catching an energy ball in her stomach, flying across the floor. Mrak Delar darted to her side to check if she was alive. While he was down, another mage hit him with a spell. Kal stepped in the way of the spell, covering Mrak Delar and Karma with his body. The energy ball didn't hurt him, but still knocked him off his feet.

"Father!" yelled Gunz, spinning in place, his sword finding his next target.

"I'm fine."

Gunz heard Kal's voice and moved into offense. "*Ventius,*" he hissed, sending a couple of mages flying, while his sword went over his head and crashed down on his opponent.

"Aw, little Fire Salamander!" Gunz took his eyes off the remaining two attackers and saw Valeria Demidova staring at him, a cold smirk splitting her face. "I was expecting you to show up here today, so I prepared something especially for you, boy!" She hissed a spell, making a circular motion with her hand.

A ring of black flames burst out, surrounding him. Gunz spun around. It was fire, but it didn't feel like his element. There was something dark and sinister about it. *If it's a fire, it should obey my command,* thought Gunz. He reached with his hand toward it but halted in the last moment. Valeria Demidova was too smart. She would know that as a Fire Salamander, he could control the fire. Elemental Fire as a weapon was useless against him and she wouldn't use it.

"Gunz, don't move!" Kal's voice was thick with fear. "Do not touch it."

Gunz heard Kal growl as he got hit by an energy ball. "Mrak," shouted the Great Salamander. "Take care of those remaining assholes while I help my son."

"Father, what is this fire?" shouted Gunz, shifting back into the center of the circle.

"Gunz, I never told you this," yelled Kal. "I thought you were still too young, and you didn't need to know that. This is the Black Fire. The only fire that we as Fire Salamanders cannot control."

"I don't understand," mumbled Gunz, staring at the black flames as they were encroaching on him.

"A Fire Salamander can conjure the Black Fire, but there is only one way to put it down. You must dissolve into it," explained Kal. "This is the only way a Fire Salamander can end his life, my boy. You touch this fire and you'll die."

"Father, what do I do?" asked Gunz, fear twisting his heart. "The circle of flames is getting smaller. Soon, I'll have no space here."

"My boy, I'm not going to let you die. I'll do it—"

"Kal, no!" Gunz yelled, punching the air with his fist in helpless fury. There was nothing he could do to stop Kal from sacrificing himself. "I'm begging you... No!"

"Kal, stop!"

Gunz heard Mrak Delar's voice and squinted his eyes to see the Ancient Master through the wall of black flames. He was standing with the sword in his hand, breathing hard. The last two mages were lying dead at his feet.

Mrak glanced back and an icy smile appeared on his face. Gunz followed the direction of his gaze and noticed that the protective shield around the monolith started to give in under Semargl's persistent attack.

"Semargl, do not stop what you're doing," shouted Mrak Delar and put his hand on Kal's shoulder. "Step away, Great Salamander. You saved me more than once. Allow me to pay this debt, at least partially."

"Mrak, no. You can command this fire no more than I can," said Kal, his voice shaking. "You will burn, Master."

"I guess, we'll see." Mrak Delar channeled his power. His eyes swirled into a multicolored blur and his body glowed with the magical energy. He conjured a shield, but unlike his usual power shields, this one was made out of water. Freezing-cold water was streaming all over his body, glistening with ice. It covered him from head to toe and Gunz couldn't help but wonder how he could breathe inside it.

In his suit of freezing water, Mrak Delar approached the Black Fire and touched it. "Obey," he muttered, ordering the fire to open for him. The fire wrapped around his fingers, licking him hungrily, but it couldn't break through his shield. The water hissed at the touch of fire and a thick cloud of dark steam rose in the air. Mrak Delar ignored it and pushed through the Black Fire. Standing, surrounded by the carnivorous flames, he spread his arms wide, creating a small opening in the wall of Black Fire.

"Gunz, I'm going to conjure the same shield around you, and

you're not going to like it. You'll be in a lot of pain, but you'll be alive," he said, his voice strained. "Luckily, you're short enough to walk under my arm. When I tell you, do it quickly and be careful. No matter what you do, do not touch this fire."

He whispered a spell, conjuring the water-shield around Gunz. Gunz grunted at the touch of the freezing water to his body, but he didn't move, waiting for Mrak Delar's command.

"Go now. And do it quick," hissed Mrak Delar. His own shield was slowly losing the battle with the black flames.

Gunz didn't wait for the Master of Power to ask him twice and slipped quickly under his arm. As soon as he was out, Mrak Delar staggered back, releasing both shields and collapsed. Kal caught him and carefully lowered him down on the floor of the cave. The Black Fire grew tighter and imploded, disappearing.

Forgetting about his own pain, Gunz dropped to his knees next to Mrak Delar. Mrak's face was pale, his lips blue from the cold he had to endure. His shaking arms were covered in blisters, but he was alive. Gunz put his hands on Mrak's chest and his forehead and gently channeled the energy of Fire through him to warm him up. Mrak Delar moaned and opened his black eyes.

"Hey, Junior, you survived," he said, the corners of his lips twitched in a weak smile.

"Mrak, what can I do to help you," asked Gunz desperately.

"You're already doing it," replied Mrak Delar. The color was slowly coming back to his face as the fire energy was working its way through his system. After another minute, he added, "You can stop now. Thank you. I'll take it from here."

Gunz watched as Mrak Delar closed his eyes and took a few deep breaths, connecting with the healing power of Earth. His burns slowly healed, leaving his skin clean and unblemished. After another moment, he stopped and sat up.

"Where is Karma?" he asked, searching around the cave.

With everything that just happened, they all forgot about

her. Gunz also turned around. He saw Karma standing by the monolith, separated from the three mages by their feeble protective shield. The shield was almost gone, and the three mages were no longer chanting. Valeria Demidova lowered her hood and nodded to the mage on her left to do the same. The mage obeyed her command and slowly exposed her face.

As she did so, Karma yelped like she was in pain and threw her whole body at the shield that was separating them. Gunz looked at the second mage and his heart thundered in his chest.

"Milana!" screamed Karma. "What are you doing, my love? How did you get there? Did they force you to perform this ritual? What's going on?"

Milana cackled, staring down at her former lover with scorn. "Karma, it's been a while, babe. Why would you think that someone is forcing me into doing anything? I'm here of my own volition."

"What?" Karma's face fell. "What do you mean?"

Milana laughed again, throwing a quick glance at Demidova. "You're such a gullible idiot, sweetie. Don't you see? Our trip to the Land of Dreams, the accidental fall into the Dark Nav? Nothing of it was an accident. It was all well planned by my mistress and myself." She pointed at Demidova.

"What are you saying, Milana?" whispered Karma, her voice trembling, tears glistening in her eyes.

"I'm saying that I'm a high-level mage. Not a helpless seer," seethed Milana, staring arrogantly down at her. "From the moment we met, everything was planned. Our meeting, our life in the Dark Nav, finding and saving that young Fire Salamander. All that was done with one purpose—to take Chernobog's attention from what really mattered. You played your part well, sweetie. I was able to steal the Axe of Perun and leave the Dark Nav unnoticed."

"No!" shouted Karma, launching herself at the shield again. "I'll kill you, heartless bitch. I'll cut that piece of coil from your chest with the very same dagger you gifted me. Semargl! How much longer?"

"You don't have what it takes to kill me, sweetie." Milana laughed. "Plus, you're still madly in love with me. You can't hurt me."

"Semargl!" hollered Karma, punching the shield with her fist and her voice got swallowed by the rocketing of the crashing protection spell. Karma pulled the dagger out and jumped at Milana.

Gunz watched Milana stepping backward, away from Karma, until her back hit the sacrificial stone. A terrifying realization engulfed him, and he jumped to his feet.

"Karma, no! Do not touch her!" he yelled, bolting toward her, but he was too late.

Karma seized Milana's throat, pushing her on top of the stone and the dagger pierced her heart. Karma let go of the dagger, leaving it in Milana's chest and staggered back. Warm streams of thick red liquid spilled from the wound, running down Milana's body, spread on the sacrificial stone. Barely visible fissures in the stone slowly got filled with the scarlet liquid, creating a complicated design. The copper smell of blood filled the cave and Karma froze, staring down at her hands, smeared in Milana's blood.

Demidova guffawed, gawking down at Karma. "Sweetheart, thank you so much! We couldn't have done it without your assistance. All the way from the beginning to the very end. To raise my lord, a blood sacrifice had to be made. But not just any blood sacrifice. A person had to give up their life willingly.

"This part was easy—Milana was so deeply dedicated to my cause that she was willing to die for it. The hard part was that the sacrificial athame had to be wielded by a person who was emotionally connected with Milana. Since you were so head over heels in love with her, you were instrumental to us.

Consider joining my ranks, sweetie. I would love to have you on my side. I'll pay handsomely for your troubles."

Karma's eyes darted to the body of her dead girlfriend; the horror of her deed reflected on her face. Tears ran down her pale face and she fell to her knees, covering her face with her bloodied hands. "I killed her," she sobbed, ignoring everything that was going on around her. "I killed the woman I loved. Oh, God..." Gunz doubted that she heard anything Demidova was telling her.

The ground trembled. This tremor was a lot stronger than the previous ones. Both Gunz and Kal swayed on their feet and lost their balance, falling on the ground. Semargl lowered next to them as dust and sand fell from the ceiling, pushing him down. Gunz scrambled to his feet, just to get knocked down by the next tremor.

Mrak Delar gathered whatever power he still had and struck Demidova. She waved her hand and the power stream dissipated. Then she reached under her robe and pulled out the Axe of Perun. Touching the pendant, she said a few words, and the pendant started to grow, turning into a large double-edge axe. Both Kal and Semargl managed to get to their feet and attacked her with everything they had.

The dark mage laughed manically, meeting their attack with the magical weapon. The Axe of Perun cut through the elemental fire like it was nothing. In the meantime, a dark mass rose above the sacrificial stone. It was growing wider and bigger, as the second mage kept chanting over it. Soon, Milana's lifeless body and the giant stone monolith were swallowed by it.

"Now!" yelled the second dark mage. "You must do it now!

Demidova twirled around and swung the Axe at the darkness that was covering the monolith. She did it three times and an ear-piercing noise filled the cave. Gunz collapsed wrapping his arms around his head to protect his hearing. His eyes watered. Through the blurry veil of tears, he saw the shape of an enormous three-headed serpent rising from the darkness. The heavy smell of sulphur invaded his senses, and he coughed, struggling to breathe.

A split-second later, everything was over. Both women and the serpent were gone, and a heavy silence enveloped the cave. Gunz got up to his feet, nausea twisting his stomach, and glanced around. Mrak Delar was sprawled on the floor, drained. Karma was quietly weeping, curled into a ball next to Milana's dead body. Kal and Semargl were back on their feet, but they both looked mortified.

Gunz ripped the shirt on his chest, exposing a new rune that was embedded into his skin. He touched the rune, sending the energy of fire through it. The rune glowed brighter with a soft white light.

"Aidan," said Gunz, hardly recognizing his own voice, "we failed. Skiper-Zmey is free again. Now it's up to you stop him."

36

~ AIDAN ~

Zane's voice still echoed in his mind, as Aidan slowly turned around to face Voron. The old warrior met his eyes and frowned.

"What's going on?" he asked, wrinkles on his forehead getting deeper. "Did you receive a message from the young Salamander?"

Aidan nodded. "It's coming," he said quietly. "They failed to stop Valeria Demidova."

Both Chernobog and Veles got up. "When did it happen?" asked Veles. He looked calm, but the storm was brewing inside him, making the magical energy field spike around him. The runes on his staff were glowing with a bright white light, providing an additional source of light in the darkness of the Nav.

"Just now," replied Aidan.

"If we're right, and Zmey is coming to the Dark Nav, this is the only place he can break through," said Chernobog, unsheathing his sword. He turned to his wintry wife and an affectionate smile changed his face. "Darling, are you sure you want to do it? Knowing your history with Skiper-Zmey, we all can understand if you choose to stay in the safety of our castle."

Morena got up and picked up her scythe. She gave a slightly arrogant gaze to her husband and shook her head. "I'm just fine here. History or not, I'm here to protect the man I love."

Chernobog's face lit up at her words. "Voron," he called his righthand man, "I need you to stay with my wife at all times. Make sure that no harm will come her way."

"Yes, my lord," replied Voron, but his body language and his facial expression showed clearly that protecting Morena was the last thing he wanted to do. He never trusted her and he would rather protect Chernobog than her.

"How can you be sure that this is the place?" asked Aidan, looking around.

He was standing in the middle of nowhere, just an empty field, barren and cold. The place was empty, void of any kind of life. The darkness was impenetrable and even the light orbs that Chernobog conjured when they arrived here, were able to illuminate just a small area around them.

"The veil that separates the Dark Nav and the entrance to the Yav where Zmey was imprisoned for thousands of years is the thinnest here," explained Chernobog. "I'm positive—this is the only place."

Just as he finished his statement, a gust of cold wind rushed through the field. Aidan opened his second sight and gasped. Even with his magical sight, he could hardly see anything, but the flow of magical energy increased significantly and the energy he was sensing was dark and malevolent. He took in a sharp breath, unsheathing his icy sword.

"The Lord of Chaos is coming," hissed Morena, excitement in her glacial eyes. She flicked her eyebrow at Aidan. "I like your sword, boy. Looks like something that should belong to me."

The ground quaked under their feet and with a thunderous bang a giant crack ruptured the field, splitting it in two. A bright yellow light erupted from the fracture, blinding Aidan for a moment. He jumped aside, raising his arm to protect his eyes. The wind grew stronger and the negative energy intensified to the point that it was hard to breathe, crackling in the air like some ominous electrical discharge.

A moment later, the light dimmed down slightly. Aidan lowered his arm and when the white spots stopped dancing in front of his eyes, he saw two women, dressed in long robes, standing at the edge of the glowing fracture. He couldn't make out their features. The light was reflecting off their skin, making their faces look like shiny white ovals.

A giant serpent with three heads was rising behind them. His body was covered in thick scales. His back was colored in swampy-green shades and his chest was shielded by thick yellowish-green scales. Zmey's eyes were also yellow with dark red pupils, and they were exuding hatred and malice unlike anything Aidan had seen before. The energy of dark magic he was emanating spread around him like a poisonous gas. Aidan choked, suppressing nausea and staggered back.

Neither Veles nor Chernobog moved, calmly watching their mortal enemy. Voron stepped closer to Morena, unsheathing his sword. She raised her arm irritably, pushing him away.

"Hello, Veles-s-s," hissed Skiper-Zmey, lowering his enormous heads down to Veles' level. "I was-s-s hoping to s-s-see you earlier at my welcome party. But you decided to s-s-send that fire-head Semargl and a couple of lizards-s-s in your s-s-stead. Why is-s-s that, old man? Am I not important enough, eh?"

"Oh, no, Zmey. You are important enough, alright," huffed Veles, the staff in his hands glowing brighter. "This is why we are here now. To make sure you're sent back in the hole you slithered out from."

Zmey lowered his head a little closer to Veles, his forked tongues flicked and disappeared. "You reek of fear, Veles-s-s," hissed Zmey, straightening up. "As well you should, as I will be the death of you."

"We'll see about that," growled Chernobog.

"And who is going to stop me? You, Chernobog? Where is your twin-brother? Where is Perun and where are the brothers Svarozhich? Just the two of you and a little Celtic half-breed? Without Perun, you stand no chance."

Skiper-Zmey barked laughing and the two women giggled, joining their master. Aidan listened to him, with horror realizing that Zmey was right. *Gwyn, Angel, where are you?* he thought miserably. *You were supposed to be here by now.*

"I guess, we'll have to make do with what we have," said Chernobog, raising his sword.

"Whoa... whoa... Lower your s-s-steel," hissed Zmey backing away, but all six of his eyes were twinkling with mockery. "I'll stop you right there, puny god of Destruction. I don't want to fight either of you. I feel... um... benevolent. It's like my second birthday today, you know?" The mouths of the three snakes stretched in a semblance of a smile, exposing huge fangs, dripping with a nauseatingly green venom. "S-s-so, to celebrate my s-s-second coming, I wish to gift the three of you your lives. Put away your s-s-swords and bend your knees-s-s. And I'll even let you rule your own little realms-s-s. Reporting to me that is-s-s, of course."

The air shimmered around Zmey and a thick black mist enveloped him. He disappeared from view for a split-second. When the mist dissipated, the serpent was gone. A tall man was standing in his place. He was towering at least eight feet tall. He had no hair, and the light was reflecting off his bald head. His eyes, just like the eyes of the serpent, were yellow with vertical slits of dark-red pupils. His hulking body was covered in unusual armor that resembled the scales of a snake and in his hand, he was holding an enormous double-edged battle axe.

He ran his fingers over the slick scales of the armor on his chest and his thin lips stretched into a wolfish grin. His teeth were small, except for two sharp canines that resembled the fangs of a viper. Despite his more or less human appearance, his tongue was forked, flickering in and out of his mouth as he smiled.

"I thought a human-like form would make you more comfortable," said Zmey, the hissing gone from his voice. "So, what is it going to be, Veles? Are you ready to submit to my rule? Bend your knee and I will leave the Dark Nav in peace."

Neither Veles nor Chernobog said anything. They didn't look like they were considering the proposal, but the anger seemed to be choking them.

"Did you forget how to say no, Veles? Repeat after me—N—O. Hell, no!"

Aidan heard a familiar voice and spun around. He saw two men who emerged from the darkness and approached them.

"Gwyn, finally," exhaled Aidan, relieved. "Angel, what took you so long?"

Gwyn ap Nudd was in his form of the Lord of the Wild Hunt, dressed in his hunter's leather pants and vest, trimmed in furs and feathers. His face was concealed by a black mask and his angled eyes were blazing with the brilliant white light through the slits of his mask.

Standing next to Gwyn ap Nudd, Angel seemed short. His long black hair was pulled back in a ponytail which was unusual for him and he wasn't trying to hide his deadly magical energy. Here, in the Dark Nav, he felt comfortable, at home.

"I can't believe my eyes! What a wonderful surprise! Gwyn ap Nudd, in the flesh," hissed Zmey, taking a step forward and exploring Gwyn with his venomous eyes. Then he hit his hips with his hands and hooted with laughter. "What happened to you, buddy? You are no longer a god."

"Don't think for a moment that it's going to help you, Zmey," retorted Gwyn ap Nudd dryly, shrugging. "I heard your offer and here is my counteroffer. Crawl back to your grave and we'll call it a day. You will never leave the Dark Nav."

"I had enough of this useless talk!" yelled Veles, raising his staff. "You're crazy, Zmey, if you think that any of us here are going to let you leave the Dark Nav and break into the world of the living."

Veles' staff blazed with a red light and a ray of his magic escaped it, slamming Zmey in his chest. He didn't fall but got pushed, sliding a few feet back. Fury distorted his face, making it look more serpent than human.

"I wanted to be nice, but we'll do it your way," he growled.

Zmey tucked the axe behind his belt and extended both his hands forward. Aidan expected to see a power-blast or energy orbs, but nothing like this happened. Visibly nothing happened, but Veles yelped and dropped his staff. For a split-second, his head tilted back, like he was sleeping or unconscious.

"No, not again," muttered Chernobog, backing away from Veles.

Veles regained consciousness and picked up his staff. But instead of attacking Zmey, he turned on Chernobog, his eyes glowing with a yellow light. He swung his staff and slammed Chernobog with his magic. Chernobog cried out and staggered back. Zmey cackled and hit Chernobog with whatever strange magic he was wielding. Both Slavic deities shouted at the same time, clashing in mortal combat with each other.

"Shit," hissed Gwyn. "I totally forgot about that..." He channeled his power and a brilliant white light surrounded him. "Aidan, we need to cleanse their system from the energy of Chaos. Take care of Chernobog."

It was easier said than done. There was no easy way to approach two gods who weren't willing to stand down until one of them was destroyed. Aidan channeled his power just like his mentor did, but he had to put his hands on Chernobog and there was no way to do it.

Zmey doubled down laughing. Both women stepped forward, energy orbs manifested in their hands, crackling with electrical discharges. At the same time, they propelled the orbs at Aidan and Gwyn ap Nudd.

Angel stepped forward and spread his arms, shielding them. A black void opened up between his arms, swallowing the energy orbs. The mages didn't stop, hurling fireballs and energy orbs at Angel, pushing him back, away from the battle.

"He is Death," shouted Valeria Demidova to the other mage without stopping her assault on Angel. "There is no known way to kill him. The only thing we can do is keep him busy and if we're lucky, we might be able to restrain him. Just don't let him touch you. He'll suck the life right out of you."

Aidan glanced around and cringed. Angel was holding the void open between his arms and it was taking a lot of his strength to maintain it. Veles and Chernobog were getting creative at trying to kill each other, now using not only their magic but also their weapons and magical artifacts they had in their possessions. Gwyn ap Nudd was trying to stop them but couldn't get anywhere close enough. Zmey was laughing manically, hitting Veles and Chernobog with his magic again and again. Chaos ruled the field.

"Dammit, Gwyn!" yelled Aidan, hoping that Gwyn ap Nudd could hear his voice over the pandemonium that broke out around them. "Give it up. You can't come anywhere close enough to these two."

Gwyn ap Nudd heard him and spun around. His glowing eyes halted on Demidova. Busy attacking Angel, she didn't notice him right away. He hissed a spell, locking her in a circle of his magic, immobilizing her. She whimpered, unable to fight his control. Gwyn came closer and seized her shoulder, his fingers digging deep into her flesh.

"Stop this madness, or I will snap you like a twig," he hissed.

"I think not." The second mage approached Gwyn ap Nudd,

fearlessly staring at him directly into his blazing eyes. "Release her or your son will die."

Aidan recognized her voice and stilled, shocked. "I expected that you were working for the other side when you started to play your games with me," he said. "There is nothing you can do to me, Ms. Bonneville, and you know it."

"I beg to differ. The Lord of Chaos taught me a few new tricks." Ms. Bonneville snickered and snapped her fingers. The Guardians' chain wrapped around Aidan's neck and he was expecting to get burnt. The chain didn't burn him. It grew thicker and heavier, crushing his neck, cutting off his air. He grasped at the chain with his fingers, realizing that it was no longer a chain. A thick silver collar was locked around his neck.

Aidan struggled to channel his power but couldn't access it. The collar was blocking his magic and there was nothing he could do to fight it. His head swam and his vision became murky. He moaned and swayed, then slowly lowered down to one knee.

"Gwyn, don't stop. Kill both of them, Father," he croaked, fighting for each breath.

"Hang in there, Son. She can't kill you," growled Gwyn ap Nudd.

He channeled more of his power and the entire field got lit up with a blinding light. Both mages cowered away from him, but Ms. Bonneville managed to keep Aidan in the clutches of her dark spell. Nevertheless, it gave a temporary reprieve to Angel and he let go of the void. Zmey cried out, clasping his hands to his face as if Gwyn's light was burning him.

In two long-legged strides, Gwyn ap Nudd covered the distance between him and Zmey. His arm struck forward, his fingers wrapping around Zmey's neck. Despite a full foot difference in height, Gwyn lifted Zmey in the air, squeezing his neck tighter. At the same time, he slammed his hand at Zmey's chest and started to chant. His deep musical voice spread through the field, becoming stronger and more powerful with every next word he said.

Skiper-Zmey groaned, growing faint as Gwyn was slowly draining his magic. Veles and Chernobog stopped their pointless fight and stood lost, gaping at each other like two people who just woke up from a mind-boggling nightmare.

Angel quietly sauntered toward the mages, but his every step was infused with rage beyond comprehension. The tendrils of darkness were slithering around him like deadly serpents and the ground shook slightly with every step he took.

"Release Aidan," he growled, his face twisted with fury. He reached forward ready to lay his hands on them. They squealed in horror, but were unable to move, frozen by the most primal fear—the fear of death.

"It's over, Zmey," said Gwyn ap Nudd. "You can't fight me. All your supporters are under our control."

Skiper-Zmey glanced faintly at Gwyn and a slow smile spread over his face, exposing his terrible fangs. "Are you s-s-sure?" he whispered, his yellow eyes fixed on something behind Gwyn's back and his forked tongue flickered in and out.

Gwyn ap Nudd glanced back, but it was too late. The temperature dropped suddenly, and restraints made of pure black ice locked his wrist and his ankles, draining his magic and rendering him powerless. The same type of restraints appeared on Veles, Chernobog and Angel. They all fell to their knees, unable to move.

"Father!" yelled Aidan as he watched Gwyn ap Nudd forced to his knees by Morena. She touched Gwyn's face and a layer of black ice covered his mouth. Then she whispered something, erecting a solid dome of black ice over him.

Aidan fought the silver collar that was still blocking his magic. Ms. Bonneville put her hand on his shoulder, holding him down. "Down, boy," she seethed, tugging at his collar. "There is nothing you can do. You're mine now and I swear I'll make you pay for every moment of humiliation I had to endure because of you. So, be a good boy and obey. I think if my lord won't mind, I'd like to keep you alive as my pet." She touched his hands and heavy golden handcuffs manifested on his wrists, locking them together and pinning him to the field.

Zmey regained his strength and walked around the chunk of ice that was Gwyn ap Nudd, to the goddess of Winter and Death. Just now Aidan noticed that Voron was lying down on the ground, covered in a thick layer of ice. In the surrounding chaos, no one even noticed when Morena disabled him. Zmey took Morena's hand, bringing it up to his lips and walked her to her husband, Chernobog.

"Morena, my love, why?" moaned Chernobog, gazing up at his wife. "I love you. I would do anything for you. Why did you betray me?"

"I didn't betray you," replied Morena, distaste curving her lips. "I was never yours in the first place. I did whatever I had to do to free myself from you and from this godforsaken place. I was the one who stole the Axe of Perun from you and gave it to Milana. I was the one who helped her escape from the Dark Nav right under your nose while keeping you busy with that Salamander. And all this time, you were none the wiser. Sad... Really."

She wrapped her arms around Zmey's neck and kissed him. Zmey pulled her closer, his fingers digging into her shapely behind and returned her kiss, turning slightly to the side so her husband could see it. Chernobog dropped his head, his shoulders hunched powerlessly. Holding Morena's hand in his, Zmey seized Chernobog's hair, jerking his head up and stared into his lifeless eyes. Then he cackled and let go. "Love can be deadly," he said shaking his head. "Even to gods."

He turned to Ms. Bonneville and Valeria Demidova and raised the Axe of Perun in the air. "It's time, my loyal followers," he said. "Are you ready? Soon, the world will be ours."

Zmey approached the glowing fracture and moved his hand over it. The air around his hand rippled like it was water. Keeping his yellow eyes fixed on the fracture, he gestured to Morena to stand by his side.

"It will take three strikes of the Axe to break the veil," he explained, his voice strangely airy and elated. "You know what needs to be done, darling. Get ready."

"Oh, I am ready, my love." Morena snickered, raising her arms up. "I've been ready since I was given to this goddamn loser to spend my eternity in the darkness of the Nav."

The space between her arms was engorged with her magic. Blue lightning bolts originated between her arms and the sky above her got even darker. Aidan tilted his head back, gaping at the sky. A dark swirling mass was descending on the field, moving in a slow circular motion like a giant tornado from hell. He didn't know what it was, but its dark energy was leaving no place for doubt—whatever it was, it was unmistakably evil.

Aidan glanced at the Head Mage. She was too busy staring at Morena to pay attention to him. He dropped his head and closed his eyes, with all his strength reaching within for his magic. It was blocked by the collar, but he was able to gather a tiny amount of it, just enough to redirect it to the communication rune that was embedded into his chest. The rune warmed and lit up just a little. He raised his handcuffed arms, pressing his hands to the rune.

"Zane, they are coming to Yav," he whispered. "Morena betrayed us. We couldn't stop them. It's over—"

A mighty blow on his jaw threw Aidan on his back. He hit the ground hard, the air knocked out of him. Ms. Bonneville ripped his shirt off his chest and gawked at the rune. Then she raised her hand and slapped him across his face.

"Who did you communicate with, boy?" she seethed, her hands clutching into tight fists. "What did you tell them?"

Aidan closed his eyes, bracing himself for the next blow but remained silent.

"It doesn't matter, Eleonor," said Zmey peacefully, a malignant smirk on his face. "No one can stop me now."

"What do you want me to do with him, my lord?" asked Ms. Bonneville, pulling Aidan up by the collar on his neck.

"Whatever. I don't care about any of them," replied Zmey with an indifferent shrug. "None of them is a match for me now. As far as this half-breed, he's yours. You can do with him as you please."

Ms. Bonneville peered down at Aidan, flicking her eyebrow at him derisively. Then she leaned forward and touched his lips with her fingers, whispering something. Aidan grunted as a piece of duct tape sealed his lips.

"Now, Aodh mac Lir, be a good boy and don't talk, unless I tell you to," she hissed straightening up and kicked him in his chest. Aidan fell back. She gloated over his helplessness for a moment, then bent down and petted his cheek. "I'll come back for you, my pet."

She turned away and marched back to the Lord of Chaos. His vision still blurry, Aidan watched Skiper-Zmey raising the Axe of Perun and crashing the mighty weapon on the air right above the fracture, like it was a solid wall. A bright line manifested in the place where the Axe struck a moment ago. Zmey raised the Axe again and slammed it down at the glowing line. Without waiting, he did it again and stepped back, holding the Axe down.

The glowing line became unbearably bright. A gust of the mighty wind rushed through the Nav and with an ear-piercing noise, the veil was torn. Zmey pushed his hands into the tear in the veil, ripping it apart. With Morena by his side, he stepped through the tear in the veil and they both disappeared on the other side, followed by the two mages.

The swirling dark mass reached the tear and followed

through it to the other side. As the dark mass was exiting through the rip in the veil, Aidan noticed that it was not a solid mass. Thousands of monsters that looked like phantom birds flew to the outside world, supported by their horrendous wings. Beside the phantoms, he saw some other manifestations flowing through the tear. They were also glowing with the evil energy, but they were different from the phantoms.

Aidan raised his hands up, trying to pull the tape off his lips. But it was no ordinary tape and without his magic he couldn't take it off. The situation was hopeless. He was disabled by the dark Guardian's magic. Gwyn ap Nudd, Voron, Angel and Veles were sealed under the mass of the black ice. On top of it, Chernobog was restrained and crushed by the pain of his broken heart.

All is lost, thought Aidan with despair in his heart and closed his eyes, allowing exhaustion to settle in.

* * *

AIDAN DIDN'T KNOW how long he was lying motionless on the cold ground of the Nav, when he felt some added weight on his chest. He opened his eyes and saw a large black bird sitting on his chest. The bird cocked its head and stared at him with its round eyes. Then it opened its wing and the shimmering glow of magic surrounded it. It hopped forward and touched the tape on Aidan's mouth with its beak. The tape slowly dissipated, and Aidan was able to take a deep breath through his mouth.

"Voron?" he asked, recognizing Chernobog's righthand man.

The bird hopped down and twirled in place as Voron took his human form. "Yes, my lord," said the warrior with a light bow. "Luckily, Morena didn't think highly of me, so she forgot that I also have magic and I can shift." He lifted Aidan's hands, probing his handcuffs with his magic.

"No, Voron," said Aidan, pulling his hands away. "I'll be fine.

Can you free Gwyn ap Nudd from the black ice? If you can give him access to his magic, he can take care of everyone else."

"It may take time, but I'll try," said Voron, heading toward the pile of ice that was covering Gwyn ap Nudd.

He raised his sword and infused it with his magic. Then he crashed it down on the black ice. At first the ice resisted his assault, but after a few strikes, a glowing fracture marred its perfectly black surface. Voron doubled his effort and a few more web-like fractures separated from the first one. After a few minutes, the icy dome trembled and exploded, propelling a bunch of icicles through the air.

Gwyn ap Nudd was sprawled motionless on the ground. The mask was gone from his face. His eyes were shut, and his skin had a bluish tint to it. Aidan gasped and tried to get up, but the magic of the handcuffs held him in place. "Voron," he called, not sure if his mentor was dead or alive.

"He's alive," replied Voron without looking at Aidan. He kneeled next to Gwyn and put both his hands over his face, channeling his magic. The ice that was covering Gwyn's mouth melted under Voron's touch and Gwyn ap Nudd opened his eyes. He sat up slowly, assisted by Voron and connected with the Nav, restoring his strength and power. His eyes lit up with the brilliant light and the ice that was bounding his wrists and ankles blown up into sparkling dust.

Gwyn ap Nudd got up to his feet and flexed his shoulders. The black mask manifested over his face and he laughed, the kind of laugh that promised nothing good to his enemies.

"I'm back," growled Gwyn ap Nudd through his clenched teeth, "and I'm coming for you, Zmey!"

37

~ TESSA ~

Tessa ran stealthily through the long corridors of the Guardians Headquarters mansion. She wasn't that late past the curfew yet. Only five minutes. But she didn't want to get caught. She was still on probation, and she remembered that Aidan paid dearly to get her this probation.

She turned the corner and was about to enter into the Apprentices' Wing when she heard a loud whisper. Tessa halted and peeked around the corner, holding her breath. Not far from the entrance into the Mages' Wing, she saw two high-level mages. They both were talking quietly, but their body language was betraying their state of anxiety.

Feeling torn, Tessa decided that she had to know what was going on. *I'll be careful*, she promised to herself, shifting closer to the mages so she could hear what they were saying. Luckily, they were so deeply involved in their discussion that they didn't notice her.

"...Eleonore has been gone for a few days already," said the first mage. "Do you know what's it all about?"

Eleonore? Oh yeah... The Head Mage. Eleonore Bonneville.

"No," replied the second mage. "And that's the problem. She disappeared so suddenly that she didn't leave any instructions on who should be taking care of the Order while she was gone."

"Don't you feel it? I'm sure her disappearance has something to do with that."

"Yes, I could feel the darkness rising for a while. What I don't understand is why Eleonore didn't send any of us to research the situation and deal with it. She even had that Celtic god at her disposal, but she preferred to run him around, doing some petty training-level tasks."

"Whatever was rising is here already," said the first mage, shaking her head. "I could sense the battle. It started a while ago —the confrontation between the light and the darkness. And the light is losing…"

Aidan is there, I am sure, thought Tessa, pressing her hands to her chest, her heart pounding against her ribcage. *This is the battle he wanted me to stay away from. The light is losing?* She felt a cold sweat running down her back. *Aidan… No… I have to be there, by his side.*

Forgetting that she was supposed to be careful, she ran straight into the Mages' Wing. She heard both women screaming after her, but she ignored them. She didn't stop until she reached Missi's room. Tessa banged on the door frantically, but no one answered. After a minute, the door next to Missi's opened up and another young woman in her pajamas peeked outside.

"Tessa, what's with all the racket?" she asked sleepily, rubbing her eyes. "Don't you know? Missi is not here. Ms. Bonneville sent her away on some mission a few days ago."

"She's gone?" asked Tessa, dumbstruck.

"Yes," replied the young woman, "and you shouldn't be here either. If the mage on duty catches you, you'll be in trouble. More than you already are…"

"Never mind that, Lily," Tessa cut her off. "Do you know

how to summon an Archangel?"

"What? Are you out of your friggin' mind? An apprentice of your level doesn't have what it takes to summon someone as powerful as an Archangel—"

Lily was still talking, but Tessa didn't listen. She ran to the Guardians' Library. Without slowing down, she kicked the door open and zoomed inside. Tall shelves with thousands of books surrounded her. Reading the labels on the side of shelves, she proceeded deeper into the library until she found the shelf labeled "Summoning Spells".

With horror, she realized that every book on this shelf was locked. She stomped her foot and kept browsing the shelf until she found what she was looking for—a thick old book in a leather bind. "Summoning Angels, Archangels, and Divine Beings" was written on the spine of the book.

Tessa tried to pull the book from the shelf, but it didn't budge, locked with a heavy chain. She needed to call a librarian, but she had no time for it. She also knew that because she was the lowest level apprentice, they would never allow her to read this book anyway.

If I break the chains, they will expel me, and Aidan will suffer for it. A thought flashed through her mind. *The light is losing the battle. Aidan may get hurt, or he could be dead. For all I know, there are ways to kill gods. Let them expel me. As long as he is alive and well, I don't care.*

She connected to her power, collecting electricity at the tips of her fingers. A low thunder rumbled in the library as Tessa hit the lock on the book with a lightning bolt. The lock broke, and the book fell into her hands.

Tessa sat down on the floor, quickly flipping through the pages until she found the spell she was looking for. She re-read the instructions a few times, committing everything to memory and got up. Channeling a little bit of her magic, she used it to draw a complicated rune in the air. Tessa observed her handiwork, comparing it to the picture in the book. The rune looked perfect. She touched it and whispered the words of the summoning spell calling to Archangel Uriel.

A shower of golden sparks erupted in front of her and Uri dropped through it, falling to his knees. He wrapped his arms around his head, staring up at Tessa, his eyes bloodshot.

"Tessa?" he moaned. "Stop the summoning call. You're killing me."

"Oh my god, it worked!" yelped Tessa. "Oh, no... how do I stop the spell? The book didn't say that."

"Goddammit!" growled Uri, his face covered in perspiration. "Say *Incanto Comlium* and that should kill the spell."

"*Incanto Comlium*," said Tessa quickly and Uri visibly relaxed, slowly rising to his feet. He grabbed the book from the floor, reading the words of the summoning spell Tessa used.

"Never use this summoning spell again, Tessa," he said quietly, throwing the book on the floor. "It's designed to torture the person you're summoning. I'll teach you how to do it properly later. Now, what did you want? Why are you summoning me when the city is under attack?"

"The city is under attack?" mumbled Tessa then she grabbed Uri's hand. "Where is Aidan, Uri? Take me to him. This is why I summoned you."

Uri stilled, gaping down at her. "Aidan is not in the city, Tessa. I can't take you where he is. Sorry."

"Uri, please," she begged, tears rising in her eyes. "I must be with him. Mages are talking... They're talking about a battle between the light and the darkness. They said that the light is losing. I feel it right here." She pressed her hand to her heart. "I must help Aidan. My place is by his side. Please! I love him, Uri!"

"Fine," he said finally. "But I still can't take you where Aidan is. I have no power to travel to that place. But I'll take you to Angelique. She's a seer. Perhaps she can tell us what's going on."

"Let's go, let's go," Tessa rushed him, seizing his hand.

Uri snapped his fingers, and they vanished from the library.

* * *

THEY MATERIALIZED behind Angelique's condominium building. Uri pressed his finger to his lips, gesturing for Tessa to be silent. As they walked around the building toward the main entrance, Tessa heard a loud howl and a scream filled with terror that followed it. Uri tensed, staring in the direction of the sound.

A moment later, Tessa felt freezing wind sweeping by. Uri grabbed her arm, pulling her toward the building.

"What's going on?" hissed Tessa.

"I told you. The city is under attack. Demons, phantoms, ghosts, you name it—it's here," barked Uri. "Dammit, too late."

He pointed up. A dark cloud was moving fast in their direction. A few terrified people were running along the street toward the building.

Golden flames wrapped around Uri as he assumed his angelic form. His golden wings opened up to full extent, and he rose in the air. Without caring who could see him, he unsheathed his sword, blazing with gold flames. As the dark cloud came within his reach, he swung his sword, channeling his power through it.

Tessa couldn't see what kind of monsters assailed Uri, but he spun in place like a golden tornado incinerating every single one of them. People froze in place, staring at the sky in awe. A few minutes later, Uri slowly lowered down next to Tessa, sheathing his sword. His wings folded behind his back and then dissipated together with his golden fire.

A woman approached Uri and reached with her hand to touch him but quickly pulled away. "I'm sorry," she said with a shy smile, "I don't know who you are... or what you are... but thank you. You saved us all." She turned around to see her friends. "I just wanted to tell you that your secret is safe with us. We're never going to tell anyone about what happened here."

"Thank you," said Uri, smiling back at her. The woman nodded to him and walked away with her friends. Uri sighed and sent a small amount of his magic after them. "In a few minutes, they will forget everything that just happened."

"Let's go," said Tessa, pulling Uri toward the building. But before they opened the door to walk inside, she heard sounds of heavy steps and turned around. Her eyebrows climbed up as she watched two medieval knights riding toward them. The knights stopped their horses and dismounted.

"Father Beaumont?" she mumbled, blinking a few times at his shining chainmail and breastplate.

He smiled. "Hello, Tessa," he said with a light bow. "I wish we had time to chat, but my friend, Luc de la Crosse, and I are slightly preoccupied at the moment."

"My lady," said the second knight with an elegant bow.

"Uriel," said Father Beaumont, sounding urgent, "what are you doing here? We need you in Parkland stat. A huge motorcycle gang of demons broke into a residential neighborhood. Akira and Yaroslav are holding them down, but we need your help. With your purifying fire, you can exorcise all of them in a matter of minutes."

Uri grunted, throwing a scorching gaze at Tessa. "I'll be there in a few minutes, Raoul. Just hang in a little while longer."

Raoul nodded. Both knights mounted their steeds and vanished. Tessa and Uri walked into the dark building. The power was down, and the elevators were out of service, so they took the stairs to the third floor. Uri halted in front of the door with the number 313 on it and knocked. The door opened up immediately.

"Uri, thank God. I was just about to summon you," said Angelique, ushering them inside her apartment.

"Not another summoning," mumbled Uri, rubbing his forehead. "What's up, Angie?"

"Uri, I need you to take me to Zane—"

"What the hell is wrong with both of you!" yelled Uri, throwing his hands in the air. "Do I look like an Uber driver to you? Did you see what's going on outside? People are dying! Vampires are working with the FBI to save humans and you want me to drive you all over the world? I should be out there, doing my job and taking care of people."

Tessa and Angelique exchanged a look and shouted at the same time. Uri pressed his hands to his ears, gazing heavenwards.

"Please, stop!" he yelled. "I'll do what you want. Angelique, Aidan is in the Dark Nav. I have no access to the realms of the dead. Can you see anything related to Aidan? Anything at all?"

"No," said Angelique, turning to Tessa. "I'm sorry, it's been a few days since I had my last vision. I see nothing. But my intuition tells me that I should be next to Zane. Now."

"Fine. I'll do what you want. I'm wasting more time arguing with you two." Uri raked his hand through his hair. "You know that if we all survive this mess, both Aidan and Gunz are going to kill me. Together."

"You're an Archangel, you'll survive," retorted Tessa. "Where is Zane now? Since you can't take me to Aidan, take us both to Zane."

"Fine. Dress warm. I'm taking you to Arkhangelsk, to Mount Karasova. It's north of Russia," said Uri. "Do it quick."

"Before you take us to Mount Karasova, can we please make a quick stop at Zane's house?" asked Angelique, a guilty smile on her face.

Uri threw his hands in the air, a low growl rumbling in his chest. "Fine. Just do it quick."

Angelique ran into her bedroom, and a few minutes later came out dressed in a warm jacket and boots. In her hands, she was holding another jacket and a small box. She gave the second warm jacket to Tessa. Uri waited while she put it on. Then he took their hands and sighed.

"God knows, I shouldn't be doing this," he muttered and all three of them vanished from the room in swirls of golden flames.

38

~ ZANE BURNS, A.K.A. GUNZ ~

In a heartbeat, the world around him became a gut-wrenching mayhem—howling, roaring, tearing at the soul and clawing at the flesh, blinding and deafening havoc. As usual in extreme situations, his military training took over and Gunz dropped to the ground, covering his head with his arms.

As he was lying down, sprawled and helpless, while all hell broke loose inside Mount Karasova, Aidan's words resonated in his mind with pain. They failed to stop Zmey two times. This was it. This was their last chance to stop him. There will be no other opportunity. It's now or never.

The roaring of the winds was unbearably loud and terrifying, but he lifted his arm just a little and peeked outside, searching for Kal or Mrak Delar. Dark swarms of sand and small rocks were swirling within the cave in a continuous nauseating motion. As soon as he lifted his arm, his face got bombarded by the sand, with the strength of an industrial sand-blaster and he had to shut his eyes.

In the split-second that he had, he didn't notice Kal or Semargl anywhere. He knew that Karma was on the other side of the cave, next to the stone monolith, so he didn't look for her.

But he found Mrak Delar right away. The Master of Power was lying on his back just a few feet away. His face wasn't protected from the winds and the dark mass of sand swirling in the cave. Blood was trickling down from the corner of his mouth.

Dammit, if he stayed like that, he'd get killed by this sand and projectiles that were flying around. Gunz lowered his arms and crawled toward Mrak Delar, holding his head as low as he could. Fighting the wind, it took him a few minutes to reach him. Keeping his eyes tightly shut, he touched Mrak Delar's face, feeling the warmth of his skin. The Master was alive. He pulled himself over Mrak Delar covering his face the best he could.

"Master, are you okay?" Gunz hissed and felt the light movement of Mrak's arm.

"I'm alive... overused my — ahhh — just need a few minutes—"

"Would Fire energy help?" asked Gunz, carefully trying to connect with the elemental fire.

"Yes..."

Gunz allowed the fire energy to flow freely through him, circulating it through the Master of Power. A few seconds later, he felt Mrak's hand squeezing his elbow and stopped. As the winds kept ravaging the cave, they stayed down in the same position.

After a while, the noise started to subside; the wind slowed down and then died out completely. The silence that cloaked the cave was bloodcurdling, agonizingly pressing on his stretched nerves. Gunz carefully lifted his arms and peeked out. The sandstorm was gone, but so was Mount Karasova.

He scrambled up to his knees and surveyed the area, awestricken. The mountain was gone. He was sitting on a piece of flat land, a small lake glistening with the reflected light of the moon just a few yards away. The broken stone monolith still remained in the middle of the area that once was a cave.

A tall bald man was standing next to the monolith. Morena, the goddess of Winter and Death was standing by his side, her hand on the crook of his arm. A sword, glistening like ice, was in her other hand and with horror, Gunz recognized Aidan's sword. Valeria Demidova and another woman were standing on either side of them, like loyal bodyguards. The man had the eyes of a serpent, yellow with vertical red pupils. In his hand he was holding the Axe of Perun. It wasn't hard to guess who he was.

Gunz started to rise, but the man wagged his finger at him, an evil smirk revealing his long venomous fangs.

"Nuh-uh, little lizard. Stay where you are. On your knees. I like you in this position."

Zmey stepped aside and now Gunz could see Kal and Semargl, both encapsulated into blocks of solid black ice. He cringed, knowing perfectly well the pain Kal and Semargl were in. Morena ran her long nail over the ice and then turned to Gunz.

"I hope you remember what I can do to you." She flicked her hand at the block of ice. "Defy me or my lord Skiper-Zmey and you'll see what else I'm capable of, Fire Salamander. Besides, you don't want your little girlfriend to die, do you?"

Angie? No, she can't be here...

Morena stepped aside and Gunz saw Karma. She was down on her knees, next to the monolith, her arms and legs set in ice. But even if she wasn't in restraints, Gunz didn't think she could fight. Everything about her—her head, bowed down to her chest, and her hunched shoulders—was betraying her true state of mind. She was broken, unwilling to fight even for her life.

Gunz sighed, raising both his hands up. "What do you want from me, Morena?"

"First of all, learn some respect, fire-worm," she seethed.

Morena pulled her arm back and struck him with Aidan's sword, penetrating his shoulder. Gunz grunted, grabbing his shoulder and bent forward. Blood spilled through his fingers, dripping down his arm. Morena snickered and pulled the sword out, forcing another cry of pain out of him.

"Now, let's try it again," drawled Morena, gesturing to him to proceed.

"What do you want from me, my lady?" Gunz repeated his questions, anger turning him inside out.

"Much better," said Morena. "Master of Power. Is he alive?"

Gunz glanced at Mrak Delar. His eyes were flooded with the blackness of his power, as the Master was trying to show him that he was ready to fight. Like the best painkiller, an angry ecstasy coursed through Gunz, and he felt the fire rising in his eyes, making them glow red.

"He's alive, my lady, but he may as well be dead," he said. As proof, he picked up Mrak's arm and let it go. His arm dropped down lifelessly. "He's hurt physically and drained magically."

Morena exchanged a quick look with Zmey and he nodded at her. She turned to Gunz, staring down at him in disdain. "Lift him and deliver him to my lord," she ordered.

"I would need to get up for that, my lady. Can't do it on my knees," muttered Gunz, hiding his glowing eyes.

"Don't get smart with me, lizard," hissed Morena. "Shut your mouth or I will shut it for you. Do as you are told!"

Gunz pulled Mrak up, throwing his arm over his shoulders. "Jesus Christ all mighty, you are heavy, man," he hissed as he dragged him to Zmey. "Now what do you want… my lord?"

Zmey grabbed Mrak's hair, yanking his head up and checked his face, narrowing his reptilian eyes. "Perfect," he muttered, letting go and wiping his hands on his pants. "You can put him down at my feet. I'll deal with him later."

As Gunz was lowering Mrak Delar down, the Master opened his eyes and mouthed just one word, "Now…"

The ground trembled, and the wind picked up, rushing through the forest and disfiguring the smooth surface of the lake. Heavy thunderstorm clouds rolled in and the bright zigzag of lightning split the dark sky. Mrak Delar rose high in the air, two energy orbs crackling in his hands.

Zmey screeched in fury, stamping his foot. A deep fracture originated where his foot hit the ground and ran toward Mrak Delar. The Ancient Master of Power laughed and sent both energy orbs flying at the same time. Both Morena and Zmey ducked down to avoid the direct impact. But Mrak wasn't aiming at them. The energy orbs smashed the ice blocks that were holding Kal and Semargl. The ice cracked and a web of fractures covered its shiny surface.

"Ignius," shouted Gunz, striking the ice blocks with the fire. The ice blew up, showering everything around with small icicles and white dust.

Kal dropped to his knees and roared, like a wild beast, reverting into a full-powered Great Fire Salamander. For a moment, the colossal lizard levitated in the air. A powerful blast of fire energy spread through the area, knocking Zmey, Morena and both mages off their feet. Kal reverted back into his human form, fire dancing around him, making him look like a human-shaped torch.

Both Semargl and Kal unsheathed their flaming blades and charged Zmey who was already on his feet. Without waiting to be asked, Gunz joined their attack. Zmey hurled a giant rock at them with unbelievable force. Mrak Delar met the rock with his power shield and the rock exploded with a loud bang that could wake the dead.

Zmey growled and hit Kal with his intoxicating magic of Chaos. But the ray of his magic never reached Kal. A brilliant white shield rose between the Lord of Chaos and the Fire Elemental. Gunz spun around and saw Gwyn up Nudd, holding the shield.

"Fool me once," hissed Gwyn ap Nudd, expanding his shield and wrapping it around Zmey and Morena, immobilizing both of them. His unnerving white eyes stopped on Mrak Delar.

"Master, I can't keep them like this forever. I need a deep hole in the ground. Do it!"

Mrak Delar lowered himself down next to Gwyn ap Nudd and connected with the power of the Earth. With one swing of his arm, he moved the stone monolith aside. His arms got pumped with bulging muscles as he lifted a giant chunk of earth in the air.

"Not enough," growled Gwyn ap Nudd. "Double it. I'm losing my grip. Do it fast."

Mrak screamed, gathering all the power he had and lifted another pile of earth, making the hole in the ground deeper. Gwyn grunted, dropping to one knee, slowly losing his battle. All of a sudden, his shield shone brighter.

"I'm here, Father," said Aidan, channeling his magic into Gwyn's shield.

Zmey tilted his head back and emitted a terrible shriek. Gunz never heard a sound as awful as that. He pressed his hands to his ears, feeling like his head was about to explode. Blood trickled from his ears and his nose. Mrak Delar dropped to his knees, wrapping his arms around his head. Gwyn ap Nudd and Aidan were still holding the shield, keeping Zmey restrained.

Angel flew over Gwyn's shield and pointed his hand at Zmey. "*Silenties*," he said quietly and Zmey fell silent. Preoccupied with Skiper-Zmey everyone forgot about the two mages. Quietly they tiptoed around, positioning themselves behind the monolith, so no one could see them. When Gunz noticed what they were doing, it was too late to stop them.

Joining their forces, the mages hit Gwyn ap Nudd with raw magical energy. Gwyn cried out and for a heartbeat his shield dropped. This tiny fluctuation in the flow of his power was enough for Zmey to break free. He rose in the air, pulling Morena up with him. Morena screeched and a frosty winter blizzard tore through the land.

Gunz grunted as thousands of tiny pieces of ice penetrated his skin. He looked around, but there was nowhere to hide. As torturous as it was, he ignored the pain.

"*Ignius.*" He made a circular motion with his hand and locked both mages into a circle of pure fire. They yelped, backing away from the flames. "Don't go anywhere." He smirked at the women. *It'll take them a while to break free.*

"Gwyn ap Nudd, I thought you were smarter than that," bellowed Zmey, anger distorting his features into a serpent-like snout. "Even if you could hold me down forever, you still don't have what it takes to restrain me. Besides, you also need this!" He showed him the Axe of Perun and cackled. "Oh, wait. Even if you had it, you couldn't use its power. Are there any illegitimate sons of Perun among you, losers?"

He peered down and cackled again. Kal and Semargl lowered their sword. With horror, Gunz realized that Zmey was right. There was no way to kill him and they didn't have the power to curse him back into his grave. They didn't even have the oak coffin they needed.

"I didn't think so," continued Zmey. "You don't have what it takes to fight me. Morena, sweetheart, would you deal with them for me? I spent too long underground. I want to explore the world of the living. See how it's changed."

Morena smirked, and the blizzard got heavier, obscuring the vision. Gunz raised his arm to shield his eyes. Through the snowstorm, he saw the giant silhouette of Zmey gaining some height. All of a sudden Skiper-Zmey stopped, as though his bald head hit an invisible ceiling. He grunted and rubbed his head, staring down.

"Going somewhere?" asked Veles. He snapped his fingers and a hoop of glowing red power wrapped around Zmey, pinning his arms to his body. Veles slashed his hand through the air, yanking Zmey down. The Lord of Chaos yelped and blacked out, as the hoop of Veles' power squeezed him tighter.

Morena squealed like a pig, jumping on Veles. The ancient god caught her in midair with his free hand and threw her on the frozen ground. She hit her head on a rock and passed out.

"Chernobog, if you please," said Veles calmly.

Chernobog started to chant. A moment later, a large oak coffin manifested in front of him. It was levitating in the air, seemingly unsupported. Chernobog walked to the hole in the ground that Mrak Delar created and peeked inside.

"Master, can you make this hole twice as deep as it is now?" he asked, shaking his head.

Mrak Delar struggled to his feet. Gunz came to help him. Mrak took a rugged breath and connected with the power of Earth. His arms were shaking with strain, but he managed to make the hole deeper. Chernobog carefully lowered the coffin into the hole in the ground and turned to Veles.

"Ready, brother."

Veles turned back to Zmey who seemed to be unconscious. He lifted him and lowered him in the coffin, conjuring a few cold iron chains to tie them over the coffin. As soon as Zmey's back touched the wood of the coffin, he screamed and rose high in the air, breaking the restraints of Veles' magic. His maniacal laugher was as painful as his magically enhanced shrieks.

"Now-now, you had your fun, boys. Admit it—it's over," he drawled mockingly, wiping his hands on his armor. "Come on... Some of you actually are still gods. You know you can't do it. So, why are you wasting your energy and trying my patience? Most of us are actually immortal, so we can exercise in this manner for a very long time. I can't really kill any of you and you don't have what it takes to curse me again. So, let's call it a day and part our ways."

"You're right," agreed Gwyn ap Nudd, rising, shaking dust off his leather pants. "I had enough, too. Even though I am not a god and I didn't start all this mess, I would like to be the one to finish it."

Before Zmey got a chance to respond, Gwyn ap Nudd gathered all the power he had and slammed him square in his chest. Aidan joined his attack. Zmey laughed opening his arms wide, demonstrating that Gwyn's power had no effect on him. Veles and Chernobog exchanged a quick look and added their power into Gwyn's assault. Kal, Semargl and Gunz joined them and an impenetrable wall of fire rose around Zmey. A multicolored hoop, blazing with blinding light, wrapped around Zmey, holding him in place.

Skiper-Zmey roared, growing in size as anger took hold of him, yet he couldn't break free. The more he struggled, the more power it required to hold him in place. Gunz glanced back at Mrak Delar. The Ancient Master was shaking his head tiredly and his defeated look chilled Gunz's soul.

"Zmey was right. You know the outcome. We need Perun and his brothers," said Mrak Delar.

"No, you don't, Master. There is one more way to force the Zmey into the coffin."

Gunz gasped and spun around at the sound of the voice, releasing his power for a moment. Surrounded by golden flames, Angelique looked airy and beautiful, and completely out of place in the deadly and vicious surrounding of the battle.

"No, no, Zane," yelled Angelique, reaching for him. "Don't drop your power. Keep it flowing. I need a moment to get ready."

Gunz turned away from her and joined the attack again, his heart beating desperately against his chest. He had no idea why Uri brought Angelique here or what she was planning to do, but a dreadful feeling of something terrible spread through him, making him weak and lightheaded.

He felt her hand brushing his hair as she walked past him, and her touch made his blood run cold. "Angie, what are you doing here?" he yelled, fear making his voice ring with desperate notes.

"I'm the only person who can do it, Zane," she said simply. "Now, let me focus."

She stopped next to Gwyn ap Nudd and closed her eyes. Her magical energy spiked around her and she went up in the air, levitating next to Zmey.

"Lord of Chaos, look at me," she commanded, her voice strong and tender at the same time. "Look into my eyes…"

Hypnotized, Zmey turned his head and met Angelique's eyes. His eyes widened and mouth opened, his forked tongue sliding in and out. Angelique flew closer to him and placed her right hand on Zmey's chest over the place where his heart should have been. A soft light encapsulated her hand. She put her left hand on Zmey's forehead and started to chant.

As she was chanting, Zmey started to change. His eyes lost their yellow glow, now resembling regular human eyes, but Angelique's eyes were shining yellow now. Angelique choked and almost blacked out for a moment but managed to keep her control over Zmey.

"Move the coffin here, Master," ordered Angelique.

The shimmering light of her magical energy kept circulating, surrounding her and Zmey. Now a thin layer of her magic was connecting her with the monster, and it seemed like their bodies were joined by it. Mrak Delar complied, with an effort slowly moving the coffin under the place where Zmey and Angelique were levitating.

"Master, faster!" she demanded urgently. "He is fighting me… He's too strong for me."

She channeled more of her magic, restarting her chant. The layer of magic that connected them grew stronger, pulling them closer, fusing their bodies into one entity. Zmey started to struggle, but still couldn't break free. He broke the original trance Angelique put him under, but he still couldn't demolish the restraints of the strange magic she was wielding.

Finally, the coffin was in place. Angelique glanced down and smiled, a sad and wistful smile. Carefully she lowered herself down into the coffin, pulling Zmey with her.

"No, witch... you still can't curse me..." growled Zmey, his fingers squeezing tighter around the handle of the Axe of Perun. "I have the Axe... it's mine..."

"I don't think so... strangely, it feels like it belongs to me. Hmm, weird, but I'm sure, it's actually mine."

"Tessa!" yelled Aidan, for a moment his stream of power wavering.

Tessa winked at Aidan and approached the coffin, extending her arm forward. The Axe twitched in Zmey's hand. Zmey growled holding on for dear life, but the Axe didn't obey his command. It burst out of his grasp, made an arch in the air and ended up in Tessa's hand.

Tessa raised her arm with the Axe up and bright lightning forked through the sky, connecting with the Axe. She rose up, air around her crackling with electric discharges, lightning bolts flashing in the depths of her eyes.

All eyes were on her, but she didn't care. The thunder rumbled above her, and she laughed, enjoying the feeling of her power. "This weapon definitely belongs to me," she shouted, her voice sounding thick with power. "It chose me, and I feel it like it's a part of my body."

"Daughter of Perun," whispered Chernobog in awe. "Impossible..."

"Close the coffin!" yelled Veles, his eyes still on Tessa.

Gunz jumped forward, spreading his arms over the coffin protectively. "No," he yelled, his chest tight with anxiety. "No, Angelique is still there. You can't!"

"Step away, Salamander," ordered Veles. "This is our only chance to send Skiper-Zmey back into oblivion. This witch won't be able to hold him much longer! STEP AWAY!"

"No!" shouted Gunz. "NO!"

Veles and Chernobog grabbed the lid of the coffin, ready to

close it. Gunz turned around and spread his body over the coffin. He looked at Angelique, his heart breaking into thousands of pieces. Her body was fused tighter with Zmey's, her right hand seemed to be deep in his chest. Her left hand blended with his head.

"Zane, you have to let them do it," she said firmly. "This is the only way."

"No, no, no," Gunz moaned, his trembling fingers threading through her hair. "No, Angie... please... it'll kill you... don't make me do it..."

"Kal, control your child!" yelled Veles urgently. "We have but a few seconds to seal this coffin."

"Gunz, my child, please don't make me control you." Kal stepped next to Gunz, putting his hand on his shoulder. "Step away, my boy."

"Father, I'm begging you..." moaned Gunz, tears running down his face. "I love her... please... control me and you'll be killing me."

"Gunz, move," ordered Angelique. "Now!"

"Fire Salamander, obey. Stand down," whispered Kal, mortified. "I'm sorry, my boy..."

Gunz dropped to his knees. Kal wasn't applying full control, but he was holding him down, his hand on his shoulder. Veles and Chernobog covered the coffin and Angel wrapped the cold iron chains around it.

"Angelique!" Gunz screamed, not recognizing his voice. His tears, clear human tears, transformed, now liquid fire escaping his lifeless eyes.

Tessa approached the coffin and turned to Veles. Tears were streaming down her ashen face and her hands were shaking. "What should I do?" she asked hardly audible.

"Three strikes of the Axe of Perun will seal this coffin for eternity," replied Veles.

"Eternity?" asked Tessa, her fingers unlocked, and she dropped the Axe.

The word "eternity" radiated through Gunz and he doubled down unable to breathe. He fought against Kal's control and the Great Salamander let him go. Gunz felt his freedom but he couldn't bring himself to move. He was kneeling by the coffin, his hand brushing over the wood. "Angie…" he whispered, fire sliding down his eyes, dropping on the dead ground.

Aidan came to Tessa's side. He picked the Axe off the floor and put it in her hand. "Tessa, I guess it's your birthright," he said. "Do what you must."

Tessa raised the Axe of Perun up, gathering the electricity in its blade and plummeted it down. Mighty thunder rushed through the land and a blast wave of wind spread around, bending the trees to the ground. Gunz moaned as if the Axe just struck him in his chest.

Tessa swung the Axe again and lowered it down. The coffin lit up with a bright red light and the chains melted into it. The coffin thrashed, coming in and out of focus for a moment. Someone screamed inside it, a terrible howl of anguish. Gunz wrapped his arms around his head, rocking back and forth.

Tessa raised the Axe one last time and hit the coffin. A bright light enveloped the coffin and when the light subsided, the coffin was gone. The hole in the ground that Mrak Delar created was filled with dirt now and the stone monolith was fixed and placed back into its original place.

Gunz walked toward the monolith and wrapped his arms around the cold stone. He wasn't crying. He wasn't saying anything. He couldn't. He slid down to his knees, resting his forehead against the stone and fire rose around him.

"Gunz," called Kal. But Gunz raised his hand up, shaking his head. He just wanted to be left alone. He didn't want to talk or to hear words of support.

He saw Veles talking to Aidan and Tessa, explaining something about the Axe. Chernobog approached him and bowed. He raised his flaming eyes staring at the Slavic deity without understanding.

"You lost someone who was dear to you, young Salamander," said Chernobog. "You loved her, and she sure was worthy of your love. Keep her in your heart, child, treasure your memories, but don't give up on your life. You owe her that much. Today, Angelique saved the world, but most of all she gave her life to save the man she loved."

Chernobog sighed and headed to his wife, the goddess of Winter and Death. She was still sprawled unconscious on the ground. The icy sword was lying down next to her. He picked it up and gave it back to Aidan. Then he lifted Morena, carelessly throwing her over his shoulder and approached Veles.

"Brother, would you allow me to deal with my wife and her betrayal on my own?" he asked.

"Yes, but don't be easy on her," said Veles with a sigh. "Your man, Voron, is waiting for you in the Dark Nav. Once you fix the veil, you need to come back and hunt down all the phantoms that your wife released into the Yav."

Chernobog bowed to Veles and vanished together with Morena.

Kal approached Gunz and squatted in front of him. "My boy, you can't stay here forever. There is nothing here for you." He touched the fire, commanding it to cease.

Gunz got up, slightly swaying and looked around. His eyes moved from Aidan to Mrak Delar and then stopped on Angel. Angel met his pained gaze and shook his head.

"I'm sorry, my friend, but Angelique is not dead. She fused her essence with Zmey's and that allowed her to control him long enough, so we could put him back in his cursed grave," he said putting his hand of Gunz's shoulder. "I swear, if it was in my power, I would bring her back for you, but it's not."

Gunz nodded, biting his lip and headed to the circle of fire that was still burning around the two dark mages. As soon as he approached them, the flames went up higher, burning brighter, fueled by his anguish and anger.

He walked through the fire into the circle and halted. Both mages cowered away from him, their fear almost palpable. Gunz stared at Valeria Demidova and his whole body went up in flames. In complete silence, he raised his hand and his sword manifested in it. He was ready to strike her down when he saw Countess Demidova standing outside the circle. No one noticed when the old lady came to the place of battle.

"Allow me," she said quietly to Gunz, her dark eyes glowing with pain and anger.

Gunz nodded and lowered his sword, extinguishing his fire. The Countess approached her daughter, staring down at her.

"Mama..." whimpered Valeria, reaching for her mother, but the Countess stepped away from her, disgust reflected on her face.

"I curse the day you were born," said the old lady coldly, looking down at her daughter. "I brought you into this world and I plagued it with your presence. It's only right that I should be the one to free the world from your darkness."

She channeled her magic and seized her daughter, sending her flying into the lake. Valeria screamed as the double bottom of the lake gave in and sucked her down. A few seconds later, Valeria Demidova was no more. The Countess stared at the lake, a look of relief on her face. Then she turned around and headed to Gwyn ap Nudd.

"Now, I'm ready to go with you, my lord," she said with a bow.

Gwyn ap Nudd drew a rectangle of light in the air, turning it into a door and walked through it, taking Countess Demidova with him.

Gunz turned to the second mage, his igneous eyes burning with wrath. She froze, terror flashed in her eyes. Before anyone could stop him, he swung his sword, instantly decapitating her. "*Ignius,*" he whispered, setting her remains on fire and then added in a low growl, "Thou shalt not suffer an evil bitch to live."

He approached the stone monolith and caressed its rough surface with his fingers. His eyes fell on Karma, who looked just as lifeless as he felt. He turned to Mrak Delar.

"Mrak, can you do me a favor?" he asked evenly. Mrak Delar nodded. "Please take Karma anywhere in this world, or any other world... Take her anywhere she wants to go, my friend."

"I'll do that," promised Mrak Delar.

Gunz turned to Kal, feeling dead inside and out.

"You were right, Father," he said, hardly moving his lips. "There is nothing left for me here."

He opened the fire-curtain of his portal and walked through it.

39

~ ZANE BURNS, A.K.A. GUNZ ~

Gunz walked out of his portal and crossed his back yard toward the door of his house. He pushed it, in the back of his mind realizing that the door was unlocked, but at the moment he wasn't capable of wondering why. He stepped inside the house and looked around. It was empty. Completely empty. He got used to the solitude of his place and he used to love it, but right now this habitual silence felt deadly.

Gunz headed to the living room. Not really thinking about what he was doing, he took a bottle of vodka and came back to the kitchen. He sat down at the table, his fingers mechanically twisting the cap off the bottle. He put the cap on the table, staring at the clear liquid inside. The sharp smell of the alcohol invaded his nostrils, and he took a huge gulp of the fire-filled liquid straight from the bottle. As the heat spread through his body, he folded his arms on the table and rested his forehead atop his folded arms.

The last moment of the fight with Skiper-Zmey flashed in his mind—Angelique's eyes, gazing at him with love, ordering him to let her die. And he did. He stepped away. He abandoned her. He let them kill her. No, it wasn't them—he killed her.

Gunz lifted his head and screamed, a terrible howl infused with more anguish than any one man could tolerate. His eyes flooded with flames and drops of liquid fire fell on the table.

With shock, he touched his flaming tears and just then noticed a small white box sitting in the middle of the table. He pulled the box closer and everything inside him died, drowning in the next wave of pain as he recognized Angelique's handwriting on the box.

"To Gunz."

He stared at the box, his hands shaking. *To Gunz?* Angelique never used his nickname. It was always Zane or his true name—Vladislav. She always told him that his nickname was given to him by his closest friends, those few men who went through war, fighting by his side. She didn't think that it was right for her to use this name. *Gunz?* He tried to open the box, but his fingers didn't obey—numb, unbending. He put the box down and took another swig of vodka before giving it another try.

Finally, he was able to open it. Inside, there was another box with a new wristwatch in it. It wasn't a standard FBI watch. It was a Russian watch, a military edition—*"Vostok Komandirskie"*. He took the watch out of the box and checked it out closely. An outline of a wyvern was clearly visible on the dark-blue face of the watch. Mishka was there. Why? He noticed that the watch had an extra button on the side—undoubtedly a panic button, installed by Jim. And if Jim installed the panic button, of course, he installed a GPS tracker.

"Mishka," called Gunz, surprised to hear how lifeless and hollow his voice was.

The wyvern materialized in front of him. "Finally, boss, you freed—," he started to say but fell silent as Gunz slammed his fist on the table. The bottle swayed, and the cap rolled over the table, dropping on the floor with a hollow jingle.

"I asked you to take care of her!" he yelled. "Why didn't you?

You had one job..." his voice trailed off. He shook his head and covered his face with his hands.

"I'm sorry, boss," said the wyvern, touching him with his wing, "she locked me in this watch as soon as I got there. I don't know what kind of spell she used, but I couldn't break free until you called me."

Gunz lowered his hands and glanced at his wyvern. His golden-red glow disappeared, and he looked grief-stricken.

"Mishka, I'm sorry, I don't blame you," he managed to say. "Don't take it personally, but I need you to leave. Just for a short while, my friend. I need to be alone..."

"As you wish, boss," mumbled Mishka and silently vanished.

Slowly, Gunz flipped the watch over. There was an engraving on the back. *"Take care of my perfect world."*

"Nooo..." he moaned, grief shredding his insides.

Gunz dropped the watch on the table and reached for the bottle, knocking the box off the table. He didn't put the bottle down until it was empty. Then he got up and went to get another bottle. As he returned to the kitchen, he saw the box on the floor. He squatted to pick it up and noticed that under the watch packaging there was something else. He pulled the box out and stared at a yellow notepad page, folded neatly at the bottom of the white box.

His body felt leaden as he lowered himself down on the floor and pulled the page out of the box, unfolding it. It was covered in Angelique's even handwriting. The world spun around him and he couldn't read a word, liquid fire dripping down on the page in his trembling hands. But the page wasn't bursting in flames. She accounted for everything, making the paper fireproof.

Gunz opened the new bottle of vodka and took a huge gulp. He wiped his face with his hands and picked up the page again. His vision cleared, more or less, and he could read now.

Gunz,

My strong, handsome boy. I love you. I loved you from the first moment I saw you, when you walked into Jim's office accompanied by Mrak Delar. He practically dragged you in. You were so withdrawn and miserable. You hardly said one word to me. But I could see your beautiful soul hiding behind the wall you built around yourself. And from that moment, I knew that you were the only one for me.

I am sorry it took me so long to tell you that, but there was always something between us—our lifestyles, magic, people and monsters, or your constant runs between two worlds. I'm glad I told you at the end and we had our time together, as short as it was. You're my love, my life, my perfect world.

I am sorry, I lied to you. I knew that the reason I couldn't see the future was because I didn't have one. I don't even know why I mentioned it at all to you that night. I guess I was scared, and I wanted to hear you telling me that everything was going to be okay.

Once I learned who your adversary was, I knew that without Perun, none of you had what it took to win this fight. Only a witch with psychic abilities like myself could control the Lord of Chaos by fusing her own essence with his and taking over his body. I just hope that I'm a powerful enough psychic-witch to pull it off and give you all a chance to lock Skiper-Zmey back into his grave and place the curse...

My love, I beg you not to hate Uri for bringing me to Mount Karasova. Knowing you, you probably can't even look at him right now. It wasn't his fault. I never told him why I needed to be there. I manipulated him a little, making sure that he would bring me and Tessa to the place of the final battle. And he was too preoccupied with everything that was going on in the city to look past my words.

Tessa is a daughter of Perun. After our first reading, it took me a long time and a lot of research to get to this conclusion. And today, when she showed up with Uri at my doorstep, begging him to take her to Aidan, my theory got confirmed. Please tell her that she needs to find her father. It's important for her and for this world. But before she can take on such a difficult task, she must learn more, practice her magic and power. In other words, she must remain with the

Guardians for as long as possible. And tell her that she can't do it alone. To find Perun and bring him back, she'll need you and Aidan at her side.

I know what you think, Gunz. You think I'm alive... somewhere. Don't. I'm dead. There is no me anymore. Do not spend your eternity looking for a way to bring me back. It's impossible. Let me repeat it again so it sticks in your stubborn head.

I AM DEAD.
Don't beg Angel to bring me back either. He can't.
I AM GONE.
Forever. And I want you to move on. I want you to be happy. So, please, don't look for me or for a way to separate my essence from Zmey's. You can't. No one can. I know that you love me, and you would move mountains for me. But Mount Karasova is one mountain you should never attempt to move.

I love you, Gunz, my strong, beautiful boy. I always have, and I always will. Even death can't change that. You gave me something, no one else could—that perfect world within the circle of your arms.

With love,
Angelique.

Gunz put the page on the floor next to him. He stared into space, unable to hear, see or feel anything but the pain that was ripping him from the inside. He picked the bottle up and kept drinking until the world around him started to spin and he felt too drunk and too numb to move.

Through the fog in his mind, he registered a fire portal opening in his kitchen. Kal and Mrak Delar walked through the portal and halted before him. Kal squatted down in front of him and put his hand on his shoulder, giving him a light shake.

"Gunz," called Kal, frowning.

"Father," mumbled Gunz and laughed drunkenly. "You controlled me... You swore not to..." He laughed again and took another gulp of vodka. "The only time when it truly mattered that you didn't... You made me kill her..."

Kal got up and threw a bewildered look at Mrak Delar. "He's drunk," explained Mrak Delar with a sigh.

"I can clear his mind," said Kal making a move toward Gunz, but Mrak Delar seized his elbow stopping him.

"Don't," he said shaking his head. "He's grieving. It's his way of dealing with his pain, Kal. Let him be."

Gunz listened to their conversation, for some reason finding it ridiculously funny. He laughed again, but the tears of liquid fire filled his eyes, running down his face.

"Look at his tears, Mrak. He's losing his humanity," whispered Kal, but Gunz registered his every word. "If we don't help him, he'll become more fire than man."

"Mrak," said Gunz raising his hand up, but had no strength to hold it and his hand fell on the floor with a dull thud. "Mrak, nothing helps… can you take away this… gut-wrenching feeling…" He laughed bitterly. "Yeah… you called it pain… but it's so much worse… Can you make me… forget. Just for a few minutes. I'm begging you."

"Oh, boy," said Mrak Delar. He bent down and lifted Gunz off the floor. Gunz didn't object, feeling too weak and numb for any kind of protests. He couldn't even hold his head up. Holding him in his arms, Mrak Delar took him upstairs and lowered him down on his bed.

"What are you going to do, Mrak?" asked Kal.

"There isn't much I can do," replied Mrak Delar with a sigh and turned to Gunz. "I can't make you forget. And trust me, you want to remember. But I can give you a few hours of peace. When you wake up, you'll remember everything, and grief still will be tearing your soul apart. There are no shortcuts around it, not even magical ones."

"I don't care… Make it stop, even if it's only for a few hours." Gunz moaned, covering his face with his hands.

Mrak Delar glanced at Kal and the Great Salamander nodded. The Master of Power touched Gunz's forehead with two fingers, whispering a spell, putting him in a deep enchanted sleep.

"Thank you..." whispered Gunz and closed his eyes, falling into peaceful oblivion.

* * *

It was the middle of the day when Gunz woke up and sunlight was flooding his room. Just like Mrak Delar said, he remembered everything. He sat up on the bed, lowering his feet to the floor and rubbed his face, feeling the roughness of the stubble on his cheeks.

"Good afternoon."

Gunz turned around and just now noticed Aidan sitting in the armchair by the closet. He was still dressed in the same torn shirt and dirty pants he had on last night. His face was covered in dust and he looked drained.

"How long have you been sitting here?" asked Gunz.

"Since last night, when Mrak Delar showed up at my penthouse and dropped me off here," replied Aidan with a shrug, crossing his legs at his knees. "Coffee?"

"Yeah, fine," said Gunz, ready to go down to the kitchen. Aidan waved his hand, conjuring two cups of Starbucks coffee, and offered one to Gunz. "Must be nice to be a god." Gunz chuckled humorlessly, taking a sip of the hot coffee.

"Not always," replied Aidan, serious. "Care to know what happened after you left yesterday."

"Not really," replied Gunz, and he meant it. "But I know, you're going to tell me anyway. So, go on."

"After you left, Semargl summoned Stribog and his sons," said Aidan quietly, carefully tasting his coffee. "You probably know of him. He's another elemental Slavic deity. The god of Air and Wind. Anyway, he came with his sons and they recreated Mount Karasova. Just like the first time, Stribog's sons brought the sands from the four ends of the Yav and they created the mountain over the grave of the Skiper-Zmey. And then Veles placed his enchantment, cursing the Lord of Chaos for eternity. It's all over now."

"I figured," whispered Gunz, squeezing the hot cup in his hand. They put a mountain over Angelique... and placed a curse. He bit his lip, feeling empty inside.

"I'm sorry, Gunz," said Aidan quietly.

Gunz nodded. "You don't need to be on a suicide watch, Aidan," he said dryly, turning away from his friend. "I don't even know how to conjure the Black Fire. Even if I wanted."

"I am not worried about that," replied Aidan, pulling his phone out. "I am here for a few reasons. First of all, do you mind if I make sure that my friend is okay, and he is not alone when he is in pain?"

Gunz nodded. "Thank you, but I'm fine. As fine as I can be in this situation, I guess."

Aidan's phone rang. He looked at the screen and smiled. "And here is the second reason I am here." He answered the phone, putting it on speaker.

"Aidan, hello." Gunz heard the familiar voice of his friend Sasha and lifted his head.

"Hi, Sasha, you're on speakerphone and Gunz is here, with me," replied Aidan, offering the phone to Gunz.

"Sasha, hi," said Gunz, staring into the screen of the phone unblinking. As nice as it was to hear his friend's voice, he wasn't sure that it was safe for Sasha to be in touch with him.

"Gunz, I know what happened," said Sasha, his voice laced with worry. "Do you want me to come over? Tell me and I'll hop on the first plane to Miami."

Gunz felt the blood draining off his face. "No," he said, a little too sharp. He took a deep breath and repeated, "Thank you, but no, Sasha. You stay where you are. As far away from me as possible."

"Why? Gunz, what's going on? You don't sound like yourself."

"Because people get hurt around me," he replied quietly. "And those who dare to love me end up dead... Thank you, Sasha, but please stay where you are." He gave the phone back to Aidan.

"I'm still in one piece and alive," noted Aidan, taking the phone from Gunz's hand.

"You're a god," replied Gunz dryly.

"Gunz, that's bullshit, man. I don't believe in all this magic and curses nonsense. If you need me, tell me and I'll be with you no matter what," said Sasha. "Aidan, please call me if he changes his mind."

"I will," promised Aidan and hung up the phone. He folded his arms over his chest and turned to Gunz. "I need to see your tears. That's the other reason I'm here."

"You want to make me cry? You don't think I had enough of it in the last few days," snapped Gunz.

"I didn't say that I want you to cry," replied Aidan calmly. "Mrak Delar said that I need to see your tears before I leave."

"Oh, that," mumbled Gunz. He took his Swiss Army knife and made a small shallow incision on his arm. A few drops of blood appeared on his skin. He showed it to Aidan. "Bleeding red. I guess, I'm still human."

"Mrak didn't say to make you bleed. He said to make you cry," objected Aidan stubbornly.

"Sorry, I'm not an actor. I can't cry on demand," replied Gunz, aggravation rising within him. "Please, Aidan. I appreciate your concern, and Mrak's too. But what I need is time. I'll be fine and back at work. I just need a few days to deal... you know?"

"Yup, and I promise, I'll be out of your hair," replied Aidan, rising. "But not before I see your tears."

He held out his fist and covered it with his other hand. Rays of purple light broke through his fingers. Aidan approached Gunz and unlocked his fingers. A small stone shining with purple light was lying in the palm of his hand. "Inhale," he ordered, moving the stone closer to Gunz's face.

Gunz took a quick breath and staggered back, pressing his hand over his nose, tears running down his face. "What the hell, Aidan!" he shouted. "This stuff is worse than ammonia salts."

Aidan ignored him. "Your tears, Gunz," he said with a soft smile. "They're clear human tears. Now I know that you'll be okay. Call me when you're ready." He snapped his fingers and vanished.

Gunz approached the dresser and looked in the mirror. His face was covered in dirt and blood, but clear human tears were running down his cheeks, leaving wet traces behind. The folded yellow page and the watch were lying on the dresser. He caressed the paper with his fingers, sadness tearing him apart.

"I'll be fine," he said, locking the watch on his wrist, but then shook his head. "I'm never going to be fine, but I'll have to learn how to live without you. I just need time."

He stared into the mirror at his reflection for a moment. Then he screamed, pulling his arm back and plummeted his fist into the mirror. The mirror broke into hundreds of shiny splinters, dropping on the dresser and to the floor. Gunz stared down at his bleeding knuckles and then lifted his eyes. A long piece of mirror was still remaining in the frame. A lifeless, exhausted face was staring back at him.

"Screw it!" growled Gunz, slamming his hand into the pile of glass on the dresser. The pieces of mirror cracked under his hand, spilling on the floor. "Goddammit! Screw it all! I'm going to find out what kind of crazy spell you preformed, Angie. And I am not going to stop until I unbind you from Zmey and bring you back!"

EPILOGUE

***

One month later
~ Aidan ~
Modern day, Chicago

AIDAN WAS PACING NERVOUSLY in front of the door in the Assembly Hall. The Guardians summoned him just a few hours ago, and he had no idea what to expect. The former Head Mage of the Guardians Order was dead. She was also branded as a traitor, quite a few of her evil deeds uncovered since the Destiny Council launched their investigation. She was the one who mutilated the two Books of Words, trying to conceal Valeria Demidova's connection with the Guardians Order and with her personally. Aidan assumed that since Ms. Bonneville was a traitor, his oath to her was now null and void.

It was the new Head Mage who summoned him. He didn't know who the new Head Mage was and why he or she needed to talk to him. At least the summoning call was gentle and the tugging at his mind stopped as soon as he crossed the border of the Guardians Headquarters.

"Aidan!" He heard Tessa's voice and turned around.

Tessa was walking toward him accompanied by Jamie, the guard. Aidan frowned. He didn't like that Tessa was escorted by a guard. She halted in front of him and for a moment just stood there, searching his face with her deep eyes. Then she rose on her tiptoes and wrapped her arms around his neck, placing her head on his chest.

He hugged her, closing his eyes, but then pulled away. "Tessa," he said softly, "are you in any trouble again? Why are you with a guard and why was I summoned?"

Tessa shrugged. "Well, since that night when I broke into the library, took a locked book without permission, summoned an Archangel and left the property without notifying anyone, I didn't do anything else wrong."

"That's all?" Aidan threw his hands in the air. "I have a feeling that after all that, they're going to put me in chains and enslave me for the rest of my life. One year of servitude certainly is not going to be enough to cover all your offenses."

"Oh, don't be such worry-worm, Aidan," said Tessa, rolling her eyes. "They're not going to enslave you. Although I must admit that the thought of you as a slave doesn't bother me as much as it should. I actually like that idea. As long as I'm your only master."

"Ha-ha, dream on," muttered Aidan, feeling a flush creeping up his cheeks.

"A girl can dream, especially since dreams are free." She laughed, patting his cheek. "It's so cute that at your age you can still blush." She hugged him, giving him a light kiss on his cheek and changed the subject. "On another note. How is Zane?"

"He's fine," replied Aidan, cringing inside. As much as Gunz was putting up a front, he knew that he was anything but fine. "He's fine, but he's not the same man you remember."

"What do you mean?"

Aidan shrugged. "It's hard to explain. When you see him in person, you'll know what I mean. It's like he is hollow inside. He was always a little distant and guarded, but I attributed it to his Salamander's nature. He could never relax, always keeping his power in check. But now, imagine that but tenfold worse."

"How is that?"

"He still didn't go back to work. Agent Andrews came to me, asking for my help to bring him back. He had not gone back to the dojang either."

"So, what is he doing? Do you know?"

"He spends his time between the Wardens Library, Riders Library in Kendral and any other library of magical books and scrolls he can put his hands on. Actually, Father Beaumont sees him a lot more than I do."

"I think I know what he is doing," whispered Tessa.

"Not hard to guess," replied Aidan, shaking his head. "But Angel told me that there are no known ways to bring Angelique back. She fused her essence with Zmey's and that can't be undone."

"Did Angel try talking to him?"

"Yes, of course he did," said Aidan. "Many times. He listened to Angel, smiling politely, and as soon as Angel was out of his house, he went back to what he was doing. And the way he fights, Tessa... he scares me. It's like he has no soul."

"What do you mean? Zane was always an excellent martial artist. What changed?"

"He still is. Now better and scarier than he was before," said Aidan with a sigh. "A few days ago, I saw him fighting a group of demons on the street. He didn't even use his fire power, just basic hand-to-hand combat. He annihilated every single one of them, Tessa. I don't think he even checked if human souls were still inside their bodies. He was precise, fast and cold. Don't get me wrong, that's the only way to deal with demons. But sometimes it feels like he has a death wish. He doesn't care if he gets hurt. He's like a perfect killing machine. Reckless, soulless and dangerous. And when he's not researching or killing, he's drinking. I've never seen anyone drink so much and not get a hangover." Aidan pursed his lips, shaking his head. "Anyway, the truth is, he never recovered. Everyone grieves in their own way. Possibly, he just needs more time."

"As soon as I get a chance, I'll go back to Florida and talk to him," offered Tessa. "Maybe I'll be able to get through to him."

Aidan chuckled bitterly. "Good luck with that."

"Are you saying that he's not going to let me in?"

"No, that's not what I'm saying," objected Aidan. "He'll welcome you into his house and he'll show you the best Russian hospitality you can dream of. But if you try to get into any kind of serious conversation, you'll hit a wall. He is not going to talk, Tessa. Not to you, not to anyone else. And as far as I'm concerned, everyone needs to back off and give him some space and time to grieve. In his own way."

Tessa nodded. "Aidan, what he said about Perun. Is it true?"

"Perun is your father, Tessa. There are no doubts about it. If he wasn't, you wouldn't have been able to use the full power of the Axe to lock the coffin," said Aidan. "Gunz told me what Angelique said and I tend to believe her words. When you're ready, we should start searching for your father."

"If my father is a god, does it make me a..." Her voice died off as she stared down at her clenched hands.

"A goddess, most likely. Since your mother was a Reaper, not a human, you're probably not a demigod. But I'm not sure," replied Aidan. "In any case, you need to stay with the Guardians and learn as much as you can. Just like Angelique said."

Before Tessa got a chance to answer, the door to the Assembly Hall opened and Jamie walked up to them.

"Tessa, Mr. McGrath," he said, "the Guardians Council is ready for you both."

Aidan headed toward the Assembly Hall with Tessa by his side, ready to fight if he had to. As soon as he walked in, he noticed that it wasn't the full Guardians Council assembly. There were only three people inside—two women and a man. The man got up and walked around the table to greet them.

He stopped a few feet away from Aidan and bent forward in a light bow. "Aodh mac Lir, it's an honor to finally meet you. My name is Quinn Allerton and I'm the Guardians Order Archmage. I'll be taking over the position Ms. Bonneville used to hold."

"My lord," said Aidan carefully, bowing slightly to show his respect.

"Before we get into a conversation, please allow me to discuss a small matter with Therasia," he said, turning to Tessa. "Ms. Donovan, I've heard mixed things about you, young lady. And I believe that we owe Mr. McGrath's presence in the Order to your previous misdoings."

"Yes, my lord," replied Tessa, throwing a wide-eye stare at Aidan.

"In the last month, you managed to add to your already impressive list of broken rules," continued the Archmage. "Breaking and entering into the Guardians library, wrecking a few locks in the forbidden section of the library, summoning a high-level divine being, and leaving your duty at the Guardians HQ without notifying your superiors. All these are serious offenses, young lady."

"I'm truly sorry, my lord," mumbled Tessa, "but I swear I had a good reason!"

"That you did," agreed the Archmage, smiling. "You did all that and we owe you our gratitude for saving our world. To all of you who valiantly fought the Lord of Chaos at Mount Karasova." He bowed to Aidan again. "Having said that, it still doesn't excuse your breaking of the Guardians Order rules."

"Please don't expel me," pleaded Tessa, pressing her hands to her chest. "I need to learn. I must know how to use my magic and power, now more than ever."

"I had no plans to expel you, Ms. Donovan. The Guardians Order needs talented members like yourself," said the Archmage, "but the term of your probation will be extended by another year."

"Thank you, my lord," said Tessa, happiness twinkling in her dark eyes. "I won't disappoint you."

"I'm glad to hear it, Therasia," replied Archmage, patting her on her shoulder. "You may leave now. I need to have a few words with Mr. McGrath. You can wait for him outside. It shouldn't take long."

As soon as Tessa left, the Archmage turned to Aidan. "Mr. McGrath, I was told about the way Ms. Bonneville treated you and I want to extend my apologies."

"Apologies accepted," said Aidan. "Ms. Bonneville was a traitor and everything she did was done to benefit the Lord of Chaos. Now that we know that, I assume I'm no longer held by the oath I was forced to give her."

The Archmage cleared his throat uncomfortably, shifting from foot to foot. "I'm sorry, but no," he said, calmly looking at Aidan. "You pledged your fealty not to Ms. Bonneville personally, but to the Guardians Order for the duration of Ms. Donovan's probation. And as such, your oath still stands."

He came closer and touched the pendant on Aidan's chest, sending a small amount of magic through it.

"Does it mean that because Tessa's probation was extended by a full year, so was my service to the Guardians?" asked Aidan, working hard not to show his aggravation.

"Yes," replied the Archmage. "For now, you're free to go back to your life, Mr. McGrath. But as a sworn member of the

Guardians Order, you must return any time we summon you. Do you have any questions?"

For a moment, Aidan was just staring down at the Archmage, fighting with the internal need to wipe him out of existence. Then he turned around and silently walked out of the Assembly Hall.

* * *

~ Zane Burns, a.k.a. Gunz ~
South Florida

COLD WATER WASHED OVER HIM, abruptly ripping him out of his sleep, turning every cell in his body into a separate tiny chamber of torture. Gunz rolled over to the other side of the bed, his back pressed against the closet door, ready to pounce on whoever assailed him.

"Dammit, Akira," he growled, his lip curving into a feral snarl as he saw the Scarlet Queen standing by the side of his bed with a bucket in her hands. "What the hell are you—"

He didn't get to finish his statement as Akira picked up the second bucket and drenched him with another shot of freezing water. Gunz cried out, covering his head with his arms and slid down to the floor. His clothes got soaked instantly, clinging to his body, and that added to his misery.

"Akira, why?" he panted, struggling to get up. "What did I do to deserve this?"

Akira walked up to him, seized his wet shirt, and easily yanked him up. She observed his wet disposition and wrinkled her nose.

"It's not what you did, Zane. It's what you're not doing," she said, shaking the water off her hand, like a cat who stepped in a puddle. "Undress and take a shower. Now! God knows, you need it."

Gunz sighed but didn't argue. Silently he headed into the bathroom. Once the door was locked, he quickly shed all the wet clothes on the floor and turned the hot water to the maximum. He stepped into the shower stall and let the firm jets of heat run down his body, caressing his skin. For a few minutes, he just stood, enjoying the hot shower.

He wanted to stay like this forever, not moving, not doing anything, but most importantly—not thinking. Thinking brought back the memories. And he didn't want to remember. Memories were painful. They were gnawing at him from the inside, day and night. He couldn't eat, he couldn't work, he couldn't do anything.

But the worst of all were the nights. Those endless, dark, lonely nights, when he would lie in his bed, unable to sleep. As soon as he would shut his eyes, he saw Angelique. Over and over, he relived that night at Mount Karasova, blaming himself for what happened to her. She loved him and trusted him, and he failed to protect her. And the thought of it was tormenting him worse than any physical torture.

Every evening, when he was coming back from the Wardens Library, walking through the dark city streets, he was hoping to meet a few demons or any other monsters, so he could fight. Physical confrontations were awakening some primal instincts in him and with adrenalin rushing through his system, he was able to give some release to the anger and pain that were boiling inside him. Fighting was making him forget everything else. So, he was walking the dark streets, deliberately searching for trouble.

Drinking was helping to numb the pain to a degree too. He would drown his sorrows in alcohol until he could think no more. Only then could he fall asleep, sometimes right there, on the kitchen floor.

Gunz sighed, remembering that the queen of vampires was still in his bedroom, waiting for him. As much as he wanted to tell her to beat it, he knew that it wasn't a good idea to get Akira angry. He quickly finished his shower and toweled his body dry. He wrapped the towel around his hips and walked into the bedroom.

Akira took in his appearance, her angled eyes stopping on the towel and smirked. "As much as I enjoy the view," she purred, "I need you to slip into something less comfortable."

"Why? Are we going somewhere?"

"Yes, I'll tell you on the way," replied Akira, heading out the door. "I'll wait for you downstairs."

Gunz changed into jeans and a t-shirt and went downstairs. Akira walked him to his car and started to drive.

"Akira," said Gunz after a few minutes of silence, "care to explain where you are taking me? I'm not in the mood to play games."

"You're not in the mood for anything. All you do is drink!" barked Akira, her eyes sparkling with anger. "You forgot who you are, Mr. Burns. You forgot that as the Great Fire Salamander you have obligations to this world—"

"I *had* obligations!" shouted Gunz, his body locked with rage. "I failed! I failed everyone who loved me and trusted me!"

Akira sighed. It seemed that his furious outburst wiped out her own anger. "Maybe you did, maybe you didn't. It's a matter of opinion and as much as I disagree with your statement, I am not going to argue with you," she said quietly, staring at the road. "Nevertheless, I trust you and I desperately need your help. And you have your chance not to fail me. So, what is it going to be, Zane?"

"You need my help," repeated Gunz, leaning back in his seat. "What could possibly happen that would make the almighty Scarlet Queen seek the help of a drunk Fire Salamander."

"Zane!" yelled Akira, throwing her hands in the air. The car swung to the right and someone honked at them. "Zane, my son is missing! I need your help to find him."

Gunz stared at Akira, shocked. "Yaroslav is missing? Since when?"

"Two weeks," replied Akira quietly.

"He's a big boy, Akira," said Gunz, shaking his head. "He probably met a nice vampire girl and wants some time away from his mommy. Plus, you have nothing to worry about. Yaroslav can hold his own."

"No, Zane, you don't understand," said Akira, and true worry made her grip at the wheel harder. "Yaroslav is my son and we are psychically connected. I can feel his distress, but I can't sense his location, which never happened before. Something is wrong."

Gunz thought for a moment. Nothing of it sounded right. "Why do you need my help, Akira?" he asked finally. "You're a queen and you have a private security company, full of highly trained vampires and upirs. So, why would you need me?"

Akira sighed. "Because I can't trust anyone in any of my companies," she said quietly. "I have a bad feeling that somehow someone from my company was involved in my son's disappearance. You're the only person I can trust."

"Well, you shouldn't..."

"Zane!"

"Fine, Akira, I'll look into it. So, where are you taking me?"

"Before I give you all the details I have, I need to make sure you're still in the right shape and didn't completely destroy yourself with the disturbing lifestyle you developed in the last month," said Akira.

"I'm fine. I promise," replied Gunz dryly, wondering if he could just jump out of this car and be done with this conversation. But Akira was always nice and respectful to him and now that she needed his help, he couldn't leave her high and dry. Besides, he kind of liked Yaroslav, and he didn't want to see him hurt either.

"Let me be the judge of it," cut Akira sharply. "You're the

only person who can help me get my boy back, so forgive me if I don't want to blindly take the word of a drunk Fire Salamander, as you put it."

She parked the car in front of the Elements Martial Arts school and waved at Gunz to follow her. Gunz looked at Aidan's school and his jaw tightened. He wasn't in the mood to see anyone.

"Are you coming?" asked Akira, staring back at him. "I don't enjoy the sunlight. So, I would appreciate it if you didn't keep me waiting."

Gunz caught up with her and together they walked into the building. The school was empty inside. He lifted his eyebrows, waiting for an explanation. She gave him a quick once-over and pointed at the back door.

"Go change, and I'll see you on the floor," said Akira, opening the glass door that led into the dojang.

Gunz changed into his Taekwondo uniform and bowed before stepping on the floor. Besides Akira, he found Aidan and Kal standing by the wall.

"What's going on here?" asked Gunz, frowning.

"I said, I wanted to test your fighting skills, didn't I?" replied Akira dryly. "So, I brought the only person I know who is better than me."

She waved her hand. The door into the dojang opened and Mrak Delar walked on the floor holding his black sword in his hand. He was dressed only in black pants that looked like a hakama, the traditional piece of Samurai clothing. He flexed his massive arms and shoulders and his eyes lit up with the red glow of elemental Fire energy.

"Are you out of your friggin' mind, Akira?" yelled Gunz, looking around at the people in the dojang. Both Aidan and Kal stared at him with an identical wide grin on their faces. "You want me to fight this mountain of muscles who is twice my size?"

"Well, I've been called worse," said Mrak Delar, a good-natured smile on his face.

"He's a Master of Power!" hissed Gunz, staring at Akira, small flames running up and down his arms fueled by his anger. "Look at his eyes! He is wielding the elemental Fire now. He can control me! How am I supposed to fight him?"

Akira shrugged her shoulders indifferently. "Did I not teach you anything in the last few months? I guess you'll have to get creative. Your sword, Fire Salamander."

"Ahh!" Gunz pulled his Swiss Army knife out, turning it into the sword and turned to face Mrak Delar.

Mrak Delar assumed a guarding stance, bringing his giant black sword above his shoulder.

"Ready?" he asked, sparks of laughter and fire dancing in his eyes.

"Do I have a choice?" grumbled Gunz but nodded.

"Not really." Mrak Delar flashed a bright smile at him and then commanded, "Fire Salamander—go!"

BOOK THREE: EXCERPT

*Read on for an excerpt from
N.M. Thorn's new book:*

The Fire Salamander Chronicles. Book 3

* * *

*~ Zane Burns, a.k.a. Gunz ~
Modern day. Somewhere in Florida... Probably...*

The roars of a demon were supposed to scare him but were mostly annoying him. Gunz watched as the demon carelessly launched his whole bulky body into a frontal attack and rolled his eyes. The monster was over six feet tall and his massive body was wrapped with a thick layer of muscles.

The demon was obviously thinking highly of himself, sure in easy victory, but Gunz knew better. No matter how much muscle-power this monster packed, how impenetrable he thought the shield of his iron muscles was, there were always a few weak, vulnerable points on his massive body. And compared to Gunz, the demon was extremely slow.

He watched the demon's fist sailing by his face and took a quick step to the side, meeting his opponent with a powerful strike into his neck. The monster choked, losing his balance. He fell down clutching his neck, his eyes bulging. In a split-second, Gunz reached him and pulled him into a sitting position. He wrapped his arm around his neck and clasped his hands, his forearm set firmly into the demon's back. He pushed with his forearm and yanked his hands, applying a brutal choke.

The demon thrashed in his arms, struggling against his hold. Gunz squeezed harder, putting the monster to sleep. Then he got up, dropping the unconscious body on the floor and turned around, staring through the net of the cage at the raging crowd. He found the eyes of Mr. Kogan, the man who owned all supernatural fighting pits in Florida and watched him flipping his fist thumb down.

A cold smirk split Gunz's face as he kneeled next to the demon and drove his fist through the monster's face all the way to the floor. The blood and brain matter splattered all around the place where the demon's head used to be. Gunz rose, staring down at his dead opponent with disdain.

The crowd exploded in carnivorous screams. The referee opened the door into the cage and approached Gunz. He seized his wrist and yanked his arm up. The blood slowly trickled down his forearm – the blood of the dead demon. Gunz pulled his arm out of the referee's grip, wiping the blood on his cargo pants and walked out of the cage.

He headed to the backroom where he could clean up and relax for a few minutes before leaving. As he walked with his head bowed down, the roar of the crowd followed him. He felt a few hands touching his arms and shoulders, but he didn't react. It wasn't his first fight and he got used to ignoring everything, never paying attention to what people around him were doing or saying.

Gunz made his way into the backroom and dropped down on the bench. The room was small and dark. A tiny electric light bulb was hanging from the ceiling, illuminating the room with a fluctuating yellow light. The thick smell of sweat and blood seemed to be permanently rooted into everything within its walls. A small dirty sink was installed in the far corner of the room and even drops of water were falling from the rusty faucet.

He leaned forward slightly and rested his elbows on his lap, hiding his face in his hands. He wasn't tired – the fight was over so fast that it hardly spiked the adrenalin in him. He felt hollow inside, indifferent to everything, inwardly wishing that the late demon put up a better fight.

He heard the phone ring and snapped his head to the side. Gunz reached for his bag and pulled the phone out, staring at the screen. *Here is exactly what I didn't need,* he thought with a sigh, but answered the phone.

"How did you get this phone number, Agent Andrews?" asked Gunz coldly.

"And hello to you too, Mr. Burns," replied Jim, ignoring his tone. "Where are you and what are you doing?"

"A little preoccupied at the moment," muttered Gunz, unwilling to get into a conversation with his boss.

"What are you doing, Gunz?" repeated Jim, softer notes in his voice. "You disabled the GPS tracker in your watch and just disappeared from the face of the Earth. This is the first time in months that you answered my phone call. Even Aidan can't sense you. What the hell are you doing, man? There are people here who actually care about you!"

"I'm doing my job, Agent Andrews," replied Gunz dryly. "You wanted me to bring the ring of supernatural underground fighting down? So, I'm doing just that. I'm trying to get you all

BOOK THREE: EXCERPT

the names and information you need to bring them down. I conceal my fire energy because I'm undercover. I believe you know what it means to be undercover, sir?"

"But Gunz—," Jim started to say, when the door into the room opened and Gunz interrupted him.

"I got to go, Jim. Try calling me in a few hours."

He hung up the phone and looked at the woman who walked inside and halted in front of him. She was tall and slim, dressed in a latest style black dress and high-heeled shoes. Her wavy blond hair was styled to accentuate the soft oval of her face and her skin was covered in a generous layer of makeup to conceal her true age. Gunz lowered his head, not willing to meet her eyes.

"Gunz, you were as magnificent as always today," she purred, her hand resting on his shoulder, slowly moving down along the shape of his bicep. "I love watching you fight, darling. You're an untamed brutal beast. I can't believe you're just a wizard."

"Um... Thank you, Mrs. Kogan, I guess..." replied Gunz without looking at her and carefully took her hand off his shoulder. "I'm covered in blood and sweat after the fight, ma'am. I don't want you to get your hands dirty."

Mrs. Kogan squatted down in front of him, pulling her elegant black dress up just enough to expose her shapely thighs. She glanced up, searching for his eyes and reached forward. Her hand wandered down his bare chest, tracing the shape of his muscles.

"Mmm," she purred, "what can be more exciting than a young handsome sweaty savage."

Her eyes were dark with lust and her hands seemed to be restless. Before he could say anything, her fingers found the button on the waistband of his pants and then pulled the zipper down. Gunz took her hand off, gently pushing it away.

"Your husband, ma'am," he said frostily, flicking his eyebrow at the door.

BOOK THREE: EXCERPT

"My husband? The thrill is gone. He doesn't excite me anymore," she replied, not paying attention to anything except him. "Just like I don't excite him. We live in an open marriage and he wouldn't mind if I had a taste of this." She grabbed his crotch and squeezed slightly. "I wonder if you're just as mighty in bed as you're in the cage."

Gunz gasped, his aggravated gaze meeting the eyes of the man in the doorway. The man in his late fifties was tall and thin, dressed in an immaculate business suit and a blue shirt. With his gray complexion and deep dark circles around his yellowish eyes, he wasn't exuding a healthy vibe. Mr. Kogan was watching his wife's fruitless advances with an uneven smirk on his hollow-cheeked face.

"Clarissa, darling," said the man, approaching his wife, and pulled her up to her feet, "go get your busy hands into someone else's pants. Hopefully someone who wouldn't mind the intrusion. Allow me a few minutes to talk to our undefeated fighter here."

Mrs. Kogan pivoted on her high heels and sauntered away, swaying her hips. "I'll see you later, darling," she promised Gunz, blowing an air-kiss to him and walked out the door.

Mr. Kogan waited until his wife left the room and shook his head chuckling. He put his hand in the pocket of his pants and pulled out a wad of cash held by a money clip.

"Your cut," he said counting out a few hundred-dollar bills and offered them to Gunz.

"Thanks." Gunz took the bills and threw them into his bag without counting.

"Oh, no, thank *you*," replied Mr. Kogan, a wide grin on his face. "You're my biggest moneymaker after all. I'm sorry about my wife's behavior. She can be a little forward."

Gunz smirked. "She wants my body. There is nothing more to it," he said with a shrug without lifting his eyes, "and I don't give a damn."

BOOK THREE: EXCERPT

"I know," replied Mr. Kogan nonchalantly and waved his hand at the bench. "May I?"

Gunz finally lifted his head and glanced at him. Then he nodded and lowered his eyes again.

Mr. Kogan sat down next to him. "Why are you doing it, Gunz? Why are you fighting every night, risking your health and possibly your life?"

"I need money," replied Gunz evenly.

"You don't care about money," objected Mr. Kogan sharply. "I watch you every night and I'm sure that you couldn't care less about money or vanity or women. None of it. You make enough money fighting in these pits to live in a five-star hotel in any city we travel to, but you live in a cheap fleabag motel. So, what drives you inside that cage?"

Gunz didn't reply. He didn't even change his position.

"Well, allow me to ask another personal question then," said Mr. Kogan. "You look like you're in your late twenties – early thirties. But I've been around the supernatural community long enough to know that appearances could be deceiving. Magic slows down the aging and there are enough immortals roaming this world. How old are you, Gunz? Are you really as young as you look?"

Gunz nodded. "Yeah, I'm twenty-nine..."

"Then what made you so cold and cynical at such young age?" asked Mr. Kogan quietly. "I see the way you kill your opponents in the cage – you don't care whether they live or die. When you fight, it's like you're begging for trouble. You're a wizard, undoubtedly you know how to use your magic, but I saw you using it only once. It's like you're inviting the pain or possibly even death."

Gunz remained silent, staring unblinkingly at his hands, covered in blood.

"Fine," said Mr. Kogan rising, "then let me do something unusual for you. After all, whatever drives you into this shithole, makes me richer. Usually Heads of the Houses don't socialize with their fighters. Not even with unattached fighters. But I'd like to treat you to dinner tomorrow night. Would you be open to that?"

Gunz lifted his head and glanced at Mr. Kogan, slightly surprised. The Heads of the Houses not only didn't socialize with the fighters, they hardly even noticed them, treating them as low-level scum, which most of the fighters were. They were the rogue demons, vampires, werewolves, dark wizards and other monsters who were trying to either make a few bucks or satisfy their thirst for blood without getting into too much trouble with local authorities.

"Thank you," said Gunz.

"Thank you yes or thanks but no way in hell?" asked Mr. Kogan chuckling.

"Yes, thank you," replied Gunz quietly. "Just please, don't ask me any personal questions, sir."

"I'm wondering what bothers you more – the questions I ask or my wife's groping technique," he muttered and laughed. "Don't answer that, please. Is there anything I can do for you tonight, Gunz?"

"Yes, sir," replied Gunz rising, "you can get me one more fight tonight."

"Are you serious?" asked Mr. Kogan, notes of shock in his voice.

"Dead serious," said Gunz. "And if they don't have a strong enough opponent for me, get me in the cage with two fighters. Or three. Whatever will get you more money."

"I'll see what I can do," said Mr. Kogan heading out of the room.

* * *

One hour later, Gunz was walking toward the cage again. The

crowd was shouting, chanting his name. Everyone was staring at him – women with lust, men with blood-thirsty hunger in their eyes. Women were reaching to touch him. But he saw nothing, felt nothing, thought of nothing, his eyes locked on two monsters inside the cage.

Carefully he probed them with his Salamander's senses and wanted to laugh. One of his opponents was a demon. Just like the demon he fought earlier today, he was tall and bulky. But the second opponent was a dark wizard, and out of all the magic tricks he could pull out of his hat, he chose to use the fire magic. Both of them were at least a few inches taller than him and they glowered down at him with arrogant smirks on their faces.

The bouncer opened the door of the cage for him, ushering him inside. Gunz stepped on the blood-splattered floor of the ring, a frosty lopsided smirk on his face.

"I'll wipe this smirk right off your face, wizard," hissed the demon. He exchanged a boastful look with his partner and they both nodded.

"Please, do your worst," muttered Gunz dryly.

The bell rang announcing the beginning of the fight and the demon charged him at once. The shouting of the crowd dimmed down and disappeared as his mind immediately got set to a high alert.

Fire Salamander – go! Gunz thought as he drove his fist into the demon's face, knocking him out cold in one punch.

Get the Full Book Online!

DEAR READER

Thank you so much for reading The Burns Fire. I hope you enjoyed the book and will join Zane Burns' next adventure in the third book of the series, The Burns Defiance.

If you would like to stay up-to-date on the latest information about new releases, special offers, and more, sign up for my mailing list. www.nmthorn.com

For more information follow me on Facebook and Instagram.
www.facebook.com/nmthornauthor
www.instagram.com/nmthornauthor/

BEFORE YOU GO...

Your reviews mean the world to me and are greatly appreciated. If you enjoyed the Burns War, please take a few minutes to leave a review. It doesn't have to be long. It can be just a few words or stars rating.

Please help spread the word by taking this small extra step and leave your review on Amazon and/or Goodreads.

ALSO BY N. M. THORN

The Fire Salamander Chronicles

The Burns Path - Prequel Novella Book 0 - for my subscribers
The Burns Fire - Book 1
The Burns War - Book 2
The Burns Defiance - Book 3

ABOUT THE AUTHOR

N.M. Thorn currently lives in South Florida with her husband and son. Owner of a digital marketing agency by day and a writer by night, she loves spending her times creating new worlds, paranormal planes of existence and anything that could be described as supernatural.

When she is not busy working with everything digital or exploring fantasy worlds, she enjoys spending time with her family, reading, painting and martial arts.

If you would like to share your thoughts, ideas or just send N.M. Thorn a message about the Fire Salamander world, feel free to contact her at: nmthornauthor@gmail.com

facebook.com/nmthornauthor
instagram.com/nmthornauthor

Printed in Great Britain
by Amazon

20469714R00246